T0274310

THE LAST CITY

THE LAST SHE SERIES

THE LAST SHE

THE LAST CITY

THE LAST CREATION
FALL 2024

THE LAST SHE | BOOK 2

THE LAST CITY

H. J. NELSON

wattpad books 

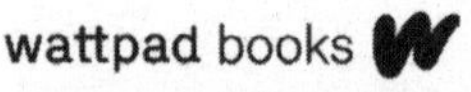

An imprint of Wattpad WEBTOON Book Group

Content warning: violence, murder, fighting, animal death

Published in Canada by Wattpad WEBTOON Book Group, a division of Wattpad Corp.

36 Wellington Street E., Suite 200, Toronto, ON M5E 1C7 Canada

www.wattpad.com

First Wattpad Books edition: February 2023

ISBN 978-1-99025-904-3 (Hardcover original)
ISBN 978-1-99025-905-0 (eBook edition)

Library and Archives Canada Cataloguing in Publication information is available upon request.

Printed and bound in Canada

1 3 5 7 9 10 8 6 4 2

Cover design by Jill Caldwell
Images © BalanceFormCreative, © Tom via Adobe Stock, © andreiuc88 via Envato, © Richard Wellenberger via iStock, © Bulgac via iStock

For my little sister, Sadie.

My dearest Arabella,

I'm not sure if this note is written out of desperation or hope, but something inside me tells me you are still alive. I barely survived the river. I knew they were following me and I had to run. By the time I managed to throw them off and made it back, you were gone. Those bastards killed Loki . . . Best dog I ever had, and he died to save me without a second thought. Why is it dogs are so much better than men?

I planned to come home and wait here for you, but Emma wasn't here. There was only some damn cat. I thought of shooting him, but she always wanted a cat, so I left him there. There was so much I should have told you, so many things I need to explain to you in person, but instead, I will leave you with the one secret I thought to tell you a thousand times but never could.

In the far north, there is a city of survivors. While the rest of the world faded away, this city has progressed. The wealthiest from all over the world gathered here. Its mark is the black spiral, the same that marks our door.

They collect women and bring them there.

No. Not collect. They hunt women, and they are sold as the world's most precious commodities.

It's there that I go to look for your sister.

But Ara, I warn you now. As dangerous as the journey will be, the city itself is a thousand times more dangerous. Our world has moved backward, while this one has moved forward. It will be a world the likes of which we have never imagined. Women will be beyond precious. It would be impossibly dangerous for you to follow me there, to help me find your sister.

And yet, I hope you do follow me. Again, I leave you with an impossible choice. Enclosed is a map that leads north, to the city I speak of. Guard it closely.

I miss you. I'm sorry. Without you, Emma, and your mother, the days are endless. Perhaps my punishment is to spend the rest of my life alone. Perhaps you are gone.

But I can't believe that. You were always the strong one, Ara. Something inside me, either faith or stubbornness, tells me that I will see you again.

Come find me. Come find Emma and we can be a family again.

All my love,
Your Father

ONE—SAM

The apocalypse only sucks if you let it.

"Teenage Wasteland" blasted out the speakers of the mall, shaking the ceiling so hard dust fell free. Late afternoon sun shone through the shattered skylights as I tilted my head back and laughed, then screamed for the hell of it.

I did it. Holy shit, I did it.

Real music shook the world for the first time in four years.

It was like the moment I'd kissed Cecelia Rose in fifth grade: the rush, the racing high, the world infinite. Like the last few years were over and the old world was back—teenage wasteland and all.

Instead of white-eyed, vicious, plague-infected animals roaming the halls below, there were small yappy dogs held by women with disapproving glares. In place of the gaggle of geese down in the food court, there was a group of teenage girls—giggling, eating fries, and laughing over some shared video on their phones. The floors were shiny white once again, freshly waxed, reflecting faces too busy to stop and admire them. My biggest concern wasn't if I could survive the winter, or if I'd have to kill the next person I saw. It was if I could muster up the courage to talk to a girl.

The music pounded, and the geese below finally decided they'd had enough, shattering the illusion when they flew by my small window overlooking the longest stretch of the mall. The birds were fat after a long summer—they'd be two days' worth of food, easy—but even with the perfect shot, I didn't reach for my bow. Instead, the ancient leather seat squeaked as I leaned back, placed both my feet atop the mountain of manuals, and sang along.

Four weeks of tinkering and scavenging parts. One expedition up to the solar panels on the roof, where I'd nearly fallen and broken my neck. Countless hours repairing wires, but now it was all worth it. I'd brought music back to our world.

I was musical Gandhi. Or rock 'n' roll Jesus.

My brother, Kaden, would have told me I was wasting time. Ara would have teased me—or told me the song was actually called "Baba O'Riley," as if that mattered anymore. Gabriel would have gone off on some rant about how we needed to prepare for winter and reassigned me to something more "productive." But there were no more clan rules.

Just Sam, the man with the plan.

If I wanted to spend the summer reconnecting the power supply to the music system in the mall, then I damn well would.

An outdated stereo system sat behind me in the small booth-like room. Before me lay a glass window with an impressive view of the mall below. I imagined before the plague a security guard must have reclined here with a cup of coffee in one hand, donut in the other, and watched the crowds below. Now the only crowds were the occasional herds of deer and the thirty-four mannequins someone had moved out of stores and into the empty hallways. I wasn't sure how it had happened; one night I'd left and the next they'd all been standing there. Still, the company was nice. I'd even named one Colborn, and used him for target practice before I wondered if naming mannequins was the first sign of losing it.

There'd been no sign of Kaden or Ara since I'd woken up three months ago in an underground bunker, barely remembering my own name, only to walk into a lawless city where the central beacon for hope, the Castellano clan, had burned to the ground. Summer was fading away, winter approaching. I'd only had Kaden's leftovers stores, most of which we'd hidden in this mall, to get me through it.

Which was why I'd a) located Kaden's favorite CD in Barnes & Noble b) decided on a new hideout, considering the smoldering state of the clan, and c) spent half the summer repairing cords chewed through by rodents, in order to d) finally hear glorious music pounding out of the mall speakers. Only someone truly awesome would hear this song and risk lawless men, infected animals, and warring clans to come to it. The music was a siren call for awesomeness, and I was the herald. Waiting. Listening. Rocking.

I leaned forward, singing the lyrics—music was probably one of the worst casualties of the apocalypse, besides, you know, women—when something moved far below.

My lips froze as I reached for my bow, when the figure crept forward. He was small, maybe even younger than my almost fifteen years. He moved from the shadows of the JC Penney and crossed to another, smaller store. He wore a dark hoodie with the hood thrown up, a small backpack, and held a long, thin object. A shotgun, maybe.

Before the plague I would have freaked over a hooded figure

sneaking around the mall holding a gun. Now I thought: *A loner. Perfect.*

Kaden always seemed to inspire people to follow him, but so far no one wanted to join me, the "skinny ginger prick." That changed today.

I spun out of the chair, pausing before the cracked mirror that hung on the back of the door. The boy reflected there wasn't the one Kaden knew—taller, wider shoulders, hair shaved close to his head. When Kaden came back, not only would he not recognize me, but he'd be impressed by the new, epic crew I'd gathered. Starting with the boy down below.

The dust that swallowed all sound now pulsed with the pounding music. Deliberately shattering the silence felt both terrifying and freeing. Like flipping off the world and daring it to come for me.

But now, finally, things are going my way. If the boy held his current course, he'd come out just past the fountain, and I could approach him from behind. I'd need to be careful; he was holding a gun and me a bow, but hardly anyone had ammunition left these days. A bow with arrows beat a gun without bullets—not that I was hoping for a confrontation. Kaden always talked people into following him. So would I. Eventually I hoped to be able to talk over the mall intercom, hype all the perks of being a part of my crew before I even met the person. But one step at a time.

A sliver of light lanced through the final door that opened into the lower level of the mall, lighting swirls of dust, the final chords of the song diminishing. I paused, waiting for the next track to play, but it didn't come. *One more thing to fix later.*

The following silence was achingly deep, like a held breath waiting for an exhale that would never come. A different person might have taken it as a warning—but I'd waited too long. This boy, whoever he was, would be the perfect first member of my brand-new crew.

I peeked out the crack of the door, to where the skeleton of some sort of small rodent mixed with the debris of old clothing and faded wrappers. Taking a deep breath, I sidestepped from the door, the whole of the mall rising around me.

The hallways stretched into nothingness, no movement, no life.

The fountain stood to my left, vines creeping up the railing to the second floor and reaching up for the sun—a grand and elegant ruin. The silence held memories: Kaden shooting my bow, and the others laughing when I outshot him; Issac handing me his Bible, asking me to use my "young eyes" to read him a passage; Jeb teaching me how to throw a knife and read animal tracks.

You're fine. They'll come back for you.

The apocalypse only sucks if you let it.

Fading sunlight lit the filthy ground. I inched forward along the wall, wondering if maybe the boy had turned around, or I'd miscalculated—when the cold barrel of a gun pressed against my neck.

Adrenaline pounded through me as a clear, high-pitched voice said, "Who the hell plays the Who over mall speakers during the apocalypse? I should shoot you right now for sheer stupidity."

His voice wasn't what I expected—younger and higher than I'd guessed. But I didn't care. He had a gun and tread like a ghost. He'd snuck up on me in the mall. My turf. And he knew who the Who were.

He was everything I'd been waiting for and more.

"Seems like a waste of a good bullet." My heart hammered, but my voice didn't break. I lifted my arms, about to turn around when the gun shoved me in the back and I froze again.

"Don't move," he said. "Throw your bow in front of you. Then slide your backpack to me. Leave the arrows on it."

I tossed my bow forward, where it clattered in the silence, then slowly removed my pack. "The backpack's not full of anything good." *Unless you count comic books.*

"I'll be the judge of that."

"Fine." I dropped the backpack and then kicked it behind me. There was a sound of shuffling, and then, the smashing of objects as everything was dumped from the bag.

"Hey!" I spun, about to tell him off when I lost the ability to speak.

A girl held a shotgun leveled between my eyes.

I should have been excited, or terrified she might be infected, or a thousand other things. Instead, all I could do was stare. Dark, nearly black hair and vivid, light-blue eyes glared at me from beneath an oversized black hoodie. Her baggy jeans and hoodie hid her form, but there was no way those eyes and lips didn't belong to a girl.

I'm getting robbed by a girl. Kaden is going to give me so much shit.

And suddenly I was hit by another memory, this one with a voice clear as a gunshot. *I think there's someone following us. I'm gonna double back and check.* Kaden had once known someone was following us—that's how we'd met Ara. Ara had also pointed a gun at him. A gun he'd somehow known was empty. I remembered how he'd handled it. Cocky. Suave. Confident.

"Listen." I raised my hands and gave her a knowing smile. "I know how this goes, your gun is empty and you're scared—"

A gunshot exploded over my head.

"Shit!" Chunks of the ceiling rained down on me as I collapsed to the ground. "Don't shoot! Don't shoot!" My voice rang high and panicked, hands trembling. I crouched, eyes clenched closed, dust coating me, the blast ringing in my ears. Finally I opened my eyes—*yup, still a gun pointed straight at me.*

"You're not gonna cry, are you?" Her voice had a sarcastic, cutting drawl to it that Ara's never had. "Because if you're gonna cry, I'll just shoot you now."

"No, I'm not going to cry," I squeaked, trying to regain a sense of dignity. Difficult to do on your knees.

"Move again and the next shot goes between your eyes."

"Not moving!"

She stepped back just enough to use the barrel of the gun to push through the contents of my bag. CDs (I mean, I needed choices for the first song to play in four years), a flashlight, a lighter, some squirrel jerky, a manual on solar panels, a Batman comic, *The Hobbit*, a *Sports Illustrated* magazine (why had I brought that today?), and a deck of cards Kaden had given me. She swung the gun back to me.

"Where's the rest of it?"

I hesitated, weighing my options before deciding I didn't have any. "It's all back in my hideout."

She sneered. "Hideout? What are you, twelve?"

"Fifteen, actually." *Or close enough to it.* What good was the apocalypse if you couldn't bump your age up a year?

She paused, a look of curiosity and suspicion on her face. "How'd you turn the electricity on?"

A slow smile crept over my face, along with a deep exhale. Girls might be a mystery that I would likely never solve, but electricity? That was science. "My dad was an electrician, he taught me a lot about old tech. The new tech runs on a different system—it hasn't run since the plague. But there are old tech solar power cells on top of the mall that survived. I had to repair them and a bunch of the wires, but it wasn't too hard."

Actually it was insanely hard. And it took me all summer.

Her eyes narrowed, something calculating there. "Could you get the power on somewhere else?"

Confidence. Channel Kaden. No, don't channel Kaden, that almost got you shot. I cleared my throat. "Probably."

Far in the distance, a flock of birds burst up and out of the mall. We stilled, and her gun turned, both of us quiet as we watched where the corridors disappeared into shadows and creeping plants. The few mannequins in the distance stood as still as us, dark, watchful forms.

But only cold wind swept down the hallway, the first breath of the coming winter.

Finally, she swung the gun back to me, something suspicious in her eyes. "Where's your crew?"

"It's just me." I puffed my chest out a bit, trying to look like a leader.

"Aren't there others living here?" Her eyes went up to the second floor, as if she expected some kind of trap.

"No, it's mostly loners who pass through." After months of talking primarily to mannequins, it felt nice to talk to someone breathing. "The Castellano clan used have their home base in the old Cabela's store, but it burned down a couple months ago. This was their turf, but now it's neutral territory."

A few of the groups who'd passed through had made camp in

the mall. I'd crept up to their camps at night, listening to them talk. Rumor had it that Gabriel, the Castellano clan leader, had set up a new clan at the Old Penitentiary—the fortress he'd always wanted. But Kaden had always told me if something happened he would meet me here, at the mall. So this is where I headed after I woke up. Also, screw Gabriel.

Her eyes swept over our surroundings: the deepening colors of the day, the breeze sweeping down through the broken skylights. She seemed to reach a decision. "Fine. Get up. Take me back to your"—she rolled her eyes—"*hideout*. Try anything and I'll shoot you."

I climbed to my feet, and then hesitated. "Can I pick up my pack and bow?"

A pause. "Yes. But hurry."

"I'm Sam—"

"I didn't ask for your name."

I scrambled to gather up the contents of the bag. Instead of holding my bow in my hands, as I normally would, I slung it over my shoulder. It was awkward with the pack, but less threatening. Only once all my things were gathered did I hesitate. What was the appropriate thing to say to a female pointing a gun at you? She wasn't my prisoner—I was closer to hers—but maybe I should offer her a drink of water at the fountain? Show her how the pump still worked after all this time? Or tell her she was safe with me?

"Are you alone?"

Wow, smooth, Sam. Really.

She cocked the gun, the cartridge falling free and bouncing on the ground. "We're all alone. *Shut up and walk.*"

"My hideout's this way." I nodded toward the small hallway I'd come through.

She swung the gun to my face. "Are you stupid? I said: Shut. Up. And. Walk."

It felt odd to turn my back on someone with a gun, but I did, checking one last time down the expansive, cavernous space, before I led us back into the narrow hallway. She followed close behind. As we walked, her words made me wonder. *We're all alone.* It had been a long summer, and each day I spent by myself, it became a little harder to believe that Kaden, Ara, and Issac would return.

Last year it felt like we'd done the impossible when our expedition team had found Ara, the first female I'd seen since the plague, and brought her back to the clan. But then everything went to shit—all because of Gabriel. He made his clan, the Castellano clan, a prison, when it should have been Ara's home. He invited Colborn and his horde of men to join the clan, despite knowing they were responsible for butchering a smaller clan in the Boise area. Gabriel might have been domineering and heavy-handed, but Colborn was a straight-up psycho. I wasn't sure of all the details, but after Ara and I followed Kaden's plan and escaped, I returned to the Castellano clan to try to free Kaden, when I was thrown from the horse. The next thing I remembered was waking up in a bunker, miles from the clan.

When I finally found my way back to the Castellano clan, the building had been burned to the ground, the people gone. Kaden, Ara, Issac—the man who'd become my father figure after the plague—were all gone. So I'd spent the summer waiting here, tagging buildings SAM WAS HERE, waiting for them to come back and for things to go back to the way they'd been. Before Kaden had ever met Ara.

The final door out of the mall loomed, and I pushed it open, letting my worries drift away. We stepped out to a golden sun sinking into the horizon, lighting a city both ruined and beautiful. Summer was gone now; fall had arrived in all her glory.

"Stop grinning, it's creepy," the girl snapped. I barely managed not to apologize as I continued forward. For the first time since coming here I wondered if instead of things going back to the way they were, I could hope for a better future—one with Kaden, Ara, Issac, me and a new girl, as a new kick-ass expedition team. Or hell, our own clan. *The Rock 'n' Roll Clan.* Or *the Teenage Wastelanders.* Or *the Sam Clan.* The possibilities were endless.

We walked down a sidewalk covered in weeds, debris, and fallen leaves, moving away from the sprawling ruins of the mall and toward my hideout.

Today, I'd heard real music for the first time in four years. I'd recruited the first member of a new team. Sure, she was pointing a gun at my head now, but we'd find common ground soon enough. The world might have become a teenage wasteland, but it took everything in me not to smile as we walked into the dying sunset.

The apocalypse only sucks if you let it.

TWO—ARA

The velvet sounds of the night whispered all around us. Somewhere an owl called. A carpet of pine needles and fallen leaves lay beneath us, the sky an ebony blanket.

Kaden rolled over to face me, the moonlight shining on his long golden curls. His lips were soft against mine. Fall's first breath was here, but I was warm with him beside me.

Then the dream changed—no longer comforting. It tilted sideways, blurring.

A crack sounded in the forest. Kaden sat up in his sleeping bag. I wanted to reach out to him, but I couldn't move. Couldn't speak. The dark forest stretched out all around, the shadows growing monstrous.

"Who's there?" Kaden called out.

Then he stood, his warmth gone. The shadows in the trees had turned into men. I was frozen, trapped, unable to move as they came closer.

"Run, Ara. Run."

~

"Ara. Ara, wake up."

I jolted awake, breathing hard. Reality hit me like a slap as cold as the wind. Kaden was gone, and I sat inside a barred cart pulled by horses, the ruins of a city passing outside. Izzie's head lay cradled on my lap, the only point of warmth on my body. She stared up at me with wide, innocent eyes that seemed too big on her small face. She'd clung to me ever since that first terrifying night when Kaden and I had been ambushed. After three years of the plague and meeting only one other female survivor, being captured, separated from Kaden, and then thrown into a wagon of women had been shocking—and astonishing.

"You were talking in your sleep again," Izzie said. "You said Kaden. Were you dreaming about him?"

"Yeah, I was," I said. Every time I closed my eyes I relived the terrifying memory. "I'm worried about him."

Kaden and I had spent the spring and summer traveling north, following my father's map to The Last City, always avoiding people as we went. Even as the nights grew colder, the leaves turning, we had been happy, cocooned in our own perfect world. Until that night. We were ambushed by men who offered us a bargain: if I would join them and their wagon of women heading to The Last City, they would leave Kaden alive—tied to a tree, with only a small knife to cut his way free, but alive. The alternative was they killed Kaden and took me anyway. Kaden's final words were that he'd find me in The Last City. It had been three weeks since I'd seen him. Three weeks of life inside this jail cell of a cart.

"Maybe he's already in The Last City," Izzie said, a tentative smile breaking over her face. At eleven, she was the youngest and most hopeful of us. "Maybe he's waiting for you."

I tugged her hat closer around her head—her honey-colored hair had been shaved short, offering little protection against the ever-present cold. "Of course he is." I didn't voice my true fear: that we would come to The Last City and Kaden wouldn't be there. That something horrible would have happened to him and I would be trapped in some new place, unable to help him.

Kaden can take care of himself. He'll be there. Just focus on getting yourself there in one piece.

I took in the area surrounding us, surprised at how much it had changed in a few hours. When I'd gone to sleep we'd traveled down little more than a muddy, pitted trench through a northern forest. Now dilapidated houses and businesses with long-since-faded signs crept up against the road. Stretching out as far as the eye could see lay the ruins of a city.

My heart suddenly beat faster, and I pressed against the chain-link to look farther into the ruins. "Izzie . . . is this . . . ?"

"The Last City?" She sat up straight, her voice tinged with excitement. "Yeah, I think we're almost there."

Longing pulled in my chest as I watched birds wheeling through the clear, cold sky. Kaden and I had journeyed for months—through mountains, through ruins, over rivers, facing desperate men and infected animals—and now I was nearly there. Now we would find each other again. I'd already heard the guards talking. They said the surviving population lived in the far corner of the city, behind some sort of wall. They'd also claimed that all the women brought to the city were protected and kept safe.

Here's hoping Kaden is already there, waiting for me with Father and Emma. It felt like a bit too much to hope for.

The cart I sat in—little more than a wooden bottom with chain-link sides and top—was pulled by four horses and currently housed eight women. Judging by the smell, the cart had once been used for livestock and had been repurposed to bring female prisoners to The Last City—just as my father had warned me. From what I'd heard from the other women in the wagon, the men who drove the wagon hunted women, making a meandering journey through cities and towns, searching for female survivors to bring back to The Last City. To my surprise, most of the women in the cart had come willingly. They believed the stories of The Last City offering sanctuary to women—and dismissed the warnings in my father's letter.

"How long till we make it to The Last City?" I called out to the nearest guard. I didn't trust them, wasn't convinced we'd be safe, city or no city. My father had taught me too well for that. In the back of my mind hummed my purpose: find my father, find the truth, find Kaden.

"We get there when we get there," he said gruffly, drawing away from the cart before I could ask more.

Izzie leaned into my warmth and squeezed my hands. Together we watched as the ruins of the city grew thicker around us—like walking deeper into the wilds of a forest made of metal and concrete and brick. There were buildings with collapsed roofs, houses scorched black, and the ever-present red X: the mark of the infected. Fall was in full effect, trees of deep gold, red, and purple adding color to the otherwise dull gray monotony. In Boise it wasn't nearly so cold in the fall, but here a piercing breeze wove through the buildings and dark clouds, blotting out the sun. Snow clung to the deepest shadows and recesses, which meant the first snow had already fallen. Every now and then we passed the remains of a bonfire, some with birds perched atop the charred remains, watching our cart pass with beady, wanting eyes.

"Do you see that?" I leaned forward and curled my fingers through the cold chain-link. There, on the wall of a house facing the highway was a mark I'd seen just once before—at the beginning of summer. Painted on the door of my house.

A black spiral. Despite the numbing cold, my blood beat hot and fast.

"What is it?" Izzie flinched back from the fencing.

I moved down the bench, not taking my eyes off the mark as we rolled by. "That black spiral. On the house. Have you ever seen that before? *Anyone?*"

She shook her head no. No one else replied.

"Hey, what does that mark on the house mean?" I called out to the guard again. He ignored me, my voice swallowed by the sounds of the horses' hooves on pavement and the low moan of the wind through the ruins.

"Anything out there?" Rosia called from the back of the cart, where she and the other five women huddled for warmth. With only one eye, and a shaved head, Rosia looked frightening at first—but she cared for the other women like they were her own family.

"A black spiral painted on a wall. Know what that means?" I tried again. My fahter's letter mentioned it was the mark of the city—so why was it out here in the ruins, and why had it been on our door? The cart rolled on, the mark gone now. Something in me desperately wanted to go back. My father trained me to always be alert, to search for the small details that others overlooked. It was the mark of a good hunter and a true survivor. And something about the spiral felt important . . . and maybe dangerous.

Rosia shrugged. "I've only seen the red X."

A flash of movement came from high above in one of the windows and I twisted my head to follow, but it was gone.

"I'll keep a lookout for it," Izzie said, distracting me. Already I wondered if I'd just imagined the movement—life in this moving prison could do that. "Maybe we'll see it again."

"Thanks." I pulled her close, shivering into her warmth, not missing the way she lit up when I did so. "Did I miss anything else interesting while I was asleep?"

"A couple of dragons fighting a unicorn. A few alien space-ships. A fountain of youth and a time machine offering free rides back to before the plague. The usual."

The older sister in me saw straight through her teasing. She was afraid and trying to hide it. Most of the other women in the cart were old enough to be my mother, but Izzie was little more than a child.

"How about I tell you a story," I said, deciding to distract her.

"Yes! One about Emma."

For a moment words failed me. It was hard to talk about my little sister—not just because Izzie reminded me of her, but because Father and I had left her when she was infected. Only because I'd found a note from my father, hidden in my childhood home, did I hope that she might still be alive. In that note, now tucked against my chest, my father had warned me how dangerous The Last City would be—and that Emma might be there. *And the black spiral on our door in Boise is the same mark as the one here. Maybe it means she really is there.* My heart soared at the thought, and finally I found words to say, "What kind of story about Emma?"

"A warm one." She snuggled closer into me.

"One summer day, a long time ago," I began, "Emma and I decided to build a go-cart and—"

"You told me this one already. Tell me a *new* story." Her voice was petulant, demanding, so much like Emma it hurt. "One you've never told anyone. A *secret.*" The others in the cart didn't turn, but I could sense they were listening now.

I settled back, and sighed, thinking hard. *A secret . . . I don't have many secrets anymore.* Over the long summer Kaden and I had spent journeying through the mountains, I had told him everything—how I missed my father, how I wished I would have said goodbye to my mother, how I feared I could never atone for leaving my sister.

In turn, Kaden had told me his own secrets and regrets. How he felt it was his fault his brother Sam and father figure Issac had died. How, if he had taken over the clan from Gabriel, maybe none of it would have happened. Maybe the only thing I'd kept from him was my fear that he would blame me for everything he'd lost. He never faltered, not once, even when I began to doubt The Last City existed. He knew me in a way no one ever had . . .

. . . except for Emma.

Which was when I realized there was one story I'd never told him. One story I hadn't wanted to. The cold wind brought scents of decay, sending a shiver down my spine. Izzie squeezed my hand—just like Emma had a day long ago.

"Once, a long time ago," I said, "Emma and I went up into the foothills. We weren't supposed to go alone, but we did anyway." I fell deeply into the memory of the girl I'd once been—one who thought she knew everything. "It was only a few weeks before the plague. Back then, I was only starting to realize that Emma was special."

"Special how?" Izzie interrupted.

"She was . . . different." I wasn't sure how else to explain it.

"All her life my father told me to protect her. Not to let others see her difference: her strength and her calculating intelligence. That was why she didn't go to school and why we didn't celebrate her birthday like other kids. We were playing in the foothills, by a deep ravine, when Emma called out in the distance, and I ran to her, terrified. But what I found . . . I think that was the first moment I realized just how far I would go to protect her."

Emma's hand wrapped around mine with a strength that belied her small frame. Together we stared down at the broken body at the bottom of the ravine. My heart floundered in my chest.

"He was trying to make me go with him," Emma said, turning to me—I couldn't look away from the man. "He was going to hurt me."

Fear reached cold fingers down my throat. "Is he . . . ?" I couldn't say the word, even though I knew. His limbs sprawled at odd angles, and a dark stain spread behind his back. Instead, I whispered, "What happened?"

"He found me in the woods and said I needed to come with him. He said he knew what I was. He grabbed my arm and tried to drag me away. I ran but he chased me so I jumped the ravine—"

"You jumped the ravine?" Anger replaced fear. The ravine was narrow, only several feet wide in places, but deep. If you missed the jump, and fell in, you were dead. Which was clearly what had just happened. Emma had jumped the ravine, and the man had tried to follow her across and fallen in. I refused to consider any other explanation.

"I was just trying to get away," she said, as if she could read my thoughts. "What do we do, Ara?"

My name in her mouth snapped me back to reality. Father told me to protect her. I pulled her from the ledge and lifted her chin. I made my voice one of steel—just like Father's. "Nothing. He was a bad man. He deserved it. You did nothing wrong. We don't speak of it again and nothing bad will happen. I promise."

My words trailed off, and I realized why I'd never wanted to tell that story. It was the first moment I'd realized how Emma was different, and how terrified that difference made me feel. There had been no horror in her eyes. She hadn't been afraid, or sorry the man was dead. I never asked her to explain how the man fell into the ravine, or if it really was an accident. I didn't want to know. I only wanted to see her as my perfect little sister, afraid of nothing . . . until the day her eyes bled and we left her.

Izzie stared at me, but I couldn't meet her gaze. Only two weeks after I'd made that promise to my sister, a plague had swept over the world, taking what I thought was every woman but me, and most of the men. When the plague had come for Emma, my father and I abandoned her. I was worse than the corpse lying at the bottom of the ravine.

"Sounds to me like he deserved it," Rosia drawled out, and Izzie and I both turned to her. "He was probably a pervert. Who talks to a little girl out in the woods? Perverts, that's who."

"Did she die of the plague?" Izzie whispered.

It was suddenly hard to speak. "My mother got it first; she left to try to give us a chance. When Emma got it, my father and I left." Izzie took my hand and squeezed, only sympathy in her eyes. Sympathy I didn't deserve.

"There wasn't anything you could have done," Izzie said gently. "Maybe she's already in The Last City, safe and waiting for you."

"Maybe." I stared hard-eyed out into the ruins, trying not to think about what I would do if she wasn't there.

But Izzie wouldn't accept my sadness—that was my favorite

thing about her. "You'll find her again. I know it. Your dad too. And handsome Kaden."

She made a kissy face, and this finally pulled a giggle out of me. Then a laugh when she wrapped her arms around herself and started to make ridiculous kissing faces. Okay, so maybe most of my stories featured Kaden, but I couldn't help it.

"You never told me how you and your father got split up," Izzie said. "Was it as exciting as with you and Kaden?"

I'd already regaled them all with the story of how Kaden and I had separated—the men who'd surrounded us in the dead of night. The bargain we'd struck. The horror of leaving him there, and the fear that I'd never see him again. It was the dream that haunted me every time I closed my eyes.

"You may as well tell her, Cherry," Rosia said from the back of the cart, using her nickname for me that I could only assume my auburn hair had inspired. "You know she won't stop asking till you do."

Izzie grinned at this. "She's right."

"It was three years after the plague hit," I said, caving beneath Izzie's devious grin. "Father and I were up in the mountains." *Just over a year ago*. It felt like a lifetime. "It had been a hard winter, and someone was following us—I think they even had an airship and dogs tracking us." I paused, remembering beneath the terror, a flicker of awe hearing the sound of airships again. "My father led them away and told me to meet up with him in three days, but he never showed. So I went back to Boise and met Kaden." I waved a hand. "You know the rest."

Rosia chimed in again. "Someone was following you . . . you mean like the perv who was following your sister?"

I stared at her in surprise, the cart jolting us over a big bump and forcing me to grab hold of the cart and Izzie. I'd never considered if there was a connection between the man at the bottom of the ravine and the men who were following my father and me in the mountains. Why would there be?

"No . . ." I said slowly, wondering why that single word felt wrong. "There's no reason for them to be connected." *Or at least, no reason I can see.* "But who knows. Maybe I can ask them both when we get to The Last City."

"Of course you can!" Izzie smiled, and then lowered her voice, full of longing. "Read your father's note, one more time, pretty please?"

The other women in the cart groaned—after I'd shown Izzie the note and map my father had left me she'd asked me to read it a dozen times.

"If I hear that letter one more time, I'm going to throw up," Rosia whined. "Why couldn't you have saved a spicy love letter from Kaden? *That's* what I want to hear."

A few other women laughed, and my cheeks burned red. I might have been a little too descriptive about our journey alone through the mountains. *He will come for me*, I'd told them all so confidently the first night in the wagon. But it had been three weeks without him. Then, yesterday, one of the women had been taken from the cart and never returned. The other women didn't speak of it—but I had a feeling that while most of these women were bound for The Last City, a few ended up elsewhere. I couldn't let that happen to Izzie or me.

"I used to have a different man for every day of the week," Rosia said with a dramatic sigh.

Beside me Izzie giggled, turning to me. "You said Kaden's blond with curly hair? Like a prince from a fairy tale?"

I didn't have a chance to respond before another woman chimed in: "I bet The Last City is full of handsome men."

Rosia cut in. "Who cares about the men? Hot water, and cheese, that's why I let them take me. And TV. I'd give my left tit to watch a single episode of TV again. Or hell, even football." More laughter, and now a few of the other women joined in, talking about old favorite TVs shows, hot showers, cars, airships, and fast food—everything we'd lost.

"But they've got it all back in The Last City," Rosia said, her voice full of confidence. "All of it and more."

A few of the women murmured, some in agreement, some in doubt, as Izzie and I exchanged a quick look. Before we could say more, the wagon slowed, and one of the men banged on the side. The smiles and laughter disappeared.

"Everybody out!" one of the men called out, slamming the butt of his rifle against the side of the cart. The sharp thunk made Izzie cringe into my side. "You've got five minutes to piss then it's back in."

On the ground, shuffling silently forward, the group of women was quieter, subdued, in a way that made me sad. A grizzled guard with a deep voice pointed to an alleyway between two tall brick buildings. "You've got five minutes in the alleyway. The back is blocked so don't try anything." The group of women shuffled forward silently, but when I passed he reached out and yanked me back. "Not you. You can piss here."

For a half second, I thought about reaching for the gun in his holster—my father had taught me how to disarm an opponent.

He was a bad man. That's what I'd told Emma of the man in the ravine. Maybe there were no good men or bad men in this world—maybe there were only the living and the dead.

But then Izzie turned back in line, her wide eyes meeting mine. Shame bloomed in my chest. My father had taught me to defend myself—not shoot a man in cold blood. "Go," I called to her. "I'll be fine. I'll go here." *And piss on the guard's shoes while I'm at it.*

Rosia grabbed Izzie's hand, giving me a worried look before she pulled her away with the rest of the group. A man with a sad attempt of a mustache came to stand beside the older guard who'd stopped me. "Why'd you keep the pretty one back?"

I stiffened at being called the "pretty one" but the older man only watched me with cruel, assessing eyes. "She's the one who talks the most," he said to the mustached guard. I suddenly wondered if my many stories had been a bad idea—I'd never imagined the guards had been listening.

"So? They all talk."

"She's different," the older one said. "Look at her, glaring at us. She's not broken."

I forced my eyes to the ground—difficult to do when the gun at the hip of the older guard practically screamed my name. *I could shoot both of them before they even knew what happened. They took me captive—it would be self-defense.* But there were too many to fight all on my own, and I couldn't leave Izzie.

"There's always one in every group," the older guard went on. "One who riles them up, makes them think they'd be better on their own, instead of being grateful we're risking our lives to protect them. Women like that are dangerous—like some kind of infection. You gotta be careful it doesn't get to the others. We shoulda sold her off like the other one."

Sold her off. So they *had* been selling off women—the words made me cold, but only more determined to get to the city with Izzie. From there I would find a way for us to be safe. I just had to make sure neither of us was sold before then. The younger man laughed at the other man's words. "You worry too much—some men like 'em fiery. Look at that hair, they want—"

But I never heard what they wanted.

Twenty feet to the left of us, a window exploded.

In a split second, chaos erupted. Gunfire shattered the day.

On the other side of the wagon, one of the guards turned to look directly at me—then spat up blood. Bullets hit the ground and walls, dirt and snow exploding all around. The guards were shouting, screaming at each other, but it didn't matter. The street we stood on was surrounded by tall buildings—we were stuck in a metal canyon with nowhere to hide. Men leaned out of the windows of the buildings above, the glint of guns flashing as they fired on our group below. The horses screamed and bolted, the cart careening down the road.

Izzie. Find Izzie.

There wasn't fear, only cold purpose. I sprinted for the alleyway where the women had disappeared. Snow and dirt exploded all around me as bullets rained down. I spun around the corner. Women huddled behind dumpsters and debris coated in ice and snow. Rosia alone kicked at a door set into the side of the building, trying unsuccessfully to force her way in. "Take cover!" I screamed at her, "Get behind something!"

"Izzie?" I called out, terrified she hadn't made it here. Maybe she was gone? But then Izzie stepped out from behind a rusted car, her eyes connecting with me, her lips forming my name. "Stay down!" I screamed.

A bullet tore into her small chest.

I watched her fall the same way I'd seen my sister die in my dreams: a thousand times over. Slow and painful and horrible.

White noise buzzed in my ears.

The gunshots, the screaming, everything faded.

There was only the vision of her wide eyes staring down at her chest. I ran to her, each step seeming to take an eternity. When I lifted her head back into my lap, just the way it had been in the wagon, her eyes stared up at mine, glassy. Unknowing.

"Izzie? Izzie? It's going to be fine. You're going to be fine." I stroked her head, the hat gone, her hair soft and fine like a dandelion's. "I'm sorry. I'm so sorry," I whispered.

Her lips moved, but no sound came out. Her silence said more than words ever could. *Sorry isn't enough. Sorry won't bring me back. Sorry didn't save Sam, or Issac, or Emma. Sorry isn't going to save you.*

I held her like that for some time—until the sounds of the battle had gone quiet and the sun slanted sideways through the ruins. The fact that I had somehow survived again felt like a curse instead of a consolation.

"Ara?"

I would have known his voice in any life. For a moment I wondered if that was what had happened: if the strange, ringing silence was the stillness of death.

Kaden crossed to my side. Only then did I look up. *He found me. Just like he said he would.* And yet, my heart broke yet again.

The cart and the horses were back, but the guards were gone.

No. Not gone. The snow, far too early for the season, had already half covered several lumps that hadn't been there before.

Whatever guards hadn't run were dead now. Once I would have been caught up in questions of whether they deserved it, but I was too tired for those kinds of questions.

The only questions I had didn't matter anymore.

Why couldn't they have waited for us to get to the city? Why did I call out her name?

Kaden knelt in the bloody snow beside me, the two of us staring down at Izzie. I remembered one of the stories he'd told me this summer about his little sister, Kia, who had died in his arms, her final request to set the horses free. I wondered what he saw when he looked down at Izzie. Did he also see another soul he'd failed to save?

Over the long summer Kaden's hair had grown long, bleached nearly white from the sun. In the dying light of the day, it spilled around the sharp angles of his face and made him look nearly angelic—the exact opposite of the gun in his hands and the dead lying all around. But Kaden was like that—able to hold on to the good through the bad. Even here, in the midst of death, his goodness was all that kept me from tilting my head back and screaming.

"Who was she?" he said softly.

"Izzie. My friend."

"Are you hurt?"

I shook my head no, reaching out with trembling fingers to close Izzie's eyes. It didn't seem right that she'd survived a plague that killed all women, only to die just before we reached The Last City. Then I reached out and took Kaden's hand in my own, holding on to him like a tether to this world.

If you're up there, Issac, take better care of her than I did.

"We need to move, Ara," Kaden said, gently. "Some of the guards got away. They might come back. We need to take the women and get them to The Last City."

I didn't get up. There was no joy at the realization that we'd nearly made it—only anger. Anger that we'd been so close. Anger that I'd failed yet again. I barely recognized my own voice. "Why did you stop us?"

"I've been tracking you for the last week. The men lied to us. They were selling women to other buyers along the way—they weren't actually intending to bring you into The Last City. I ran into another group that was looking to set an ambush and stop them before they could sell any more women." His voice sounded heavy and sad. "None of the women were supposed to get hurt."

I couldn't look away from Izzie. In life she was small. In death, she seemed barely more than a child.

"Kaden!" Someone called. Kaden reluctantly stood, leaving me beside Izzie with the strange, sudden ache to ask them all to leave.

"This Ara?"

My name drew my eyes up against my will. A slender man stepped out into the alleyway—a rifle slung across his back, two pistols at his hips. He walked with a fluid, swaying grace I didn't see often in men. And then he pulled down a mouth scarf and head covering, and I saw why. It wasn't a man. A young woman with thick black hair, warm brown skin, and full lips stared straight at me.

I remembered what I felt the first time I met Gabriel's little sister, Addison—the wonder that came with realizing I wasn't alone in the world. It was the same feeling as when I'd been thrown into a cart of haggard women.

It wasn't what I felt looking at her.

"You killed her," I whispered. I wasn't sure if I was talking to the beautiful dark-haired woman, to Kaden, or maybe, worst of all, to myself.

"It was an accident, Ara." Kaden reached out to me—but I pulled away. "Talia didn't—"

"She was just a child," I yelled, anger exploding out of me, not caring when the other men by the wagon turned to stare at me. Then, just as suddenly as it had come, the anger disappeared, replaced by grief.

Why did I call out to Izzie? She'd come out from hiding when I called her name—I killed her the same as whoever pulled the trigger.

My breath came in heaving gasps. It felt like I was a bystander, watching myself break down, unable to do anything to stop it.

"I'm sorry for your loss," Talia said, though her voice didn't sound it. She swam in and out of focus, her voice coming at a distance. "We've wasted too much time . . . early for snow . . . need to move . . . back before dark . . ."

Only when she was gone did I finally open my eyes, finally let myself take a deep, heaving gasp. To do what I needed to do: say goodbye. Again.

"Ara—" Kaden began, but I held up a hand, cutting him off. I pulled out my father's letter, a small thing that had given her so much hope, and set it on her chest. Snow already gathered on her small form. *There's nothing you can do for her anymore.* I stood and forced myself to walk away, imagining her eyes watching me as I went.

Kaden walked beside me as we made our way back to the wagon, the snow drifting down, already masking the violence here. Fresh blood stained Rosia's shoulder, but it didn't slow her from gathering the other women around her, crying and hugging each of them. To my shock, they all crawled back into the wagon, Talia helping them climb back up. Then Talia turned, her gaze locked on mine as she held a hand out to me.

I stiffened and drew back. *No way in hell am I going back in there.*

Talia's eyes narrowed, but before she could say anything, Kaden broke in. "Ara can ride with me. My horse can hold us both."

Talia didn't respond, though I could tell from her pursed lips she had more to say. Kaden pulled me away from the wagon.

As we walked, the snow began to thicken, the wind picking up as the sky darkened. *It shouldn't be this cold. It shouldn't snow in the fall.* My thoughts felt disjointed, detached from my body. This far north it was a harsher, colder world. Or maybe the world had stopped caring about the rules altogether. Kaden pulled off his jacket and settled it over my shoulders. I shivered into the sudden warmth. With the storm pulling us closer, I bowed into his body. His arms came around me, holding me close.

"I'm sorry," he said. "Forgive me."

I couldn't speak, crying against him as he held me. With his arms around me I felt both whole again and irreparably broken. This was what I wanted, all I thought I needed, but still my heart felt broken.

Behind us, someone cleared their throat, and we broke apart. A teenage boy with acne and blue hair stood behind us, holding the reins of a massive black horse. "Talia wants to leave. She said storms like this can get bad fast. She thinks we can make it back before the gates close." There was clear skepticism in his voice. He tossed the horse's reins to Kaden, and I caught a full look at his outfit: even more bizarre than having blue hair in the apocalypse. He wore a long leather trench coat with a sword at one hip, a pistol at the other.

"Ara, this is Harrison," Kaden said, gesturing to the teenage boy with blue hair. "He's part of Talia's team—I was going to try to free you myself before I ran into them. They probably saved my life."

Harrison grinned at me, and I saw something else odd I hadn't seen in years. He had braces on. *Damn, braces in the apocalypse. That sucks.* He caught me staring, and seemed to misinterpret my gaze because he drew the sword at his hip. "It's a samurai sword. Sick, huh? I named her Jessica."

I was spared answering when Talia strode by and snapped, "Put that stupid sword away."

Harrison immediately obeyed, though I heard him mutter, "Her name is Jessica," as he made his way back to his horse.

Talia's voice lifted above the storm. "Let's move out!" Her voice echoed between the buildings. At once everyone sprung to obey, even Kaden. The man who drove the wagon saluted her as she passed, nothing ironic or mocking in the gesture.

The wagon had already begun to move, at least ten men walking alongside it—most of them without horses. In one smooth motion Kaden mounted the black horse, and then held out a hand to me. I let him pull me up.

Atop the horse, even with my arms wrapped tightly around Kaden, the world felt unsteady. The snow swirled all around us, masking the ruins, so that I could almost pretend it was the remains of Boise around us, and we were riding Kaden's old horse, Red. *Ahh Red, I do miss you.* Part of me hated that the world we lived in now moved on so quickly—daring to love a horse, a city, or another human being was a risk in this world. You never knew how long it would last.

"What's it like?" I called over the growing snowstorm. "The Last City."

"Like nothing you've ever seen."

Then we charged after Talia, riding toward The Last City and leaving Izzie buried in the snow behind us.

I'd gotten too good at saying goodbye.

THREE—ARA

"We're here."

At the sound of Kaden's voice, I lifted my head from where I'd buried it against his shoulder. Snow swept through the ruins, the sun nearly set. Even so, the massive wall before us was unmistakable, running in both directions like a scar across the land. The top rose above the buildings around it and blazed with lights, pinpricks burning through the night.

"Welcome to The Last City, Ara," Harrison said, his blue hair filled with snow. "Prepare to trade the plague for some good old-fashioned oppression."

I didn't even spare him a glance, too caught up in staring at the massive wall. Twenty minutes earlier, our small group of riders had parted ways with the wagon of women when the road split. They followed the main highway while we took a quicker path that cut through the ruins and Talia insisted would get us there before the gates closed. I'd barely had time to raise a hand to the women in the cart before they rolled down the road and into the darkness. If Izzie had been with them, I would have insisted we all stay together. But the despair of losing her still coursed through me—along with the cold realization that maybe they were better off without me.

Now our small group of four horses and five riders all stood on the crest of a hill, staring down at the massive wall cutting through the ruins. I wrapped my hands tighter around Kaden's waist. "Have you been inside?"

He shook his head. "No. After I met up with Talia's group, they left a few men to follow the wagon, and then we went to get more men and weapons for the ambush. I only saw the wall."

"We were lucky to come across him," Talia said. "He was about to try to break you out with no weapons, no escape route, no clue really." She paused, as if she expected some kind of thank-you. *Keep waiting for that.*

The wall cut directly through the ruins, clearly an addition to the city. Before the plague it would have been an interesting structure, but now it felt like finding the Great Wall of China on the moon. "How did they build it?" I said, equally impressed and unnerved.

"Same way history always builds walls," said Ronnie, the last member of Talia's team, in a deep, slow baritone. Unlike Harrison's colorful appearance, the only notable thing about Ronnie was his sheer size and horse to match. "On the backs of innocents."

"No one who makes it to The Last City is innocent." Talia's gaze cut to Kaden and me—I was surprised at the guilty shift in my stomach. "Come on, lovebirds. Join the monster or get eaten by it."

Her horse leapt forward, and the other horses needed no urging, racing down the hill after her. Even with Kaden's warm body pressed tightly against mine, my stomach dropped out beneath me. I'd forgotten what it felt like to ride a horse: the terrifying power, as if you were flying over the ground yet completely out of control.

As we drew closer, I could make out forms walking across the top of the wall, all heavily armed. Blinding lights lined the structure, growing even more brilliant with the darkening sky and falling snow.

It felt like staring into an impossible future—or maybe it was a past I'd thought was lost to us forever. If they had electricity, who knew what else they'd brought back, or maybe never even lost. It felt wrong to hope for a better future when I'd just said goodbye to Izzie, but I couldn't help it.

Our group rode until we came to a path carved through the snow, ruins on one side and the black wall rising on the other. Far ahead of us streetlights burned along a cleared highway.

"Hold up!" Talia yelled as our path ended at a massive gate set into the wall—one that was currently closing. Then, in what felt like an unnecessary addition, "We've got a survivor with us—a woman!"

At those words a few of the men by the gate—all heavily armed—turned to our group. Behind them the main gate slammed shut with a resolute thud, audible over the wind and snow. As we rode closer, I saw there was a much smaller door to the side of the gate. It seemed more like a tunnel, wide enough for only a single person to pass through, with bars on the front and a metal grate that I guessed could slide across and seal the wall completely. Unlike the massive main gate, the smaller tunnel was still open.

Our horses slowed as we approached. Now that the sun was

fully gone, the cold of the night bit even deeper, and the lights of the wall seemed otherworldly. Kaden's breath clouded as he whispered, "Talia said new arrivals have to walk inside the tunnel. They'll scan us there, and then, once we clear, we can pass through into The Last City."

I could hear the false confidence in his voice. A whole summer spent in freedom, just the two of us, and now I was asking him to willingly walk through bars and back into a world governed by men. *It'll be worth it though, if Emma and Father are there. If the truth is there.*

We dismounted, and with a nod from Talia, Harrison and Ronnie took the four horses and started down the road that must have led back to the stables—in the swirling snow it was hard to see far. Kaden, Talia, and I made our way to the door at the side of the looming gate.

As we drew closer, I saw what Kaden meant about being scanned inside the wall. There was a turnstile with bars from top to bottom across the door, so that only one person could walk in at a time. Once you went through, you couldn't go back. Beyond it lay some sort of tunnel that I guessed had bars on the other end. *So they can keep you contained if you test positive.*

"Long live the Chancellor," one of the guards said to Talia, setting his fist over his heart.

Talia's grin soured, but she copied the gesture, something mocking in her voice when she repeated back, "Long live the Chancellor."

I exchanged a glance with Kaden, but there wasn't time to discuss it—one of the guards already gestured Talia forward through the door. She pushed her way past the metal bars, disappearing into the metal tunnel as one of the guards muttered, "Cutting it a bit close tonight, Talia?"

"You know me," she called back. "Besides, I've got a bounty to collect."

She'd better not mean me. Kaden watched Talia disappear into the wall with tense, worried eyes. At least inside it looked dry and warm. Now that we'd stopped moving, the sun gone, the wind cut straight through my jacket and my ears and nose burned with the cold.

The guard pointed the scanner at Talia's eyes and a small beep sounded. "Clear. Next." He sounded as bored as I felt anxious. A screech then a clunk came as Talia pushed her way through the metal bars and into the tunnel.

That's it. Just one scan and I'm in The Last City.

"Do you want me to go first?" Kaden said.

I shook my head. "No, I'll go."

Kaden squeezed my hand, and I walked forward, pushing the bars. Inside, without the cold of the wind and storm, I instantly felt warmer. A large, concrete hallway expanded all around me, the metal chute a small part of what almost reminded me of the inner corridors of a football stadium. The guard lifted the scanner to my eyes and said, in a bored voice, "Long live the Chancellor."

He stared at me, and not sure what else to do, I repeated the words. "Long live the Chancellor?"

This seemed to appease him. I shot a glance back at Kaden as the guard lifted the scanner.

Traveling through the mountains all summer and into the fall.

Everyone we'd lost. Issac. Sam. Izzie. It was all about to be worth it.

And then the scanner made a different sound than Talia's—a sort of angry triple beep. The guard stared at the machine for the longest ten seconds of my life.

No. Please, no.

The guard, a young man with freckles and a crooked nose, shook the machine, and then held it up to my eyes again. I felt paralyzed, terrified, as the same angry sound echoed in the concrete cage.

For the first time the guard looked at me—really looked at me. Another guard, and then another came to his side, the tension building as I stood in the barred tunnel, utterly alone.

"Ara?" Kaden called out, and I glanced back at him as a slow metal grating began to close over the bars that held us apart.

"Kaden?" The grating slowly crept forward, cutting off the night into a smaller and smaller sliver. There was nothing he could do to move forward or me back.

"Ara! Ara, I'll get in tomorrow, I promise—"

His voice was cut off as the metal slammed resolutely closed. The noise of the storm was suddenly replaced by the low murmurs of the guards and the soft buzzing of the lights above—electricity. It would have been incredible, a miracle to me, if I hadn't been trapped here with Kaden outside.

More and more guards gathered, a few of them talking into a sort of radio, muttering words I couldn't make out. Another guard showed up with two other scanners and repeated the same process, with the same result. Slow, cold panic began to grow in my chest.

"It's going to be okay."

I turned to see Talia, safely outside of the second set of bars, hanging back from me. *She's scared of me. Scared I might be infected.* I took a step closer to her, oddly satisfied when she startled back.

"Could you piss off?"

I wasn't even sure why I was angry at her, but I was. She'd shown up, out of nowhere, and now Izzie was dead and I was trapped inside a cage, separated from Kaden. The last person I wanted help from was her.

Talia acted as if she hadn't heard me. "Trust me, I've seen what they do to people who test positive—this isn't it." Her brow furrowed, and she took another step back. "This must be something new."

Something new? Great, that makes me feel so much better. More and more guards gathered, their whispers growing as they looked at me and the scanners. I felt like an animal at a circus, unable to escape. The tension in my chest felt ready to burst, when the mood of the room suddenly shifted.

There, at the end of the long hallway, two guards opened a set of double doors, holding them wide. A man dressed differently than all of the guards, in a gray suit of all things, strode through. He was older, straight-backed, and moved with a clear, commanding purpose.

At once the murmurs silenced, several new phrases echoing again and again as he passed: "Hail Chancellor" and "Long live the Chancellor." Layered together it sounded like some sort of bizarre chant. The men parted before him, creating a corridor through the crowd straight to me.

"Should I be worried?" I whispered back to Talia. But when I turned, she was gone, the only hint of her presence a door at the end of the hallway closing.

"Coward," I muttered, though had I been able, I probably would have followed. I'd survived the apocalypse by hiding, only fighting when I was backed into a corner. *Like I am now.* I stood tall, took a slow deep breath, and slid my hand to the pocketknife

I'd buried in my coat jacket. I'd survived Gabriel and his ruling of the Castellano clan. I'd survived Colborn. Whoever this man was, I would survive him too.

He drew closer, walking beneath the lights, and I got the first good look at his face—and my breath caught in my chest.

No . . . it can't be . . .

I recognized him.

We'd never met in person. I'd only seen him once in a picture my father had shown me, but I remembered it instantly: a middle-aged man with his teenage son, an arm slung over his shoulders, their faces so alike they could have been twins if not for the age difference.

But Father had told me he was dead.

It can't be him. I'm dreaming. Or seeing things. The shock and the cold have finally gotten to me.

And yet . . .

The guards parted as he strode the final few feet forward. His gray suit was tailored to his tall, thin form, everything about him sharp and neat—nothing like my father, who always smelled of the woods, with clothes faded and lined with weapons. He came to a stop a few feet from me, closer than the guards had. Again, I saw the clear resemblance to my father—the high forehead, the sharp cheekbones, the bright, curious eyes—but that was where the similarity ended. My father was always smiling, laughing, whistling. This man's face was cold, foreboding, a careful circle of space around him.

"Walter?" I said. His eyes flickered in surprise, and I said the word I never believed I would: "Grandfather?"

A slow, disbelieving expression worked over his face. A few seconds ago I'd seen only a resemblance to the man in the picture.

But now, standing before me—my father's smile broke across the face of a man I never thought I would meet.

"Arabella." Awe and shock alike rang through his voice. "Welcome to The Last City."

FOUR—KADEN

"Hey, Kaden, look!" Sam's face lit with delight as he tilted a comic book up to catch the sunlight streaming in through the windows.

"What is it?" I didn't move from my spot by the window, or lower my gun from its position trained on the street. When Issac said Sam needed to continue his education and broaden his horizons, a bookstore wasn't exactly what I'd envisioned.

"It's a Batman comic," Sam said, consumed with turning the pages, his bow forgotten on the table beside him.

"Batman worked alone—that meant he was always vigilant. Always alert and watchful," I said, hoping Sam would pick up on my hint. He didn't. Gabriel wanted us back at the clan tonight. At this rate we'd be late, if we made it back at all. As much as I loved pissing Gabriel off, I wasn't sure books were worth it. Then again, I hadn't seen Sam this happy in ages.

Issac finally returned from the stacks, his pack loaded with books.

"Let's go," I said, eager to move on.

But he stopped me, and held out a book of his own. "Here. This one is for you."

Curiosity made me stop, and look down at the cover. "Where the Red Fern Grows?" *There were two red dogs and a boy on the front, and I tried not to scoff. "Let me guess, the boy grows up and the dogs die? Pass."*

Issac laughed. "Yes, it's about a boy and his dogs. But mostly it's about working as a team. And the ones we leave behind."

I didn't read books before the plague, but I'd started to during those couple of years in the clan. I told Sam it was because we no longer had TV or football or social media, but really it was because of Issac. But I hadn't read a single book since Issac had died, not even the Bible he'd given me. It reminded me too much of him. For Issac, every book held a different lesson.

Standing before the massive wall, I wondered what lesson Issac would construct from this situation. Would he think everything we'd been through was worth it? A clan left burning in our wake. Countless lives lost. Months spent journeying through the mountains and then, just when Ara and I had drawn close, the two of us taken captive *again*. Ara and I had both sacrificed so much to follow her father's map here, to The Last City. And I'd lost her the moment she'd walked through the front door.

"Okay. Yes, sir. Thank you, sir. We will do that." Ronnie, Talia's second, hung up the phone outside the wall. He towered over me, reminding me a bit of the massive Clydesdale horse he rode—yet somehow he had the smooth rosy cheeks of a twelve-year-old boy. I stared at him as he stood there, barely resisting the urge to shake him.

"Well?" I couldn't keep the panic out of my voice. The doors had sealed shut twenty minutes ago. I'd run down the road and begged Ronnie and Harrison to come back to the wall to help me demand entry. Instead, Ronnie had slowly picked up the phone and talked to the guards inside while I tried not to rip the phone from his hands.

"Well what?" Ronnie stared at me with calm brown eyes. The night should have been dark with the swirling snow, but the wall's lights blazed above us, blinding us to the shadows that lay beyond.

"Where is Ara?" I demanded. "Is she okay?"

"She's fine. Apparently, she knows the Chancellor. We'll be getting three times the normal reward."

Harrison whooped and thrust his sword—which I refused to call Jessica—into the air. "Three times! Did you hear that, K-man?" He slapped me on the shoulder; I barely felt it over the shock coursing through me. First that they had turned Ara in for a reward—they definitely hadn't told me that—and second that Ara could possibly know someone here. "Why didn't you tell us you knew the Chancellor? We would have turned you in for a reward too!"

"I *don't* know the Chancellor," I muttered as I stepped out of the reach of his sword. My entire plan to fly under the radar and never meet the ruler of The Last City had blown up in the first ten seconds of getting here. But Ara couldn't know the Chancellor . . . could she? The closed gate and wall loomed above me, offering no explanation or passage forward.

"Maybe we could use the reward to get our own place that's not a dump," Harrison said excitedly to Ronnie, both of them already turning and walking away. "Or maybe we could all get our own horses. I swear I could have outrun my last horse. Or maybe a better sheath for Jessica—she could rust in this weather."

"Wait!" I ran after the two of them. I'd once led an expedition team, and then nearly a clan. Surely I could get two men—one of whom had braces, acne, and a sword he'd named—to follow me. "Talia went in already," I said, skidding to a stop before them. "She was with Ara. Aren't you worried about her? Isn't she your leader?"

Harrison and Ronnie's eyes slid together, then away, both of them suddenly quiet. Ronnie finally said, with that slow, deep trudge, "I'm the leader. Not Talia. That's what it says on the expedition team papers."

"I wouldn't lose sleep over it. They're *women*." Harrison winked at me. Somehow being winked at by someone with braces in the apocalypse wasn't remotely comforting. "They're the true survivors in this world—not us. And Talia doesn't like the Chancellor. She probably made herself scarce."

"You're saying Ara's alone with the Chancellor?" My voice crept higher. "Who is he?"

"The ruler of The Last City," Ronnie said simply. Then, almost as an afterthought, he added, "I would advise not getting on his bad side. Or any side. Best never to meet him."

Harrison swung his sword in front of him so that I was forced to jump out of the way—clearing their path. "Don't worry, he's *super* old," Harrison said, the two of them trudging by. "I'm sure you're still her number one."

I stood there, alone in the swirling snow, as they left me to stare up at the blazing, impossible lights. All summer I'd doubted the map and letter that Ara had clung to. But for a moment, standing before these walls, I'd allowed myself to believe we'd finally found a sanctuary. A safe place.

Now I wondered if this was only the beginning of another

clan, another Gabriel, another place that would seek to imprison and control Ara—but on a terrifyingly enormous scale. *And if it is, then you're going to need all the help you can get.*

"Wait!" I called out after Harrison and Ronnie, running to catch up with them. Outside of the reach of the lights, the night was bitterly cold and dark. "Can't we break in somehow?"

"It'll open in the morning." Ronnie shrugged his massive shoulders.

"What about the women in the wagon? Where will they be taken?"

This time Harrison answered. "They've got safe houses out here for women, to hold until the gates open, but even Talia can barely get in them—they won't let you in. They'll take them to the Sanctum tomorrow. Relax, if your girl knows the Chancellor then she's in the safest place in the whole world right now."

That's exactly what I'm afraid of. I cast a final look back at the wall that seemed to bisect the world: ruins on one side, and something different, new, and equally terrifying on the other.

~

The stables were warm and rich with the scents of horses and hay. After all the time Ara and I had spent sleeping on the ground in the mountains, it felt like a luxury bedding down in the hay. Or it would have, had Ara been here.

"Just don't think about it," Ronnie said, as if that were possible. He took up half the stall on his own. "She'll be fine. Probably eating steak and potatoes right now."

Harrison moaned. "No talking about food."

We'd been given a small ration of some smoked fish and dried apples. Even though Ronnie was twice the size of Harrison, it was the latter who'd whined at the small portions.

"I still don't get why you aren't worried about Talia," I said. From what little I'd seen of her, Talia was fierce, but she was still a lone woman in a city of men. "Aren't you all a team?"

Harrison squinted down at his sword, polishing a nonexistent spot before he answered. "Talia's got more lives than a cat—don't think you could kill her if you tried. They'll both probably have a whole harem of new boyfriends before dawn." He winked at Ronnie, who just shook his head.

"You're sure we can get in tomorrow?" I said.

"Gates open at dawn," Harrison said, seeming irritated that no one had laughed at his joke. He turned over in the hay, presenting me with his back. "Then you'll wish you were never in a hurry to get in. All men have to go through citizenship and defense training before getting placed in a job."

"Defense training?" *Sounds like something Gabriel would cook up.*

Harrison shrugged, unable to ignore me despite his turned back. "Basically boot camp but with lots of propaganda thrown in. Teaches you all about how the Chancellor saved us, how we'd die without him, how without him there'd be no plague flower or new tech or electricity and the world would be a dark, broken place, blah, blah, blah. Just say 'Hail Chancellor' a bunch and you'll be fine. Now shut it. Jessica needs sleep."

With that ominous bit of information, the two men fell silent. Ronnie whittled at a piece of wood before he yawned and settled down in the hay. Harrison polished his sword with a rag for a few minutes before he too yawned and then began to snore. The sounds of horses, creaking wood, and the storm outside weren't near enough to still my racing thoughts. Sleep evaded me, straw poking into my back as I stared unseeing at the rafters. How was it possible Ara knew anyone within The Last City? Old fears I thought I'd forgotten—of Colborn reaching for her, of Gabriel with his hands on her waist and mouth pressed against hers—swirled and haunted my restless dreams, until I suddenly came violently awake, a cold hand clamped over my mouth.

I jerked away, reaching for the knife at my waist. A hooded figure loomed above me, a single lantern hung in the center of the barn lighting him from behind. But then my eyes adjusted and I recognized the mocking eyes and slim form.

"Talia!" Anger replaced fear as I shoved my knife back. "I could have hurt you."

She held a hand up to her lips, and then glanced over the edge of the wooden stall, to the noises of the barn beyond. The storm howled outside the barn, a horse nickered softly, no other noises rising. Still, her caution brought me fully awake and alert.

"Did they open the gates?" I whispered.

"No." She crouched low beside me, the wooden door to our stall at her back. "Not for a few more hours. That's why I came here. I know which horses are fastest—I can help you steal one. I'll draw you a map. There're faster ways south than the way you came. Take the highways, there'll be men, but as long as you have a horse and a gun, and travel light, you should be safe."

I stared at her in confusion. "I'm not leaving Ara. The people on the phone said she knows the Chancellor—she could be in trouble."

Her eyes shifted nervously. "I heard that too. That's why I think you should leave. They've been saying she's his granddaughter."

His granddaughter. Shock coursed through me. Of course

Ara had told me about her father, and that he might be in The Last City. But Ara had never told me she had grandparents still alive—or that one might possibly be ruling The Last City.

Ara doesn't keep secrets from me, I wanted to say. Instead, I kept quiet. Her father had kept so many secrets from her—it was entirely plausible she hadn't known.

"Isn't that a good thing?" I finally said. "If Ara's grandfather really is the leader of The Last City, he'll protect her. Maybe that's why her father sent her here. To keep her *safe*."

Talia's eyes narrowed. "Sure. Because all women want is to be locked up and kept safe."

"You were the one who said The Last City was a place where we would be safe."

When Ara and I were both surrounded, the men had promised her safety—so long as I was tied up and left behind. It took me nearly two damn days to cut my way free of the ropes and another agonizing week to find the wagon. But then I was outnumbered, with only a single dull knife. I'd been about to throw caution to the wind and attempt to rescue her regardless when I ran into Talia and her group. After a tense exchange, she explained that the men were selling women along the way, and her orders, from the Chancellor himself, were to stop them and bring the women safely to The Last City. Talia had likely saved not only my life but also those of the women in the cart. How could that be a bad thing?

"It is a good place—in some ways. For some people," Talia finally said, "so long as you keep a low profile, and know who your friends are. But Ara is the Chancellor's *blood*. That changes everything. You can't hide from that."

"Why? Why does it matter?"

"The guards were talking about Ara—her test came up Invalid. That's never happened before. To *anyone*. The best survival strategy in The Last City is to lie low. Recite the stupid sayings, kiss-ass to the officials, follow the rules, swallow your pride, and keep any thoughts to yourself. Surviving means joining the monster—not fighting it. And definitely not testing as the first Invalid ever."

I barely heard her, because a strange sort of pulsing fear had made my mouth go dry. "My test came up as Invalid too."

The two of us stared at each other, different emotions flitting through her eyes, as the storm battered the barn outside. "When?" she finally said.

"After the men tied me up, and Ara was already in the wagon, one of them held up a scanner to my eyes. He said if I was infected he'd spare me a slow death and kill me right then. But it said Invalid. He thought the scanner was broken."

Harrison coughed and muttered in his sleep, and we both felt silent. She looked deep in thought when she said, "Do you remember what happened to the machine they tested you with?"

"He tossed it. It's still out there in the woods somewhere."

Talia nodded at this, looking deep in thought. "Good. We'll make sure it stays lost."

"If Ara also tested that way, it has to mean something . . . right?"

She stared at me, her brow furrowed, and then finally smiled—not what I was expecting. "You know, Kaden, when you insisted on joining our team to save your girl, I thought for sure you'd die in the first five minutes. And then I thought your girl was just another princess bound for the Sanctum. But maybe I was wrong."

"Maybe? Wow, thanks."

She rose just enough to glance over the closed stall door, then sank back into a crouch. "You sure you won't go south?"

"If Ara is inside those walls, that's where I'm going."

She gave a low laugh. "Careful, Kaden; not all princesses want to be saved."

Her tone was teasing, but my voice wasn't. "Ara will always want me. And I her."

She stared at me, something assessing in her eyes. Then she reached into her pocket and lifted out a sort of lanyard with a card at the bottom. "Then take this. It's a shortcut into one of the side entrances where you're supposed to do your own scan—but you can skip it by using this. Be *careful*—they monitor all the entrances. If you only go in once, and stay in, you might be okay. As soon as dawn breaks, be at the side entrance—it's a half mile past the main one, next to the ruins of an old movie theater. Ronnie and Harrison will show you where." She paused, and considered me with a critical eye. "Maybe have Harrison cut your hair first; the blond curls stand out too much. And for the love of God, remember that citizen training is about blending in and conforming, not standing out."

Right. So another clan all over again. I reached out and took the card—it was simple, red on one side, black on the other, with the words *One City. One People. One Ruler.* printed in bold, with a barcode beneath the writing.

"Why all the secrecy?" I buried the card in my pocket. "If they took Ara to the Chancellor for testing Invalid, why would it matter if I tested that way too?"

"I'm not sure—but I'm going to find out." The smirk left her face, some deep warning buried in her eyes. "This isn't some hick clan where you can buy your way in with a fishing pole and some beet seeds. Secrets and connections are just as valuable, if not more so, as food and supplies. The quicker you learn that, the longer you'll survive here." Then she stood and opened the stall door. A creak sounded. She froze, her head whipping sideways at a sound—but it was just a horse moving in the stall beside us.

Only then did I think of what should have been my very first question. "Wait, if the gates are still closed, how did *you* get out here?"

Even in the dark, I could make out the flash of her smile. "Good luck, Kaden." Then she disappeared down the long center aisle of the barn. I waited in tense silence, expecting some kind of tussle as she tried to steal a horse, which would inevitably come back to us. But no noise came. Only the low howl of the storm battering the walls.

Eventually I turned over to find Harrison with one eye open, watching me. "Women," he muttered, shaking his head as he closed his eyes. When it was clear he wasn't going to say more, I settled back into the hay to wait for dawn.

Two Invalid tests. A grandfather who ruled a city I hadn't even entered yet.

Talia was right about one thing: The Last City was full of secrets.

FIVE—SAM

"Walk faster."

I stumbled as she shoved her loaded gun—now being used as a prodding stick—into my back, and bit back a retort. My experiences with women were narrow, but I was pretty sure this was over-the-top.

The dying sunset lit the ruined city shades of red and orange, and the trees that had once grown in neat rows around the parking lot had become a forest-like hedge. Only the pavement prevented nature from swallowing this place whole.

We walked between long-abandoned cars, so covered in dust that you could no longer see inside their shells. A few silver airships also hid beneath leaves and weeds, still shiny despite the seasons passing. I'd once tried to break into an airship, to access whatever new tech lay within, but it was too tightly sealed. The new tech was lost to us—at least until someone figured out how to turn it back on. *Who knows though. Today it was music and a new team member; tomorrow it might be new tech and a girlfriend.* Kaden would have told me I was being overly optimistic.

"We're going this way," I said when we came to a split in the sidewalk, then risked a glance behind me. At my movement she swung the gun toward me. I lifted my hands. "Sorry."

"Just walk."

I'm walking, geez. A small game trail wove through the waist-high grasses and weeds that had sprung up between the cracks of the pavement, a cool breeze bringing scents of sagebrush and decay. Some of the trees had already turned red and gold, heralding the end of summer. Birdsong carried over the open area, and somewhere in the distance a coyote howled.

We passed by a few of the old department stores, their signs faded and insides trashed. I'd already been inside the Old Navy twice this summer for longer pants. Finally we crossed the last street, and I smiled at the glory of the building before.

"Here it is. Home, sweet home." I didn't even try to disguise the pride in my voice. The Castellano clan in the old Cabela's had been impressive—but Gabriel's clan was all about survival and efficiency. My hideout was wholly my own. It was more than just a place to hoard supplies and stay warm. It was about remembering what humanity once was and could be again.

"Barnes & Noble?" Her voice dripped with scorn. "Are you serious? This is your hideout?"

"This is where I found the manual to fix the sound system," I said, disappointed she hadn't seen the immediate genius of it all. "Plus no one ever looks here." And Kaden would know to look for me here.

She stood beside me, a frown on her face as she held her gun and stared up at the faded exterior now covered in vines. What I really wanted to tell her—or anyone—was that if we wanted to fix the world, everything we needed was in this bookstore. *This* was where salvation lay—not in weapons, or canned foods, or all the other pointless places people looked.

The floor-to-ceiling windows had grown dirty in the last few years, but they still let in enough light in the day to shine upon the rows and rows of books. *She just needs to spend some time inside, then she'd understand.*

With that hope, I smiled at her, and at once she swung the gun toward me. "Why are you smiling? If this is some kind of trap, I swear I'll blow your brains out."

"It's not, I promise." My voice squeaked a bit, so I cleared my throat and forced it lower. "But we should get inside. We don't want to be outside once the sun goes down. That's when the infected animals hunt."

"Fine." She gestured impatiently. "Move."

I walked us to the side door, which I'd disguised behind a dumpster and other mounds of junk. To get past it required turning my head, and shimmying behind the dumpster along the wall. She glared at me, forced to point her shotgun straight up as we both squeezed through the small space. When we'd both made it through I pulled the door shut behind us, then turned back to the gun pointed at me.

"Can we lose the gun-pointing thing?"

"No."

"Fine. But can you at least make sure the safety's on?"

She glanced down at the gun. "It's not. And don't tell me what to do."

Was Ara like this when Kaden and I met her? I couldn't remember. With no other option, I turned and made my way through the rows of books, the dying light leaking through the massive windows lining the front. When I first started living here, I'd spent a good amount of time trapping the rodents that kept eating the books. It made me feel like a protector of earth's history. It was meant to be only temporary of course, until Kaden and Ara and Issac came back, but until then, it was nice to have a place all to myself.

The old bookstore café stood in the very center of the store untouched, covered in dust, waiting for people who would never return. No scent of coffee lingered, but the wooden, papery scent of books still triumphed over the scents of dust and rot.

"My hideout's in the back." She didn't respond, but she also didn't threaten to shoot me again. *Maybe I should call it something cooler than a hideout? Fort? Mini-clan? No, that's worse.* We walked silently through the shelves, until I pushed through the door marked EMPLOYEES ONLY, and then paused.

"It's darker back here, and a little cramped. It'll be pitch-black as we go down the hallway. But I've got a pull light in my room." I paused, suddenly wondering how exactly this was going to work.

"What?" she said, eyes narrowing.

"Nothing." I cleared my throat and moved ahead into the hallway. She followed after me, and then the door closed, sealing off the dim light from the sun, leaving total darkness. *Please, please don't shoot me.*

"If you give me your hand, I'll lead you." My heart pounded, my throat dry. *What if speaking is giving her a target?* "It's not too far."

A pause, and then, "Fine."

Slowly, I reached forward with my hand. She jerked back at my touch, but then, after a moment, her hand reached out again and took mine. Her grip was surprisingly tight. We walked together through the darkness.

"Sorry it's so dark," I said, speaking into the silence. "I managed to get light in my own room, but the best defense I have is not letting people think anyone's back here. And putting lights in here definitely would."

"Do people come through this area?"

"Sometimes. That's why I'm careful not to keep things too clean out front. I don't want anyone to know I'm here." *Except for Kaden. But he'll know where to find me.* "This is it. I'll pull the light."

I dropped her hand and opened the door. Nerves crept up my throat as I pulled the light switch for the single bulb I'd managed to rig to the solar panels. Then I stood in the center of the room, wishing I'd cleaned up.

Books littered the floor, posters covered every inch of the wall, and several model airplanes hung from the ceiling. In the corner my only table, taken from the coffee area, was covered with the board game Risk, and the lone chair held a guitar and several "teach yourself to play" books I'd given up on almost instantly—music wasn't really a talent of mine. She looked over my sanctuary with hard eyes, saying nothing.

"I wasn't really expecting someone." I swung my hands at my side, desperately looking for something—*anything*—to do besides stand there and look stupid. My eyes landed on the heater in the corner. "I'm gonna turn on the heat."

It wasn't really that cold, and I'd planned on saving the small battery-powered heater for the coldest winter nights, but I needed something to do. I crouched before it while I made a mental list of everything and anything I'd left on the floor or hanging from the walls. Still she said nothing.

"Are you into comics?" I blurted out. She didn't respond as I hurried to clear off the chair for her. "Never mind. You can sit here—if you'd like," I quickly amended.

She bent and picked up a comic book from the top of one of my bigger piles, and frowned down at it.

"They're original Batman comics," I said into the silence. *Really, really valuable ones.*

She lifted a single brow—something I'd never quite managed to pull off. "Looks like good kindling to me."

"*Ha*. Good one."

When she dropped it back into the pile, I carefully moved the whole stack under my cot, just in case. She sat on the chair, laying the shotgun across her lap, gazing up at my collection of model planes hung from the ceiling. I'd always loved planes; I'd even done a solo scouting expedition out to the airport this summer. But it was far enough away that I'd been forced to spend a sleepless night in one of the planes. The airport held too many memories of the before-days: I'd only ever been there with my mother. The summer she'd died, her eyes white and weeping blood, it had made sense that the world ended too. But Kaden had come for me. Kaden would always come for me.

I cleared my throat, no idea what to do next. What would Kaden have done? Then it came to me. Food. Offer her food. *Girls like food, right?*

"Are you hungry?"

She shrugged and I took that as a yes. One of my plastic bins held the remains of my dehydrated food. As I rummaged through them I took the chance to discreetly sniff under my armpits—and then instantly regretted it. Kaden always said a natural scent was better for hunting, but now I wished I would have ignored that particular piece of advice.

"I've got chicken and dumplings or beef stroganoff." I held up two bags that said they had four servings each, but I could easily devour in one go. "Which do you want?"

"Beef."

We didn't speak as I boiled and poured the water into her pouch and then handed it over with one of the three forks I owned. She was careful not to touch my hands as she took the meal, then set it on top of her gun. She'd pushed back her hood, revealing nearly black hair pulled back in a tight ponytail, a few strands falling free. It was glossy and thick—clearly she bathed. Unlike me. That *also* didn't seem like a safe thing to mention.

You're welcome for the food. I hope you like it. It's really tasty. I was saving it for my brother, but this seems like an occasion to celebrate too. Again, I tried to remember how Kaden had talked to Ara, always smiling and teasing. Instead of inspiring me, the thoughts had the opposite effect, making me stumble when I spoke.

"Are you looking for anyone?" I winced at the question, but she didn't even look up from her food. In her defense, it was good food. "I've been looking for my brother, Kaden, and his girlfriend. I mean, kind of girlfriend. I guess I don't know what he would call her. Do they still have girlfriends anymore?" *Oh my God, shut up, shut up, shut up.*

Her fork paused halfway to her mouth. I thought maybe it was shock, or surprise, at my words. After all, I'd spent three years without seeing a woman before I'd met Ara. But when she spoke, her voice was cold and absolute. "There're no other girls left."

There's you, I wanted to say. "There's at least two others that I know of." I felt almost proud telling her that, but if I'd expected some sort of excited reaction, I was disappointed. If anything, her eyes became colder.

"How do you know they're still alive?"

I paused, considering. "They were the last time I saw them. And they survived the plague so . . ." I trailed off, feeling stupider with every word.

Her gaze was withering. "Then they're probably dead. Besides, it's stupid to look for people. People leave and disappoint you. Better to be alone."

"You don't really believe that, do you?" The words tumbled free before I could stop them.

Her eyes blazed up to mine, her voice cold. "Yes. I do." She paused, took another bite to eat, and then lifted her chin, voice haughty. "I'm looking for . . . some*thing*. Not someone." It took everything in me not to speak, to wait for her to continue, but finally she spoke, so soft I barely heard her over the thrum of the heater. "A city that survived the plague."

I'd heard rumors, everyone had, but even Issac had dismissed them. "What kind of city?"

"A lost city," she said, as if that explained it.

"Like Atlantis?"

It was the wrong thing to say. Her voice became mocking. "No, not like *Atlantis*. A real city, not a stupid made-up one."

"I could help you, you know," I said, desperate for her to know I wasn't making fun of her. "I've got the books in here, and—"

She cut me off. "You shouldn't be so eager to help everyone you meet."

"I'm not eager to help *everyone* I meet." *Just, you know, lost, pretty girls*. I'd also gotten into the habit of feeding a scraggly cat the remains of my kills, but mentioning that wouldn't help my point.

We fell into silence again. After we were done eating, I cleaned my bed free of books and magazines. My cheeks burned bright red when I said, "You can take the bed. I'll sleep on the floor."

I thought she would protest, or maybe just shoot me, but instead she stood, holding her gun the way I remembered my grandmother clutching her rosary. She sat down on my cot as I moved out of her way, giving her as much space as the small, cluttered room allowed.

"I'm going to get my spare sleeping bag out." Narrating my actions seemed the safest way to go. She didn't respond as I dug in the bins and found a yoga mat and one of the spare bags that I'd been saving for Kaden.

"I'm going to pull the light. It'll be dark," I said. She didn't respond.

A soft click, and then darkness. Outside the sounds of the night grew—howls and creaks and creatures—but for the first time in months, I didn't curl into a ball and try to shut it all out with memories of the past, or the pages of a book. Instead, I stretched out on the mat and wondered what she was thinking.

She had been wandering the ruins alone. Which meant, unless she was some kind of superhuman robot like in my comic books—who half the time developed a conscience and got lonely even though they weren't human—she must have been at least a little lonely. After all, she didn't have to follow me back to my hideout. She was the one with the gun pointed at me.

That line of reasoning gave me the courage to whisper into the darkness, "I'm not sure if you caught this earlier"—*when you were trying to shoot me*—"but my name is Sam."

"I don't care what your name is."

The lack of a gun, or at least the hope she couldn't aim in the dark, made me bold. "I just think it would be easier, if I—we—have something to call each other." I thought back to the time Mom had let me get a dog. We had to get rid of her, because my dad was a "whiny jackass" in Kaden's words, but she had the same glossy black hair as the girl. "My dog's name was Callie."

"Do I look like a dog to you?"

I flushed red, glad for the darkness. "No. Sorry. I just meant—Sorry."

There was the sound of her shuffling in the blankets, and I sent up a prayer that she had the gun's safety on, or better yet, wasn't holding it while she slept. Gabriel would have lost his mind; he was always going on and on about knife safety and gun responsibility, the kind of talks that made Kaden roll his eyes and pretend to vomit. But even Kaden was careful when our expedition team was given a gun—which didn't happen often. That was why he was so enthusiastic about me practicing the bow. It was a lot harder to hurt yourself with a bow—though not impossible, as some of my fingers could attest. But now I wondered if Kaden had foreseen the day when we wouldn't have ammo, and would need to fall back on other weapons—the same way we'd been forced to fall back on old tech. I'd almost fallen asleep, lost in memories and thoughts of a different time, when she suddenly broke the silence.

"You can call me M."

M.

Maybe not a whole name, but it felt right. The girl with the gun, searching for a lost city, with only a letter for a name. I smiled, and rolled over in the blanket, then said into the darkness, "Good night, M. I'll see you in the morning."

She didn't respond, but it didn't make my smile any less. For the first time in a long time, I felt hopeful enough to send up a real prayer to Issac's God. He hadn't seemed to be listening much these past few years, but maybe the girl, M, was proof that he was still out there somewhere, watching and waiting, hoping humanity would do better this time.

Please let her still be here in the morning. Please let her decide to trust me. I didn't want to ask for too much, like for the girl to tell me her full name, and maybe even become friends, but I sent up a final request just in case.

And please don't let her shoot me, or herself, in the night.

SIX—ARA

I paced the inside of the cell, the guards outside watching me with wary eyes, silent but for the occasional murmurs. All night it had been like this. The men at a distance, watching me like some sort of wild animal. At first I'd yelled—demanding to know what had happened to Kaden, for Walter to *come the hell back*—but after a while I fell silent and set to pacing. Walter, my grandfather, was the bloody Chancellor of this city and he'd left me in a cell. My brief conversation with him had replayed in my head all night.

Arabella. Welcome to The Last City.

Is my father here? And Emma? He said he would be here.

I closed my eyes, a throbbing in my forehead growing as I pictured Walter's face, the slow sadness that gave me the answer before he even spoke.

I'm so sorry, Arabella. You are the first of your family that I've seen in twenty years.

It's just Ara, not Arabella. And my father said he would come here. He might have gotten lost, or delayed somehow. He will come.

We will have time to talk over all of this in the morning. For now it's safest if you stay the night here. Even if you didn't test positive, we can't break protocol. We've never had an Invalid test, but I'm sure it can be explained. I promise I will have everything sorted quickly.

And then he'd left me here. Ten minutes after being reunited with my long-lost, supposedly dead grandfather, the old bastard had abandoned me.

After an hour, they'd opened a section of the bars to reveal a room with a cot and tiny bathroom—essentially a prison cell, complete with a dish of food someone slid through an opening in the wall and then slammed shut after. It reminded me of the first night I'd spent in the clan, in Gabriel's room. The thought of another Gabriel, another clan, brought a flash of fear that I quickly buried. *This is my grandfather. My own blood . . .* That was better, right?

After the shock, anger, and concern faded a bit, I'd tried to sleep—difficult considering the radio station that played nonstop from some speaker in the walls I couldn't see. Hearing music again was like being brought back to another time, but to my surprise, it wasn't the music that held me captive. It was the man's voice that came on between songs.

The man spoke about The Last City: the brutality of life outside the city, and the advancements and progression inside. Mostly, he talked about the Chancellor. I learned how the Chancellor had discovered and mass-produced the plague flower, whose petals gave a temporary immunity to the plague and was the whole reason for The Last City's existence. He explained how, before the plague, the city had been called Thule, and The Last City was merely a nickname because of the city's commitment to self-sufficiency and independence in case of disaster—an almost self-fulfilling prophecy. I listened as he explained how the Chancellor had emerged from the chaos brought on by the plague and united the city survivors with the discovery of the plague flower. At first, they'd only had enough flower to protect a few hundred, but slowly they expanded, using the local university greenhouses and labs as a home base. They managed to turn the new tech back on in a small, surviving part of the city, and built a wall to protect both the flower and the survivors within. Over time, people began to journey to The Last City, and production of the flower grew. There were also recordings of other men, and even a few women, who spoke of the horrors they'd endured outside the wall, and the new life the Chancellor had given them here. *No wonder he can't be here with me; he sounds busier than God.*

I drifted in and out of restless sleep in the cell-like room, thankful that Rosia and the other women in the wagon had gone their own way. If The Last City was really everything the man on the radio claimed it was, I didn't want my Invalid test hurting the other women's chances to find a home here. One of the guards had said they'd be taken to a protected building for the night, and then transported somewhere safe within the city. I hoped he was right.

As morning drifted closer I came back into the main area, my body on high alert. The men, a mix of old and young, watched me with the same wary fear as last night. I was no longer the lone woman in the clan, protected and honored. I was something different here: *Invalid.*

More food slid through the slot in the prison cell, but I ignored it, remaining in the tunnel area where I could watch the guards. It was nearly dawn: surely Walter would return soon. I placed my head against the cold bars and tried to tune out the words on the radio—currently discussing how many lives the Chancellor had saved by discovering the plague flower and building the wall. Not once all night had the word *Invalid* been mentioned.

Just because a test gave a strange result doesn't mean anything. Just because an old man told you that Emma and Father aren't here doesn't mean anything—even if he is your grandfather. I almost believed myself.

The guard closest to me, slumped in a metal chair, suddenly straightened. A voice crackled low on the walkie-talkie clipped to his vest, and he leaned in to listen. Then he answered back, "Copy that."

He stood, and turned to the other men, raising his voice. "News from the Chancellor." The room instantly quieted, all eyes turning to him. "We can lift the lockdown. The gates will open as normal today, and expeditions are all green-lit to go out. The Council determined the Invalid diagnosis isn't dangerous—it's because she shares the same blood as the Chancellor. The test was based on his blood."

An audible sigh of relief went through the guards. It felt like a weight had lifted off my chest. *Always a good day when you learn you aren't patient zero for some new plague.* The chief guard—whom I'd taken to calling Slump—bent back over his radio and said, "Escorting the prisoner outside the wall now."

Prisoner? I frowned as Slump unlocked the door to the cell. It swung open with an audible creak, and then he looked at me expectantly, as if he and his other companions hadn't spent the entire night ignoring me.

"The Chancellor has cleared you," Slump said unnecessarily. "He's asked for you to meet him outside the wall. Inside Thule."

Thule? I didn't move. "What about Kaden?"

He reached into the cell, and hauled me out before I even thought to resist. "That's above my paygrade."

I stumbled as he dragged me forward, burying angry words. Even though I'd been "cleared," the other guards fell back, giving me a wide berth as we passed. I thought we would go back out, but instead, we finally crossed to the other side of the wall . . .

To the side that opened into The Last City.

After a whole night of waiting, I was going to see what lay beyond the wall. My heart beat faster as Slump stopped before a metal door and scanned his lanyard.

All our long months of traveling I'd been waiting for this moment. I remembered the first time Kaden had brought me to the clan: the sheer, pulsating life within. The clan was a declaration of humans uniting to do more than just survive.

So, what then was an entire city?

Slump opened the door to the outside world. I stepped out, my heart rising like the golden dawn before.

A massive, glorious city stretched out before me. The kind of city that had once existed before the plague. The kind of city that shouldn't have existed now.

Red brick and sandstone buildings rose around me, peppered with tall pines and trees full of fall colors. It might have looked like a college campus, if not for the heavily armed men riding and leading horses through the dawn. Lights glowed within the buildings closest me, the streetlights just now flicking off. There were no burned-out, decaying buildings. No red Xs.

The city sloped down before me, the wall running in an enormous half circle with one side cut through by the river. Cleared streets wove between the buildings, and smaller footpaths twisted through groups of pine. Most of the buildings nearest me were two or three stories, with ivy winding over red brick, and large arched double doors. In the far distance, I could make out skyscrapers, but they were farther downriver, outside the wall.

Smoke rose in dark trails across the city, but it was clear from the electricity and biting cold that most of the buildings must have had another source of heat. Standing there in the morning cold, watching men emerge from buildings and call out to each other, my heart broke in a way I wasn't prepared for. I suddenly remembered everything I had lost. Emma's laughter, her smile. Father dancing with Mother in the kitchen, the warmth of the stove, the hum of the refrigerator, the noise of the television and its blue glow in the night. Not just my family, but my whole world. An entire way of life I had taken for granted until it was suddenly gone.

I took a few steps away from the wall, wanting to see more. The buildings closest to me were a strange mix of old and new. There was the red brick and sandstone, with almost gothic architecture, but in some of the gaps that had once existed between buildings, new structures had sprung up. These were made mostly with wood, all unpainted and rough-looking. It created, in places, a line of uninterrupted roofs. Hung from several of the new buildings were brightly colored posters, the closest of which read LONG LIVE THE CHANCELLOR!

The wall sliced through everything, imposing and out of place. I'd come out to the left of the huge gate, where I could see men lining up—maybe the gate would be opening soon. Just when I wondered if I should walk down into the city, or better yet, make for the main gate and go find Kaden, I saw Walter walking up one of the streets, two burly men flanking him. My chest tightened—not in fondness, but more in preparation for battle. He needed to know that leaving me locked up "for my own good" wasn't something that could happen again.

"Good morning, Ara," Walter called out, his voice ringing through the cold morning air. "Welcome to Thule! Or The Last City, as most call it now. I suppose it's better than The Lost City—I was never fond of that nickname."

"Good morning, Chancellor."

I'd resolved to call him that instead of Grandfather. Grandfathers didn't leave their granddaughters in a cell all night, wondering what the hell was happening.

Despite his age, he moved quickly up the hill. "Apologies for last night, and please, I would much prefer Grandfather. Or at the very least, Walter. Everyone calls me Chancellor, but not everyone is my granddaughter."

And I'd prefer if Kaden and I had found The Last City in a tropical paradise filled with free pizza and everyone I loved. But I forced myself to be pleasant. If the plague had taught me anything, it was that sometimes flattery got you more than fighting—especially with powerful men. I'd only just entered The Last City, and I could already see that Walter ruled here in a way that even Gabriel hadn't managed.

"Fine, *Walter*. When you left me in the cell all night, Kaden was left on the other side of the wall. I'd really like to see him."

"Yes, I was told—Kaden came through this morning at dawn. I had him personally placed in the citizen training class we reserve for our best and brightest. The first day they go easy on them—it should only be a few hours and then he'll be brought to the Outpost. It's a group living house I thought would be a good fit for you both."

The swiftness of his response took the wind straight out of my sails. "Citizen training?"

Again, he smiled. "All new male recruits to the city are required to complete a monthlong training course. We train them for defense of the wall, teach them our rules, and then find them an appropriate job within the city. After living in the ruins, it takes some time for people to realize we're all expected to work together here. A few people choose not to stay after completing our training. It helps to make sure everyone in The Last City knows and serves our purpose."

"Which is?"

Again, he gave me that wide, disarming smile. "To live in peace and prosperity." He gestured to the city beyond. "Come. I will give you a tour of the city—a citizen class from the Chancellor himself."

The way he said it sounded like I'd won some great prize. Then again, maybe I had. I'd spent the last few months just trying to survive. This was The Last City—humanity's final holdout. My heart beat faster as together we walked deeper into the city.

"This part of the city was the old university." Walter gestured to the buildings with the elegant arches and spires. "Before the plague I was the Chancellor here. The labs and greenhouses we had on campus were instrumental to the plague flower and food production—really the campus saved us. It's why we first started building the wall here, to protect our greenhouses."

As we walked through the old college buildings, and toward the line I'd seen gathering at the gate, I felt like I was on some sort of bizarre campus tour led by my grandfather. *Well, I always did want to go to college.* When we reached the line of waiting men I got my first glimpse at the men here who weren't guarding the wall. They were rough-looking, heads and faces mostly covered in thick wool hats and scarves, most holding guns, machetes, knives, or other homemade weapons—definitely not college freshman attire. Besides the heavier winter clothing and snow boots, I didn't see much difference between the men here and the men of the Castellano clan.

"What are they waiting for?" I said.

"The gates to open." Walter nodded at the gate, a look on his face like I'd missed some joke. "It took a bit longer today with the Invalid scare." *Ahh, Invalid scare. Me.* "Many of the men who can't find jobs within the city go out during the day and search for supplies we can't produce inside the city. They return by nightfall and trade what they've found for food or plague flowers."

Without fail, every man we passed placed his fist over his heart and murmured some iteration of "Hail Chancellor," "Long live the Chancellor," or simply "Chancellor." None of the men addressed me. Instead, their eyes flitted to me and then quickly away, as if they were afraid to look at the girl standing beside the Chancellor. *They couldn't know I tested as Invalid . . . could they?* At the clan, I knew why men watched me. Here I wasn't sure.

Then I saw a woman standing in the line. Two long gray plaits showed from beneath her hat. She stood with one hand laid easily against a machete on her hip, a black spray-painted gun across her back, like some kind of elderly postapocalyptic Viking. Two men stood at her side, the three speaking with thick accents I couldn't place. As we drew closer, they fell silent, murmuring "Hail Chancellor" as one as we passed. I was barely spared a second glance.

"The women here are allowed to come and go?" I said when we'd moved on. *There was a woman just standing there.* I couldn't stop the strange, warm sensation filling my body. A woman who wasn't a prisoner. A woman who was *free*.

"Of course. The Last City isn't a prison. All citizens are free to come and go—the wall is a precaution against the plague and people who would threaten our peace, nothing more. In fact, we recently opened the ruins for scouting expeditions." Walter gestured to the last few people in line: a man on horseback with multiple limp cloth sacks hanging off his mount—presumably ready to be filled. "I'm sure the line will die down in the next few weeks, when things start to get picked over. Once summer hits people will roam farther, but for now the cold brings everyone back by nightfall."

"I heard them talking about the wall on the radio—that some people were against the wall originally."

"Yes, our city is filled with people from every walk of life, and the world over—it's why we have citizenship training for newcomers. We can't afford the kind of division cities once had."

"Would you like me to greet you with a 'Hail Chancellor'?"

He laughed at my tone—a sound that reminded me so much of my father it hurt. "While I have a council of advisors, we found that the city needs a strong ruler. One person to unite behind. The greeting isn't necessary."

Memories of Colborn and Gabriel churned inside me, and of the way power corrupted men. I didn't say anything, but Walter chuckled regardless. "You look exactly like your father when you disagree with something—I can see the disapproval in your eyes and mouth."

This surprised me—I wasn't used to anyone but Kaden reading me. But since he already had, I didn't see a reason to lie. "I guess I've seen what happens when one person has too much power."

"What alternative would you suggest?"

"What about a leader elected by the people?"

"And how did that go before the plague? Did the leaders elected by the people protect them or care for them? How about when the plague came? Did those individuals sacrifice their lives and well-being to help those they ruled over?"

The world had fallen so quickly . . . and yet, even before that, it seemed like leaders only looked after themselves and their own. The poor got poorer and the rich got richer. "No. I guess not."

"Here within these walls, my people are safe and well, my decisions are absolute and swift—because they need to be. The plague has given us no choice. One city, one people, united beneath one ruler."

They were the words I'd seen on a poster. It sounded so perfect. Yet I shuddered to think what all of Boise would have looked like united beneath Colborn.

Except this was my grandfather, and he was partly right. I had watched the world fall. What Walter, the Chancellor, had done here was incredible—who was I to judge how he'd done it?

The area we walked through was mostly industrial buildings that looked as if they had been repurposed into housing. Men came and went in the early morning sunshine. Most of the windows were smashed or boarded over and many of the walls were spray-painted with graffiti, yet when I could see inside, I saw clear signs of life. Beneath the fresh layer of snow were piles of refuse and garbage that no one seemed to give a second glance.

Finally I could wait no longer. "What about my father? And Emma? You're sure they aren't here?"

"No one enters or leaves this city without me knowing," Walter said as we passed by an old gas station where the metal overhang had created a protective covering for a group of makeshift tents beneath. "Your father and Emma would have tested as Invalid, and I would have been notified immediately."

The fact that he thought he knew everyone who entered and exited this city wasn't comforting. I wondered if I should press him, or question him further, or if it was better to pretend contentment. "I just worry about him," I finally said, deciding to hold back. For now.

"It's a long journey from Boise to here. A thousand things could go wrong. If your father said he would come here, then give him time." He swept a wide hand out to the city rising all around. "Lucky for you, The Last City is a beautiful place to wait."

I thought on his words as we walked down the snowy streets, the radio station playing some soft and sweet piano melody that echoed between the buildings. As the city awoke, the scents of horse manure, baking bread, and the cold river all mixed together. It was beautiful—wondrous even. Part of me desperately wanted to call this place home.

But without Emma and Father, I wondered if it would ever be enough.

~

Humidity hung hot and heavy in the air as Walter and I walked side by side down the rows of plants in the biggest greenhouse I'd ever seen. Walter had spent the walk here explaining that the plague flower gave a temporary immunity to the plague, but was only effective when fresh. Without access to cars or airships, transporting it over long distances was near impossible.

Opaque glass showed the snow-ridden streets outside, but

inside the massive greenhouse, it felt like we'd stepped straight from a northern winter into a tropical rain forest. The men working in the greenhouse stopped working to watch Walter and me, murmuring "Hail Chancellor" as we passed. Walter greeted each with a slight smile.

"Is this all powered by new tech?" I asked when we'd finally passed the group of workers and stood alone. The greenery stretched all the way up to the ceiling, on huge rotating planters.

"Yes. After the first year we disabled our airships—they took too much energy, and we no longer have oil for cars. We use horses mostly for transportation now—we grow a sort of green moss that keeps them docile and fat in the winter."

"The new tech failed in Boise. How did you keep it running here?"

He gave me a sly look that I was beginning to recognize. *He's clever, and he knows it.* "It shut down worldwide, as a sort of failsafe. It takes a massive surge of energy to turn it back on. We're lucky to have a nuclear reactor here and used it to get power started again."

A surge of energy: Would that be possible elsewhere? His words brought a flood of possibilities. The clan. Home. We could turn it all back on again. I tried to picture Gabriel's face if I came back and told him I knew how to get the new tech power back citywide. *Hey hubbie, sorry I fake-married you and burned down the clan. Would you forgive me if I could get the power back on?* The more I thought of it, the more appealing the plan sounded: so long as I could find Emma and Father first.

Walter led me to another section of the greenhouse, and I was surprised to see two armed guards outside the door.

"Chancellor," they said together, and then opened the door.

Unlike the other greenhouses, this one was filled only with flowers blooming a shade of red that was as deep and rich as fresh blood.

"The plague flower," Walter announced proudly. "We were able to produce a temporary cure in the blood of one person—but giving that blood to others was impossible. The plague flower was our solution. They propagate the immunity across the entire species. We send the flowers daily to food production stations across the city, rotating what section gets it when. Come, try one." He picked a flower and handed it to me.

"I just . . . eat it?" He nodded, and I put the small flower on my tongue, tasting faint earthy sweetness. "Whose blood?"

He didn't respond, so I repeated the question. "Whose blood do you feed the flowers?"

Finally he turned to me. "Mine."

"Can I see?"

He hesitated again. "I suppose I can show you the water tank."

He walked us over to a huge water tank, hoses running out in every direction. He stared down at the swirling water, his voice soft when he said, "Most of my colleagues gave their lives to find the cure. And your grandmother. It was a sacrifice that saved the world. The plague flowers are all but sacred here—the entire existence of The Last City revolves around them."

The dark water made a low rumbling as it churned and frothed. I wondered if he spilled his blood directly into the water—barbaric but fitting. Maybe the cost to save the world was paid in blood. I stared up at the vast rows of flowers, the blinding lights and soaring ceilings made the room feel like some kind of church. They seemed like such a small, fragile thing to hold back a world of darkness.

"What happens if they stop working? Or you run out?"

"Then The Last City ends." He seemed far too calm for a man admitting how easily his city could fall. "Come. There's one more thing I'd like to show you."

The wind felt twice as cold when we left the warmth of the greenhouses behind and walked a long bare street. The two bulky men still trailed us, and this time I noticed while most people greeted us, there were others who gave us a wide berth, or went a different way entirely rather than pass by Walter. We passed more of the posters I'd seen originally, some with Walter's face printed in shades of red and black. It all made me wonder why my father had never spoken of him, and yet had sent me here. What other secrets had he kept from me?

We passed beneath a grove of bare trees before Walter drew to a stop. There, to the left of the street, was the first expanse of open area I'd seen in the city. Looming out of a sloping lawn filled with trees of red and gold stood a massive cathedral, arching spires dusted with snow. It looked like something straight out of a storybook—or it would have, except for the heavily armed men standing just outside the wrought-iron gate.

Then, there, on the brick wall that lay beside the gate, I saw it again.

The black spiral.

The mark I'd seen in the ruins. The mark I'd seen on the front door of my home.

My heart beat faster: if the mark had been on my home, on the road, *and* here, that had to mean something. "What does that spiral mean?" I said.

Walter's lips flattened, his eyes flinty when he glanced at the spiral. "Some people use it to mark their houses in the ruins—to let others know they mean to journey to The Last City." He waved a dismissive hand, and for the first time, I sensed he wasn't telling the whole truth. Because if what he said was true, then why would the symbol be inside The Last City? "I thought you would want to know where the women who were with you in the wagon ended up." Walter gestured to the cathedral. "They have all decided to join the Sanctum."

If I were being honest, thoughts of Kaden, Father, and Emma, as well as my blood testing Invalid, had wiped the women from my mind. But looking at the wide sloping lawn, the cathedral beyond, I was suddenly ashamed I hadn't asked about them before. "Are we going in? Can I see them?"

"No man may step onto the grounds. Not even me."

"What if they want to leave?"

"All citizens within The Last City are free to leave it. But in a city of men, most women feel safer within the Sanctum. A few take jobs elsewhere. You met one such woman."

He said it with pride, though I wondered if he'd be so proud if I told him how fast she disappeared last night. "Talia?"

"She's one of our best expedition leaders. And she has brought back more women than anyone else. Captured women are more likely to trust another woman." *Yeah, well, not all of us.* "It's not a perfect system, but I hope you can help with that."

"Me?"

"You are your father's daughter—I can see how you question everything." My cheeks burned but he only chuckled. "It's a good thing. Ruling The Last City is a massive, complicated task. I could use your help." He gestured to the cathedral. "Of course, it would be unfair of me not to offer you a different alternative."

I shuddered at the thought of living in some old church,

cloistered inside like a nun. Even though Rosia and the others were inside, I was surprised by the cold feeling I got looking at the building. The silence of the lawn, the arching spires—it felt cold, wrong. *A beautiful cage is still a cage.*

"Are they already inside?" I asked.

Walter nodded. "Yes—all but one who had a small wound and went to the hospital first. You're welcome to visit her tomorrow. The other women were the first wagon to come through the gates this morning—the safety of our female residents is our number one priority. I was told they all chose to join the Sanctum together. They should do well there; it's a tightly knit community. Most women choose to join—but a few don't."

I heard the undercurrent in his voice. The ones who didn't join were the loners, the different ones. Like Talia. Like me. But if Kaden couldn't be there, then neither could I. "Could I go check on them later?"

"Of course. I will assign you a female guide to show you around The Last City. She can bring you. I figured you would want to speak with the young man you came with first."

The young man I came with. I guess that was one way to put it. I nodded, staring at the building before I pulled back from the bars. Even if it wasn't for me, I hoped Rosia and the others had found what they were looking for. "I don't want to stay somewhere Kaden can't."

"I thought you would say that. Onward then, to our final stop."

No movement came from beyond the gates, and I gave the silent cathedral and the black spiral a final glance before I followed him.

We walked down into more industrial streets: filled with decrepit warehouses and fences topped with barbed wire. It looked like a once-beautiful city that had been repurposed into a darker, more dangerous version of itself. Even the vibrant graffiti held sinister messages: "Repent, sinners!" "We are the forgotten," even "Death to the Chancellor." I glanced at Walter when we passed the last message spray-painted on a brick building. He didn't even blink. *Guess you've got to be made of strong stuff to rule the world's last surviving city.*

Between many of the buildings lay trash, discarded furniture, and shelters where men had used the solid wall of the building to create some sort of temporary dwelling. Deeper in a few of the alleyways, men gathered around metal trash cans with fires burning inside. I even glimpsed a stray dog, lean yet bright-eyed as he rooted through the dirty snow.

Finally Walter stopped beside a large red brick building, vines crawling up one side with two large pines framing the front door. The street outside it looked cleaner than the others—or at the very least, there were no bars on the windows, and the small buildings that sprung up on either side of it appeared solid. Above the aged wooden door, someone had painted, in messy capital letters, THE OUTPOST.

"This is where I leave you," he said. "I believe it was once an old sorority building, but someone tore down the letters. Everyone calls it the Outpost now. Many of our newcomers come here."

"You aren't coming in?"

"No. I have neglected my duties long enough. But, as I said, I will make sure you have a guide to help you find your way around, and find work within the city. And I sincerely hope you'll come by my house. I hope we can get to know each other better."

"I will."

He held out his hand, but I stepped past it and wrapped my

arms around him, surprising both of us. Even if I had my questions, even if I would keep looking for Father and Emma, I didn't want this to go the way of the clan. I wanted to give The Last City a chance—and that included Walter. "Thank you, Grandfather . . . for everything."

His hands hesitated, and then settled around me. "Welcome home, Ara."

SEVEN—ARA

The sounds of distant laughter and voices greeted me as I opened the door of the Outpost, scents of wood and well-worn carpet rising all around. My memories of sorority houses in movies were of shiny white floors and cream-colored carpets—the exact opposite of this place. Dirt and grime clung to every surface. *Maybe it was a frat house, not a sorority.*

To my left was a sort of lounge area, with a glass case that still held a few trophies now mixed in with an array of canned foods and ammunition. To my right stood a large room with a battered piano in the center, covered in books and weapons. An array of maybe thirty cots surrounded the piano, all with backpacks, shoes, and clothes strewn at random. It reminded me a bit of the clan—or at least, the clan without Gabriel.

A stairwell opened into an even dirtier downstairs, lit by buzzing fluorescent lights, a single open room jammed with men laughing, talking, eating dinner. If not for the wide span of age ranges it might have seemed like some bizarre college gathering.

Most of the men looked to be in their early twenties, a few seemed barely more than children, and a handful at most looked like they could be over thirty. Regardless of age, nearly all wore a startling mix of weapons. Rifles, pistols, knives, spears, even a few machetes. There was a distinctive stink that made me pause on the stairwell, and wonder if maybe I should rethink life in the Sanctum.

"Drink! Drink! Drink!" The men at one of the tables chanted as a man at the end downed a pitcher of amber-colored liquid, raucous cheers erupting as he slammed it back onto the table.

Then I saw him—his blond hair catching the light. Warmth filled me, and relief so intense I almost ran to him. His back was to me, he had new clothes on, and something else—he'd cut his hair short. *A few hours away and he cuts his hair!* Sitting beside him on the long bench sat a slight figure with her long dark hair flowing free, and the warm, happy feeling diminished a bit. Of course Talia was here. I stepped out of the dim stairwell and into the light.

At first no one noticed. Then one man punched another, until a man pointed to me and slurred, *"Look! A girl,"* then promptly fell backward off his bench. The room roared with laughter as I paused, frozen by a room of curious faces turning to look at me.

Then Kaden turned and his eyes caught mine. There was no hesitation. He vaulted off the bench, running to me, and swept me clean off the ground. His mouth pressed against mine—in front of a now-cheering room.

When he pulled back, my cheeks burned red at the whistling and applause, but my smile matched his. Kaden was happy and here with me—what mattered beyond that?

"Missed you, Princess," he whispered and kissed me once more on my forehead, before he set me down and turned back to the room. "Everyone—this is Ara!"

My face burned. There were shouts of welcome, and drinks raised as Kaden pulled me away from the others and back up the stairs.

"Where are we going?" I said, breathless. He didn't answer, flashing me a smile. We climbed three flights of stairs, to the very top floor of the building. There was a long central hallway and numerous doors that branched off both sides, almost like a hotel. We walked to the final door in the hallway, and he opened it.

"What's this?" I stepped into a small room with steeply slanted walls, a single bed, and a massive window dormer.

"This is our room."

"Our room?" The words felt strange on my tongue. The whole time we'd been together we'd either been traveling, trapped in the clan, or fighting to survive. The idea of just having someplace safe, to lie down and sleep, to talk . . . I wasn't sure I even knew how to do that. His arms wrapped around mine from behind, and I leaned back into his chest, staring at the room in wonder.

"Are you all right?" he said after a few moments of silence.

"I think so. It feels . . . strange. I guess I've gotten used to not trusting anyone or anything."

"Well, it's definitely an upgrade from sleeping bags on the forest floor," Kaden said. Then he surprised me again. "How did it go with your grandfather?"

Did everyone know? I supposed life in The Last City might be more like the clan than I imagined: secrets were impossible to keep. I shrugged, settling for some piece of the truth. "Fine, I guess. He said my father and Emma aren't here."

"Do you believe him?"

"I don't know him . . . but what reason would he have to lie?"

Kaden was silent at this; I took it as tacit agreement. I gently pulled from his arms and turned to face him, wanting to read his expression. His smile was careful, strained, but his touch, when he reached out to brush my hair behind my ear, was as gentle as ever.

"I know you want the truth," he said, "but sometimes the truth comes with a cost. Are you sure this is what you want?"

"I can't leave without knowing if my father or sister are really here. I just need some time. To find out if he's telling the truth and to look around the city."

"And if we don't find them?" His voice was gentle, but I knew what he wanted. I was the one who'd wanted to come here. And now that Walter had said that Emma and Father weren't here, I wasn't sure where that left us. How long could I ask Kaden to pursue my family and my truth when he'd already left his home, and lost his family, for me?

I leaned forward and stood on my tiptoes until my forehead pressed against his. The promise I spoke wasn't given lightly. "If we can't find them, we leave in the spring. Go back to Boise and build a new home there together. I promise."

Kaden. The truth. My family. That was all I needed and wanted. I prayed that I wasn't reaching too far, wanting too much.

He lips pressed against mine, gentle and then more insistent. For the first time in a long time, I let myself forget everything, and lost myself in only that moment.

~

Lunch was still in full swing when we came back downstairs. Kaden took me to the table he'd been sitting at. A couple of the men introduced themselves, a few others heckled us for taking so long, but overall they seemed a friendly bunch. I recognized the two men from Talia's team: Harrison, the teenager with braces, the leather trench coat, and vivid blue hair; and Ronnie, who barely seemed to fit on the bench. And of course, Talia, who watched us both with a sort of smug expression on her face. Each of them welcomed me to the Outpost with a sense of pride.

"Thanks," I said when Talia slid a full plate of food in front of me—potatoes, a strange sort of lumpy burger, and greens.

Talia squeezed onto the bench beside me. "The cook is a cranky bastard, but the food isn't too bad. He even said they got an extra shipment of food now that the Chancellor's granddaughter will be staying here."

I looked at Kaden in surprise, but he only shrugged, his eyes tight at the edges. *Great, so everybody knows then.*

"The burger's crap—it's all from the greenhouses," Talia went on without pause. "Some kind of mashed bean that they add those nasty bugs to." Her voice held none of the awe Walter's had when explaining the wonders of "insect protein production."

Ronnie shook his massive head. "I miss cows."

Harrison laughed. "We've still got you."

Ronnie punched him, nearly knocking him clean off the bench.

Talia rolled her eyes, unconcerned as she focused on me again. "Ignore them. I do. It'll be nice to have another woman here. Someone civilized." She leaned over, speared her burger, and ate it straight from her dagger.

Right. Civilized. I took my first bite of the burger. It definitely wasn't meat—but I'd been hungry too many times to complain about a full meal in front of me.

"So Ara, I heard you got your own personal citizen class from the Chancellor this morning. Learn anything interesting?" Talia said.

There was some kind of hidden meaning in her voice I didn't understand. It made me cautious. "Considering I haven't been to a normal class, I wouldn't know the difference."

Harrison laughed and slapped Kaden on the back. "Yeah, Kaden, how was citizen class this morning? Give us all a refresher on the Chancellor—did he discover the moon?" There were a few low snickers at the table, but Kaden didn't laugh.

"They talked about how the city was formed, and how the wall was built. Mostly it was about the Chancellor." Kaden's voice was careful, but Harrison's wasn't.

"Kaden's downplaying it—he'll be breathing, weeping, and shitting Chancellor stories by the end of the training," Harrison said.

"You're just mad you almost failed the physical," Talia said, her voice smug.

Harrison's ears turned bright red—interesting against his blue hair. "I didn't *almost* fail. My officer was an ass and you know it."

The two set to bickering, and I turned to Kaden, lowering my voice. "I forgot to tell you. My grandfather said there's a way to get the new tech power back on with a surge of energy. It might be possible to get it back on in Boise."

Kaden's eyes suddenly became distant, accessing: the look of an expedition leader. "Sounds like Gabriel's wet dream," he finally muttered. "Even if we got it back on, I hardly think we'd get a warm welcome."

"What'd you do?" Harrison said.

The others at the table suddenly fell silent—I'd thought we were talking privately, but Kaden only laughed. "Ara burned the clan down before she left."

Harrison choked on his food, while Talia lifted a single brow. "Respect."

"I didn't mean to burn it down." I sent Kaden a hard look. "It was only supposed to be a small decoy fire."

Kaden grinned, not bothering to keep his voice down even when I stomped on his foot under the table. "She also fake-married Gabriel, the clan leader, seduced him, only to sedate him with horse tranquilizer."

My cheeks burned red as the whole table laughed now. "I didn't *seduce* him," I muttered. "It wasn't that dramatic."

Kaden's laughter held a dark edge now. "He deserved it." His voice became thoughtful. "Still, it'd be a hard journey back to Boise in the winter. Better to wait until spring." I was thankful that he seemed to be on board with that plan now—and hoped it would be enough time.

Talia nodded as if she had some sort of say in his decision. "The citizenship training is only a month. It's hard, but most people are so happy to be here they'll do or say anything. Just don't volunteer for the Captain's class—he trains men to the bone. And his teams go out all year, even in the winter."

I had a sudden sense of foreboding. Walter had said he was putting Kaden in some sort of special group. What if it was the one she was talking about? But I said nothing—I wasn't sure if I trusted Walter, but I definitely didn't trust Talia.

"Are the men who were at the gate today part of expedition teams?" I said.

Talia scoffed. "Those are scavengers. They might as well be buzzards picking at the rotting carcass of the ruins."

"Wouldn't mind if we could go out a few times," Harrison muttered, earning himself a dirty look from Talia.

"We aren't scavengers." Talia's voice was ice-cold. "We do sanctioned missions or not at all."

I sensed another fight about to break out. Before it could, I turned to Ronnie. "What job do you have, Ronnie?" Surely there had to be other, safer jobs that Kaden could take in The Last City. The thought of him leading expedition teams into the ruins without me made me nervous.

"In the summer we do sanctioned missions," Ronnie said. "But in the winter we mostly do security. Classified security."

"Actually, we mostly look at security cameras and foota-ARRG—" Harrison bellowed as Ronnie elbowed him in the ribs.

"*Classified* security." Ronnie went back to eating. "And we don't take newbies."

I exchanged a glance at Kaden. He smiled back. *Guess we're newbies now.*

"Don't fret, Ara," Talia said, something mocking in her voice. "Kaden will be busy with training, but I was assigned to show you The Last City." My fork froze halfway to my mouth. Of course it was Talia that Walter had assigned to me—she was the only other woman I'd seen in the Outpost. Still, I wished I would have realized it sooner and asked Walter for someone else. "I'll keep you so busy you'll wish you'd never left Boise at all," she went on.

Might not need to do anything to make me wish that. Kaden caught my eye and lifted a brow, as if silently asking what I thought of spending my days with Talia.

In response, I turned to Talia. "I saw a black spiral symbol in the ruins. And today, on a wall outside the Sanctum. What does it mean?" I left out Walter's explanation—I wanted to hear hers. I wanted to know what kind of guide she would be.

Her smile reminded me of a cat with a bird caught in his jaws. "Everybody in The Last City has their own theory—it's practically a rite of passage. Once you have your own story, you belong here."

It didn't escape me that she hadn't answered. Harrison cut in. "Most people think it started as a symbol left on their houses to tell others they were coming to The Last City. But I think it's because there's a whirlpool beneath the city, somewhere in the tunnels."

"There are tunnels beneath the city?" Kaden said.

"Full of more secrets than there are rats in the ruins." Talia turned to me and grinned. "I'll show them to you both. No one knows The Last City like I do."

Harrison leaned toward me and muttered under his breath, "True. And no one's a bigger pain in the ass."

~

Kaden and I sat side by side on the windowsill of our room, legs dangling free. From up here, the city was picturesque, dark trails of smoke drifting into an eggshell-blue sky, the roofs dusted in snow. Music drifted up from a cracked window from the floor below us, but I wished the man on the radio would come back on. He had just finished a story about the Chancellor and his work on genetics before the plague. Everything about Walter sounded impressive. Which only increased my confusion—why hadn't my father told me about him?

"Did you ever think we'd hear music again?" Kaden suddenly said, interrupting my thoughts.

I pushed away thoughts of The Last City and Walter and focused only on him. "I never really thought about it." I'd been too busy trying to survive, to find Emma and Father, to think about what we'd lost.

Kaden stared out over the city, playing with the ring on the necklace around his neck—the one Issac had given him. "Sam always believed we'd get it all back on. He even had a stash of CDs. I didn't even know people had those anymore. I never really cared beyond survival, but Sam always had hope. I wish he could have seen all this."

Something about the dark, withdrawn look on his face scared me. A few times over the summer Kaden had gone silent for days at a time. Only the constant movement and vigilance needed for life on the road seemed to keep him from slipping into a dark place. I knew he blamed himself for Sam and Issac's deaths, but I didn't know how to make him see it wasn't his fault. "Maybe he does see it," I said softly. "Maybe he and Issac are together up there, watching and laughing at us."

"Wonder what Issac would say about Walter and Talia?" Kaden said.

"Probably that we need to pray for them."

This drew a laugh out of him. I didn't say what else I was thinking: that maybe my father and sister were up there with Issac and Sam too. Maybe I'd brought him here for nothing. But I was tired of talking—instead, I pulled Kaden toward me. His lips met mine, and I threaded my fingers through his hair as he pulled me closer. It was one of the things I loved best about Kaden—he never did anything halfway.

When he finally pulled back, his voice was low and rough, his grin wicked. "You know, having our own room isn't the worst."

This time I laughed. "Are you saying you could get used to life here?"

It was the wrong thing to say. Kaden's face fell. "Ara . . . I—"

I cut him off before he could say more. I needed him here. Maybe it was selfish, but I couldn't do this without him. "Just till spring—then we go back. With you in the training class, and me working with Walter, we can find out if he's hiding something." I'd already told him privately that the Chancellor had placed him in the Captain's class. To my surprise, it hadn't fazed him. "And I'll see what Talia has to show me in The Last City. Even if Walter is telling the truth, that he hasn't seen my father, it doesn't mean he couldn't have missed him. My father had a way of . . ."

"Disappearing?" Kaden filled in.

"Exactly."

Kaden nodded, turning back to look over the long stretch of roofs. "The citizenship class doesn't worry me—Ronnie said it's basically boot camp. But I am curious what the Chancellor's team does in the ruins."

I bit my lip, holding back my words of concern, but Kaden read them anyway. He lifted my chin, his voice soft now. "I'll be careful. And if this isn't the place for us, we go back to Boise in the spring." I heard the longing in his voice—but he'd agreed to stay, and that was all I needed. I had until spring to find the truth, and I would make use of every moment until then.

"You'd make the long journey back with me?" I knew what his answer would be, but I wanted to hear it anyway. His green eyes lit up and he pulled me to him, my heart dancing to a different rhythm than the music.

"I'd go anywhere with you."

EIGHT—SAM

Dawn crept in through the windows as I moved silently through the shelves of books, trying to remember a book I'd seen weeks ago and dismissed. All night I'd thought about what M had said. About her search for a lost city. Then, in the early morning, it hit me. If her lost city was real, then chances were it was in a book. I knew of just the one.

I found the shelf with a collection of books published by local authors. My hands trembled as I pulled the book free. A cloud of dust erupted, as if it were some sacred ancient treasure, and I, the brave archeologist, was unearthing it.

"What the hell are you doing?"

M's voice rang clear and sudden as a gunshot. I nearly dropped the book as I spun. She glared at me from beneath the dark hoodie—pulled up again. Holding up the book, I tried not to look guilty while also wondering if it would work as a shield.

"I was thinking about what you said," I said. "About your search for a lost city. And then I remembered this book, *Local*

Superstition and Conspiracy Theories of the American Northwest. I saw it a while back and dismissed it, because I figured it'd just be all about Nessie and Sasquatch, but, then, this morning, I thought if any book was going to have a mention of a lost city, it would be this one. So I got up early and found it for you."

The silence stretched out as I extended the book and waited for her words of praise and appreciation—maybe even a smile. Instead, her eyes grew colder.

"Sasquatch?" Her voice was a razor.

Too late I realized maybe I shouldn't have compared her lost city to finding Sasquatch. "Not that the city is *like* Sasquatch, it's just the first comparison I thought of. A lot of people believed in Sasquatch around here, there's some really compelling evidence." *Oh my God, shut up.* "Never mind, forget that I said anything about Sasquatch. I haven't even opened it yet, so I honestly don't know what's in it. I thought maybe you'd want to do the honors."

"The only Sasquatch here is you." She hiked the gun over her shoulder. "Forget what I said last night. I'll find the city on my own."

"No, wait. I can help you!"

I stepped forward—a mistake. She had the gun back out, and aimed at my chest before I could take another step. My hands didn't even tremble when I held them up. I was getting better at this. "Look, all conspiracy theories start with a piece of truth. Please, M. Let me help you."

The gun didn't waver, and neither did she. "I don't need *help*. And if I did, the last person it would be from is you. Follow me out of this building and I will shoot you."

She took a step back, then another, walking backward with

the gun pointed at me until she disappeared behind a bookshelf. My heart thundered, panic coursing through my veins. *Don't let her go. Stop her!* But how? She was holding the gun, not me. I wasn't Kaden—I didn't have the power or even desire to take her captive.

The book.

I looked down at the work in my hands. This whole summer, I'd protected my books. When my faith in Kaden wavered, I turned to my solemn belief that the future and hope of humanity lay here, in these shelves. It was time to test that belief.

The pages trembled beneath my fingers as I opened it to the table of contents, with all the anticipation and fear of a man opening the book of life. Each moment was another step away from her, another step toward the awful, horrible loneliness I couldn't go back to.

It won't be here. I'm going to be alone and useless—

I saw it.

"Thule, The Lost City, page forty-three!" I shouted, my voice ringing out through the stacks, wanting to laugh and cry at the same time. "It's here! Wait, M, it's actually here! The city is in the book, I swear!"

I ran through the store, careening to a stop in front of her.

"You're lying." Her left hand rested on the door, but she didn't pull it open.

Because I saw the same hope bursting in my chest reflected in her eyes. "If I'm lying, you can leave. I won't follow. But if I'm telling the truth, can I make you breakfast?"

~

Hours later, the afternoon sun lit upon the many piles of books M had pulled from the shelves, far outpacing my attempts to reshelve them. Her destruction had yielded nothing—except for a few books that referenced the lost city of Atlantis. Those she had stacked in a separate pile that she called the "burn pile," to my increasingly nervous laughter.

M threw another book down, making a disgusted noise as she looked over the pile of books. "Read me the passage one more time. Let me close my eyes and think."

"Yeah, sure. Right." I cleared my throat, risking a single glance at her as I picked up the original book. The shotgun lay abandoned on the table behind her, a fact I was careful not to mention. Her dark hood shadowed her face, her dark hair pulled back severely from a face of sharp, feminine angles. She cracked an eye open. "Hello? Sasquatch?"

It took me a moment to realize she was calling me Sasquatch—not the worst nickname. *Not the best either.* "Sorry." I opened the book, and cleared my throat once before launching into the short except.

"'The Lost City of Thule was originally mentioned in ancient Greek and Roman literature as a far northern place, something akin to the edge of the map marked with monsters, meant to symbolize the danger that lies beyond the edge of the known world.

"'However, there is also a modern-day city known as Thule, sometimes referred to as "The Lost City." This was both because of the immense secrecy of the leaders of Thule and its unique and nearly self-sufficient design.

"'Thule was known for its early use of nuclear energy—coupled with hydroelectric power from the river it is built alongside—as well as some of the first uses of "new tech." The immense power reserves made it a hub for researchers and scientists, known for startling scientific discoveries, as well as a university with a world-renowned research center for genetics and disease. However there were also whispers that, like the creators of the atomic bomb, the leaders of Thule dabbled in sciences better left untouched.

"'Nearly ten years ago, Thule announced they had produced the first human clone grown in a laboratory. There was outrage around the world, but before the "girl" could be shared with the world, she disappeared. The leaders of Thule claimed she was stolen, but of course, many simply believed she never existed at all.

"'For more information, consult my next work: *Mysteries, Men and Monsters*.'"

M let out a noise like a growl, and strode over to me. I froze, but she only ripped the book out of my hands and flipped to the very back.

"Asshole!" she yelled as I flinched away. "Why didn't he just include everything he knew here! Just trying to sell more books." She turned on me, eyes blazing, as if she suspected I was somehow a part of this plan. "Did you check and see if any of his other books were here? Or if there was some sort of address we could go to?"

"I've checked—there's not any here." I attempted to mimic the slow, gentle way Kaden spoke to the wild horses he sometimes broke in for the clan. This was the only book by this author in this store—I was sure of it. Still, I glanced over at the information desk and sighed. "I've never missed the internet so much."

She was pacing now, back and forth. As she did, I picked up another book I'd added to my own personal pile—for comfort, not research. I ran my hand over the mix of colors on the cover, smiling as I remembered my mother reading the book to me as a child. "Kinda reminds me of in *The Sorcerer's Stone*, where Harry, Ron, and Hermione spend so much of the book trying to figure out who Nicolas Flamel is. If they'd just had the internet they could have figured it out in five seconds."

"For the love of God, shut up." M pinched her nose, her head tilted back. She stayed like that for a solid minute, face scrunched up, while I wondered if she'd explode if I suggested she take some deep breaths. *Nah. She'd probably just shoot me.*

Finally, she spun back to me. "All right. Change of plans. Do you know of any other bookstores in the area?"

"There was a library at the university." Then I cringed, adding a bit quieter, "It was close to the river, so I bet it's underwater now." Her nostrils flared, and so I quickly added, "But there were some other local ones." *Think! THINK! Mom always liked books—where did she go?* "Well, there was Rediscovered Books, and Once and Future Books, but they were both downtown—"

"So they're also flooded. What else?"

I hesitated. "The Borah clan was in one of the old high schools, but . . ." But Colborn's horde had razed the clan to the ground, and I highly doubted they'd decided to save the books. It was only when I thought of the old high schools that I realized that there was another, much easier source for other books. "There's the Ada Community Library," I said, proud I'd remembered it. "It'd be a trek out there. But it was standing last time I saw it."

And it was the only library I actually knew the location of, because it wasn't far from where I'd grown up.

She paced back and forth. "Do you think you could get the computers working there?"

I hesitated, torn between being honest and risking being shot. "It depends . . ." *But probably not.*

She stepped closer to me, my heart beating faster even though her voice was scathing. "Can you at least try, Sasquatch? Or are you too afraid to leave your precious little hideout?"

I cleared my throat and set down the Harry Potter book. Then I rose, thankful for the inches I'd gained this summer, wondering if I really did look like a Sasquatch now. *Better than the ginger troll.*

"Absolutely I can."

NINE—ARA

The next day I woke to the sounds of people in the hallway outside. I lay there for a moment, watching Kaden sleep beside me. His skin was deep gold, but now that his curls were gone, his face clean-shaven, he looked like a whole different person. He didn't even want to be here, and yet the men in the Outpost had accepted him in a moment. Maybe I shouldn't have been surprised: he was a man. He would take their citizenship class and become one of them.

In contrast I was the first person to test Invalid, a woman who didn't want to join the Sanctum, and the daughter of the man who told me to come here, yet hadn't come himself. Belonging to this city didn't seem possible for me.

You don't want to live here, I chided myself. *All you want is your family and the truth. It doesn't matter if you belong or not.* I slid off the bed and made my way to the large window at the peak of the small attic room. The walls were steeply slanted—Kaden had already hit his head twice. The only furniture other than the bed was a solid wooden dresser, which we'd pushed in front of the door last night because there was no lock on it. Still, someone had painted the walls a soft blue, and the bed was covered in quilts. There was something homey about the room, even if it was only temporary.

Dawn crept through the curtainless windows and showed a view of the snow-covered streets below. The interlocked roofs of the crowded buildings and the horses and wagons reminded me of some sort of snow-covered, industrial London. But no matter how beautiful this room, or this city, I knew it would never be home without Father and Emma. We had come all this way on the promise we'd find them; I felt foolish and naive that I'd brought Kaden here for nothing. Yet another plan ruined.

There's still time. They could still be here.

I made my way back to the bed and ran a hand down Kaden's back. He stirred, then turned, his eyes still sleepy when he smiled at me.

"Morning, beautiful," he said, his voice rough from sleep. A sudden jarring knock sounded on the door, and we both turned as the handle jiggled. The dresser worked and the door stayed closed.

"Hey lovebirds!" Talia's taunting voice came from the other side of the door. "Stop lovebirding and get dressed. Breakfast is almost gone and we've got work to do, Princess!"

"If she calls me Princess one more time," I muttered.

"Maybe you could give her a chance? She did save our lives." Kaden practically leapt out of bed—he always was more of a morning person than me.

"Then maybe she should call *you* Princess."

Kaden laughed, and a few minutes later we pushed the dresser out of the way. Talia lounged against the wall, tapping her foot as if we'd taken an hour.

"Finally," Talia muttered, and tossed Kaden a small cloth bag that jingled with the sound of change. "Your cut."

"For what?" Kaden eyed the bag with suspicion.

"For helping bring in Ara's group of women to The Last City."

Kaden opened the bag and pulled out a handful of quarters. One side of the quarter still bore George Washington's face, with the word LIBERTY written above him. But the other side no longer held an eagle. Instead my grandfather's face stared up at me, the words ONE CITY, ONE PEOPLE, ONE RULER stamped around the edge. *My grandfather's face is on a coin. The surprises just keep on coming.*

"Don't spend it all in one place," Talia said to Kaden. "Every coin is good for one plague flower—but watch for unstamped coins. If it doesn't have the Chancellor's face on it, it's not worth anything."

"If it's got an eagle, it ain't legal," Harrison called out as he passed us in the hallway. More men were beginning to emerge from the other doorways, some calling out sleepy greetings to Talia, others nodding to Kaden. Most ignored me. "Come on, Kaden," Harrison said. "I'll walk you to citizenship training. You don't want to be late. Trust me."

Kaden bent down and kissed me. "Keep your eyes open out there," he said, soft enough that the other men in the hallway couldn't hear. "Love you."

"Love you too," I said.

They'd barely started down the stairs when Talia pulled another pouch from her side and tossed it to me. I caught it with surprise. "The Chancellor wanted you to have this." Then she turned, walking away from me down the hallway and threading between men pulling on coats and an astounding amount of weapons. "C'mon."

There was only one large community bathroom with showers on the second floor—Kaden had stood guard when I showered last night, but when Talia and I walked through I understood why so many women went to the Sanctum. There were naked men *everywhere*. Even with my eyes trained on the floor, my cheeks burned red.

"You get used to it," Talia said, then yelled, "Attention! There are two women entering the bathroom! Guys, move it or lose it!" Men jumped out of her way so fast I didn't want to know what she'd done to prove it. I resolved from now on to shower only in the dead of night with Kaden guarding the shower.

Still, even a bathroom filled with men was a vast improvement compared to a summer spent bathing in freezing mountain rivers. The luxury of turning a tap and watching clear, clean water flow free was one I wouldn't take for granted again.

We left the house an hour later. The breakfast everyone had rushed to eat had included fresh eggs, a luxury Talia claimed was sent because I was here. Ironic, because they were gone by the time we got downstairs. I didn't care—the strange bug patties and potato hash were more than fine. *Any* food was more than fine.

"Are you showing me more of the city today?" I asked Talia as we left the Outpost. A biting wind howled between the buildings and I pulled the new, fur lined coat Talia had given me tighter against me. The bare branches of the trees shook above us like skeleton fingers. Talia glanced over her and I followed her gaze: the two men who'd followed Walter and me yesterday now trailed behind us.

She lowered her voice. "You need to ditch the extras first."

"How?"

"Your problem. Not mine."

Great. I've got an unhelpful guide and a grandfather who assigned people to follow me without even telling me. Can't anything ever be easy?

At least as I followed her I got to see more of the city. The more I saw, the more I suspected Walter had deliberately shown me the nicer parts of the city yesterday. Rotting garbage lined the streets, the smell barely held at bay by the cold, and more than one rat scurried away as we approached. Talia set a quick pace and I was forced to step carefully to avoid greasy-looking puddles and glass poking out of the snow. As the sun rose, more men on horseback passed us on the road. Most ignored us, but a few sent curious glances our way before being deterred by the sight of the two hulking, heavily armed men trailing us.

Talia called out greetings to a few men, but didn't slow or introduce me. We crossed beneath several sets of traffic lights hung with thick ivy and dangling icicles. Cars sat abandoned beside the road, most covered in enough snow I could only make out their general form. A few were cleared off, and just when I was about to ask Talia why, a pair of men emerged from a van without wheels, then locked it behind them. *They must live inside it.* Not a bad idea, really.

A few blocks later we came to a large brick building with an automatic door. In place of a receptionist, a young man sat on a metal chair in the main foyer, a machine gun laid casually across his lap.

He immediately warmed when he saw Talia. "Good to see you, Talia."

She didn't smile back. "We're here to see the woman brought in last night." Only now did I remember Walter had said one of the women was injured, and brought here instead of the Sanctum. Was this place some sort of hospital?

He picked up a clipboard. "She's in the main room." His eyes slid to mine, and widened. "Wait, is that—"

"The Chancellor's granddaughter?" Talia smirked. "Sure is. Look sharp, he'll be by soon."

I didn't miss the sudden fear in his eyes, or that the moment we passed I heard the low sound of his voice over a walkie-talkie. I couldn't make out his exact words, but I got the gist. He was warning the others that the Chancellor was coming.

A set of swinging double doors opened to a large, long room lit by fluorescent lights with cots and dividers between them. Voices murmured softly, the scent of bleach hung in the air, and somewhere a machine beeped.

Seeing it all made me think of Emma. Not because she went to the hospital often, but the opposite. She never went to the hospital: that was one of Father's rules. I remembered the day she'd cut her arm with Father's hunting knife and how he had stitched it up himself. When I asked why he hadn't taken her to the hospital, he said he didn't trust doctors to do something he could do himself. But then six months later I'd gone to the hospital for a broken arm. A broken arm was a different matter than a few stitches, but still, it was one of those odd memories I hadn't thought to consider until now.

"I'll wait here." Talia pointed at a red line painted on the floor in the back third of the room. "The side across the red line is reserved for the female patients."

As I walked down the long room, men lying on other cots

watched me pass with interest. A few had cuts and scrapes on their faces, another a splint, but none bore white eyes weeping blood. *Of course not. They don't let the infected in here.* Recognition flickered in some of the men's eyes, and made me walk faster and stop examining each of them. *Could they know I tested as Invalid? Or was it that I was the Chancellor's granddaughter?* It didn't seem possible that word could have spread so quickly. When I crossed over the red line, an elderly female nurse with a kind smile appeared.

"You must be here to see Rosia," she said.

"Yes. Thank you." The nurse walked me past row after row of empty cots. As I passed the dividers I glanced inside each. Some naive part of me hoped to see the flash of Emma's dark hair. *Walter said she wasn't here. Of course she wouldn't be somewhere as obvious as the hospital.* Still it was hard not to hope.

We came to the back corner, all the other beds empty, except for the last, where Rosia lay. I smiled when I saw her.

"Hey Cherry. Knew you'd miss me," Rosia said. Bandages wrapped around her shoulder, mostly hidden by a hospital gown, and a clean white strip covered her missing eye. She looked cleaner and better fed than she ever had in the wagon.

"Good to see you out of the wagon." I sat on the chair beside her cot as the nurse discreetly left us. "You okay?" I nodded at her shoulder.

She shrugged and then winced. "One of the bullets nicked me, didn't even notice until one of the other girls pointed out the blood. Can't complain. The better question is how are you?"

"What do you mean?" I said, suddenly tense. Did she already know I'd tested as Invalid—did everyone?

"The Chancellor came by earlier." Her eyes darted one way

then the other, as if checking we were alone. "He thanked me for helping bring the women safely here. Asked about you. Tried to get me to convince you to ditch Kaden and join the Sanctum."

So Walter's been asking around about me. I wasn't sure what to make of that. Was it the concern of a caring grandfather, or the manipulations of a ruler? "What'd you tell him?"

"Jack shit."

I laughed. Only now, standing beside her, did I see how tired her smile looked. It made me think the loud, brash woman in the cart had been an act for the others. I wondered if I should tell her the truth: I didn't know what to think of my grandfather. The first rule my father ever taught me to survive the apocalypse was to trust no one. Had he meant the same of his own father?

"It's all right, Cherry," Rosia said gently when I didn't respond. "I figured if any of the women in the wagon wouldn't join the Sanctum, it'd be you and Izzie."

Emotion thickened my throat, both at the thought of Izzie and that once Rosia joined the Sanctum, I might not see her again. Because seeing Rosia here had shown me the true reason I wouldn't join the Sanctum: I had failed the women in the wagon. Izzie had been mine to protect and now she was dead. I didn't deserve to join the Sanctum.

I wondered if Rosia saw the sadness in my face, because she reached out and took my hand. "It wasn't your fault, Cherry. Just promise me you'll be careful out there. I don't know about this Chancellor, but from what I've seen of the world, and men, things don't magically get better."

I nodded, and then, because I had to at least try, "You sure you want to join the Sanctum? We're thinking of leading an expedition back to Boise in the spring. You could come with us."

She patted my hand, her old grin spreading across her face. "'Course you are, Cherry. You're a fighter if I ever saw one. But I'd only slow you down. The Sanctum is where I belong now."

You're a fighter, too, I wanted to say. *Come with me. Trust me.* But I had said the same to Izzie, and then I had left her buried in the snow.

"Then I'll miss you," I said, heart heavy. "And you'll always have a place with me if you change your mind." I bent over and gave her an awkward hug.

When I was close, she whispered in my ear. "So did you find your father and sister?"

"No. He said they weren't here." I didn't have to explain who "he" was.

"The girl I met in the wagon wouldn't take no for an answer. Would she?"

"Hell no."

We talked for a bit longer, and then the nurse returned and it was time for me to leave. As I crossed the red line on the floor, back to the men's side of the room, I wondered at Rosia's words. Walter might be my grandfather, but that didn't mean I had to accept that my father and sister weren't here.

When I reached Talia she surprised me, throwing one arm around my shoulders and leading me down a hallway to the back. "Walter will be here soon. Last chance to jump ship." Her eyes darted one way then the other down the hallway. *She's nervous. That's new.*

"I'm staying," I said, wanting to stay all the more now.

"Suit yourself, Princess. I'll see you later tonight then."

"No, wait, aren't you—" *My goddamn guide!* Too late. She'd already pushed open the door and disappeared out into the cold.

I exhaled in frustration. The two large men who had followed us were now watching me from the other end of the hallway. They made no move to follow Talia. Of course they didn't. They were here for me, not her.

I watched her go, before something outside caught my eye. In the parking lot behind the hospital, a green glow reflected off the snow. A glow that reminded me of something so far in the past it didn't seem possible. *It can't be . . .*

I pushed open the door, walking out into the cold and moving in the opposite direction Talia had. A field of snow stretched behind the building. It looked like an old parking lot, mostly empty but for the few covered shapes of cars in the far back. The ground was filled with strange, glowing green lumps. The ones farther in the distance were coated in snow, but the closer ones were covered in thick green moss, bright against the white-and-gray landscape.

The snow crunched beneath my feet as I made my way closer. There was something familiar about the green glow—and the shape of the lumps. It wasn't until I stood over one of the lumps that I realized what lay below the glowing green moss.

A body.

It felt like my brain was stuck on static. I could make out the arms and legs and divots of the face—all covered in thick glowing green moss. The closer ones glowed brighter, untouched by snow, and the others were covered beneath snow, the glow just barely visible.

What the hell?

The two guards followed behind me, but for once I didn't care, trapped in my swirling thoughts. I'd seen this same glowing green moss before. After Kaden and I had kayaked through Boise's flooded town. It had been on the walls of the top floor of the

Birmingham Medical Testing Center—where a man had attacked me. So why was it here?

"Hail Chancellor," came the voices of the two men behind me.

I didn't even turn, annoyed yet not surprised that Walter was here.

"Ara, so happy to see you again," he said.

I didn't move, instead staring out at the strange graveyard before me, and the uneven field beyond. I'd thought the snow had drifted into strange shapes. Understanding made me sick. The parking lot was filled with bodies.

"Fascinating, isn't it?" Walter said when he came to stand alongside me.

Not the word I would have used. "What is this place?"

"A graveyard, of sorts. We call it the green plague—a joke really. It's a bioluminescent moss we created in our labs. Originally it was created as an alternate light source in place of electricity to be used in the tunnels beneath the city. But then we discovered its decomposing abilities. Disposing of bodies was a problem for us originally—it's too cold most of the year to dig, burning takes enormous amounts of energy and fuel, and leaving the bodies in the ruins attracts infected animals." He actually smiled as he looked down at the bodies on the ground. "Now we don't have to even move them. It takes most of the smell away too. In ideal conditions, and with the right placement, it eats them down to the bones in less than a year."

A cold breeze blew up some of the snow, the cold cutting straight to my core. If this moss was created here, then how did it end up in Boise? Was that lab some sort of outpost from The Last City? And why had my father had a slip of paper with its name in his backpack?

Could I simply ask?

Intuition kept me quiet. Walter might look like my father, but they were clearly two very different men. My father would have never looked at a field of bodies and smiled. *Then again, he'd clearly kept secrets from me.*

"I'd love to see the lab where you made this," I said, finally looking away from the graveyard. I didn't even need to fake my interest. "Could you take me?"

He looked thrilled at my request. "Of course. Your father was one of my best scientists back in the day. I wouldn't be surprised if you have the same talents."

"He was?" This was a surprise to me.

He shrugged, his smile almost nostalgic. "Charles and I had many disagreements, but we shared a love for bettering the human condition. How we did that might have differed. But I don't want to make those mistakes again. The vision I have for The Last City—I hope it's one you'll come to share."

"I'm not sure I could be happy without my father and sister." I stared out at the field of bodies. When, exactly, had humanity become a problem to dispose of as quickly and efficiently as possible? "If I'm being honest, Kaden and I have been talking about heading back to Boise in the spring."

He nodded, his brows furrowed. "I see. I'll just have to think of a way to keep you here. I'll have my men bring you to my lab first thing tomorrow."

He guided me inside, then walked me back to the Outpost. Long after he'd gone, the graveyard of bodies still lived in my mind. *I'll just have to think of a way to keep you here*. I wondered what Walter would say if he knew the real reason I stayed; for a mystery three generations deep. The green moss, the black spiral,

Walter—there were too many connections back to my father, back to Emma, back to home.

I wasn't leaving until I found the truth.

~

The next day I went alone to Walter's lab. Kaden had come home last night exhausted from his training, and then left before dawn. He seemed, if not happy, at least not miserable. I'd told him about the green moss, but even he wasn't sure what it meant. Either way, he warned me to be careful.

Talia hadn't made an appearance this morning, so today I walked down the streets with one of the men leading, another behind. As we walked, I tried to appreciate the city for its beauty; the snow-covered buildings, the glow of electricity, the Wild West feel of wagons and men on horseback riding down the streets. I even saw a few repurposed cars pulled by horses. Compared to the territorial, brutal clans in Boise, it was a miracle—yet even so, The Last City was a city with sharp edges. Talia had told me there was a curfew at dusk, and warned me not to leave the Outpost after dark. Even though there was a police force, and a few surveillance cameras still working, it was clear that justice here was paid for in blood.

The men led me to a massive, modern-looking building. I wasn't sure what I'd expected, but it wasn't this. While most of the other buildings showed wear, with chipping paint and ragged roofs, this building rose proudly, at least four stories tall, with floor-to-ceiling windows and black siding that reflected the dull winter sun to nearly blinding effect.

One of the guards scanned his lanyard and opened the door

for me. I took a deep breath and then walked into a brightly lit room flush with activity. With the electricity lighting clean floors, computer monitors glowing, and men talking and chatting, it felt like walking straight into the past. The plague had left dirty fingerprints on the rest of the city—but here, it seemed like time had gone forward instead of back.

Walter walked toward me in his quick, energetic stride, wearing a white lab coat today instead of a suit. "Thank you for coming, Ara. Please, come, there's so much to show you!"

"Thanks for having me." I kept Kaden's words in mind, saying little as I followed after Walter. He seemed to have transformed into an energetic college student in an old man's body, gesturing to every little thing and speaking so fast I didn't catch everything. Walter explained the first floor was dedicated to genetic testing and coding—specifically for the plague flower. "We want to make sure the flowers we produce continue to be as effective as they were in the beginning."

"Do you think you'll ever find the cure?"

He gave me a wry smile—as if this was an odd question to ask. "The Last City's entire structure is built upon the plague flower—it's the basis of our currency. A cure would collapse the city."

"But then you wouldn't need the city, or the wall, or the flower."

"Or would we need it more than ever?"

Of course not, I wanted to say, but then paused. When the world had fallen, my father had tried to protect me by taking us far into the Idaho wilderness, but even so, I'd seen what people had done to each other over scraps of food. I remembered the vast clouds of birds settling over the city. People hadn't come together in the end—they'd torn each other apart.

With his unsettling question echoing in my ears, we left the first floor behind, and took an elevator down. I watched as Walter lifted the lanyard around his neck and lifted it to a sort of scanner. There was a sort of rust-red smudge on the card.

He caught me watching. "It's a drop of my blood. My lab can only be accessed by a specific genetic code. One of my brighter ideas, don't you think?"

I had no idea how to answer that, so I nodded and said, "Sure."

The elevator door opened to a room completely different from the lab above—but I didn't step forward. My heart thundered as I stood there paralyzed, remembering the last time I'd entered a lab just like this. In Boise. Kaden and I had kayaked through the flooded downtown. I'd gone upstairs in the dead of night, opened the door with my blood, and then was attacked by the man inside. The man who'd known my last name, and known my father. Kaden had killed him before I got any answers, and we'd left a dead man on the floor.

Fear held me rooted to the spot. *It's not the same place. No one is trying to hurt me here.* Yet there were the same giant vials full of green water that made a soft whirring noise, and the green moss grew across the walls in branching tree-like patterns.

"This is my own personal lab," Walter said, not seeming to notice the panic warring inside me, "where I continue the work I did before the plague."

Move, Ara. He'll notice you're being weird. I forced my legs to unlock, walking stiffly into the room, despite every instinct screaming to flee. Thankfully Walter seemed all too content to hold the majority of the conversation. And the farther I moved into the lab, the more differences I saw between his lab and the one I'd seen in Boise. It was bigger, more lived-in, and filled with more equipment. *And no one who's trying to hurt me.*

I passed between the green columns of water and found an entire wall of small box-like cages, hundreds of them, stacked on top of each other. About half of them were full of white rats, the other half empty. I bent to look inside one, then jerked back when a rat lunged against the side of the glass. My heart thundered, unnerved by the animal. Its eyes weren't white, but even so it clawed at the side of the glass, making frantic, jerky movements.

"What kind of work did you do before the plague?" I finally managed.

"We were modifying the DNA in animals," Walter said from the other side of the cages. "Every disease and imperfection in humanity stems from faulty DNA. Most men saw the plague as a tragedy. I saw it as an opportunity."

I made my way past the rat cages. I'd killed, skinned, and eaten more than my share of small furry things, but I didn't like seeing all those rats in cages, locked down here beneath the earth. Maybe even more unsettling was Walter calling the death of millions an opportunity. "An *opportunity* for what?" I asked.

"To do better than God," Walter said, his voice nearly reverent, his gaze full of pride as he bent to tap one of the cages—the rat inside attacked the glass in response. "There are so many diseases born into our DNA. But what if they weren't? What if every single person was born perfect? What if, instead of greedy, selfish creatures, humanity worked together perfectly and selflessly?"

Farther down the same wall was another wall filled with the same box cages, only smaller and holding mice. While some seemed normal, others attacked the glass like the rats had as I passed. *These things don't look perfect. They look like monsters.* All around us the green waters surged and trembled, casting an eerie green glow on everything, as if we were stranded beneath an ocean.

As Walter showed me the rest of the lab, I wondered if the one in Boise had been some sort of outpost for The Last City. An outpost that my father had known of. *If only he were here. If only I could ask him.* My father had once told me to go back to the beginning. But now I wondered: What if it wasn't my beginning? What if it was his?

"How goes your quest for perfection?" I tried to keep the skepticism out of my voice.

"Great things take time," Walter said. "But The Last City is the first step in the journey." Then he gestured me forward, back to the elevator—apparently the tour was done. "Come, I've prepared lunch for us at my place. It was once the dean's house; it has an impressive collection of books if you'd like to borrow some."

"I would." I watched the green-lit lab until the doors closed, unable to dismiss the feeling I hadn't seen or asked nearly enough.

~

That night I paced the small attic bedroom as I told Kaden everything I'd seen in Walter's strange underground lab, and then the dean's house—a sprawling mansion set on a hill with a view over the city.

"It just doesn't make sense," I muttered. "Why is that green moss here *and* back in Boise? The lab Walter showed me—it might as well have been a carbon copy of the one back home."

"Did you tell him you recognized it?"

"No." I paced back to the window. "Do you think I should?"

"No. But I do think you should be careful. Just because he's your grandfather doesn't mean he won't hurt you if you get in his way."

"Get in the way of *what* though?" I sighed and then flopped down on the bed beside him. Even here, in our small safe haven, when I closed my eyes I saw only green. "I wish you could have seen him talk—about how the plague was an opportunity. It was like he was . . . Not mad, but *obsessed*."

"We could leave now. Go back to Boise." His voice was careful, but I didn't miss the underlying hope. Guilt tightened my chest. I was more entrenched here than ever. I couldn't leave now. Not without the truth.

"No. Walter definitely has secrets. Plus you should have seen the lunch we had: ham and cheesy potatoes and fresh bread and strawberries. He definitely doesn't mind keeping things from his people. I know he's hiding something. And if you can learn anything from the citizenship training, or even go on an expedition with them, then maybe you can see something I'm missing." I sat down on the bed beside him. "If we don't find anything by spring, then we'll go." I was confident it wouldn't take that long.

"I'm with you. You know that."

"I know."

He pulled me closer to him, when I caught him stifling an enormous yawn. I suddenly felt guilty for monopolizing the conversation. "Enough about Walter. How was the citizenship training? Any leads?"

"Not really. It reminds me of some sort of weird mix of football camp and propaganda nightmare. I yelled 'Hail Chancellor' so many times today I can't decide if I hate or love him."

"That's probably the point." I snuggled in beside him, staring up at the cracks and lines across the ceiling—wondering why I automatically envisioned the patterns the green moss had made on the wall. It made me want to talk about anything else. "I walked by the Sanctum on the way back here."

"Oh yeah? Considering joining and leaving me behind?"

"You know I wouldn't join without you."

"How about I quit my citizenship training, buy a wig, and come with you?"

"You think you can pass for a woman?"

"Hi, my name is Kayla," Kaden said in a ridiculous falsetto, "and I'm looking for a strong man with lumberjack arms."

I giggled, and then reached out to trace the stubble across his jaw. "You might need to shave before we try this plan." He wrapped his arms around my shoulders, pulling me against him.

Here, warmed by his arms, the truth about why I hadn't gone inside the Sanctum finally surfaced. "I couldn't bring myself to go in. After Izzie . . ." I trailed off. After Izzie's death, I didn't want to face the women again. Rosia would protect them now—that wasn't my job anymore. I'd already failed them once.

Kaden pulled my chin up to meet his eyes. With the sun setting outside, a roof over our heads, and Kaden's green eyes looking into my own—I wanted it all to be enough.

"I'm sure they're all fine and happy in the Sanctum," he said. "Remember my first tip for surviving the apocalypse?"

I laughed. "You mean that there is no surviving because we're all going to die?"

"Exactly." His fingers traced my jaw, burning fire, as he bent and kissed me. When he pulled back, my cheeks were flushed, my smile matching his own. It was enough—for now. "So you might as well enjoy it while you can."

TEN—KADEN

The blue light of the television bathed the room in cold light.

"The hell did you just do? Are you stupid?!"

I was already running to the back door when the bottle shattered against the wall just a few feet away from my head. My dad's voice grew louder in the dining room, but I'd already swung open the back door, halfway across the lawn before the fear even registered.

Stupid, I chided myself. I knew better than to bother him when he was drinking. I also knew better than to buy him glass bottles. But it had been a while since I'd lived with my dad for any longer than a few days.

My heart beat an unsteady rhythm as I crossed the dark lawn. Kia, my half sister, and my two stepbrothers weren't here. They stayed with their mother most of the time, and now I remembered why.

I paused in the shadows beneath the trees, listening. Nothing but the Montana wind. When I was sure my father hadn't followed, I ducked into the shadows of the barn. Red's head lifted from his stall, nickering softly in the light of the barn. The warm, heady scents of horses and hay brought a wave of relief.

"Hey Red." I reached out and scratched the beautiful horse's forehead. I'd spent every last penny I had buying him, money Mom would have wanted me to save for college. Too bad she didn't get a say anymore. That was the one perk of living with my dad: he didn't give a shit about anything but the ranch. It was no wonder his second marriage was falling apart. At least in Boise, Sam needed me. No one needed me here. I was basically another ranch hand.

Red's ears swiveled forward, and he pushed at the stall door in a way that made me smile. "No running tonight, boy. Just need a place to crash." I fed him a handful of oats from the bin, his warm lips flapping against my hand, my heart rate slowly returning to normal. Then I climbed up into the loft. I'd left a sleeping bag there a long time ago. The mice had chewed on the bottom, but it would do for the night.

I pulled out my phone, scrolling through a few girls' names before I stopped on Sam's. I hit the call button before I could wimp out.

"Kaden!" Sam answered, his voice an excited squeak that made me smile. "I've been waiting for you to call. How are you? How's Montana?"

"Awesome," I said, lying. There was no use in admitting how homesick I was—there was no going back now. "I bought a horse."

"A horse?! Wow, really?!"

"Yep. He's huge too. Almost seventeen hands."

"No way! So unfair. We had to give back Callie." His voice trailed off, and I knew he was thinking of Mom. I'd had a giant fight with Gary, Sam's idiot dad, about said dog. He said he was allergic—I said he was just a whiny asshole. I'd expected Mom to back me. But she hadn't. And when I'd suggested that maybe I should go live with

my dad, that maybe things were too crowded now that Gary had moved in, she'd agreed.

My own mother hadn't even fought for me.

Sam had gone silent on the other end of the line, so I made my voice light. "Yeah, well, Gary's a whiny bitch, so I guess in some ways you still have a dog."

Sam laughed on the other end, and then his voice went softer. "When are you coming back?"

His words hit me like a punch to the gut. I didn't know how to tell him I wasn't.

"Sam? Sam, who are you talking to?" Mom's voice rose in the background.

"I've gotta go," Sam said.

"Yeah. Me too." I paused, and then said, "Hey Sam?"

"Yeah?"

"Someday we'll get a dog, and a horse, and live in a stupid-big house together without anyone else to tell us what to do. Okay?"

"Okay."

~

I wasn't sure why the memory of Sam, and that stupid dog, came back to me now, in a courtyard full of the winter wind and men training. Maybe it was because only here, without Ara, did I realize how utterly and completely I'd failed Sam. I'd never gotten him that dog, or that house. I'd put him in a clan where we were always told what we could and couldn't do. Funny how quickly safety could become a cage.

"Who do we serve?" the Captain yelled.

"The Chancellor!" I answered with the class of fifty men, barely resisting the urge to roll my eyes.

"Who are we?" the Captain called.

"One city, one people, one ruler," we answered. I'd already had to run extra laps for not shouting loud enough—and it wasn't even noon.

"One hundred jumping jacks, let's go!"

The group started to count the number. I shadowed the others, trying to lose myself in the physicality and turn my brain off. I'd never thought, just a few days after making it to the fabled Last City, I'd be both ready to leave and lying daily to Ara. *It's hard work, but not too bad. I'm already starting to get to know some of the men. Really, I'm enjoying it.*

But what the hell was I supposed to tell her? That citizenship training was some sort of bizarre propaganda boot camp with leaders who clearly enjoyed tormenting the city's newcomers? That I didn't care about whatever "truth" Walter was hiding or if we ever found her dad? I loved Ara, so I'd do this for her. I'd gone through worse.

"PUSH-UPS! NOW!"

I hit the ground with the rest of the class, sweat running down my face even in the cold courtyard. Our class of men was evenly spaced out in a courtyard between buildings. To one side was what I'd taken to calling the obstacle course from hell: a torturous mix of ropes, ladders, sprints, and even a fun section to crawl beneath. I was used to physical challenges—enjoyed them even. But playing sports, working on a horse ranch, or even leading an expedition team was all about working toward a common goal I believed in. The common goal here seemed to indoctrinate us into an authoritarian dictatorship. It didn't help that said dictator was my girlfriend's grandfather, who I was supposed to be digging up dirt on.

"Kaden! Who do we serve?" the Captain yelled at me.

"The glorious, wonderful, not-at-all-overhyped Chancellor!" A few of the men closest to me snickered—then quickly fell silent. "I'm thinking of naming my firstborn after him," I added. I knew better, but after days of this I couldn't help it.

The Captain smiled at me—he had a strange, humorless look where his eyes narrowed and his lips lifted. A look that didn't bode well. "Run the obstacle course again. Let's see if you can find any respect there."

"Yes, sir." Inwardly I groaned, but outwardly I was careful not to show it. This was what Ara wanted, so I would do it. *Then we head back to Boise in the spring. This is better than being holed up somewhere and starving. Barely.* I made my way across the courtyard to where two other unlucky men were also in line—one of them had laughed when one of the officers had stumbled. The other was a lanky boy that barely looked more than sixteen. I wasn't sure what he'd done. Maybe it was just the terrified expression on his face. There was a time where I would have made my way over to him, joked about how absurd this all was, and taken him under my wing.

Instead, I got in line behind them, as straight-backed and silent as a soldier. Ara wanted me here—I wasn't here to create another expedition team or make friends. The boy glanced back at me. I could tell he wanted to ask me something, but I didn't meet his eye. I knew what happened to the men I took under my wing.

"You're up," one of the officers said to me, and lifted his stopwatch. "Let's see you do it in less than ten minutes this time."

"Yes, sir." I suddenly wished I'd run the course a hell of a lot slower this morning, instead of lapping several of the men in front of me. It took everything in me not to lean over to the young man and tell him hard work was never rewarded, just to see him smile. Sometimes a smile was all it took to get men through—but no. That wasn't me anymore.

"Go," the officer said, and I took off. The first day had been easy—we'd sat in a classroom, learned about the Chancellor. But this was some sort of special class that the Chancellor and Captain handpicked. I know Ara thought that was what I was here for—to make friends with important people and uncover whatever secrets Walter was hiding. In truth, I was only here until she found what she needed here. I was ready to get the hell out of here the second she was.

At the thought of Ara's face, and my lack of honesty, my hands slipped from the bars I'd done so easily this morning. I fell hard—the cold ground felt like falling onto cement. There was some ugly laughter from the man behind me. I was in danger of being lapped and definitely wouldn't beat my time from this morning—which might mean I'd be forced to run the course again. I pushed all the worries away and focused only on the rhythm of my body and the physical challenge before.

"Passing," someone called from behind me. My pride surged for a moment, but then I hung to the left of the track to let them go—

Sam.

Gangly limbs. Red hair.

I fell hard. This time the ice cut deep into my hands. I didn't even notice the pain, twisting my head up, desperate to see Sam again. Instead, the boy with gangly limbs passed me by.

No. It's not Sam. It's the boy from earlier.

My heart thundered, adrenaline pulsing through me as he passed. The young man glanced back at me, as if he was debating whether to come back and help me. He seemed to think better of it and kept jogging. *Good for you. Best avoid me. Maybe you'll survive this world.*

I climbed to my feet, trying to shake the image of Sam from my head, and yet also desperate to hold on to it. The other boy looked nothing like Sam—just the long limbs and right age. Yet my heart still ran ragged, my bleeding hands trembling. For a moment the sun had caught his hair and made it seem like Sam's. For a moment, I'd seen my dead brother, and was right back in the endless hole of grief I almost hadn't survived.

"Back in the course!" One of the officers was yelling at me. I barely heard him.

I'd dreamed of Sam countless times throughout the summer. A few times I'd even thought I'd heard his voice and laughter coming from the trees or hills. But always Ara was there. Always she pulled me back.

"Cadet! Get moving or you're out of the class!"

I finally realized it was the Captain himself who stood before me. I straightened to my full height as he continued to yell some very colorful obscenities I would certainly not be telling Ara. *No, really, the class is going great. I think the Captain even likes me—he has some nicknames just for me.*

"Why the Chancellor himself requested you to be here is anyone's guess," the Captain spat out, and then he tossed a cloth at me. "You're getting blood everywhere."

I stared down at my hand, and then the snow, now covered in bright red spots. He nodded to the med tent. "Get cleaned up, and then run the course again."

"Yes, sir," I said. I was almost thankful to see the blood and feel the pain—anything to distract from the pain of remembering Sam and all my failures. I made to pass him, but he caught my shoulder.

"Hail Chancellor," he said, his eyes narrowed, watching me closely.

You've got bigger demons than this. Just say it.

I was surprised by how much I didn't want to. I'd once let Gabriel rule the clan when I could have taken it from him. Who knew what would have been different if I had taken responsibility instead of running from it. Maybe Issac and Sam would still be alive. Maybe we would all still be in Boise, laughing at the notion of some fabled lost city. *And maybe you would have never met Ara.*

This *wasn't* the clan. Walter wasn't Gabriel. And yet, when I muttered, "Hail Chancellor," I wondered why I felt like, yet again, I was making the wrong choice.

~

Later that night at the Outpost I stood under the frigid flow of water from the shower until my body began to tremble. It had been a long, brutal, exhausting day. But that wasn't why I didn't get out.

I wasn't ready to face Ara.

All summer I'd had two goals: make it to The Last City; protect Ara. But now that we were here, I'd watched how she had found a new purpose exploring and uncovering whatever truths lay here.

I didn't care what dark truths lay buried here. In fact, I wanted them to stay that way: buried.

It was the first time I'd ever felt like I was so much older than Ara. She followed her father's word with a sort of biblical devotion I would never understand. When my own father's eyes turned I'd injected him with horse tranquilizer, a mercy kill, and then burned the house he lay in. I never looked back. My family was gone—Ara was all I had left now. And yet I felt as if I could no longer hide from the ugly truth I'd spent the whole summer running from.

Sam and Issac were dead because of me.

How could I ever lead a new team when I'd failed the only one that mattered? How could I protect Ara when I'd failed to protect them?

Somehow this city had become a quest that was hers instead of ours. Her grandfather ruled. Her father had left her the note. Her sister might be here. But Sam and Issac were cold and buried and rotting beneath the earth.

I turned the water off, stopping the freezing flow, my body still trembling as I tried to push the image of Sam out of my head.

There is only the peace that you find. That was what Issac had told me. He believed that peace was here, or maybe that God was still here. I wanted to believe that too, that I would see them all again someday . . . but I didn't know how. Issac had left me here, alone, far before I was ready for him to go. I didn't know where his peace was. I didn't know how to find it.

The cold felt as if it had worked its way into my bones, even after I got dressed and made my way down to dinner. Talia watched me with curious eyes, clearly picking up something that was off, but I wasn't ready to talk to her. I saved all my energy for when Ara finally strode in, her cheeks pink from the cold, her eyes blazing with the energy and drive they always did. Like a fire burned inside her. And when she kissed me, and then sat at my side, I knew what I had to do.

I wouldn't build a new team. I wouldn't put down roots here. But I would be here for Ara. I wouldn't let her see the way the deaths of everyone I'd failed suffocated me, like a weight slowly dragging me deeper and deeper into darkness.

I would be there for Ara the way I hadn't been for Sam and Issac.

I would protect her with everything I was—or I would die trying.

ELEVEN—SAM

For the third night in a row, I woke to M screaming.

Rain pounded on the ceiling, the distant sounds of thunder rumbling, like the storm was trying to break through the bookstore's roof. We'd spent a few days inside Barnes & Noble, poring over the books on the shelves, looking for more references to a lost city, M trying to learn everything she could about power and outlets. *Try* being the key word. No matter how patiently I explained things, M snapped often and demanded answers I doubted even my father could answer. *How does the new tech work? Could you get the airships running again? Why the hell not? Are you good for anything?*

I explained that the new tech ran on some sort of system no one knew how to turn on anymore—only the old tech, machines of steel and oil and wires, could be accessed. She only grew more frustrated, so I didn't tell her about a book I'd found specifically about new tech. There *was* a way to turn it back on, with a massive surge of energy, but that was only theoretical and far beyond my scope. On the bright side, we'd gotten over all the gun-pointing nonsense. Now she only muttered threats under her breath.

The first time she'd screamed in her sleep and I'd tried to help her, I'd knocked over two piles of books before I managed to pull the light switch. Then, when I leaned over the cot, she hit me so hard my cheek throbbed the entire rest of the night and following day. But now her screams rose again, and I couldn't stop myself, rising from my spot, pulling the light switch and making my way across the crowded floor of my room—over comic books, novels, and discarded clothes—until I stood beside the cot.

"Don't," she muttered, still caught in the dream. "No—please, don't!"

I reached forward, shaking her shoulder, ready to spring back at the smallest movement.

"M, wake up," I whispered. "M! It's just a nightmare."

She lurched upright and I jumped back, retreating to the farthest corner of my small room as the cot squeaked beneath her. Her breath came in shallow, heaving gasps, loud enough to be heard over the noise of the storm. A pile of comics pressed against my leg, threatening to tip as I tried not to move.

I counted slowly to thirty, and then, when her breathing had slowed, I whispered, "I have them too." She turned to look at me, as if she'd forgotten I was there. "Nightmares about the end," I added.

It was the wrong thing to say. One moment she was a girl waking from a nightmare, and the next her angry exterior snapped back in place, her eyes finding mine with a malice that rivaled the outside storm.

"They aren't nightmares about the end," she hissed. "We've waited long enough. We're leaving. Today. At dawn."

"I haven't taught—"

"You're a shit teacher. Maybe you're doing it on purpose so you have to come with me." She glared at me, like she'd finally discovered my plan. I seriously doubted I would still be alive if that really were my plan. It had taken me all summer to play a single song in the mall—trying to teach someone in a week what I'd learned from years of helping my dad and months of trial and error wasn't exactly easy.

"But it's raining," I said slowly.

"Does it look like I give a shit?" She jumped out of bed, somehow glaring down at me despite the fact I was quite a bit taller than her. "And this is Idaho—it'll be done in five minutes."

The thunder rumbled outside, and though some might have seen it as a warning, excitement grew in my chest. I smiled into her glare. "All right. I'll get two backpacks ready."

~

It took another four days to find the library, a fact M reminded me of nearly every minute. I might have grown up in the city, but everything looked different now. Some sections had burned to the ground. Street signs were covered in weeds, or missing altogether. And there were sections I didn't dare enter: where I knew other clans ruled. My pride took a hit when I realized I wasn't nearly as good at navigating the city as Kaden. If I ever did return to the clan, it wouldn't be as an expedition leader.

Which was why on the fourth day, when the library finally came into view, I couldn't bury the rising elation—and relief—that it was still standing.

"That's it," I said pointing, barely resisting the urge to let out a "whoop!" and fist pump.

"Don't look so happy—it took you four damn days to find a library. I could have found an actual Sasquatch in less time."

Her words stung—even if she was right. I wasn't Kaden. *But I got the power back on and played the first song since the plague. And I found a book about how to turn the new tech back on—even if I don't understand it, I have the basic theory. That's got to count for something.* Even Gabriel, with all his dreams and planning, hadn't managed either of those things.

"Let's go check it out," I said, about to step forward, when M's hand caught me in the chest. I froze—she never touched me. In fact, she was very careful to keep a no-contact zone between us. But now she pushed in front of me.

"I go first."

"You sure? I've got my arrows and . . ." Her withering gaze cut me short. I pulled an arrow free and nocked it, wanting to insist that I should go first, then decided to let her have it her way. She was holding the gun after all. And if the last few days with her had taught me anything, it was that arguing with M was pointless.

A small parking lot overgrown with weeds lay on one side of the library. Together we pushed through waist-high grasses and weeds to where a set of concrete stairs opened up to the double doors of the front entrance. From below I could see the first of the doors had shattered, covering the stairs with broken glass. M started quietly up the stairs, but when I followed each piece of glass seemed to crunch beneath my feet. She turned, glaring at me as more glass crunched underfoot.

"Sorry," I mouthed. I might have been the best archer in the clan, but in the last year I'd grown what felt like a foot. Stealth wasn't exactly my strong suit.

She shook her head, and then stepped through the first set of the doors. I wondered if we would have to break the second, but when she pushed, it swung quietly open. *Maybe some romantic librarian left the doors unlocked, wanting humanity to have the blessing of knowledge.* I smiled at the thought, and then followed M deeper into the cavern-like library.

Muddied light leaked in through the windows. Scents of paper and mildew hung heavy in the air. It was clear people hadn't been here in a long time. A tinge of remorse churned in my chest for all the books forgotten and unprotected here.

A staircase led downstairs, and this time M let me lead as we moved down into the darker basement area, lit only by windows on the far side. There was a trail of raccoon paw prints through the tiled area, but other than that, there was no sign of life. Finally I lowered my bow, the muscles in my back and shoulders aching.

One of those little bells sat on a desk. I rang it, watching as M jumped and swung back to me.

"Welcome to the Ada Community Library!" I said in a chipper voice. "Could I help you find anything today?" She scowled at me, but this only made me smile wider. "Maybe we could start with the author's name . . . or maybe they have a local authors' section, or maybe—"

She was already walking away from me, heading back upstairs. "You stay down here. I'll look upstairs."

"But this is the kids' section!" I called after her.

"Exactly."

~

The sun was sinking when M and I sat across from each other in a pair of matching armchairs in the teen section, a small area sectioned off from the rest of the library. We'd looked through what felt like nearly every book in the library twice. We'd even searched in the back rooms. But there was nothing.

Worse, all the computers were gone, and the electrical system was a mess even my father couldn't have repaired. Whatever M was looking for, she wouldn't find it here.

I sat down across from her, nervous that she would be angry and blame me. But her face was only pensive. "You said the bookstores downtown are flooded," she said. "What do you think the chances of turning on the electricity there would be?"

"Depends where and what you want it for. There's only one place I know of downtown that had the electricity working. It was at the very top of a building that we searched for medical supplies. Some sort of new tech was still powering it."

Her eyes suddenly zeroed in on me. "You said new tech didn't work anymore."

I shrugged. "I said I didn't have a way to turn it on—it takes a massive surge of energy. But if it had never turned off—"

"Do you think it's still on?" She cut me off.

"Could be."

"Were there computers there?"

"Ummm, I think so?" I tried to remember back to the trip I'd made last year with Kaden, Ara, Gabriel, and Issac. The truth was I didn't remember much about the building. It was all overshadowed by the river monster that had nearly killed me. I hadn't actually been to the top floor. But Kaden had mentioned it later, and how odd it was that there was still something powering that floor of the building. "Kaden said there were, but I didn't see them. It was on the top floor."

"What was the building called?"

I paused, trying to remember the name. "Birmingham Testing Center . . . or something like that."

She stared out the window, at the setting sun. Then her eyes cut back to me. "All right. New plan. You take me to this building and get us up to the top floor."

I hesitated, the full scope of what she was asking flashing through my mind.

We'd need to cross the city. The closer we got to downtown, and the river, the more clans and people we'd face. Even with a bow and a gun we were still just two teenagers. Then we'd need kayaks to cross the flooded downtown filled with treacherous currents that grew colder by the day. All the kayaks from the clan had either been destroyed or moved, which meant our only option was to find the two kayaks Kaden had hidden at the edge of downtown for his personal use—if they were even still there. Not to mention the last time I made this trip, my entire expedition team was attacked by some kind of river monster and I had nearly died. *So no big deal.*

Her sneer was back. "What is it, Sasquatch? Scared? Or just think you can't do it?"

"No. I can do it." *But if I can't, I'm going to die trying. Or more likely, we both will.* I didn't want to sound like a coward in front of M, so I bluffed. "I'm trying to figure out what I get from this arrangement?"

Her eyes hardened. "You mean beyond me not shooting you right now?"

"Beyond that would be great."

She looked out over the books, running a strand of her dark hair over and under her fingers in a way I wished I had the courage to. Her gaze came back to mine. "If you find how the new tech is powering the building, then you could bring that knowledge back to your clan. They'd welcome you back with open arms."

They would already welcome me back with open arms. "I don't want to be a part of the clan—not while Gabriel leads."

She smiled, a look that was equal parts terrifying and mesmerizing. "Then get rid of him."

"I can't just get rid of Gabriel—he's the leader of the clan. His family practically founded it."

Her sneer was back, and she held a hand out to the stacks around us. "So? I thought you were a reader. Pick up literally any historical book here and it'll tell you that bastards stay rulers—until you bring them down."

"I couldn't do that."

She shook her head, something disappointed in her gaze. "Then maybe all you're good for is reading books and turning on the electricity."

"Maybe."

I didn't let her see that her words hurt me. Because they didn't . . . much. All I really wanted was for Kaden to come back, for things to go back to the way they were—but M couldn't help me with that. The library darkened as we sat there, the stacks of books and bright murals on the walls fading, the sounds of the night growing. I cleared my throat. "If I'm going to risk traveling through a city with warring clans, infected beasts, and people who want to kill me, then I demand two things."

Her eyes narrowed. "And what's that, Sasquatch?"

I held up two fingers. "First, I want you to stop threatening to kill me. And put the safety on your gun." I put down one finger. "And second, I want your real name. M has to stand for something."

There was a flicker of surprise in her eyes, and then a slight rise in the corner of her lips. "That was three things." She sat up and reached out a hand, bridging the space between us. "But I'll take it. Once you get me to the new tech, I'll give you my real name."

Her fingers tried to crush my own as we shook, and I responded in full. Then she pulled her hand back and lifted her gun, pushing the safety on. "Happy, Sasquatch?"

"Ecstatic."

"Great. Now let's set up camp."

Together we pushed two of the faded couches into one of the small back rooms. It wasn't cold enough to risk a fire, so we used the last of the fading light coming through the lone window to eat some of our dried food, and then each laid a sleeping bag across a couch and crawled in. I was surprised when M left me the longer couch—I was quite a bit taller than her, but somehow I'd expected her to take it. M leaned her gun against her couch so that it pointed up at the ceiling, the safety on. As far as camps went, it was one of my better ones.

The night deepened, the scents of books comforting me almost as much as M's presence.

"One more thing." I turned over in my sleeping bag to face her, the night too deep to make out anything beyond rough shapes. "Any chance we could nix the whole 'Sasquatch' thing?"

Even in perfect darkness, somehow I knew she was smiling.

"Not a chance."

TWELVE—ARA

A couple of weeks passed in The Last City and Kaden and I found an odd sort of rhythm. He returned each night from training, quieter than normal, insisting he was just tired. Judging from the myriad bruises on his body, I didn't doubt it. I spent time with Walter, or on my own, exploring the city and trying to understand the vast, complicated machinery of thousands of people living and working together. Always looking for clues about the lab, for information about my father or sister, for whatever secrets Walter might be hiding. But there was nothing to find. The truth was as mysterious as my father's note: *go back to the beginning*. We'd found The Last City, but now it felt like we were stuck in the middle of a story, and I couldn't step out to find the beginning or the end.

The worst part of it all was the growing distance between Kaden and me—but I supposed after a summer spent only in each other's company, maybe some distance was inevitable. I hoped once Kaden finished the training we'd have more time together. I could tell that my quest for the truth was one he tolerated more than shared—but how could I ask him to do more, seek further and deeper, when he'd lost his family and left his home for me? Tonight he fell asleep almost immediately after dinner. I lay there beside him, staring out the window, thinking of Walter and my father, and how two men from the same family could be so different.

Then again, Emma and I were always different. No one ever picked us out as sisters. But it never diminished our love for each other.

I drifted into dreams of my sister running forever away from me, of her strange, intense eyes, her particular ability to see things I couldn't, until a knock on the bedroom door startled me awake. Kaden froze, his soft breathing silenced. The sun was long gone, the night velvety black outside the window. The ever-present radio played somewhere in the house, but otherwise the night was quiet.

Kaden slipped out of bed, grabbing the gun on the dresser while I picked up the knife under the bed.

"Who is it?" Kaden said, his voice low.

"Housekeeping," Talia's voice came from the other side of the door. Kaden gave an annoyed sigh, lowered the gun, and opened the door.

"What do you want, Talia?" he said.

Talia breezed past him, like this room was hers.

"Please, come in and make yourself at home," I growled.

She ignored me. "I've got something I want to show you two but we have to ditch the guards. Harrison and Ronnie are going to make a distraction in five minutes. Are you in?" To my surprise it wasn't Kaden she addressed the question to—it was me.

I glanced at Kaden, and he shrugged as if to say, *it's up to you.* Though I'd normally be opposed to extra time with Talia, I wasn't getting anywhere in my hunt for the truth on my own. "We'll meet you downstairs in three," I said.

"Make it snappy, we've only got one shot." Talia winked at me, then left as fast as she'd come. I watched her go. At first I hadn't trusted her with Kaden—because what girl wouldn't be interested in him? But she hadn't even looked at him standing there shirtless. He was already pulling on warm clothes, and I hurried to follow.

"We definitely don't trust her, right?" I said as I pulled on my jacket and boots.

Kaden was putting on a holster and several knives, and I wondered if he was delaying the question. Talia had risked her life to help rescue me and the other women in the wagon. But it was hard for me not to also associate her with Izzie's death. *Maybe that's just my own guilt though.*

He seemed to choose his next words with care. "I don't think we should trust anyone in the city except for each other." I wondered if there was a subtext there. *Including your grandfather.*

"Do you think it could be something to do with Emma or my father?" My heart beat faster at the thought.

"Maybe . . . though I doubt it'll be that easy."

"What part of this has been easy?"

"Being with you is always easy, Princess." He winked at me and opened the door. "Except for when you're setting things on fire."

A few minutes later we crept into the front foyer. Talia stood beside the front door, a finger held to her lips. Outside the front windows, I could make out two men standing just outside the front door. *Let's hope Talia doesn't also like fire.* Judging by the look Kaden shot me, he was also worried about what kind of spectacle Talia had cooked up.

Then, visible outside the large front windows, two men stumbled down the main street. They sang some raucous song so loudly I could hear it even from here. One of them was huge, and the smaller one had blue hair that gleamed beneath the streetlights.

Ronnie and Harrison.

"Hooome, home on the range!" Ronnie sang in a deep baritone, tilting back and forth at such dangerous angles I would have been impressed had I not suspected this was all an act. Harrison sang a completely different song, in a falsetto that made me wince. Talia leaned against the front door, slowly turning the knob but not opening it yet.

"Get ready," she whispered.

When they'd reached the front of the house, Harrison and Ronnie's voices escalated. The shadowed forms of the guards moved from the door to the street.

"You two!" one of the guards called out. "It's after curfew!"

"C'mon, Princess," Talia said, slipping out the door. Kaden and I followed after. Harrison and Ronnie bellowed and fought in the yard, the two guards trying unsuccessfully to separate them as we slipped into the night.

At night the city was a different beast than its daytime counterpart. The crowded, bustling streets of the afternoon held an edge in the darkness. It was eerily quiet, as if the vast, clear sky of stars above had swallowed all sound. There was a curfew in place, no one was meant to be out after dark, but even so I saw the shadowed forms of people move quickly out of our way, as eager to avoid us as we were them. In the day, the city was dangerous, everyone armed and wary; at night it felt like anything could happen here, and not in a good way. A few windows glowed with the light of electricity, and a few streetlights were lit, but Talia seemed keen to avoid these, leading us across streets and through alleyways by moonlight alone.

Every so often, Talia paused, and I noticed, in the distance, the uniforms of night guards passing beneath the few glowing streetlights. *I wonder what would happen if they caught us*. Maybe I would find out what kind of protection being the Chancellor's granddaughter really gave me. Tonight I was thankful they went their own way and we continued on undetected.

After maybe twenty minutes, Talia stopped beside an old building, the lights off inside. "This is it." She pointed to what looked like the door to a root cellar, set into the ground. "Ladies first?"

Before I could step forward and prove I wasn't scared, Kaden's hand landed on my shoulder.

"I'll go first." He heaved open one of the heavy doors. Steep stairs descended into thick darkness. He caught my eye, and then pulled his small handgun free.

"That won't help you down there," Talia said with a smug smile.

He caught my eye, and must have seen the concern there because he smiled at me. "Burning daylight," he said, then started down the steep steps.

I made to follow him immediately but Talia caught my arm. "Give him a second, it's a tight fit. There's nothing down there that will hurt him."

I pulled my arm from her grasp. "You might be my city guide, but don't think for a minute that means I trust you."

Talia stepped closer, all the way up to me, until our breath mingled, and I wanted to step backward—but I didn't. I wouldn't cede ground to her. She whispered, "Princess, that might be the smartest thing you've ever said."

Then she spun, her loose hair slapping me in the face as she disappeared into the hole behind Kaden. I stood there for a moment in the moonlight, annoyed. I'd wanted to put Talia in her place, and yet somehow I felt like she'd put me in mine.

"Burning daylight," I muttered and ducked into the darkness after them.

Steep steps descended into a sort of underground cellar, where Talia and Kaden were waiting for me. We hadn't brought a flashlight, but I saw now that the glowing green moss grew over the walls of the basement. *Great. Let's hope no bodies come with it.* In the far corner of the cellar, a tunnel lined with the same green glow led away from the direction of the street.

"What is this place, Talia?" I said quietly.

Talia gave me her catlike smile. "The one part of The Last City that Walter doesn't control." Then she started down the tunnel without another word.

I exchanged a look with Kaden—in the green glow his eyes were a vivid, almost impossible green. "What do you think?" I said.

"I think this is a bad idea," he said with a sigh. "Terrible, actually."

"So . . . full steam ahead?"

"Sounds about right."

I started down the tunnel, Kaden close behind. The tunnel sloped slightly downward as we walked, and then, to my surprise, leveled out and widened, until we could walk comfortably.

Before long, I heard a low rumble ahead—water, maybe? Then, with a single sharp turn, the tunnel suddenly opened up, and I was left speechless.

Before us lay a vast underground cavern, roughly the size of a football field, with what looked like a bazaar in full swing. Scents of meat and bread perfumed the air, steam rose from below, giving the chamber a warm, humid feel, and the sound I'd thought was water was actually the low hum of hundreds of voices. The cavern was packed full of makeshift wooden stalls, people flowing between them, and there were floodlights mounted at regular intervals on the walls, giving the room the brightness of noon. After the cold night air, it felt like stepping into a new, colorful, chaotic world. Talia had already sauntered down the final set of stairs cut from the stone and joined the frenzy.

I turned to Kaden, surprised when his hard look didn't match the wonder in my eyes. "What's wrong?" I said.

He shook his head. "Nothing." But I could tell he was unsettled, and didn't want to be here. The same way he didn't want to be in The Last City. The thought of losing him terrified me almost as much as never seeing my father or sister again did.

"C'mon. It'll be an adventure." I took his hand and pulled him after me, not giving him a choice.

We made our way into the tide of humanity. Some stalls were crammed with old tech items: flashlights, batteries, weapons of all sorts. Some stalls were selling outdated magazines and newspapers. Others had canned food items I hadn't seen in years, and clothes and shoes. I heard the sizzle and crackle of oil, and smelled the scent of nuts and meat cooking. Some of the vendors smiled at us, calling out prices or haggling with others. *Too bad I didn't bring that bag of coins.*

"Kaden, look." I pointed to a stall with only one item spread out on a white tablecloth: bright red petals. *Plague flowers*. There were even a few plants in their own pots. Without Walter's blood, I wondered if they did anything. The man behind the table held a rifle casually in his arms, and even though the petals were spread out before him, I had the sense it wouldn't be wise to ask how effective the petals were in front of a crowd. Kaden seemed to have the same thought, because his hand met the small of my back, guiding me after Talia.

"What is this place?" I said to Talia when we caught her beside a stall full of gleaming knives.

"Full moon bazaar," she said, as if that explained everything. "You're lucky you caught it." *Lucky. Right, that's me.* She went back to bartering with the stall owner, as Kaden and I exchanged a look. The room was lit from the sides by massive lights someone had set up, but I could still make out the green glow of the strange moss behind it.

At least a few hundred people filled the area, talking, laughing, bartering over goods, some even holding mugs filled with some kind of alcohol. They all wore the arsenal of weapons I'd come to expect, but most of the weapons were sheathed, or laid beside stalls, as if no one expected to use them here. Even Talia, who usually walked with commanding purpose, not giving anyone the time of day, was different here. I watched as she tossed her hair over her shoulder, then reached out and touched the arm of the man she was bartering with. His cheeks turned bright red, and they seemed to reach an agreement.

"Is there a reason you brought us here, Talia?" Kaden stepped into Talia's path before she could start off again.

"Of course." She nodded to the far corner of the marketplace, outside the glare of the floodlights. "There's an underground market here for newcomer women's blood—people think that because Walter feeds blood to the plague flowers, maybe women's blood fed to the plague flower will cure them. Total shit, of course, but it didn't stop me when I came here."

Kaden had stiffened beside me. "You want Ara to sell her blood?"

Talia shrugged. "It's how I got the money to start my expedition team—sold as much as I could till they wised up and realized it wasn't doing shit." She stepped forward, taking a piece of hair between her fingers before I pulled away. "I'd say the blood of the Chancellor's granddaughter herself, the first Invalid in the city, should come at a nice premium. After all, the most precious thing in The Last City is secrets."

Before Kaden could speak, and inevitably turn down the plan, I spoke. "If I do trade my blood for secrets, do you think someone might be able to tell me if my father and Emma are here?"

"I didn't say that. I said you could trade your blood for *secrets*." She leaned in closer, her eyes mocking. "That's the thing with secrets: if you know what they are beforehand, they aren't a secret."

Behind us, a group of men had started singing some sort of drinking song—their revelry a perfect contrast to our small group. Kaden's eyes held only worry, his jaw hard with the words I knew he held in. Almost as if she could sense my hesitancy, Talia said, "But if you just want to go back, keep sleeping in your attic, and playing princess . . ."

"No," I said. "Let's do this." Finding Father and Emma. Finding the truth. Nothing else mattered. Kaden sighed beside me, but he didn't try to talk me out of it. Maybe he knew he couldn't.

"Follow me," Talia said, then turned down the winding pathways between the stalls.

"You know," Kaden muttered, "when I said you should give her a chance, this wasn't what I meant."

"It'll be fine," I whispered back, hoping I was right. Talia took us back to a far corner of the cavern, where a crevasse hollowed out part of the wall. An old man sat in the small opening, his shoulders hunched, eyes closed. Before him, on a thin, dirty blanket, a single potted plague flower sat.

"How do we do this?" I whispered to Talia.

"Just cut your hand, and then feed it to his plague flowers." Talia pointed to the potted plant. "Then you get three questions. So make sure they're good."

I drew my smallest blade, and then pressed it against my palm.

"Small cut, please, Ara," Kaden said, clearly unhappy with this.

I barely even felt the blade, so focused on what I would ask as I let my blood leak over the flowers.

"Ask your three questions," the man said, and opened his eyes. I nearly startled back—they were pure white. My hand went instinctively to the dagger at my hip, but there was no blood leaking from the edges. He wasn't infected, just blind.

I forced my hands to my side and took several deep breaths before I said, "The Chancellor told me my father and sister weren't here." I wondered if there was a way to say this that didn't sound treasonous. "But I'm worried he might have . . . missed them. Can you think where someone would hide in The Last City if they didn't want to be found?"

His answer came immediately. "Men often hide in the ruins to escape the Chancellor's gaze. They can still trade for the plague flower, but they hide outside the Chancellor's authority." His words brought up a possibility I'd begun to fear—what if Walter was telling the truth, and my father was out in the ruins, hiding, waiting for me? How would I ever find him? The man continued. "There are also rumors that a powerful man who left The Last City returned when he shouldn't have and is now hidden away." Hidden away? As in captive? I didn't want to waste another question and ask him to elaborate, because I couldn't imagine my grandfather holding his own son captive.

I stored his cryptic answers away, and focused on my next question. "What does the black spiral represent?"

Lit by the green moss, the effect on his white eyes was eerie. "Deep underground, in the natural tunnels beneath the city, lies a whirlpool. Some people claim that if you jump in and hold your breath long enough, it'll bring you up outside the city walls. Others claim it can't be survived—yet it is still preferable to life here. Others say it represents the darkest secrets of the Chancellor, and his all-consuming ambition. Only you can decide the answer for yourself."

That was pointless. Thanks for nothing. I took a deep breath, thinking carefully. What was most important to know about Walter?

And then it came to me. "Who are Walter's enemies?"

He lowered his voice. "There are whispers of a man who escaped The Last City within the last few days. They're hunting him in the ruins, but trying to keep it a secret. Rumor is they'll be sending the Captain and his team after him soon."

My legs suddenly felt weak—was it possible the man who'd escaped was my father? Now it felt like I had more possibilities than ever: he could be the man who'd returned and was hidden away, the man hiding in the ruins, or the man who'd recently escaped. *Or none of the above.* Which made most sense? "Do you know who the man who escaped is?" I said.

He reached out and picked one of the flower petals, setting it on his tongue and closing his eyes as if savoring the taste. "A man with more secrets than you, Invalid girl. That's four questions—we're done here."

THIRTEEN—KADEN

Ara stared up at me, her eyes concerned. "You don't have to do this."

The sun crept into the shadowed stables, lighting Ara's hair a golden red, the sounds of horses and impatient men just outside. Even if there were other women in this city, she still drew the eye of every man she passed. *And I'm going to leave her here. I am so, so stupid.*

We both agreed that there was some small chance her father and sister might be somewhere in the ruins, but that we shouldn't tell Walter we were looking for them. Which meant we needed a covert way to go look and see who the Captain was hunting. Talia had somehow convinced Walter that I should graduate from my training early and go out with the Captain's next expedition. The only thing we disagreed on was Ara remaining in the city while I searched the ruins.

"If I see or hear anything that might be a lead on your father, I'll come back and we can go out together," I said, trying to remember my own arguments for why she should stay. "This is a good thing—the Captain knows the ruins better than anyone. If your father is out there, we'll find him."

She looked out at the men waiting for me, and then back to me, her lips pressed tightly together even as she nodded. There was one more reason I wanted to go on this expedition. Within these walls, I felt trapped, confined. Every day the walls grew a little higher. Over the past few days, I'd seen Sam two more times. I wanted to feel the power of a horse running through the ruins, outside the wall and this world of careful rules Walter had created, and chase away my brother's ghost. Maybe in the ruins I could find the peace Issac spoke of. Maybe I could escape the demons that haunted me.

"Promise me you'll be careful?" she said.

"Careful?" I pulled her tight against me. "That doesn't sound like me."

"I mean it. Don't make me steal a horse and come after you."

The horses snorted outside the barn, pawing the ground, impatient to leave, but there was one more thing I had to do first. The cold chain of a necklace lay around my neck, bearing the ring Issac had given me just before he died. I lifted it from my neck, and placed the necklace over Ara's neck. A strange ball of nerves turned over in my stomach. I hadn't intended to give it to her now—I'd wanted to wait for the right time. Ask her father and be all traditional like Issac would have. But neither of them were here anymore, and I was done waiting.

"Marry me," I blurted out.

Her eyes flicked up to mine, shocked. "What?"

"Marry me," I said again, slower now, forcing myself to breathe.

She looked down at the ring, turning it over in her fingers, an agony of time passing before she said, "The last time I was supposed to get married it didn't go so well." Finally, her eyes came back to mine, a slight, worried smile there. "Besides, does marriage even exist anymore?"

I took her hands in mine, holding them for a long moment before I said, "You're searching for your truth: about your father, about Walter, about this city. I support that. I support you and I'll go to the ends of the earth if you ask me. But the only truth I want, the only truth I need, is you. That's what that ring represents to me. That's why I want you to have it."

"You already have me forever," she said softly. "Why get married?"

I smiled at her stubborn streak; of course I'd want a woman who didn't want to be married. "Because that's what people used to do when they were in love? And because I don't think we should give up on everything from the world before." Or at least, Issac and Sam hadn't. They'd always been dreamers, readers, believers—it was something I envied them. Something I hadn't appreciated until I'd lost them. "Issac gave me the ring, and told me to give it to you. He believed in stuff like marriage and God and love." I stared down at her hands in mine and said softer, "I guess I want to believe in something again."

She was quiet for some time, and I was terrified to look up. But when she spoke again, her voice was as determined as always. "Ask me again."

My gaze rose to hers. And when she smiled at me, something euphoric and light bubbled up inside my chest.

"Marry me," I said for the third time.

She stepped closer, and I saw the teasing tilt of her lips, the flush of happiness in her cheeks, the answer before she even said it. "Okay."

I felt weightless, like the grin on my face would never leave. “Good enough for me.” Then I pulled her against me, and tilted her face up to mine. I kissed her, and for a moment there was no city, no plague, no lost family—only us. Only *this* truth.

When I pulled back, her smile matched my own.

“You should go,” she said.

“I should.” Instead, I leaned in to kiss her again.

Finally she pulled back. “Go,” she said, shoving me playfully.

This time I did, from the shadows of the barn and out into the dawn breaking over the patchwork city. My new expedition team stood saddled and waiting, the Captain at the front. I had almost no information on the mission—the Captain had only said we'd get more details at the gate. With no word to me, or introductions to the other men, he kicked his horse and the group rode forward. *Might be a bit too much to expect a congratulations from this lot.*

“Guess that's us, Storm,” I muttered to the black horse I'd ridden last time I'd been in the ruins. No one else had given him a name, so I figured “Storm” was fine. Even if he wasn't Red—no horse would ever be—there was a sort of joy that rose in me when I swung onto his back. Like a weight lifted off me that I hadn't realized had settled there. Not peace, but an unburdening of sorts.

Our group followed the main road that ran through the city. It was still early so the road was mostly clear. The Captain slowed as we approached the final stretch that met up with the wall, the hill slanting upward and the crowds thickening. Many people were on foot, with packs on their backs—apparently they'd recently opened the ruins to teams on foot.

“Nice day for a ride,” I said to the man beside me. “How often do you guys go out?”

The man I'd spoken to, big with a shaved head, gave me a slow, cold look, and then pushed his horse forward. *Guess I've got some work to do in befriending my team and uncovering Walter's secrets.* Deception wasn't exactly my strong suit.

We reached the gates, crowded with people trying to leave, and the men dismounted. I followed their lead, pulling Storm after me, as we all made our way up to the opening. Guards were posted at intervals, scanning people as they came and went in the chaotic flow. I suddenly tensed: Talia had said our group wouldn't need to be scanned because we were with the Captain, but what if she was wrong?

"Kaden!"

I turned, shocked to see Walter parting the flow of the crowds. *Well, I guess now I know what getting more information at the gates means.*

"Chancellor," I said, when Walter drew level with us. The flow of people continued around us, as if we were a boulder in a stream. "I didn't think you'd be here."

I wasn't sure why I was surprised—Walter seemed to be everywhere at once. But I couldn't deny his timing today was impeccable. The guards who had been approaching our group simply passed us by.

"Please, call me Walter." He reached out to shake my hand, and I smiled, knowing full well I wouldn't stop calling him "Chancellor"—it felt too much like putting my guard down. "Glad you feel ready to join the team. I have no doubt your expertise will be needed out there."

"Anything to help The Last City." *Anything to find Ara's truth and leave this place forever.*

The Captain came to stand beside us and joined the pocket of space we'd created in the flow of people. I didn't miss that the guards hadn't scanned him either. *Guess the Captain's team really does get special privileges.*

"What can we do for you, Chancellor?" the Captain asked.

Walter smiled, the look of a good politician. "I have a sensitive mission for you today."

From his pocket he brought out a small device that looked like a walkie-talkie, with a glowing screen. I caught a glimpse of a young man with wide, haunted eyes—definitely not Ara's dad—before the Captain tucked it out of sight. So, the man we were hunting wasn't Ara's father. *Too late to back out now.*

"We'll see to it, Chancellor," the Captain said. He stepped back into the flow of people, remounted his horse, and started out the gates. The other men guided their horses after him, rejoining the flow of people. Storm's head came up, watching the others go, but I held him back. Once I would have followed without question. But I'd let Gabriel lead the clan, and Issac and Sam had died because of it.

"Chancellor?"

He turned, his smile not faltering.

"What'd he do? The man we're hunting?"

"His name is Septimus. He killed three men and escaped the city a week ago. A patrol sighted him in the western ruins, but he was able to evade them. Talia insisted you were an experienced tracker. But if you don't think you can handle it—"

"No. I can help."

"Good man," he said. Something about his condescending tone made me stiffen. The fact that a single order from Walter was enough to doom a man . . . it felt like all the mistakes I'd made in the clan all over again. But I wasn't here to help or protect anyone but Ara. My goal was to find her father out there in the ruins—whoever this other man was, I couldn't help him. I gave Walter a final nod, then swung atop Storm, rejoining the tide of humanity spilling out of the city.

I looked back only once, to see Walter watching me go, statue-like in the flow of people, a small circle of space around him none dared to enter.

~

The sun sank toward the horizon as I crouched beside the embers of the fire we'd found in the ruins.

"Well, tracker? Should we head back for the night?" The Captain stood in the remains of an old gas station, using his boot to kick at the carcass of some small furry creature mixed into a pile of faded candy bar wrappers and rusted cans. He'd said little all day, as we'd ridden through the ruins. I could feel his cold eyes on me now.

I didn't respond, turning a log on the fire over, the embers flickering as a cold wind blew in from the shattered front window.

"Tracker? You hear me?" the Captain said again, louder, despite the fact that I knew he knew my name. "We need to head back if we're gonna make it before the gates close."

"This fire is fresh." I stood to face him, coming to a spontaneous decision I hoped I wouldn't regret. "Hours maybe. He's close by. We should camp here for the night."

He stared at me, and I braced myself, waiting for him to explode. Instead, he surprised me. "You think we can catch him in the morning?"

"With the snow, there's bound to be tracks. If he hasn't gone south yet, it's because he doesn't have supplies. He's likely bunkered down somewhere close—we can look for smoke in the morning. If he knows we're close and spooks now, he'll freeze to death in the night. Either way, it shouldn't be too hard to find him."

I wasn't sure why the lies came so easily. Maybe I'd gotten too used to not trusting others. Or maybe since Sam and Issac died I'd lost faith in humanity. Whatever the reason, a day of tracking had brought me to one simple conclusion: Septimus *wanted* to be found. His fires were obvious; so were his camps, with clear, deep prints in the snow leading to each. If he'd really murdered three men, why not head directly south? Why linger in the ruins? It was possible the encroaching cold trapped him here, but there were enough caravans moving through the ruins that he could have joined one. This wasn't a hunted man: this was one playing a very dangerous game. A man that Walter wanted quietly killed—and one I wanted to talk to. Plus, I needed more time to find clues, if they were out here, about Ara's dad.

"We should set a guard," I finished. "Just in case he comes looking for supplies."

"Fine. I'll tell the men."

I followed him out of the gas station and back into the growing cold. In the distance, the sun sank behind the buildings. I ran a hand over Storm, murmuring softly to him as I pulled him through the wide door frame of an old laundromat—where they'd decided to keep the horses from the bitter cold of the night. Until I'd ridden Storm through the ruins, I hadn't even realized how much I missed this. But these men weren't my old expedition team—not even close. Issac was the best outdoorsman I knew. He would have known what Septimus was up to simply by examining the first footprint.

"I wish you were here, old man," I whispered. Storm's ears perked forward. His head turned to mine with wide, deep eyes. It reminded me so much of Red I couldn't help but lean forward and talk to him the same as I had my old horse.

"What do you think, boy?" I murmured to him. "You think he's just stupid, leaving behind all those fires and tracks?" Storm didn't move, his liquid eyes watching mine. "Yeah, me neither," I muttered, and then gave him a final pat. "Me neither."

Across the way, the other men had broken into an apartment building and started a small fire in the grate, eating cold food we'd brought from The Last City. They spoke in soft voices then fell silent when I came in and shut the door behind me. I was used to earning my place—I'd done the same in the clan—but I wondered if this was something more. Walter had assigned me to this team before I'd completed my training, and they knew I was with his granddaughter. Maybe they thought I was some sort of snitch, or that I wasn't prepared to be here. *To be fair, I'm only here to see if I can find Ara's father or something Walter's hiding.* It made me even more determined to appear a hardworking, committed part of the team.

"I can take the first watch," I said into the cold silence. The men turned to the Captain. He sat in the armchair nearest the fire, smoking a cigar. He blew out a ring of smoke, before he turned to me and smiled—a look that was as warm as the winter wind howling outside.

"I'll take it with you."

~

Outside a slow, soft snow fell, the same as it had the day the little girl Izzie had died. Sometimes I thought about her out there, her body cold and unburied. Why hadn't we buried her? I had buried Kia, leaving a part of my heart in her small grave I didn't think I'd ever get back.

Part of me wanted to go back, to find the girl's body, but I knew I wouldn't be able to—I didn't know this city like I did Boise. Even if I did, the ground was frozen solid. We were so much farther north, the cold cutting deeper, the snow reaching higher. It was a harsher world up here.

Across the road, the rest of the men slept, the fire inside giving the house a golden glow. The Captain stood in the arched entryway, a dark form just visible from the light of the moon. My bedroll lay on the single bench in the back of the laundromat we'd found for the horses. It would be a cold night, but the crowded warmth of the horses would make it bearable.

A biting wind blew over the city, but even after a hard day of riding, I wasn't tired. Energy coursed through my body. With the fire in the house, and the clear horse tracks that led here, we may as well have put up a big neon sign advertising our whereabouts. Still, no sound came from the darkness. No movement.

Yet something told me we were being watched.

An hour, maybe two, passed like that. The light of the moon reflected off the snow, giving just enough light to make out the empty street.

A surge of disappointment filled me when the Captain finally made his way from the doorway over to me—our shift was over. Septimus hadn't shown. Maybe I was wrong.

The Captain paused in the street, and then raised a hand, motioning to me and pointing down the street. The disappointment disappeared.

He'd heard something. Adrenaline flooded my body.

Septimus was here. I was right.

I pulled out the gun they'd given me for this mission, and then left my post to follow the Captain into the night. It wasn't ideal, finding Septimus with the Captain, but it might be my only shot. Maybe I could reason with the Captain. Convince him to bring Septimus back to the city, or at least question him.

The world came into sharper focus, the shadows darker, as the Captain pointed away from camp, pacing down the road with his gun drawn. Suddenly it felt like every shadow hid a possible enemy. The Captain turned the corner, and I cast a final glance back at the warm glow of the fire behind the window, before I followed.

Turning the corner, the night deepened. The hair on the back of my neck prickled. *We shouldn't leave the horses unprotected. We shouldn't be this far from camp*. But the Captain kept pacing confidently forward. Where the hell was he going?

"Shouldn't we wake the others?" I called softly to him. "For reinforcements?"

"We can take him alone."

I glanced over my shoulder—something was wrong here, even if I couldn't say what.

I wanted to go back to get the the others, but I couldn't just leave the Captain out here, alone in the snow, stalking a criminal. If he died, then the other men would never accept me. And I'd never know why Walter wanted Septimus dead.

"We should go back," I called again, looking over my shoulder. The uncomfortable sense that someone was watching us made every tiny noise in the night seem predatory. Again, the sense that something was wrong rose. The moon lit the snow a dull gray.

And then, finally, I saw it.

The Captain wasn't following tracks. He wasn't following anything. He was just walking forward.

He was leading us away from camp.

Which was when I realized that he'd used the shadows of possible enemies all around to distract me from the only one that mattered. The one right in front of me.

His gun came up at the same moment mine did.

My breath, my heart, all pounded fear. *You are so, so stupid.*

"You shoot me, and we both die," I said, not lowering the gun, staring down at him over the barrel.

"Your gun's full of blanks."

I wanted to curse myself to hell and back again. Instead I didn't break eye contact, afraid to move. "A blank can still kill at this range."

"A bullet definitely will. I'll take my chances."

The snow swirled around us, the cold swallowing all noise, all violence. *Well, Issac, I might join you a bit sooner than expected.* Still, this wasn't the first time a gun had been aimed at me. "So, you shoot me, and I shoot you, we both die out here in the snow. What exactly does either of us gain?"

His gun didn't waver. "Doesn't matter what we gain. Orders are orders."

Cold crept down my spine. *Orders.* Someone had ordered him to kill me—and I bet I knew who. "You don't have to do this. We can work this out. You still need me to find Septimus."

"You've got us close enough. You already showed your hand; he's desperate, cold, low on supplies. My men can do the rest. Better to finish this now."

There, in the shadows behind him, a piece of the darkness

detached itself from a building. It took everything in me not to move, not to turn my eyes. But I saw in his face that he'd made up his mind.

"I'll tell the girl you died honorably," he said.

The piece of darkness leapt forward—swinging something long and thin as I dove sideways and the Captain's gun fired.

My heart thundered, breath ragged.

Not shot. I'm not shot. I would know if I'm shot, right?

My hands ran quickly all over my body, but besides my ragged breath, I found no bullet hole. I was still alive. Undeserving, lucky, and stupid—but alive.

I climbed slowly to my feet. Spread-eagled on the ground lay the Captain. A dark stain spread out over the snow beneath him, his eyes empty. A young man stood over him, his chest rising and falling, a crowbar gripped in his bare hands.

Then the young man turned to me, and even in the darkness, even with a dead man at his feet, I knew who it was.

"You must be Septimus."

FOURTEEN—SAM

"What used to be here?" M stood in what was once a proud Cabela's building, staring at the few charred beams.

"The Castellano clan," I said. An autumn wind stirred the leaves inside the blackened remains of the building. "Gabriel, the clan leader, named it after himself. Which pretty much tells you all you need to know about Gabriel." *And the clan.*

"This was the Castellano clan?" Her voice held a hint of surprise. The Castellano clan was once the most powerful clan in the city. Today the wind scattered the ashes, moving through the sad leftover shell—beams that reached up to nothing, a perimeter fence fallen into disrepair.

"It didn't always look like this."

I tried to remember the impressive way the building had once towered over the parking lot—a magnificent hunting lodge for survivors. Whatever I thought of him personally, I had to admit that Gabriel had built something impressive here. Even Kaden hadn't wanted to step into his role.

"Where is the Castellano clan now?" she said.

"Up at the Old Pen, across the city on the other side of the river. It's one of the few places in Boise with geothermal heat and greenhouses." Or at least, Gabriel had always talked about moving there, and some of the men I'd eavesdropped on this summer had said they'd relocated there—I hadn't cared to check. It was Gabriel's fault that Kaden, Ara, and Issac were all missing. The last thing I wanted to do was see him again. A tin cup lay nestled in some of the fallen leaves. I kicked it, sending it bouncing across the parking lot.

I led us past the clan's remains and toward the small storage shed a quarter mile away that Kaden had kept hidden right under Gabriel's nose. For some reason I didn't want to linger here. "So, I showed you my old home. How about yours? Where'd you live?"

"This Gabriel, he's still the leader of the clan?" M said, ignoring my question, the same way she'd ignored every question about who she was or where she'd come from.

"I haven't checked up on them, but yeah, I'd say so. Kaden liked to call him the cockroach clan leader—impossible to kill."

She snorted as I remembered the words she'd said about Gabriel in the darkening library, nonchalant and vicious in equal measure. *Bastards stay rulers—until you bring them down.* As if it were such an easy thing to do . . .

Was it?

M froze, and I stopped, so lost in thought it took me a heartbeat longer to hear what she had.

Hoofbeats.

For a moment my heart soared—the memory of Kaden riding Red and returning to the clan rose. But then I caught M's eyes, wide with fear, and reality set in.

Someone was coming.

Hooves hit the pavement in the distance, rapidly drawing closer. We were still in the large stretch of the open road—not enough time to run back into the encroaching trees. But enough time to hide here. M was already lifting her gun, but I pushed it down, motioning beneath a rusted truck.

"Don't—it might be someone from the clan. Hide underneath the truck and I'll talk to them."

She glared at me. "I'm not hiding. What if they take you hostage? Or shoot you?"

"Then you're on your own." I cast a desperate look over my shoulder, begging now. "Please, M. It might be someone I know. Trust me!"

To my surprise, she actually listened, crawling beneath the truck. Metal scraped against pavement as she pulled the gun beneath with her. "I'll shoot you in the foot if you're lying," she hissed from underneath.

The staccato drumbeat of a single horse on pavement drew closer. It was hard not to hope that Kaden wouldn't be the one riding the horse around the corner. So few of the clans had horses anymore—it was one of the things that had set the Castellano clan apart. Chances were, even if it wasn't Kaden, it was someone I knew.

And if not, well, I guess I was about to figure out how much M trusted me.

The cold, the wind, the distant clan, all came into sharp relief as I stood on the road, my bow on my back, a calculated risk to present a friendlier figure. More trees and weeds had sprung up this summer. Without the clan to beat them back, the once metropolitan area had fallen beneath the foliage.

Please, please, be someone I know.

A long-legged chestnut horse rode around the corner. The tension in my heart burst. Not Kaden, but I recognized the horse. She was one of the first mares Kaden had captured for the clan, and one of the best long-distance runners we had. It only took another half second to recognize the rider and when I did I smiled.

"Liam!" I waved both hands in the air, wanting to laugh and cry all at once. "Liam!"

Liam pulled the horse to a stop forty yards away, his hand going to the holster at his hip, his eyes weary as he stared at me. Then he pushed the horse forward, slow, prancing steps as she whinnied and fought the bit, wanting to run again. Only when he drew nearer did his blue eyes widen in surprise, then shock.

"Sam?"

"Who else?" I laughed. He slid from the horse and pulled me into a crushing embrace, his gun forgotten. After a moment he pulled back, taking me by the shoulders and looking me up and down like he couldn't believe it. He'd once been taller than me, but now I was surprised that we stood eye to eye.

"How in the—" He cut off, shaking his head. "Everyone thinks you're dead!"

"Dead?" *Why would they think I was dead?*

"Colborn said you were and then you never came back." He paused, looking me over. "You alone?"

I shrugged, resisting the urge to glance over my shoulder at the truck M hid beneath. "For now. I'm meeting someone downtown." The lie rolled off my tongue easier than I thought it would—maybe M was rubbing off on me. "Have you seen Issac, Kaden, or Ara?"

The excitement on his face slipped away. He hesitated, looking away for a moment, his voice low when he spoke. "Nobody's seen Kaden or Ara since the night the clan burned down."

"And Issac?"

This time he pulled the wide-brimmed cowboy hat from his head—a hat Kaden had given him. It moved round and round before his blue eyes met mine. The laughter that usually filled his face, that made him so well-liked in the clan, was replaced by something else. "Someone found Issac in a field, a few miles from the clan. Shot through the stomach. Just after the clan burned. Colborn's body was there too. Some kind of fight went down . . . I'm sorry, Sam."

My mouth felt dry, my heart pounding so loud I could hardly hear him. "But he's okay, right? You fixed him up?"

I knew the answer before he spoke it—knew from the moment he said I'm sorry, even if I couldn't fully believe it. "Issac is dead, Sam . . . I'm sorry."

Issac is dead.

That couldn't be right. Issac had found Kaden and me. Issac had survived the plague. Issac survived everything. He was the father I'd found after the world ended. He couldn't just be gone.

"I'm sorry, Sam," he said again. His voice seemed to come at a great distance. "We lost a lot of good men because of Colborn. But he's dead now. The clan is safe again, because of Issac."

A numbness filled me, a dull ringing noise drowning out everything else. I'd been waiting all summer for Issac to show up, to walk through the doors of the bookstore and embrace me. During the long, lonely summer, I'd doubted that Kaden and Ara would return, but never once Issac. Issac was constant, loyal . . .

. . . and gone.

It took a few moments before I gathered myself enough to meet Liam's eyes again, my voice rougher and deeper. "And Ara and Kaden?"

He shook his head, running his hands through his hair—hair that had thinned considerably since I'd last seen him. "Gabriel sent out a few expeditions originally, looking for them. But no one found anything." He shrugged, then looked down the long, empty road and sighed. "We've never had an expedition leader better than your brother. If Kaden doesn't want to be found, he won't be."

I nodded, surprised at the grief roiling in my chest—and a new, stranger emotion. Violent, red-hot anger. Had I been holding something breakable, I would have crushed it. When M had said to get rid of Gabriel, I couldn't imagine it—now I could. Issac wouldn't have died if Gabriel hadn't allied with Colborn. Kaden was right to hate him; Gabriel had started all of this. Gabriel was the reason I would never see Issac again.

Liam's hand landed on my shoulder, and I started, almost surprised to find him in front of me. "Kaden thought you were dead, Sam. He never would have left without you if he'd known you were still here. Give him some time. Kaden was always an adventurer—but he'll come home. He'd kill me if he knew I'd left you out here though."

He smiled, and I saw a flash of the old Liam—the kind man whom Gabriel had named as his second, because he cared deeply for people. Not like Gabriel, who only wanted power. Liam was selfless. *Like Issac was.* Again the pain hit, nearly bending me double.

"Why don't you come with me?" Liam said gently. "I'm delivering peace treaties to some of the other clans, letting them know that we're looking for new members. We can get you back in the stables, or on an expedition team. We're in the Old Pen now. It's got a well and greenhouses and geothermal heat, so no more freezing our asses off in the winter. We could really use you."

Of course Gabriel could use me. That's what Gabriel did. He used people, and when he was done with them, they died alone in a field or disappeared forever. But Liam was Gabriel's second, and I wondered if maybe there was a line drawn between us I hadn't seen until now. "I'll think about it . . . but I really do have to go downtown now."

He nodded, though something in his eyes said he didn't quite believe me. "A few of the men have been talking about rounding up the horses in the foothills, rebuilding the herd Kaden started. Kaden always had the touch for it. You could take over for him."

"Nah, I'm done working with horses. Keeping my feet on the ground." The thought of replacing Kaden was oddly repulsive, even though I wasn't exactly sure why. "Need a bit of a break from clan life."

Liam was quiet for a moment. "I can understand that. You've always got a place there though, if you change your mind."

"Thanks Liam. I'll keep that in mind." *And a lot of other things too.*

Then he did something he'd never done to me before. He held out his hand, and after a moment of hesitation, I reached out and shook it. Then he stepped back and put his hat back on. "You're a good man, Sam. It's good to see you. If Kaden does come back, where should I tell him to find you?"

"He'll know where."

He accepted this without question—after all, Kaden had been the man you went to if you needed something difficult found.

When he swung up on his mare I suddenly remembered something about Liam—he had grown up in Boise. He'd already turned the horse to go when I called out. "Liam?"

He turned the horse back, her hooves dancing on the concrete, ready to run. "Yeah?"

"Have you ever heard of a . . . lost city? Up north? Or, um, any cities that survived the plague?"

"Every city fell after the plague."

"But before that. You never heard of a city—" I paused, hoping M didn't shoot me where I stood. "Called Thule?"

"The name isn't familiar." His eyes darkened. "I know some men talked about a far north place where the plague hadn't hit, but I wouldn't believe it." He hesitated, then said, "Men will always make up fairy tales about places that don't exist. It's the things we build that we can trust in." *Sounds just like something Gabriel would say*. "Hope to see you around, Sam."

"You too, Liam."

He rode away. Long after the hoofbeats had faded, I stood there wondering at his words. Kaden would have gone with him but I wondered if Issac would have picked the same path as me. Of everyone I knew, Issac would have been the one to believe M, to seek out a city that existed only in book pages and whispered stories. Faith, he would have called it.

Faith.

It felt like that was all I had left.

~

It was several long minutes after Liam disappeared before M came to stand beside me.

Her eyes watched me, hard as always. "I thought you were gonna go with him."

"And risk being shot? Never." But I couldn't look at her as I said it. All summer I'd wondered about the clan. I hadn't returned because Ara, Kaden, and Issac had all risked so much to escape it, and I knew Kaden would look for me at the mall first. But maybe also because I was afraid to learn the truth. Now that I knew it, it was worse than I'd imagined.

Suddenly the quest to find this city felt like more than just an obligation to a girl I liked . . . it felt like the only thing I had left.

Together we made our way to the storage shed, the entire conversation with Liam replaying in my head. For the very first time, I wondered if Kaden could be dead too. I dismissed the thought. Kaden couldn't be dead—he was like Gabriel. Maybe not a cockroach, but a true survivor.

But he didn't believe the same of me. I wasn't sure why that hurt, but it did.

At the storage shed, it took me a few minutes to find the key we'd hidden and move all the debris placed in front of the shed to keep others out. M gazed curiously at the mountain of supplies, lit by the sun, when I finally opened it. I pulled out my final set of arrows, and some fresh socks. As I tugged, a small package fell free. My heart jolted when I recognized the writing.

Issac's elegant cursive was written across the top: *Sam*. He'd left something for me. My throat felt thick as I stared down at the writing.

He can't be gone.

How could he leave the world and I didn't know it?

M watched me with curious eyes. I doubted I could read whatever was inside without crying, so I tucked the small package inside my jacket. Then I dug out the last of the freeze-dried food and stuffed it into my backpack. Maybe I should have been worried about the dwindling reserves, and if they'd get me through winter, but I suddenly didn't give a damn. I didn't belong to a clan, to an expedition team, or to a family. If I starved, it was no one's problem but my own.

When the shed was locked again, we both hefted our packs, and weapons, an odd moment of silence as we stood outside the shed. Below us the city stretched out, the mountains rising above it all in the distance.

A lot of ground to cover. A lot of things that could go wrong between here and there.

And yet, I wasn't afraid.

I was angry.

I was angry that Issac would never come back. The best man I ever knew, who believed in mercy and grace, had died in an empty field and I hadn't even known it. I was angry that Kaden had chosen to believe Colborn. Chosen to believe that I was dead and then picked a girl over his own brother. I was angry that a cockroach ruled the clan, and that I was too cowardly to return and do something about it. I was angry that my only friends in the world were books and a girl who wouldn't even tell me her full name.

I was angry that I was alone, and it was all my fault.

M looked out at the city, and then at me, something cautious, and maybe pitying, in her eyes. "I'm sorry about your friend Issac. And about your clan."

I shrugged, refusing to look at her, or anywhere but the horizon, which had suddenly become a bit hazier. My voice came out low and thick. "Guess I don't really belong anywhere now."

"Join the club."

It didn't make sense, but her words—and their brutal delivery—made me feel better. Maybe I wasn't as alone as I'd thought. As I looked down at the city, it finally hit me: Issac wasn't ever coming back. He was gone, to the heaven and God he spoke of. A God I believed in too, because of him.

At that moment, I realized I wasn't going back to my bookstore. That chapter was over now. Whatever happened, whether The Lost City was real or not, it was time to find a new beginning.

"You ready?" I said. "All we need are the kayaks now."

"Actually, I'm regretting this whole thing." But she ruined her cold delivery with a smile.

I tightened my straps, and then took the first step leading us away from the shed and to whatever lay beyond.

"Great. Let's go."

FIFTEEN—ARA

I stood on the wall, watching as the sun set and Kaden didn't return. As the night grew darker, so did my thoughts.

He didn't come back.

One of my ever-present bodyguards approached. I hadn't learned any of their names, because they rotated often and rarely spoke directly to me. They were like shadows, always following, never speaking, so I was surprised when he addressed me now. "I've been asked to bring you to the Chancellor's house for dinner."

I didn't turn from staring over the darkened ruins—compared to the bright lights scattered in the city behind me, the ruins before were cloaked in velvety darkness. Kaden was an expedition leader. He knew what he was doing. Even so, I wondered if The Last City was a beast neither of us was fully prepared for.

When I made it to Walter's house, I found him sitting at the same table where he had his Council meetings. I'd sat there for a few of them, but I wasn't allowed to speak. Tonight my plate had venison alongside an apple and mashed potatoes with actual butter in it. Beside it stood a golden goblet with my ration of red plague flowers. I stared at the cup, rotating it in my hands before I set it back on the table. *You didn't speak up with Gabriel. You let him and Colborn bulldoze you. This is your chance to build a better world. Don't lose it.*

"Grandfather," I said, deciding to call him that instead of my usual *Walter*. "How often do people need to take the flowers for immunity?"

He looked up from the papers he read beside his dinner, as if surprised I'd spoken—we usually ate in silence. "We recommend our citizens take them twice a month." I'd already seen those closest to Walter, myself included, receive the flowers far more often—though most others received them far less. Men were willing to brave the lawless ruins, filled with infected animals, just to find something to trade for plague flowers. I'd seen a man trade a working rifle for a single flower. Walter explained it was the only way to keep the city running, and to equitably distribute a scarce resource. Now I wondered if the scarcity of the flowers was deliberate.

"This is the third time I've gotten them this week," I said. "Most people in The Last City only take them once a month, if they can even afford that." I paused, and then, my voice a bit harder, "If you make the cure with your own blood, why do you need to take them at all?"

He smiled at me the way you would a child. "Officials take them more often, to increase our immunity. I take them as an example. The city looks to me, so I must guide the way."

Seems like a giant waste. Especially when tonight, I was the only one to see. "But why don't we consume less, and give more to others?"

"Ara, I appreciate that you want to change things, but realize that The Last City is as fragile a thing as the flowers in your cup. Say the Council takes less, grows infected, and dies. Then what? Without us running the city, the greenhouses might fail. Thousands could die." He lifted his glass of flowers, the gold around the rim catching the light. "The entire economy of The Last City is built around this flower—it is the most precious commodity in the world. It's also how we ensure that everyone works and serves to the fullest capacity. But there is a limit to what we can produce."

"But why not distribute that amount equally?" I said, feeling stubborn and bullheaded. "Why give the leaders more than we need? Why give me any? I've survived so far without it—what if I don't need them and am taking it away from someone who does?"

"That is a risk we cannot take. We must protect our leaders at all costs. Imagine what would happen if we didn't maintain the strict discipline and protocol within The Last City. Do you remember what happened when the world fell?"

That was the problem. I did remember the horror of those first few weeks of the plague. The screams. The gunshots. The madness. And then, worst of all, the silence. The Last City perched even more precariously. Without Walter it could easily become anarchy, everyone trying to hoard the plague flower for themselves. The city would fall. Chaos would rule.

He lifted his cup of flowers and held it up to me, as if in a toast. "Leadership isn't easy, Ara. It requires sacrifice and hard decisions. I hope you can come to trust my decisions."

"I just wish I could be more helpful here."

"You are helpful. You are a symbol of hope. People see you and believe in our future. Just give it some time."

A symbol. I might as well be the princess that Talia accuses me of being. I stared down at the floating red flowers that Walter drank so easily. For the first time I wondered if I had judged Gabriel too harshly. He'd done horrible things, but he'd also stepped up and taken the burden of other people's lives on his shoulders. He was willing to sacrifice anything, even his life, to protect the clan. *The clan I burned down.*

Was I really the one to judge what was right or wrong here?

I lifted the cup and drank it. Walter was right: I didn't know the city or what it took to rule it. The thought of Kaden, out there in the ruins, braving the cold and the elements, made me feel both guilty and determined to do better. If he could survive the ruins in the dead of winter, then I could survive being a powerless symbol. Maybe the cost of finding the truth was fading into the shadows.

I left my plate of food and made my way to the tall windows, where I could just make out the wall in the distance. "Are you sure it's normal that they didn't make it home tonight?"

"Of course. He's fine," Walter said. "This happens all the time."

Even with the electricity burning through the night, my body rested and well-fed, something churned inside me that I had never felt in the forest with Kaden. Something like a trapped bird fluttering inside a cage.

"I just can't see him staying out there, knowing I'd worry."

"We've gotten reports of packs of infected animals, some big dogs, even an infected moose. They probably found a fresh trail. Everything is fine."

There were moments where Walter looked so much like my father I almost felt like I'd gotten him back. Then there were other moments, like right now, that I knew he wasn't telling me the truth. Except, wasn't that also like my father? He'd had so many secrets, so many things he'd never told me.

"Grandfather?" I said. His eyes had gone back to the papers before him as he ate food again and ignored me. "You told me that you would tell me more about my father when I'd gotten settled." Still he didn't look up. This time my voice was almost cold. "I'm settled."

He dabbed his mouth with his napkin, and then set it aside. "What do you want to know?"

"Why did he tell me you were dead?"

"Because to him I was. Your father never believed in the ideals behind The Last City: to stand apart from humanity. To reject the greed and waste that the rest of the world so willingly embraced. Even before the plague we strove to be a world within ourselves—fueled by our own power, growing our own foods, pushing the bounds of human research. I told your father, even growing up here as a child, that if he ever left, I couldn't be responsible for what happened to him after. I meant that. Charles chose his path."

My father grew up here. In The Last City . . . or whatever it was before it became this strange place. I wasn't sure why that realization felt so impossible, but it did. I'd always assumed he didn't talk about his childhood because it had been a bad one, not because he was hiding it from me. I leaned against the window, the cold, steady pane of glass comforting against my racing heart and the sensation that the ground itself was tilting. "Why did he never tell me?"

"Charles and I . . . well, my wife, your grandmother, Arabella, used to say that we were so alike that we butted heads on everything."

Arabella. I was named after a grandmother I never knew. For a moment words stuck in my mouth, the shock resounding to my core. "What happened to her?"

"She died after your father left." For the first time, his voice was hard. I wondered if there wasn't also blame hidden there.

I set my bare hand against the glass, trying to emulate the steady cold I felt there. Somehow the more I learned about my father, the more I realized how little I knew him, and the more it felt like everything I'd ever known was a lie. When I spoke my voice seemed to come from a distance. "I don't understand why my father didn't tell me he grew up here. Why would he keep all this secret? And why did he leave?"

Walter got up from the table and joined me by the window. We stood side by side, our reflections hazy compared to the brightness of The Last City beyond. His hand settled on my shoulder—I resisted the impulse to shake it free.

"Your father dreamed of a life beyond Thule," Walter said. Somewhere in the house the radio played—words I'd learned to tune out. "I'd hoped in time he would return."

"Maybe he still will."

Walter smiled. "Of course." But I wondered if his words were as doubtful as my heart. Once I'd followed my father's words into the ruins of Boise; and then into the mountains, journeying north to find him and Emma.

"How come you never went to look for him?"

He was silent for a long time. "Sometimes sacrifices have to be made for the greater good. Sometimes the individual tree must fall to save the forest."

"Is he the tree in this scenario? Or am I?"

He gave me a sad smile. "Neither. I've come to care for you, Ara. I would sacrifice more than I would have thought possible to protect my only granddaughter."

Only granddaughter.

He said the words like a kindness, like he thought I would turn to him. Instead, I froze.

Because I wasn't his only granddaughter.

He'd just forgotten Emma.

"You mean because Emma's dead?"

The look on his face was still, frozen. Then he corrected himself. "Of course not. I meant the only granddaughter here."

He's lying to me. He knows something and he's covering it up. I knew it the same way I knew the sun would rise in the east tomorrow: all the way to my bones. My whole body stiffened; my fingers clawed at my side.

I turned back to look at the reflection of myself in the mirror, not wanting him to see my reaction. Outside, the city grew darker, my reflection clearer. Staring at the girl who looked back at me, I realized she was no longer the one who followed her father through the mountains. The trusting girl who'd believed her father, and then her grandfather, was one who'd only had things taken from her. I didn't want to be her anymore. I couldn't.

The truth. Kaden. My father. Emma. That was all that mattered now.

"Ara? Are you all right?" Walter's voice was full of concern I no longer trusted. I was surprised at the woman who turned to him, cold on the outside, flames burning inside.

"I'm going back to the Outpost."

Kaden would have known my false smile in a second, but

Walter didn't. Of course he didn't. Sharing someone's blood didn't mean they knew you.

"Of course. The guards will escort you back. Have a nice night."

Two of his guards followed me back to the house "for my protection," though I suddenly chafed under their constant supervision. Maybe it was time I took Talia's advice and ditched them. The streets were cold and dark as I walked back to the building.

Then a scream pierced the night.

A flickering orange glow rose up out of the houses near the river. Once such a thing would have sent me in the other direction, but tonight I wanted the truth. I wanted to see what The Last City really was.

"Let's get back to the house," one of the guards said.

"I'm going to go help," I said, staring at where the flames now licked higher.

"Our orders were to—"

I bolted, running toward the screams. The guards called out behind me, but I didn't slow down. An entire house burned through the night.

There were people screaming, calling out, but as I came closer I saw that there was already a small fire engine there—drawn by horses. They were holding hoses, but no one was doing anything to douse the growing flames.

A crowd gathered at the edges of the street. I drew nearer, surprised when I saw the Viking woman I'd seen my first day in The Last City. There were streaks of ash and dirt on her face, her back straight, and face grim as she stared at the burning house.

"What happened?" I came to a stop beside her.

I was surprised at the anger on her face as she turned to look at me. In the flickering oranges and reds thrown by the flames, I nearly drew back.

"You don't belong here," she finally said. "Best run along to Grandpa."

The two guards caught up to me, one of them grabbing my arm and pulling me away. I let them, because before they'd arrived, I glimpsed something on the side of the house, beneath a sheet of roaring flames.

The black spiral.

~

Back at the Outpost, I ignored the raucous noise coming from the basement and instead made my way upstairs to our small attic room.

Only granddaughter. Walter was lying: he either didn't believe Emma and Father were out there, or knew where they were and was hiding it from me. And now Kaden was missing too.

"Whoa, weird mood in here."

I jerked upright. Talia sat on the windowsill, one foot dangling out the window, looking fully comfortable perched on the ledge of a three-story building.

"Can't you use the door like a normal person?" I snapped.

"Dumb and Dumber would see me. And I have something interesting to show you." She grinned wickedly, and I knew exactly where this was going.

"I already saw the burning building. If I show up there again they'll chuck me in it. No one wanted to talk to me."

She rolled her eyes. "Of course they didn't. That house was burned down because the people inside were plotting to overthrow Walter, and you showed up with your guards." So did that mean the black spiral was a sign of rebellion? Could I trust anything Talia said? "Did you really think they'd be happy to see you, Princess?"

"Don't call me Princess," I growled at her.

"Or what? You'll set your guards on me, take away my cure, and throw me in Grandpa's dungeon?" She threw a dramatic hand across her brow. "Please no! Save me!"

My voice was cold now. "What do you want, Talia?"

She leaned out the window, so far it was hard to stop myself from grabbing the back of her shirt and yanking her back in. *Or pushing her out.* "Just a little adventure out in the fresh night air."

"I've had enough adventures to last a lifetime." *Only granddaughter.* The words echoed in my head, an unending chant.

"Whatever," Talia sighed, though her smile was wicked, as if she could sense the swirling dilemma inside me. "When you're ready to get your hands dirty and see The Last City for what it really is, let me know." She ducked her head out the window.

Only granddaughter.

"Wait!" I called out.

She paused on the windowsill, leaning back in, "Yes, Princess?"

"That house tonight. It had a black spiral on it. You told me it means something different to everyone. What does it mean to you?"

There was something cold in her eyes, the usual mocking humor gone. "To me it means Walter is hiding something. I want to know what."

I paused, fighting against the urge to say nothing. But I'd suddenly found myself with no allies—what other choice did I have? Walter was lying. My father was nowhere to be found. And now Kaden was gone.

"I saw the black spiral outside the Sanctum when Walter was with me," I said. "He looked so angry to see it there. And now Kaden is missing." There was a flash of surprise in her eyes—she hadn't expected me to say that. "Kaden would never not come back to me, not unless something happened. Today Walter called me his only granddaughter. Why would he do that, unless . . . unless he knew my sister was . . ." I couldn't finish that sentence, turning away, embarrassed at the tears in my eyes. My voice was barely a whisper when I spoke again. "I came here to find my family, and now everyone is gone. Kaden included."

I squeezed my eyes shut, forcing my fist against my traitorous eyes to make them stop, when I suddenly felt her arms around my shoulders.

She held me for a moment, and then whispered, "I also had a sister who disappeared."

Neither of us met each other's eyes as she pulled away and went back to the windowsill. "I didn't know that," I said, using the back of my hands to wipe my eyes. "How come you didn't tell me?"

She shrugged, taking a small knife out of her boot and carving something into the windowsill, taking her time when she answered. "I wasn't sure I could trust you before. But if Kaden's gone . . . well, I think I might know why."

"What do you mean?"

"Kaden's test came up as Invalid," she said, her knife pausing for a moment. "The same as yours. I gave him my lanyard so he could get into the city without Walter knowing."

My mind reeled as I stared at her. *Why had Kaden never told me he also tested as Invalid?* "Why would that matter? Walter said my test came up as Invalid because the test was designed from his blood . . . Do you think he's lying?"

"Don't know. Don't care. All I care about is that the Invalid test is something Walter doesn't want in the city. And clearly you're part of it."

I paused to consider her words, thinking back to Kaden, and then to Walter, and finally to Talia. "Why didn't you tell me this before?"

"Because I wasn't sure if you were with Walter or not. People who turn on him are denied the cure, or they disappear. Or sometimes, like tonight, their house 'accidentally' burns down. But now you're like me."

Like Talia. Great. But I didn't say that. Because for the very first time, I felt as if I were seeing the real Talia. One who wasn't smiling, or teasing, or mocking. A girl who'd survived the end of the world just like me.

"So what now?" I said carefully.

Talia sheathed her dagger, and I saw she'd carved what was either a small *T* or a number one into the window. "You come with me. Before the watch changes." She threw a foot over the window ledge.

"Out the *window*? Isn't there some other way a bit less suicidal?"

She jumped. I gasped, and jolted forward—before I remembered there was a flat section of roof outside. It was also covered in snow, and only about a foot wide. She grinned up at me. "Are you coming? Or should I go fetch your pumpkin carriage and white horses?"

I gritted my teeth, ready to tell her off, but then she ducked around the side of the dormer, climbing the steeply pitched roof. I stared after her in disbelief, weighing my options. *Kaden needs you. You won't find him, or the truth, just sitting here.* Before I could dwell on just how stupid this was, I grapped a jacket and climbed out after her. The wind cut straight through me. I shuffled around the side of the dormer, ice cutting into my hands as I scrambled up the steep roof.

Well, Kaden, I hope whatever you're out there doing isn't as stupid as this.

I followed Talia up to the peak of the house. Only then, when she paused at the very top, did I dare to look around. My breath caught. The drop was dizzying, but the view beyond was worth it. Snowy rooftops, a distant river, and the golden glow of electricity all stretched out beneath the light of a full moon. It would have been perfect, if not for the smell of smoke in the air.

Talia walked down the peak of the house, toward the house beside it, one of the new builds that had sprung up in between, set only a few feet apart.

Just when I was about to ask Talia how she intended to get to the ground, she began to run.

"Talia, no wait—"

Too late. I watched as she leapt through the air, careening over the chasm between the buildings, before landing on the opposite side.

She's crazy. She's actually crazy.

She turned back to meet my eyes. The wind tore at her hair, pulling a few dark tendrils free. I hadn't tied mine back, and it swept around me like flames, daring me forward. As if asking how much I really wanted the truth.

Guess it's time to find out if I'm crazy too.

I took a few steps backward. My heart thundered in my chest. I closed my eyes and pushed aside all the voices that told me this was a stupid, terrible idea.

Emma had jumped the ravine without hesitation or fear. Because she had to.

I opened my eyes and ran, then leapt. Terror rose in my throat as I soared over open air. I hit the opposite roof hard. Then I felt myself falling backward, the iced roof slick, sheer terror surging—

—until Talia caught me, yanking me back from the edge.

We stared at each other in shock, both of our eyes wide in the moonlight. Adrenaline pulsed through my body, the clear, cold air burning through my lungs as the rooftops, and a whole new world, stretched out around us.

Suddenly we were both laughing. Standing there beside her, lit by moonlight and madness, I realized that Talia was crazy—but so was I.

"Not bad, Princess. Let's go."

SIXTEEN—KADEN

Snow fell slow and thick as Septimus and I both stared down at the Captain. The flakes were the only movement beyond my soft white clouds of breath.

No breath came from the Captain.

Finally, I turned back to Septimus. He hadn't confirmed his name, or spoken at all, but who else could he be? His face was all hard angles, his dark hair shorn close to his head as it had been in the picture. He stared down at the Captain, his eyes wide and disbelieving. Walter said he'd killed three men during his escape. I'd expected some sort of hardened criminal, not this man who barely looked out of his teens and like he might burst into tears.

"Is he dead?" Septimus whispered.

"Yeah."

His eyes finally lifted to mine. "I didn't mean to kill him." His voice held a pleading tone, the crowbar now limp at his side. Suddenly, it was Sam standing in front of me. Wide-eyed, trying not to cry, looking to me for guidance.

I swallowed, turning to the shadows of the city to erase the image. *Not Sam. Sam is dead.* This young man looked nothing like Sam: muscular with golden-brown skin whereas my brother was all lanky limbs, freckles, and red hair. *Or had been.* Even though he'd just killed a man, I couldn't dismiss his boyish innocence.

"I didn't mean to kill him," he said again, dropping the crowbar—it barely made a sound as it fell into the snow.

"He was going to kill me." He flinched at my words. "And his men will be after us both next. We need to move."

But he didn't move—he just stared down at the body. His dark hair was full of snow, and I wondered why the hell he wasn't wearing a hat. Far too late, his eyes lifted to mine. I was relieved to finally see suspicion beneath the shock. *Sam was always too quick to trust others.*

"Why was he trying to kill you?"

"I wish I knew." *But I'm guessing it starts with a* Walt *and ends with an* er.

The silence stretched out between us, somehow louder after the gunshot. The snow continued to fall, collecting on the Captain's body as if to remind me we were wasting valuable time.

"What happens now?" Septimus whispered.

I glanced over my shoulder—the snow wasn't coming down hard enough to cover our tracks. The men would follow us right here if they'd heard the shot. Still, it'd take them a few minutes. I suddenly had nothing in the whole world but the clothes on my back.

"We see if he has anything helpful on him." I crouched in the snow beside the Captain. After a brief hesitation, I reached forward and checked for a pulse I already knew wasn't there.

The snow burned cold beneath my knees as I emptied the

Captain's pockets and tried not to look at his empty eyes that seemed to judge me even in death. Cigars, a lighter, some jerky, and the device Walter had handed him, where I'd seen Septimus's face.

Septimus watched from several feet away. He reminded me of a stray dog with wide eyes, tracking my movements, ready to spring away at a moment's notice or come closer if I asked. When the Captain's pockets were empty, I picked up the device again, turning it over in my hands, not sure how it worked.

"Use his finger," Septimus said. "It'll unlock the screen."

I looked up at him in surprise, and his eyes flicked away from mine. I stared at the Captain's hand in the snow. *You already robbed his body, and he's already dead. Issac would understand. Maybe.* Before I could think any more about it, I lifted the dead man's finger, pushed it against the reader, and released it the moment the screen flared to life.

Septimus's face flashed across the screen. Below it, his name and orders to shoot on sight.

"What does it say?" he said, clearly wanting to come closer but hesitant to bridge the few feet between us. The gun lay in the snow on the other side of the body, untouched. Part of me was surprised he hadn't gone to pick it, or the crowbar, up.

"It's got your picture," I said, and tilted the screen to him. "Below it says: 'Septimus, Dangerous, wanted for the murder of three men. Shoot on sight.'"

"Does it say anything after 'Septimus'? Any other identification?"

It wasn't the question I'd expected. Was he afraid they might find his family? "No. No last name . . . that is you, right?"

"Looks like it."

Another strange answer. One I didn't have the time to pick

apart. I hesitated, wondering if I could get to the gun before he could, and if my next question was wise. *Guess I left wise behind a long time ago.* "Did you really kill three men?"

His eyes went to the Captain. "Four now . . . but it's not what you think."

It never is.

My fingers moved on the screen and the next picture came up. I suddenly couldn't speak.

There, staring back at me, was me. I wasn't looking directly at the camera, but it was a picture taken sometime within the last couple of weeks without me even knowing. Below it, no crime was listed. Only the words: *Kaden Marshall. Shoot on sight.*

Frozen, unable to comprehend, unable to process, I stared at the picture until I realized Septimus was holding something out to me.

The gun.

He'd just picked up the gun.

He could have shot me and I wouldn't have even noticed.

Not just that, but he held it hilt-first out to me, a strained look on his face, as if he couldn't stand to touch the thing.

"Thanks," I said, slowly taking it.

Septimus shrugged, and then crouched beside me in the snow, the haunted look in his eyes not matching his otherwise youthful appearance. "What did you do?"

"I have no idea . . . do you?"

"No."

I shook my head, lost in thought. Was it possible this was all a mistake? Walter had been kind, generous even, to me and Ara both. From the way he looked at her, I could tell he cared for her. What would he gain from removing me? Maybe I should have known by now that leaders always had their own hidden agendas. I'd assumed Ara being Walter's granddaughter made us safe. I'd never considered if it put me in danger. Or her.

The snow fell slow, taunting me as I tried and failed to come up with a new plan. I couldn't go back to the Captain's men and try to explain. The way the group had fallen silent around me, the way they'd refused to learn my name—it all made sense now. They weren't afraid of me because they thought I was some kind of spy for Walter. They hadn't learned my name because you didn't name an animal right before you killed it.

"Strange, isn't it?" Septimus said, his voice oddly pensive, as if we weren't both crouched above a dead man. "Wondering why the world wants you dead when you aren't sure yourself?"

"Sure." A sudden thought hit me. "Is that why you saved me?"

He shrugged. "I started setting the fires, knowing a group would come to track me. I was hoping to steal some supplies—I took one of the scanners from the last group. But then I saw a new picture come up. I thought this new group would be tracking you, so I started to set even more fires, to give you time to get away."

So I was right, he was trying to be found. It was little consolation now.

"Then I saw you, with the group," he went on. "I couldn't understand why your picture was there if they were working with you. I thought maybe there was some chance at forgiveness." He looked down at the Captain. "I guess it makes sense now."

Does it? Because to me, nothing makes sense now. Somebody wanted me dead—probably Walter. While I'd had men try to kill me plenty of times in the past few years, this was the first time I didn't know *why* someone was trying to kill me.

But if being an expedition leader had taught me anything, it was that you had to make fast decisions. All that mattered now was getting Ara out of that city and away from Walter. The truth didn't matter—only survival.

The familiar weight of some strange burden I thought I'd lost with Sam settled back onto my shoulders as I rose to my feet. There was something about the way Septimus watched me, waiting and expectant—the same way Sam had. It made me want to warn him that people who followed me tended to end up dead.

"You escaped from The Last City?" I said. He nodded. "Do you know a way inside that isn't through the gates?"

"Yes, but it's dangerous."

Of course it is. "If you show me the way in, I'll help you steal a horse." As I spoke, a new plan began to form in my head. If Walter, or someone else in The Last City, was trying to kill me, I couldn't go back in through the entrances I'd used before with Talia's card—there were guards and cameras everywhere. I certainly couldn't waltz in through the front gate. My Invalid test would give me away in an instant. *Why didn't I make Talia show me the hidden entrances when I'd had the chance?*

"The stables are outside the wall," I went on. "You can go south to Boise. There're plenty of clans down there that would take you. I can even give you a few names."

He was silent for ten agonizing seconds, staring out into the ruins as if he could hear something I couldn't. I wondered what I would do if he said no. When he finally turned back to me, I was surprised by the iron in his voice. "I'll show you the way in, but only if we go together."

Why the hell would you want back in? But I didn't get to ask anything else, because his head suddenly turned, staring out at the dark mass of buildings. "They're coming," he said softly.

Nothing but the cold wind called to me, yet I didn't doubt he was telling the truth. I looked down at the Captain. They would find him here, and even if they found Septimus's tracks, I would look guilty.

Was I?

There wasn't time to wonder because now I heard the voices too. Septimus turned and ran. I took a step after him, then stopped, turning back to the dead man on the ground.

Septimus had admitted to killing four men. Even if he killed the Captain only to save me, it didn't change the fact that he was a killer.

A vision of Sam, lying broken on the ground, and then Issac left in an open field, flashed before my eyes.

Good men didn't win in this world.

I followed Septimus into the night.

~

Septimus and I crouched beneath the windowsill of one of the apartment buildings overlooking the road below—where flashlights now spun over the ruins. I'd taken the Captain's device without thinking—only now did I wonder if that was a mistake. But we already had so little, I didn't want to give it up. Maybe it would come in handy.

In the darkness, I couldn't make out Septimus's features, just the soft white clouds as he exhaled. His hood was up now, but the cold hardly seemed to affect him. Or maybe the tremors running through my body weren't about the cold so much as the team of armed men hunting us below.

"Stay here," he said, barely breathing out the words.

He was gone before I could stop him.

Well, he's dead, I thought as I crouched in the corner of the room, hands tucked tight against my body for warmth. Waiting there in the cold, I couldn't help but wonder why I'd placed my trust in a man I'd watched kill someone within the first ten seconds of meeting him.

He knows how to get back into the city. But was that really it? The time ticked by as I tried, and failed, to make some kind of new plan. It was too damn cold to think.

When the wood creaked behind me I nearly jumped out of my skin—but then there, Septimus stood behind me, two packs swung over his shoulder.

"I couldn't get a horse," he said simply.

I stared down at the packs. "You stole these from them?"

"You want me to give them back?" There was an uncertainty in his voice, like he thought he'd done something wrong but couldn't figure out what.

"Hell no." I grabbed one of the packs, the weight comforting as I dug out another jacket for me and then tossed Septimus a hat. "But put a hat and gloves on first. I'm cold just looking at you."

His hands were steady, not shaking with the cold like mine as he pulled the hat on. Even though he'd just got back, he already moved toward the exit. "I left some tracks leading the other way. We should head for the river. I've got a place there to hide and rest where we'll be safe. We can lie low till they move off."

"How do we get into the city?"

He hesitated, not answering my question. "It's a two-day walk back—longer if we have to stay off the roads and watch out for the men hunting us. We should go now."

I wondered if I should push him—demand he tell me

everything. Instead, I held back. Maybe it was that leftover protective older brother instinct. He would tell me when he was ready, and trying to force him to now wouldn't help.

"Well then, we're burning daylight," I said instead.

He stopped, staring at me with a confused look.

"Wasting time," I said.

He nodded. "Right. Burning the daylight. Of course."

I almost laughed as he led us out of the building, and then the wind whipped away all humor. Together we walked through the ruins, two shadows bonded by darkness and death.

SEVENTEEN—SAM

A mist hung over the gaping fences and weary houses of the abandoned neighborhood, lit with a soft pre-dawn light. It felt like anything might emerge from the mist—castles or spaceships or enchanted kingdoms—not that I would have ever admitted that to M. I'd woken her before dawn and we walked across the quiet city now, the fog holding the world in silence. Vines and weeds had swallowed some of the houses whole. In some ways, Boise had become a lost city all on its own.

"All clear?" M called softly. I nodded, leading us across the dew-heavy grass. A week had passed since we'd left behind the ruins of the clan. Even though M still tried to hold me at a distance, we were starting to get to know each other. Night after night, she screamed in her dreams, and night after night I woke her, silently holding her until she turned over and went back to sleep. In the morning, we both pretended it had never happened.

The last few nights I'd caught a few new words—*green water* and *prisoners*—but I didn't dare broach the subject with her in the morning. It felt too much like eavesdropping on something private, and I didn't want to lose the way she huddled into my body in the darkest part of the night. Whatever demons haunted M, I understood. I had enough of my own.

"We aren't far from the building where the kayaks are stored," I said as we passed a two-story house with all the windows blacked out, an ugly red X spray-painted across the door. Almost all of the doors in this neighborhood were marked with a red X: the sign of the infected. This was one of the neighborhoods that had been hit first and hardest. Others tended to avoid neighborhoods like this—a fact I'd used to ensure we crossed the city undetected. It made for a meandering path, and M constantly complained it was taking too long, but I didn't care. It was worth the delay to circumnavigate the other clans' territories and not run into others. "We should find them today."

"You said that yesterday."

I shrugged—I did that a lot with M. "The closer we get to downtown and the river, the more men there will be. We need to be careful."

She stared up at the sky and sighed, as if wishing for patience, but didn't protest. A cool wind blew, shaking the trees, a few leaves drifting down around us. The sun rose higher as we walked, burning away the mist. After a few hours, I was forced to cross out of the neighborhoods and onto what had once been a crowded four-lane road. I vividly remembered the stretch—there was an old bowling alley my mom had taken me to for a birthday party. Today a cold wind whistled down the road instead of traffic. A deceptive calm hung over the remains of business so overgrown with weeds and ivy that I could no longer read their signs. Except for one.

The lone sign stood proud and tall, watching over the ruins as if no one had told it the world had fallen. After checking the road was abandoned, I led us beneath the golden arches.

M paused beside me, the two of us looking up at the giant *M*. The roof had fallen in on the fast-food restaurant, but the sign looked as if it could power on at any moment. *Maybe I should put that on my list next. Turn on the McDonald's sign. Unite the city with the shared loved of burgers.*

"Worst thing about the apocalypse," M said, surprising me, "is no more fast food."

"Or that all food is too fast now," I said, thinking of a herd of deer we'd seen yesterday—I'd barely fitted an arrow before they were gone.

She laughed. "True."

"Remember cheeseburgers?" I said with a sigh. "Like really greasy ones with extra cheese and onions and a toasted bun?" It was easy to remember it all standing beside her.

"Don't forget ice cream. With caramel and chocolate and whipped cream with a cherry on top."

"Chicken nuggets that come in a box. No plucking required. And french fries."

M closed her eyes and moaned, then lifted her arm, extending her gun up to the golden *M*. "I would trade my left hand—no, my left hand and this gun—for a single hot french fry dipped in ketchup."

The sight of her head tilted back, eyes closed, made my cheeks burn red. *Get it together, Sam.* Without even thinking, I blurted out, "Yeah, I'd trade my bow for a burger."

She turned from the sign to look at me. I'd thought of a dozen comparisons to her eyes during our time together—the blue of an ocean, the ice over water, a jagged piece of the sky. None of them explained why every time her eyes met mine, my heart pounded, my throat went dry, and anything that came out of my mouth was guaranteed to be stupid.

I expected one of her sarcastic comments as she stared at me. Instead, to my immense shock, she tilted her head back and laughed. It was a full-throated, joyful noise that changed her face completely. I was so relieved I joined her. Then she shook her head, a smile still in place as she set off again with no warning. Even though I was leading, I had to hurry to catch up.

"You know what else I miss?" she said as we walked. "All the things adults used to tell us would kill us. Guess what, old farts? It wasn't any of those things that got humanity. Y'all are dead and I'm still here."

I laughed at her cruel assessment. "My mom was always on me about excessive screen time. And high-fructose corn syrup."

"Exactly. Nobody ever died from too much screen time."

We kept on like that, discussing everything we missed about the before world, and the few perks of life after the apocalypse. I began to fill in a few details of her life before. She'd grown up in this city. She'd had a good life before this. Parents who loved her—even if they hadn't quite understood her. I knew that feeling. My mom loved me, but the way she had picked my dad over Kaden, and the cold way she'd kicked him out, it always made me wonder if I was next. When I explained that to M—that even before the plague I'd tried to be like Kaden, because he knew how to survive even when people deserted you—it was like she understood me in a way no one else ever had.

For the first time, I felt like we were just a girl and a boy walking through a city. Like maybe the plague hadn't ended everything good in the world.

~

We walked the rest of the day, moving parallel to an old path I'd taken with Kaden and the crew. M hadn't offered any background about how she'd survived, but from the way she moved—always alert and watchful—it seemed entirely possible that she'd lived the last four years entirely alone.

We passed an old movie theater overgrown with vines, down another wide street, and then back into some of the suburbs. I hadn't been this way in a long time, and turned the corner to find an enormous oak tree fallen across the road. I was about to climb it when suddenly I was yanked backward by my jacket.

"What the—" M's hand clamped hard over my mouth, and I froze, the warmth of her body pressed against mine. Even as my heart pounded, my body registered every place her form touched mine.

Then I heard them.

Voices, in the distance, moving closer.

Our eyes met, a silent message passing between us. My whole body hummed with adrenaline. She lifted her gun, but I shook my head. I jabbed a finger at the nearest house, where a section of fence had fallen over. It looked like a twisted spiral: one half standing and overgrown with weeds, the other fallen enough to allow us to climb over and hide behind the erect part.

If you have the choice, run instead of fight. It was one of Kaden's apocalypse rules I put to good use.

M ran for the fence, staying low, as I followed. The voices grew louder, but they didn't lift in alarm. *Please say they haven't seen us.* Together we climbed over the fallen section of the fence. We crouched in the shadows of the fence, my heart pounding in my ears. The voices grew louder.

A small hole in the fence offered me a view of the road as my heart pounded louder and louder. My body screamed to run, but a single glance at M told me she wouldn't follow. She stared through a gap in the fence, laser-focused on the approaching group.

No. If I wanted to run, it would be on my own. And I wouldn't leave M.

A soft, metallic click—M removing the safety on her gun. Almost against my will, I pulled an arrow free, that familiar tingle through my fingers and shoulders as I set it against the bow.

The footsteps grew louder.

The first man stepped into view.

Neither M nor I moved. I didn't even dare to breathe. From between the cracks, the group of men came into view, maybe ten total, their faces painted like skulls, a marking I had never seen in any of the other clans in Boise. *Could it be a new clan? Or one of the old clans chose a new marking?* I'd been out of the loop all summer, and only now did I realize that might not have been a good idea.

Two of the men held chains. At first I didn't understand—until I followed the trail of the chains to a man in the center of them. The chains connected to a metal collar around his neck. *They have a prisoner.*

Then I started back from the fence, nearly dropping my arrow.

The prisoner's eyes were white.

They had an infected prisoner.

M didn't move, but something like rage flickered in her eyes. The bow trembled in my hands, instincts warring inside me. *Always kill the infected.* A rule of the clan. *No. Protect M.* The only rule that mattered now.

I didn't have time to make a decision. The men didn't stop, oblivious to our presence as they moved past our hiding spot and farther down the road. For several minutes the two of us sat in silence, my heart pounding loud in my chest, trying to understand what I'd seen and failing.

"I've never seen a clan with painted faces, have you?" M finally said, burying the lead.

"No, their prisoner, was he—"

"Infected? Looked like it."

I stared at her, unable to speak. "I . . . What . . . How . . . Why?"

For the first time, it was M who shrugged. "Very few people survive the plague—but if they do, they have white eyes for a few weeks after, if they clear at all. As long as his eyes aren't weeping blood, he's not contagious anymore."

Part of me wanted to demand how the hell she knew that. The wiser part tried to keep my cool and act like Kaden. "Why keep him around at all?" My voice came out an octave higher than I'd intended. *So much for being cool.*

"They think he has the cure in his blood. He doesn't though."

"How do you know all this?"

She stood, the gun in her hands, as she checked down the road. "Because I survived the plague. And someone tried to use my blood to cure others. But it didn't do shit."

It was like staring at something impossible, words coming out of her mouth I couldn't comprehend. *She'd survived the plague.* I hadn't even known that was possible. She strode off, and I jumped up, my mind going a million miles a minute. "You . . . What . . . Wait, M—"

She spun, her eyes blazing. I stumbled back, because I knew that look. I was seconds away from having a gun leveled in my face.

"You might think that surviving the end of the world is some kind of adventure," she hissed, "but it's not for me. Every choice I make is life-or-death. Every person I meet is an enemy who could take me captive, kill me, or worse. I don't owe anyone, including you, a single thing. So I will give you exactly one more question."

The wind grabbed tendrils of her dark hair, her blue eyes like the low burn of a flame. *I don't want anything from you. I don't want to take you prisoner—I just want you to be happy.* All things I couldn't say. So instead I whispered, "Are you okay?"

She took a half step back, tears in her eyes before the hard shell snapped back in place. "Honestly, Sam, could you try to act a bit more like a grown-up and less like a Sasquatch all the time? How did you survive in this world before me?"

Her words didn't hurt, because I understood the pain she was hiding. There had been a time I had wanted to lash out at the entire world—when Mom died and Kaden hadn't yet found me and brought me into the clan. Only M hadn't found a clan: she had been infected, taken captive, and then escaped. No wonder she didn't trust me, or anyone else. I could never understand what it was to be a woman in a ruined city full of men. All I could do was help her now.

So I stepped by her, and her angry words, and continued down the road. "That sounds like two questions," I said over my shoulder. "I'm only available now to answer one. But maybe, if you're really, really nice to me, I'll tell you my middle name."

She caught up to me, her eyes glancing at me, and then back at the road several times before she said, "It's not Sasquatch?"

"Good guess. But no. It's Milo."

"Milo? Ugh, that's terrible. Sasquatch Sam is much better."

"It was my grandfather's name, but I think you're right. I'll look into having it officially changed."

"Best thing about the apocalypse," M said. "You can change your name to whatever you want."

I smiled, wondering if I'd ever find out what M actually stood for. I hoped so.

Just like that, the argument was left behind. We walked side by side again, and even if I couldn't quite put my finger on it, it felt like something had shifted between us. Something for the better.

We saw no other men as we continued through the ruins. I turned over the information she'd given me as we walked. If it was true that people could survive the plague then I wondered if it was my responsibility to bring that information to others in the city. *But I have new responsibilities now*. I didn't want to think of the future, or the responsibilities that lay there. Only the person beside me now.

It was nearly dusk when we crested a hill and a group of buildings I recognized rose in the distance. I grinned, almost giddy with the thought of how M would look when I showed her the hidden kayaks. The smile slipped away as I saw a trail of smoke rising into the sky.

"Don't tell me you're lost again," M said as she came to stand beside me.

"No, I found it." I sighed. "But so did someone else."

EIGHTEEN—ARA

Talia leapt over the gap between two rooftops, and without even hesitating—or thinking about how stupid this was—I followed, sprinting, jumping, flying, and then crashing into the roof on the other side. She paused only a moment to pull me up, and then we were off again.

The cold wind stung my nose and ears, but even if the night was freezing, and a single slip could mean death, I couldn't stop the joy pulsing beneath the fear. For the first time since I'd stepped within the walls of The Last City, I felt *free*. Insane, idiotic, but filled with a burning, bursting lightness that I couldn't remember feeling since . . .

Well, since Emma.

In the moonlight, with Talia leaping ahead, all the bonds and restrictions of being a woman in a world full of men fell away. I was no longer coddled, protected, and watched. No longer Invalid. Talia didn't give a shit about keeping me safe.

I felt like Emma—jumping over the ravine. Unafraid.

Unstoppable. Was this what it felt like to be her? To be unafraid of death?

"Come on, Princess!" Talia called out ahead of me, laughing as she leapt across another roof. I ran to follow. I would never have admitted it to her face, but Talia was as agile as a cat. *And as temperamental as one too.*

Ahead of me Talia leapt across a several-foot gap, and then slid down the roof to where it leveled out. Adrenaline pulsed in my chest and my breath came in quick white clouds. I followed less gracefully—my hands already bore a few deep scratches and grazes, but I didn't care. Better this than sitting at a table where my words didn't matter.

Talia's footsteps crunched on the gravel of a flat roof below, then she approached the edge of the roof—a gap so wide there was no way she could jump it. Instead of jumping, she lowered herself over the side and started down a rope that someone had attached just under the roof. The whites of her teeth showed as she shot a grin up at me.

"Come on, Princess. Don't tell me your nerve disappears at midnight."

"Funny."

The rope she climbed down looked ancient and weather-worn, but it could hardly be more dangerous than jumping onto snowy rooftops. I waited until she hit the ground, then followed.

When my feet touched the ground, I turned to find Talia lounging against the wall of a narrow alleyway. "Can we just skip whatever princess joke you're going to make?" I said before she could speak.

She grinned. "As you wish. We're here."

Here? We were in an alleyway between two brick buildings,

nothing noteworthy except a distant streetlamp that didn't reach fully into the darkness. As far as a city-ending, secret reveal, it was a bit of a letdown.

She made her way across the alleyway to the door, and knocked three times. The door creaked open, a sliver of light spilling into the alleyway. Ronnie peered out suspiciously, as if we might force our way past him. Considering he weighed more than both of us combined, it didn't seem likely.

"Password?" he said.

"For plague's sake, Ronnie." Talia pushed her way past him. He grinned as he opened the door fully. A shiver ran through my body as I stepped inside—the room was stiflingly warm. It looked a bit like my high school's computer lab, with dozens of monitors and dim fluorescent lighting. All the monitors had been arranged along two long, thin desks, and there were only two chairs, one in front of each section of monitors.

Harrison stood up as I came in, his hair seeming to glow an even more vibrant shade of blue beneath the light of the computer screens. "You barely missed one of the patrols," Harrison said. "Even Jessica thought you were cutting it close."

Talia waved a lazy hand, as if dodging patrols was something she did all the time. "They always go at the same time—they really are too predictable."

"Wait." I gestured to the computers, just now putting together what this room was. "Did you bring me here to see surveillance footage?"

Talia shrugged. "Got a problem with that, Princess?"

"I just thought this was some kind of . . . rebellion."

Talia laughed, and too late I wished I would have stayed quiet. "First of all, this isn't *Star Wars*. This is the end of the world. I already told you: you don't fight the monster. You join it."

"I don't want to join the monster. All I want is the truth."

"And what are you willing to do for that truth?" Talia said, her voice suddenly gone cold.

"Anything."

"Excellent. Then we can help each other."

Behind her, Harrison stood, his sword held at his side. "I still don't think we should trust her. She's the Chancellor's granddaughter."

Talia surprised me, throwing her arm around my shoulder and pulling me into her side. "Exactly. In a world where secrets are currency, Ara's filthy rich."

I wasn't totally sure I agreed with her, but either way, Talia was the only one bringing me closer to the truth. It was time to leave the princess behind for good. "Look, I know Walter's lying to me. My father is gone, my sister is gone, and now Kaden is too. I want the truth the same as you." And then, because I was desperate, their faces still skeptical, I added, "Plus, as his granddaughter, I can find out things no one else can. I don't have much power"—*or any*—"but I have access to places other people don't and an excuse to be there. He would never suspect me."

Harrison still looked suspicious, but Ronnie gave me a slow, thoughtful smile. "A spy on the inside . . . I like it."

Talia nodded as she stared at me—something too predatory for comfort in her eyes. "It's the missing piece to the puzzle: a person whom Walter trusts."

Harrison shook his head, like he still didn't agree, but Ronnie gestured with one massive hand to the dingy room. "Welcome to the Abyss, Ara."

Harrison ruined his own sulk by cutting in. "I thought we'd

decided on the Dungeon. Dungeon makes more sense for Jessica."

Talia steered me away from the two as they started to argue.

"Swords don't get a vote. And dungeons are *underground*," Ronnie said behind us. "Plus Talia said I was the leader so I get to decide."

"If Talia *says* you're the leader then you aren't really the leader. And I say Jessica does get a vote."

The two of them bickered while Talia brought me to a corner of the room, near a single fold-out metal table piled with some canned foods. Beside it was a small kitchenette area with a rusted sink. The water ran a shade of rusty red, but I drank it anyway, so cold my teeth ached. *Water from a faucet. Electricity. Computers.* Even after living in The Last City a few weeks, it all seemed so miraculous. Talia turned my hands up, and made me wash the cuts out with soap.

"You okay?" she said, so gently the boys couldn't hear.

"I'm good." For the first time in a long time, I wasn't lying.

Her expression became serious. "And you're ready for what I have to show you?"

"Yes."

"Okay, then brace yourself." She suddenly spun back to Harrison and Ronnie, still arguing. "Oi! Shut up! Both of you!" They fell silent instantly. "Pull up the feed you found."

The sound of typing keys filled the room as images flashed across the monitors. *Guess we know who the real leader is.*

"Got it," Ronnie said.

"I've got mine first," Harrison said a half moment later, clearly about to argue before Talia cut him off.

"Shut up! Look, here." Talia motioned me closer to the screen, and then pointed to a group of women being offloaded from a wagon. Unlike the earlier screens, this was some kind of recording. "Recognize them?" she said.

I stared at the woman and then started. "Those are the women from the wagon. But Rosia isn't there . . ."

"This is the group that was brought to the Sanctum," Talia said, "but look what happens before they get there." I watched as the wagon stopped and two women I recognized, Celina and Tiana, were separated from the rest of the group. A group of guards guided them into a brick building, and they disappeared within. The wagon continued on without them.

"Walter said all the women were brought to the Sanctum . . . where they would be safe." *Right, safe.* Why did I never check if he was telling the truth? *How stupid am I?*

"Some of them were," Talia said. "We were able to find a log of the women who entered the Sanctum, but those two never showed up on any registry in the city. I followed the woman you saw in the hospital, Rosia, and watched her go in a few days later. Her name and picture were logged in the Sanctum registry. But those two women never reappeared. Their names were Celina and Tiana right?"

I started at her words. "Yeah, they were. How did you know that?"

"That night when you first got here, when you and Kaden were separated, I went back out and checked on all of the women we'd rescued. I had some . . . growing suspicions, so I wrote down all their names—I wanted to be sure they all made it. But they were never even registered within The Last City. It's like they don't exist."

"Maybe they made an error?" Even I could hear how ridiculous I sounded.

Ronnie cut in now. "Then they've been making a lot of errors.

This has happened before—people lose family members. They go out on expeditions and never come back. Or women who were brought here are never accounted for."

You said you wanted the truth—even if it's some dark, twisted thing. But I still wanted to be sure we weren't jumping to conclusions. "It's a tough world out there," I said. "People get sick, lost, infected, and a thousand other things. Doesn't mean there's some kind of dark, scary secret thing happening. Maybe The Last City is exactly that—the last city in a fallen world. How do we know Walter is hiding something?"

"I thought that too . . ." Talia said, leaning back against the desk. "We can't exactly accuse Walter of anything, and who knows, maybe some of them are people who decide to leave the city and return to the ruins. But then we found an old blueprint of the city—a blueprint that shows a vast underground network. One that most people don't even know exists and we can't access."

Talia nodded to Harrison, and he switched the screen to a picture of a silver metal door. "We can't get past this door. There're dozens of them, but there's no keyhole, no way to force it open. It's powered by some sort of new tech they've still got running."

The breath caught in my chest.

I'd seen a door like that before. When I opened one at Birmingham Medical Testing Center in downtown Boise. Harrison and Ronnie were arguing again, but I tuned them out as I stared at the door on the screen. I knew exactly how to open it. But if I did, then I was directly moving against Walter. Despite what Talia said, this felt a lot like fighting the monster. A very powerful monster who seemed capable of anything and might be my only blood relation left in the world.

Ironic, considering the means it took to open the door.

Before I could say anything more, Talia surprised me. "There's one more thing, Ara. I wanted to wait to show you, until I was sure you were with us."

Talia nodded to Harrison, who sighed, as if he'd lost some argument without even speaking. "We were searching through the files of the missing people," she said, "trying to figure out what was happening, and well, we found this . . ."

Kaden's image flashed across the screen.

And below it were three words I couldn't believe. Three words I read over and over again, trying to understand.

Shoot on sight.

"When did you find this?" I stared at the words until they blurred on the screen. Until the cold fear gripping my chest loosened enough for me to draw a shaking breath. *It can't be. Walter wouldn't have.* Yet the evidence was staring right at me.

Ronnie's voice came soft behind us. "A few hours ago."

He lied to me. Walter lied to me. He said Kaden was fine, knowing there was an order out to kill him. A slow, burning fire built inside me as I pictured Walter, sitting calmly beside me, knowing Kaden was out there somewhere in danger. Had he been the one to give the order? Why? "Did you find anything on my father or Emma?" My voice trembled. If he was lying about this, who knew what else he was lying about?

"No," Talia said. "But we think that the underground network is some kind of a massive research facility beneath the city." *Like the lab he showed me.* "Hundreds of people could be held down there. If we can get down there, we hope we can figure out why people are disappearing. Once we know what they're doing, we can find a way to stop it."

"What about the field of bodies behind the hospital?" I pressed.

"How do we know people aren't just dying and being left there?"

Talia sighed. "Honestly, Princess, if I had all the answers, I'd give them to you. That's why I want to go down there."

I still wasn't sold. "How does this all help Kaden?" I said.

"Kaden could be down there."

He could also be in a thousand other places. He could also be dead. I paced away from her, my footsteps and the soft whirl of the computers the only noise. Finally, I stopped before Talia. I didn't know what to believe about my grandfather, or my father, anymore. But I believed in Kaden. And if this helped find him, then it would be worth it.

"What do you need me to do?" I said.

Talia motioned to Ronnie, and he pulled up a new video. "There's only one of those doors in the city that isn't guarded." The video zoomed in on an empty stone corridor.

"If it's unguarded, why haven't you tried to get through it?" I said.

"Because it's in the Sanctum," Talia responded, some hidden emotion in her voice.

Ah, of course it is.

"We need your help to get through." Talia pulled a card from her pocket, with a streak of red on it. "The guards use a different kind of lanyard—they've got some sort of bio-code on it that expires. We've tried stealing them, but they never work. Maybe you could see if Walter had an extra or—"

"No. It's not working because the blood on the card isn't fresh," I said.

Kaden's picture on the screen seemed to stare straight at me. I wondered what he would do if he were me. Then again, Kaden had no family left to betray because of me.

"Whose blood?" Ronnie finally said, his voice full of doubt.

"Walter's." I stepped over the point of no return. "I can get you through that door."

Talia laughed nervously. For the first time she looked at me with something like fear, instead of disdain. "Princess, as much as I appreciate you going rogue, you can't just steal Walter's blood. He's got guards, and security and—"

"We don't need his blood." The cuts and scrapes on my palms tinged with pain as I turned them up, a few pinpricks of bright red welling up. "We've got mine."

NINETEEN—KADEN

Once, as an expedition leader, I would have been at the front as Septimus and I walked through the ruins full of crumbling buildings. I would have been alert to all the sounds and movements in the night. But tonight, the cold seemed to creep into my bones, as all-consuming as the thoughts swirling inside me. The Captain had just tried to kill me—and now his entire team was hunting me.

Maybe I'd lost my touch. Maybe I wasn't cut out to be a leader anymore.

Septimus stopped, and I nearly walked into him. Then I saw why he'd stopped.

Three houses down, a moose stepped into the moonlight. It was so tall it dwarfed the rusted cars buried in the snow beside it.

"What is that?" Septimus said, his voice full of awe.

"A moose." *It's the middle of the night, it shouldn't be up now.* Then its head turned toward us. The moonlight showed white eyes with twin tracks of weeping blood.

The hair on my neck rose, fear bringing the frozen parts of my body back to life. *It's infected.* I reached out and grabbed Septimus's jacket, pulling him slowly backward. "We should go," I whispered. The infection made animals bigger, more aggressive, and I didn't want to test a small pistol against a full-grown infected moose.

"Can it see us?" he said. The words were a mistake. The animal's head suddenly jerked toward us.

Then it charged.

"RUN!" I grabbed Septimus by the collar and thrust him in the direction of a narrow alleyway between the buildings. We sprinted down the alleyway. I could hear the moose behind us now. My eyes flicked from door to door, until I saw one cracked open.

"There!" I smashed into the door, Septimus following behind. I turned and was rewarded with the terrifying sight of a full-grown moose smashing into the door frame. The building shook like an earthquake had rattled its foundation.

"GO! GO!" I shouted at Septimus. The two of us leapt over chairs and furniture, sprinting down a narrow hallway, before we burst into the moonlight on the other side of the building.

I put my hands on my knees, breath coming in heaving gasps, while Septimus stared at the building we'd come through with wide eyes. He reminded me of a tourist who didn't understand why it wasn't okay to pet the buffalo. "What was wrong with that thing?" he whispered.

"It was infected," I said in disbelief. *How had he never seen an infected animal?* When I could finally breathe again, I turned to Septimus, half exasperated, half angry, "Why didn't you run?"

He shrugged. "I've never seen a creature that big. I thought you would use the gun if it were dangerous."

"If?" I wasn't sure why, but I started to laugh. Something about the way his brow furrowed, the sheer innocence of him, reminded me so much of Sam that it hurt. I kept laughing, until I had to put my hands on my knees and bend forward. *You're losing it, man. Pull it together.*

"Why is that funny?" Septimus stared at me like he didn't get the joke.

I shook my head, wiping tears from my eyes. "Septimus, here's my first tip for surviving the apocalypse: assume everyone, and everything, is trying to kill you." Then I lifted the pistol. "Second tip: this little gun couldn't take down a full-grown infected moose. If you can't outrun whatever plague-infected monster is chasing you, just shoot whoever you're with. Then outrun them."

He turned to look back at the house we'd come through, then suddenly back at me. "Are you saying you would have shot *me*?" When I started to laugh, he shook his head and started down the snowy street lined with decrepit apartment buildings. "You're joking. I thought so."

This only made me laugh more. The run had gotten my blood pumping, and life returned to my limbs once again. When my laughter finally trailed off I said, "Septimus, you want to know my most important tip for surviving the apocalypse?"

He shot me a dubious look. "Yes?"

"You can't," I said bluntly. "No one can. We're all going to die one way or another—so you may as well laugh when you can."

"What if you can't find anything to laugh at?"

"Look harder. Or try a mirror."

He nodded, that serious look on his face. "I will keep looking."

"You do that, Septimus," I said. "While we're at it, here's

another tip for surviving the apocalypse: if you have the choice, run instead of fight."

"I wasn't the one who needed to shoot someone to outrun a moose."

I laughed, and this time Septimus joined me. Despite having almost died not once, but twice in his presence, I decided I liked the kid. Somehow in a few hours with him I'd found a camaraderie that I hadn't with anyone else over several weeks in The Last City. *I guess survival does that to people: binds them together or tears them apart.*

We walked farther through the shadowed city until I heard the distant sounds of the river. The temperature dropped even more as we came closer. The buildings grew more crowded, businesses cropping up with faded signs, cars buried beneath the snow like sleeping monsters that would never again awaken.

Then we came to a wide-open stretch of land I guessed was once a parking lot.

"We're here," Septimus said when we'd crossed it. I wasn't sure what I was expecting—maybe an old bunker or the ruins of a house. It definitely wasn't this.

Before us loomed iron gates, the likes of which I'd expect to see in front of a mansion. Over the gate hung a sign with ominous swirling letters. WELCOME TO SPOOKHOMPTON AMUSEMENT PARK. The energy coursing through me at the thought of food and rest abated as I stared past the gate, into the looming shadows of the park.

"Um, Septimus, don't take this the wrong way, but this looks like a creepy-ass amusement park."

He smiled, completely missing my tone. "I know. The patrols never enter." He frowned. "I'm not sure why."

"Probably because it looks like the perfect place to get murdered," I muttered. Before I could protest, or suggest we find another place to camp, he tossed his backpack over the gate. *Ah, yes, into the creepy park we go. Huzzah.*

"The other places all have barbed wire on top," Septimus called back as he began to climb the gate. "This is the best place to go unless you want to swim in the river." He looped a foot over and then jumped from the top, landing so neatly on the other side I wondered if maybe in his previous life he'd been some kind of gymnast. He watched me through the gate with the same puzzled look Sam would give Issac when he said he was too tired to play another game of soccer.

"I wouldn't recommend the river," Septimus said slowly. "I nearly froze when I left The Last City."

"The *river* is how you got out?"

He gave me that strange, cryptic smile again. "Yes. My whole body turned blue. Funny, right?"

I sighed and shook my head. "Sure, Septimus. Sure."

"Are you coming?" he said, still not seeming to understand my hesitation.

Welp, Issac, this is it. I've finally become the old man following the young into their foolish plans. If only you were here to see it and laugh.

I pulled off my backpack. On the other side of the gate, to Septimus's left, stood some sort of decrepit ticket booth. Deeper in the park, long-abandoned rides loomed out of the darkness. *So, Ara, the good news is I found an old amusement park for us to explore. The bad news is I'm stuck here with a man who's a murderer and fugitive and there's a team of people hunting us. Also would now be a bad time to admit I'm afraid of clowns?*

"Burning daylight," I muttered, then heaved my backpack over the gate. Climbing over wasn't nearly as easy as Septimus had made it look—especially with half-frozen fingers. My jacket and pants were both ripped in two separate places by the time I scaled the top. I meant to climb down, but instead slipped and fell. Even with the new layer of snow, hitting the ground felt like landing on concrete.

I followed Septimus down a winding path through the park. The dark shapes of forgotten rides towered over us, mixed in with smaller booths for food or games, some still standing, others bowed beneath the snow. The once-bright colors had faded, bleached away by the weather, and the wind made odd scraping and clunking noises echo through the park.

"How'd you find this place?" I whispered as we walked. My head snapped toward each new creak and rattle. *Just the wind. Just an abandoned place. Definitely no clowns left.*

"The river washed me up here. One of the lights was on . . . it was like a beacon in the darkness."

Oh please, for the love of God, say the light wasn't on in some sort of clown funhouse. I didn't tell Septimus that following a bright light through the darkness generally wasn't a great survival technique idea—it didn't seem like the kind of thing he would get. We wove through some smaller building, a food court with tables piled high with snow, until finally he opened the door to a building set in the back of the park.

I braced myself for something terrible. Instead, a wave of heat rolled out to meet me. *What the hell?* I stepped into total darkness. Then blinding light burst to life, so overwhelming I lifted a hand against the unexpected brightness. Even after weeks of electricity in The Last City, the light still felt unnatural.

When my eyes adjusted, I found we were in a sort of break room, with two battered couches facing each other, a small kitchenette in the corner with a sink and microwave, and a wall of lockers on the far side. A few brightly colored costumes hung from some of the lockers. I instantly decided if we needed to make a fire, any and all clown costumes went first.

"You've got electricity and heat?" I made my way over to the sink in the corner. "Almost takes the fun out of surviving in the ruins."

"Running water too."

I turned the tap on, shocked when clear water flowed out. "Damn. If we weren't in a creepy park, I'd say we'd hit the jackpot."

Behind me, Septimus moved a cloth over the crack beneath the door, and I noticed there was cardboard and duct tape over the single window to keep anyone outside from seeing the light. *Maybe he's not hopeless then.*

"Any idea how this place has power?" My ears and fingers burned as they slowly thawed, but the pain didn't stop me from drinking my fill of icy tap water before making my way over to a stack of canned food on the table.

"None," Septimus answered.

From what little I knew of the power in the city, it seemed like they'd shut off most of the ruins, and funneled power only to the section where The Last City stood. But maybe this place had slipped through, or ran on some other sort of grid. So long as Walter didn't know or couldn't find us, I didn't care.

My stomach growled, suddenly ravenous. "What food options do we have?"

Septimus gestured to the pile of canned goods. "Just these. The microwave works, and I found some old bowls. I've been eating them one at a time. There aren't any great combinations."

I smiled at the sudden memory of another time, of Issac's voice. *Come on, Kaden, I taught you better than that. You can't put jalapeños in the chili. I have to sleep next to you the next few days.*

Then Sam's answering laugh. *I think we should put the peaches in too. We can call it apocalypse stew.*

"Kaden?" Septimus's voice startled me. I realized I was staring down at the cans on the counter, unmoving and unspeaking.

I cleared my throat and pushed all the memories away. I was alive, not freezing, with food in front of me. In the apocalypse, that was about as good as it got. So I lifted as many cans as I could in my arms and turned to Septimus.

"All right, time for my first apocalyptic cooking tip. Expiration dates are always to be ignored. Issac always said: 'If it's in a can, eat it, man.' The second cooking tip is that *anything* can be combined. Now come over here and let me teach you how to make my world-famous apocalypse stew."

~

An hour later, we each lay on one of the two well-worn couches in the room. The scent of chili and jalapeños filled the room, a faint burning sensation still clinging to my tongue. I felt sleepy and warm, the horror of the last few hours of the night faded. The gun lay on the table between us, but I'd decided there wasn't a point in setting a guard. Not with just the two of us.

"What is cotton candy?" Septimus said into the silence. "One of the signs said 'cotton candy for sale' and I wondered . . ."

"You've never had cotton candy?" Disbelief colored my voice, distracting me from my dark thoughts. When he didn't respond,

I finally said, "It's kind of like a fluffy candy? They make it out of sugar and spin it, and it's sort of like a cotton ball."

"And you *eat* it? Sounds terrible."

I laughed. "Only because I'm explaining it badly." I hesitated, wondering how to ask this. "Where are you from?" I knew people came from all over to come to The Last City. The cold didn't seem to affect him the way it did me; Maybe he came from farther north? But surely Canadians had cotton candy? Except his accent wasn't Canadian. It was . . . Actually I had no idea where it was from. We'd had visitors come in from all over to visit my hometown in Montana, but I'd never thought to listen to how they spoke.

There was a long silence, then when he spoke, it felt as if the door had blown open, the cold cutting straight to my core.

"My first memories are waking up in a lab, beneath The Last City."

My first memories. The horror of those words echoed inside me. "What do you mean?" I finally said.

"I remember shadows. Whispers. But nothing solid: no family. No words. Nothing specific. It feels like I didn't exist before I woke up there."

Again, I lay still, trying to absorb what he'd said. My first instinct was to deny it. *How* was that even possible? But something about the way he'd said it: the absolute vulnerability, the tortured look in his eyes . . . I believed him.

I believed him, and that was terrifying.

When he didn't go on, I said slowly, "You think . . . that they . . . ?"

"Did that to me? Yes."

Wow, well, I guess we finally found something creepier than this park. "Do you think they can undo it? If you can get back?"

He paused, and then: "No. It's hard to explain." He lifted his hand, lit by the lone light we'd left on in the back of the room. "I know things. Like I know this is a hand. I knew I needed to find warmth or my body would die. I know the names of things: snow, wind, fire, food. Yet sometimes when I see them, it feels like the first time ever experiencing them. I feel . . . empty. Like this park. Everything is here, but there're no people or memories to go with it." Frustration filled his voice, his hand making a fist. "It feels like I'm waiting for something, but I don't know what."

I stared at him, wishing he would laugh or tell me he'd got me good. But he stared in silence at the weblike cracks branching across the ceiling. I burrowed deeper into the ratty blankets we'd found, wishing Ara was here with me, or better yet, that we were back in Boise and had never found this damned city in the first place. At least back then, when someone was trying to kill me, I knew why. The wind howled outside the door for some time before I said, "Why would you want to go back?"

"To stop them from doing this to someone else."

For the first time, I had the strange feeling he wasn't telling me the full truth. I didn't push the matter. Septimus had saved my life when he just as easily could have done nothing. So I pretended that this was all possible: that someone in The Last City had wiped his memory, and that he wanted to go back to stop them from doing it again. Then I tried to imagine it was me—the thought caught me like a punch in the chest.

Would it be better to forget Sam and Issac? To lose the haunting blame and endless pain? To never have to wake up and for one split moment think about telling them something, only to remember they were gone?

No. I don't want to forget. I couldn't give up the pain because that would mean losing them all over again. It was something I didn't like to think about, so instead I tried to do what I did best—think of a plan. "You must have some idea why they're trying to kill you."

"Without remembering who I am, how could I? The better person to ask is you."

His dark eyes turned to me. It took me a moment to realize what he was asking. "You want to know why someone just tried to kill me?"

"Yes. Any theories?"

Tons. And all of them are totally ridiculous. But seeing as this whole thing felt ridiculous, why not say it aloud? "My best guess is that it had something to do with Walter, the Chancellor of The Last City. His granddaughter, Ara, is my—" I paused. *Fiancé* didn't seem enough to encapsulate what Ara was to me. "I came to the city with her. I asked her to marry me."

"Do you think he disapproves enough to kill you for that?"

It wasn't funny, but I laughed anyway. "No. And unless you also asked her to marry you, it could hardly be the same reason for us both."

"I have never met a woman." He said the words so simply, so honestly, that I couldn't hide my disbelief.

"Never? Like even before . . ."

He only shrugged. "If I have, I have no memories of it. What is she like?"

It took me a moment to adjust to the shock of his words, and remember that not so long ago, I hadn't seen a woman for three years. I thought about how to describe Ara: Independent. Fiery. Beautiful. My everything. But saying those words aloud, when I didn't know where she was, or if she was safe, would hurt. Instead,

I said softly, "Let me put it this way: we'd better hurry up and get back to the city before she burns it down looking for me."

"And she's the Chancellor's granddaughter." He trailed off, his voice pensive. Just when I was about to ask him what he meant by that, he said, "Is there anything else, besides her gender, that marks her as different from others in The Last City?"

A spring in the ancient couch dug into my back as I wriggled to find a comfy position. There was one thing. Something I'd wanted to ignore but couldn't any longer. "She tested as Invalid. Walter said it was because he designed the test after his blood . . ."

"But you don't believe him?"

"It would make sense, except for the fact that I also tested as Invalid. But I kept it a secret." I wished now I would have pressed Talia for answers; but Ara didn't seem to like her, or me spending time with her, and I didn't want to poke the tiger. Either tiger.

"Why keep it a secret?"

I sighed. "Because Talia told me to."

"Talia, another woman?"

"Yes."

"It seems all your problems start and end with women."

A laugh startled out of me. "It was like that way before the plague too." Then I shook my head, a headache forming at my temples. "It's definitely possible he could have found out. He told Ara that the Invalid test didn't matter, that it was only because they shared blood."

"Does Ara know you tested as Invalid?"

I sighed. "No. I didn't tell her. I didn't see any reason to make a big deal out of it when it was Talia's theory in the first place." It just didn't make sense. *Why* would he want to kill me for having the same result his granddaughter also had? What could possibly be so dangerous about an Invalid test? The wind howled outside, trying to force itself in. Yet it already felt like my thoughts were a storm within me.

"Do you think he would kill over this test?" Septimus said, echoing my thoughts.

"What else could it be?" The couch squeaked as I shifted, unable to lie still. "I didn't want it to be true, because . . ." It was hard to get the words out, and when I did, they were a choked whisper. "Because if it is, then Ara's next."

I need to get back into that damn city—and then Ara and I can both get the hell out of there. We never should have left Boise. Thinking of her hometown made me think of Ara's father.

"It's just all so—strange." I gave up on sleep and sat up, speaking low and quick now. "Ara just found out that her father had once lived in this city—but he left because he disagreed with Walter about something. Then years later a plague breaks out—and his daughter is immune to it. Then her father mysteriously disappears when they're being tracked by people with airships and dogs—too many resources for the end of the world. Then he sends his daughter back to that same city he grew up in. The only city that's survived thanks to some miracle flower cure. So what am I missing here? What am I not putting together?" I closed my eyes, trying to resist the urge to punch something. *Where's a damn clown when you need one?*

"Maybe the missing piece to all this is Ara's father," Septimus said softly.

Abruptly all the frustration left me. I groaned, and flopped back onto the squeaky cushions. "You sound like Ara. I swear her father is harder to find than God, and just as omnipresent. I can't decide if I hate him, appreciate him for giving me Ara, or even believe he's real."

"Are you talking about Ara's father or God?"

I laughed. "Neither. Both."

"If we survive, will you introduce me to her?"

"Easy there, Romeo—she's taken. And we *will* survive. I didn't come this far to die now."

We were both silent for some time, lost in our own thoughts. I thought maybe Septimus had fallen asleep when he said, "Do you have memories of before the plague? What was it like back then?"

I sighed, thinking of that world, and the boy I'd once been. "Frantic. Bright. Wonderful."

"Tell me?"

So I did. The long, cold hours of the night passed as I told him stories of before: of the cars and airships, of the movies and fast food and schools and the pulsating, wild vibrancy of life before. The vanity, the greed, the wonder, the way it all seemed like it could never end. Until it did.

I meant to only tell him about the bright days, but I surprised myself, telling him of my sister, Kia, who I'd held with bleeding white eyes. How I'd burned down my father's house and left with only my horse Red and a few supplies, to make the long journey to Boise to find Sam. Meeting Issac, the man who changed everything for me and my brother.

Then I told him about my family before the plague, and the family I found at the end of the world. Issac's unshakable faith, his love for Sam and me, and finally the way he had died, selfless until the end. "The last thing he told me was 'There is only the peace we find.'" I shook my head, smiling. "So like the old man. I bet he knew I'd spend the rest of my life trying to figure out what he meant."

"And did you? Find his peace?"

Usually I would have joked, but his voice was so honest, so like Sam's, it drew a different response. "No. But I'll keep looking. Maybe that was his whole point. Maybe you have to keep looking for it."

"Like humor?"

I really did laugh at this. "Yeah. Humor, peace, and the love of a woman. The three things hardest to find in the apocalypse."

He nodded, and then a smile crept over his face. "Maybe your problem is that you're looking alone. Maybe it takes two to find peace and humor." He frowned. "I'm not sure what it takes to find the love of a woman."

"Neither does the rest of the world."

We laughed together, warm, happy, and well-fed, the darkness held at bay. For just a moment, the world felt as bright as it had once been. As I lay there, a strange thought struck me. I wondered if I'd found a small bit of Issac's peace here, in an abandoned amusement park, with a man I barely knew, without even knowing how.

TWENTY—SAM

Together M and I crawled across the flat roof of a building at the very edge of the flooded downtown, the water only a few buildings away. From up here, I could see where the water stretched out, reflecting the moonlight. It looked almost like an expanse of black pavement betrayed only by the ripples from the wind. On our side of the water, just across the street from us, was the building where Kaden and I had stashed the kayaks. A building that was currently occupied.

"I see at least two men," M whispered.

"I see three. And there could be more we can't see."

In the year since I'd last been here, the side of the building that had once been some sort of glass window display had been removed, the opening deliberately widened. Now the men below used the opening in the wall to create a sort of oven.

The fire from the oven lit the men below in shades of orange and red. There was a big man with dark hair, a man who walked with a slight limp, and inside the building, I thought I'd seen the movements of another.

"What are they doing?" M whispered.

"Smoking fish, I think." Even if I couldn't make out exactly what they were doing, the sharp scent of fish and smoke left only one possibility. It was something we'd done in the clan, but for them to do it here made me think they were loners. Still, attempting to steal from three men when there were only two of us was already insane—let alone not knowing if there were others in the building.

"What's the plan?" M said, flat on her belly beside me, her hood hiding her face in shadows. The wind that had followed us all day now cut deep. All I wanted was to go back inside, get warm, and eat. Why couldn't I have met M before the plague, when mini golfing or going to a movie was an acceptable nighttime activity, instead of risking our lives for *kayaks*? Dread rose in the back of my throat at the thought of what M was going to say when I told her there was no way we could get to those kayaks.

I decided to start with the good news first. "That's definitely the right building." *What else can I say that won't make her shoot me?* "I can't see the kayaks, but maybe that's how they're getting all the fish." The figures below moved in shadows lit by the flickering flames. "But these men definitely aren't with the clan—Gabriel had a system of fish traps, and we had a few men who specialized in fishing. Plus if this was his operation, there'd be more men here to guard and to bring the fish back. It's dangerous out here at night—the scent could bring predators or other people in." *People like us.*

My warning that these men were likely prepared for people to try to steal from them didn't seem to register with her. "Are there any other kayaks or boats we could use stashed around here?" she said.

"Maybe. There was another sporting goods store, but we'd have to backtrack and it was on the other side of the city. That's assuming anything is still left there. We could also try to build something ourselves—"

"No." She cut me off. "You're sure this is where the kayaks are?"

"Yes."

"Then we're getting them."

Was Ara this impossible with Kaden? I didn't think so. Even though I knew it wouldn't help, I tried to make her see reason. "There're at least three men down there, M. Maybe more we can't see. We're already outnumbered, and if they're willing to be out here, with an open fire, they've got to have weapons."

She didn't even blink. "You, me, and the gun. Three on three."

"M . . ."

Her nostrils flared, and she finally turned to me, her voice hard. "Is there any other way you can think to get to the testing center?"

My voice was pleading now. "If you'd just give me a few days, I could figure something out."

"We don't have a few days." Then she did something that shocked me to my core. She reached out and set her hand on mine. "Please Sam. Help me."

It took a good ten seconds for my brain to restart. When it did, I stared down at the men instead of her. "I want to help you, but this is suicide. Please, just let me think of another plan. A little time, that's all I'm asking for."

Her hand drew back. She stared down at the men below, her eyes hard. I wanted to tell her that I would do anything for her: that if she went down there, against all my advice, I'd be right there beside her. Instead, I stayed quiet. My fingers grew numb as I waited.

Finally she gave a terse nod. "You have until noon tomorrow to think of something. Then we do things my way."

"I can work with that." Relief flooded my body.

She didn't meet my eye as we made our way back down into the building, but I let it go. I focused instead on making camp for the night. It wasn't the sort of building Kaden or I would have chosen normally: there were no beds, couches, or food, just several cubicles and desks, with yellowed paper scattered throughout. The only vending machine had been shattered, the contents raided. We couldn't risk a fire, so we bedded down in a conference room with windows that showed a view of the flooded downtown.

M accepted some dried deer jerky from me with no comment, even though I wanted to tell her the story of how I'd shot the doe—my first big-game kill on my own. I figured it was better to focus, so I let her eat in silence as I stared out the dirty window at the star-filled sky, and tried to think of a plan.

As soon as she was done eating, M crawled into her sleeping bag and turned her back on me, offering no assistance or ideas. Kaden would have known what to do. He always knew what to do. That's why he was the leader of our expedition team. I was—what? Good with electricity and books? Not exactly helpful here. Even if one of us could create a distraction, neither of us could carry two kayaks away without help . . .

On and on my thoughts spun.

Until I woke, the soft light of pre-dawn leaking the windows. It was too early to wake up, yet something had woken me. Raised voices came from outside.

M?

I turned over. Disbelieving shock hit me.

The room was empty. M's sleeping bag and supplies were gone.

She went without me.

Panic brought me fully awake. I leapt up and grabbed my bow

and arrows. I always slept in my shoes and jacket, but I abandoned all else as I charged down the stairwell, then burst out the last door.

The view in front of me was disorientating. The fire had escaped where it had been contained earlier, and now flames danced inside the building, smoke pouring out of the opening where the fish hung. Crashing and cursing came from inside. A gunshot ripped through the air and someone—a man—screamed.

And then another voice, female, raised in panic: "Sam!"

Her voice burned through me.

The night was still heavy, dawn just on the horizon, but the fire gave off its own light, urging me forward. There was no hesitation in me. I crashed through a wall of dead fish. Clouds of dark smoke billowed as I moved into the building, and then stumbled on something warm and solid.

A man with dull eyes stared up at me.

Fear sliced through me, but not for me. For M.

"M!" I screamed into the billowing smoke. The room was large and long, once a storage site for camping equipment, now filled with flames licking up the far wall. Though every instinct screamed against it, I moved deeper into the room, arrow nocked, the bow tight with tension. The sound of a grunt and thud of bodies came ahead, and I stepped around some sort of long counter—

—to see a man sitting astride M, his hands wrapped around her throat. Her face purpled as she clawed at his face and neck.

An arrow took him through the neck.

It happened so fast—one moment his hands wrapped around her neck, the next he jerked back. I barely registered that the shot was mine. The *kill* was mine.

He made an awful gurgling sound as he fell to the ground, clutching at his neck. *Clean kills, Sam. Don't let the animal suffer.* Kaden's voice. Or was it Issac's?

"Are you okay?" I bent beside M, pulling her up. She nodded, unable to speak. Then she pointed behind me. I spun, expecting another enemy. Instead, the smoke roiled and billowed as I saw them.

The kayaks.

It's too late! I wanted to scream at her, but she was already moving. Somehow I knew the only way she was leaving this burning building alive was with a kayak.

"Back door!" I yelled at her. I slung my bow over my shoulder then ran to the remaining kayak, tore it from the wall, and charged through the flames after her. The smoke burned like lava down my throat, but all I could think of was the man I had just killed.

We burst out of the black smoke onto the opposite street. I swallowed air in choked, heaving gasps. Behind us the building roared in flames, the heat so blinding it seemed impossible we had emerged from within.

M stumbled, making for the water. I followed after.

Only when my feet hit the cold water did I finally drop the kayak. Embers had fallen on my jacket, burning straight through it. I waited only as long as it took to remove my shoes and bow before I plunged face-first into the water. The cold took my breath away, hurting and healing in the same moment.

When the burns on my feet and arms subsided to a dull ache I half crawled, half staggered my way to shore. Then I stripped off my shirt and pants with shaking fingers. The dawn pinked the farthest edges of the sky, the rest of the sky as dark as the water, while I stood there, half naked and shivering, and watched the building go fully up in flames.

I just killed a man. A man who, for all I know, was guilty of nothing beyond using the kayaks Kaden and I left there.

"You should have told me the plan." I spun around to look at M. Blistering anger, like the flames of the building, roared inside me.

She turned away from the flames, and faced me. I saw what I hadn't before: guilt. That single look from her felt like a punch to the gut. It wiped away my anger in a single blow, and replaced it with something much worse: betrayal.

"You were going to leave me," I whispered, shocked at how much it hurt and that I hadn't understood the moment I awoke alone. "That was your plan: take a kayak and go?" *After everything we've been through?*

I wanted to cry, or better yet, let the blistering anger return. Anything was better than the way she couldn't meet my eye and the horrible knowledge that after everything we'd been through, she didn't care.

"I thought . . ." My voice was ragged from smoke and exhaustion. *I thought what we had meant something. I thought I meant something.*

I didn't expect what she said next. "I'm sorry, Sam."

Sorry doesn't change anything though, does it? I couldn't look at her now. I didn't want to see what had likely been so painfully obvious this whole time—that she didn't care. *You are so stupid. If you were smart you would get the hell out of here right now. She doesn't care for you—she's using you. That's all.*

A massive crack sounded behind us. We both turned to watch as part of the building, now roaring with flames, fell in on itself. If the men inside had been alive before, they weren't now.

But I knew the man I'd shot was dead. The moment the arrow entered his neck he was dead. Or maybe it was before that. Maybe it was the moment he'd tried to hurt the girl I was in love with.

I knew what Kaden would say. He would have told me it wasn't wrong to defend ourselves. That just because we did bad things, it didn't make us bad people.

Kaden was always so good with words. And promises that went to shit.

"Stay here," I said to M, too angry to bother explaining, or even to check if she actually would. I stalked away from her, taking my shoes and bow with me, heading back to the building where I'd left my sleeping bag and supplies. I wondered if she'd still be waiting when I got back, hating that I hoped she would.

When I returned to where I'd left my things, I watched the flames climb higher in the building across from us. I dug out my few remaining clothes—dark jeans, a black T-shirt, and an army green coat—then pulled them onto my shivering body. *Guess I finally got that bath I needed.* The thought was angry, bitter, and tired. Like me now.

When I was dressed in dry clothes again, I made my way back. To my surprise M had both kayaks perched at the edge of the water, her bag loaded in one, with a paddle leaning against each.

"I'm surprised you waited," I said, sounding as angry as I felt.

"Me too," she said softly. "But I figured we should finish what we started."

Her blue eyes watched me, the color of ice on a stream, beautiful and sharp, ready to slice me open and leave me bleeding. There was blood on her chest, a burn on her cheek, and standing there in the dawn, I didn't think I'd ever seen anything more beautiful.

Or terrible.

Standing before her, burns on my arms and blood on my hands, I finally saw the truth. Kaden was never coming back. No one was coming to save me. The path I took was wholly my own—and so were the consequences. I killed that man. That was my choice. So was the choice I faced now.

"You comin', Sasquatch?" M said. Her hands were already on the kayak, ready to launch it into the water, but her eyes were on me. If I followed her, I would venture into the dark water that had almost killed me last time.

And yet, I knew my answer. "Yeah. I'm coming."

I launched my kayak into the water and M followed. My strokes broke the surface, sending out ripples as the water grew deeper, the streets and sidewalks receding below. I looked back, just once, at the burning building, the flames roaring higher and higher, a black plume of smoke reaching into the growing dawn. A man I'd killed lay forgotten inside. Only then did I finally understand why Kaden was never coming back.

He'd found someone he'd let the whole world burn for.

TWENTY-ONE—ARA

Talia and I moved through the city, quietly, side by side. We'd spent all last night planning, and then returned to the Outpost at dawn. Talia had even blown a kiss to the flabbergasted guards out front when we'd waltzed through the front door. I'd been all for marching to the Outpost right then and there, but Talia wisely insisted we get some sleep first.

Now I felt like some sort of nocturnal creature as we walked through a city nearing dusk. At times Walter's manor on the hilltop came into view, the setting sun lit behind it. Every time I looked at it, an ember of anger flared brighter inside me, burning away the cold and fear. Talia was right to call me a princess—I'd sat safely inside those walls, doing nothing.

The closer we drew to the Sanctum, the more nervous Talia became—running her hands through her hair repeatedly, her eyes flashing over her shoulder. I felt the opposite effect, sinking deeper into coldness.

I'll show you what your only granddaughter can do.

Whatever secrets Walter was hiding, I felt as if they were finally within reach. The door beneath the Sanctum couldn't be a coincidence.

"I can't believe I'm about to do this," Talia whispered, as the spires of the Sanctum peaked over the roofs of the house. Two guards stood outside the gate, guns in hand.

"Any last words?" I whispered as we drew closer.

"Maybe we should pick another door. We could take out the guards or—"

"No. You were right to want to come here. I want to see the Sanctum. I should have checked it out when I first came here. Or at least visited the women in the wagon."

Talia clenched my hand harder as the guards turned—they'd finally spotted us.

"Ara. I have something I need to tell you," she whispered, her voice high-pitched and unlike her. "Something I haven't been fully honest about."

Her legs slowed, but I pulled her along. We weren't backing out now. "Whatever it is, you can tell me once we're inside."

"That's the thing," she whispered. "I have been inside."

"What?" My foot caught on a crack in the sidewalk and I nearly fell. "Why didn't you tell me before?"

"Because I thought if I did, you wouldn't come."

Oh, great. That's not ominous at all. "Well, it's too late now. We're going in." Still, I couldn't resist asking. "Why'd you go in? Were you thinking about joining?"

She gave me a typical Talia glare. "Never. I got a day visitation pass to look for my sister. She wasn't there."

"And why, exactly, did you think telling me this would make me not want to go in now?"

She didn't answer, twirling a lock of her hair in her fingers over and over again. I'd never seen Talia with anything but blistering confidence. Seeing her unnerved made me doubt everything. Meanwhile the Sanctum only grew larger.

Only granddaughter. I steeled myself. "Talia, look at me." Her eyes finally came to meet mine. "Whatever is in there, we'll face it together. We get in, look for Emma, and if she's not there we go through the door tonight. We'll be there a few hours at the most." She nodded, letting me pull her across the final street and onto the sidewalk that led up to the gate. Then, because I couldn't resist: "What's it like in there?"

Talia shivered. "Like a living nightmare."

"Isn't the Sanctum supposed to keep women safe?"

"Sure it keeps them safe. And silent. And obedient."

The gates loomed, and it got progressively harder to pull Talia along. The guards watched us, speaking in low voices, but not leaving their post.

"If we do this, just promise me one thing," she whispered. "Don't leave me there."

Emma's bleeding eyes, then Izzie's small form left in the snow flashed before my eyes—I pushed them both away. I wasn't leaving anyone else behind. "I promise."

Together we stopped before the gate and I declared, with a confidence I didn't feel, "We've come to join the Sanctum."

Both guards stared at me. We'd already discussed visiting versus asking to join. Talia claimed we'd see more if we asked to join—only now did I realize I should have asked how exactly she'd known that. The guard on the left murmured something into his radio. I'd tucked my hair beneath my hat, but even so, there was a flash of recognition in both of their eyes. *They know who we are*. But we'd planned for that too—expected it even. It was why I hadn't told Walter before. I wanted a real look at the Sanctum before he had a chance to hide anything.

For a moment I thought they would deny us, or worse, that they'd reported us to Walter, but then the gate creaked open. Neither of them spoke as we passed, walking up the hill toward the Sanctum. With every step the twisting spires loomed closer.

I tried not to flinch as the gate slammed shut behind us.

~

The eerie sound of voices singing together came from inside the Sanctum, golden light spilling from arched windows as we approached. Talia held back from the massive wooden door, so I knocked and then stepped back to wait.

"Maybe we should go," Talia said.

"We aren't leaving." To prove it, I took her hand in mine, forcing her to stand beside me.

Standing there on the front doorstep, I felt like a princess trying to enter some beast's castle. The door was ancient, wooden, and imposing, and behind us the wide lawn stretched out, filled with bare trees and unsullied white snow. Before Talia could speak again, the door creaked open. A woman appeared, dressed in all black.

"Welcome to the Sanctum. Please, come inside." She had a soft, floating sort of voice—eerie in the deepening dusk.

Talia and I exchanged a look, fear in her eyes, determination in mine. I pulled her inside as yet another door closed behind us. For the first time, doubt rose in me: if we couldn't find our way to the door to get out of here, Ronnie and Harrison couldn't help us.

Kaden was gone. There was no one to come save us if we failed. *No one but us. That'll have to be enough.*

"Follow me, please."

Talia shot me another look as we followed the woman in black through a large entrance hall, past where the voices rose in song. We came to a small back room that smelled of wood and dust. It was filled with clothes hangers, each holding the same black dress the woman was wearing. She must have seen the distaste in my eyes, because she said, "We ask all newcomers to discard all clothes, weapons, and memorabilia from the outside world. We live only in peace here."

Talia glared at me, but I simply said, "Of course," and did what she said, stripping down to my underwear and then discarding the many weapons I had concealed under my clothes. Talia's eyes were hard, tossing her pants at me when she took them off. I ignored her. After we both stood before her in only the long black dresses—which was going to make running and staying warm in the cold difficult—the woman smiled.

"Wonderful. Please follow me to your living quarters." The woman gestured to a staircase at the end of the hall. "For the Chancellor's granddaughter, we have one of the larger rooms for you both. I'm sure you'll find it accommodating."

Talia exchanged a look with me, and I swallowed. *We planned for this. We knew it was likely they'd recognize me.*

"Actually, um, Sister," I said, trying to remember what people had called nuns, "we're really hungry. Maybe we could go to the dining hall."

"I am not a nun. You may call me Regina." She paused, her head going to the side, listening: the voices had stopped. "They've just finished. I suppose you two could join them for dinner."

We made our way back to the main entrance, and I started as I watched the flood of women, all dressed in black, coming out of the main chapel area. Talia grabbed my hand, squeezing painfully as together we watched the flood of faces pass us by. I was shocked at the number: two, maybe three hundred women walked past. But never the one face I wanted to see.

Emma, where are you?

Dark hair flashed, and my heart rose, only to plummet when a curvy woman with brown eyes turned to me. Not Emma. Then I saw a familiar face . . . with one eye.

"Rosia!" I said, soft but urgent. "Rosia!"

Her head turned slowly to mine. There was no recognition in her gaze. No spark. Just the empty gaze of a person who seemed not fully there. A living nightmare—that's what Talia had called this place. For the first time I understood the sentiment: something was deeply wrong here. Rosia kept going, and then an older woman, clearly meant to bring up the rear, walked by us and frowned.

"Come now, girls. Don't lag behind."

"Sorry," I muttered, yanking Talia forward to follow the line. What the hell had they done to Rosia? Yet as we walked, I wondered if there was something wrong with all the women here. The people in line were oddly quiet, heads bowed, the only noise the soft shuffle and movement of all the bodies. No laughter. No whispered gossip. Talia waited until we were farther down the corridor before she whispered, "They aren't here. Can we get the hell out of here now?"

"No. I could have missed her." We kept following the line. My unease grew. "How come none of them are talking?"

"I told you, this place is a living nightmare. Everyone is like that here. They're just . . . empty."

The hair rose on the back of my neck. "Do you think they're doing something to them?"

"Clearly. That's why I left as soon as I figured out Una wasn't here."

Una—it was the first time I'd heard her sister's name. My heart sank as I thought of everyone we were trying to help. My father, Emma, Kaden, Una. But I didn't want to abandon Rosia here. There had to be something I could do to help her. "Just give me till tonight. If we don't find Emma or Una, then we go down the silver door when everyone's sleeping."

Talia sighed, her face unhappy. "Fine. But don't eat the food."

"Why not?"

"Because it's fattening." She turned to glare at me. "Why the hell do you think?"

Great, so not only did I never check on the women here, they're also being brainwashed with the food. "Can you please stop keeping secrets from me?"

"Sorry, Princess. That's kind of what I do."

~

Dinner was an eerily quiet affair. I'd found a spot next to Rosia, but she hadn't so much as glanced at me. I would have been terrified out of my mind, but the sinking sensation that Emma wasn't here overwrote my fear. The only people who talked were at a table at the top of the room. Talia caught my eye when I picked up the spoon beside my bowl, and shook her head no. I hadn't been intending to eat it, but I was at least going to pretend. I watched as she took her bowl of soup and dumped it into her neighbor's bowl, and then settled it back in front of her, the spoon in hand.

I would have laughed, if not for the fact that the person beside her didn't notice. No one at the table did.

Adrenaline pumped through me, made worse by the fact that I could only sit there in silence and occasionally exchange looks with Talia, then look back at my hands in my lap. I copied Talia's movements, emptying my bowl into the person's next to me, and then, on impulse, reached over to Rosia's bowl, and emptied it into the container at the center of the table. She did nothing.

Beneath the table I took her hand, and squeezed it hard. "Don't eat the food," I whispered. "Don't eat the food, Rosia."

I'd sat on the side where her eye was stitched closed, so I couldn't make out if she'd heard. But she didn't eat any more; she simply sat there, doing nothing. Only once did another woman meet my eyes who wasn't Talia. She looked at me for only a moment, confusion in her eyes, like she'd woken to find herself in some sort of strange dream.

"Don't eat the food," I mouthed at her. Her brows furrowed and then she went back to staring at the bowl before her.

Regina found us again after dinner. "How was your food, girls?"

"Good," Talia and I murmured in turn. My stomach tightened at the lie.

"If you'll follow me to your room," she said. We followed her, going up more stairs than I cared to count, and then finally into a small room with two metal-framed single beds, decorated only by a wooden table with a glass jar holding a single shriveled flower.

"There is a bathroom attached. Please remember wandering is not allowed in the Sanctum." She left, and I went to the door, waiting a full minute before I tried it. *Locked.*

I turned back to Talia, who cocked an eyebrow at me. "Don't say I didn't warn you."

"Umm, you didn't. Until we were practically already here, remember?" I sat down heavily on the bed beside her. "What the hell is wrong with the women here?"

She wrapped her arms around her knees, pulling them to her chest. It made her look small and young—new for her. She didn't speak for some time. Then, "I was only here for three days, but I think they brainwashed the women somehow. It started to feel like my brain was getting sort of . . . foggy. All I can think is there's something in the food. I stopped eating and felt more and more like myself. That's when I realized I needed to escape."

"How come you never told anyone? Or tried to do something?"

Her eyes were hard when they came up to me, her voice razor-sharp. "Sure, because Walter would have listened to me? He's probably the one who ordered it in the first place. You've seen what happens to people who rock the boat. I would have disappeared like everyone else."

"Sorry, I didn't mean . . . Sorry."

She shrugged, something miserable in her expression. "You don't fight the monster. You join it." Her eyes closed, her voice a whisper now. "I hoped that by becoming an expedition leader, saving women, I could make up for not helping the women here . . . I guess I just wanted to forget it."

I nodded, closing my eyes and lying down on the bed beside her. "Maybe we can still help them. Maybe there will be something in the tunnels that can help us." I cast a look at the locked door. "Any chance you know how to pick a lock?"

"Nope."

"I guess a decoy fire would probably just burn us all to a crisp . . . How did you get out last time?"

"You're not going to like it."

"Try me. Anything is better than staying here and doing nothing."

She gave me her catlike smile, and then waltzed over to the window and swung it open. She swept a dramatic hand at the lawn below. I stared at her in confusion, then at the sprawling lawn beyond. Finally it hit me.

"Please tell me you aren't serious."

"Told you you wouldn't like it."

I came over to the window and leaned out. A dizzying drop greeted me. A thin ledge ran along the edge of the window and so far into the distance I couldn't see where it ended. The night beyond was inky black, taunting me with its secrets. If Kaden was out there, if he needed me, then I had to do whatever it took to find him. Including this. I pulled back in and looked down at my dress.

"If we're gonna do this, we need to figure out how to climb in these dresses."

~

Walking on the roofs of the city was one thing: if you fell you might die.

If we fell from on top of a cathedral, death was a guarantee.

Talia and I both tore our dresses, tying them around our legs. There wasn't anything we could do for warmth, but we only had to climb across the peak of the roof to where another hallway offered windows Talia said she could open. Then back to the room with all our clothing and supplies, and then down to the silver metal door that tunneled beneath the city.

This is nothing. You've done far more dangerous stuff than this. I tried to believe that as the wind whipped my hair, trying to tear me from the narrow ledge and toss me off the side. We'd left everything untouched in the room, and even pushed the window closed. It would look like we'd disappeared into thin air. *Thin air.* The thought made me dizzy at just how far the ground was beneath us, as if the air really were thinner. *No, don't think like that.*

Finally the ledge ran into a large hallway window. Talia edged alongside it, trying to get it to open.

"It's locked!" she whispered, her eyes wide, "It wasn't locked last time!" I stared through the long, empty hallway and then down at the little switch that would let us inside. *No one to save you except yourself.*

Then I closed my eyes, balanced on one leg, and kicked with the other. Pain bloomed through my foot, even through my boots, but I ignored it, relentlessly kicking until the glass shattered and I finally reached through and flicked the switch to open the window. The jagged edge of glass caught my hand on the way back and I gasped at the sudden sharp pain.

"It's open," I muttered, clutching my now-bloody hand against my chest. Talia forced the window open, helping me to climb inside after her. The two of us landed silently in a carpeted corridor, quiet but for the wind now whistling through the window. There was no hiding the evidence of our escape now. Glass littered the hallway, and blood ran down the gaping hole.

"So much for them not knowing how we got out," I said. Beside me Talia had already ripped a piece of her dress off and wrapped it around my hand. She tied the hand off with a pull that made me gasp.

"This way," she said.

Together we ran light-footed down the silent corridors. My hand throbbed, and if it came to a fight, I wasn't sure how much help I would be. But there wasn't anything I could do for it now. Talia seemed sure in her decisions, leading us down the staircase and back near the entrance. Soon we came to the room where our clothes and weapons had been left.

With only one good hand, I didn't try to take the dress off, just pulled my pants up underneath and put the jacket over. I probably looked absurd, but it hardly mattered. All of the weapons we'd left here earlier were gone.

"Come here," I said on impulse, taking Talia's hand and smearing blood across it.

"What are you doing?" she said, shocked.

"In case we get separated. Now you can open the door too."

"We won't get separated—let's go."

Again we passed through the darkened corridors, two shadows moving quietly but swiftly. At intervals the lights above burned bright, terrifying to pass beneath.

Finally Talia opened a side door that revealed a steep staircase spiraling down. The farther we descended, the colder it became, until my breath came in clouds.

At the bottom of the staircase, in a dimly lit stone corridor, stood the gleaming silver door.

The same type of door that I'd seen almost a year ago in the Birmingham Medical Testing Center, back in the flooded downtown ruins of Boise. When I opened the door with my blood, the man inside knew me. He'd known my father. He'd wanted my blood.

"Is it too late to change my mind?" Talia shifted from side to side, like a flickering flame, never ceasing to move. In contrast I felt as cold and unmovable as the door in front of us, terrified what truths lay beyond.

My bandage had already soaked through—I winced as I brushed my hand across the door. The metal door looked nonporous, but just like at the testing center, the blood somehow melted into the door.

Talia drew in a sharp breath. "We could just go back. Leave The Last City and forget men altogether. Retire to a small cottage by the woods, become hermits with a dozen cats—"

"Hush."

I pushed the door open, shocked when instead of a corridor like the one we were in—cold, dim, and made of stone—we were faced with a long white hallway. Fluorescent lights glared above, several doors on each side like some kind of hospital. It stretched out before us, a terrifying invitation.

"Hermits live longer than princesses," Talia whispered, hanging back from the door.

"Neither of us is becoming a hermit." I grabbed Talia's hand and pulled her forward. The soft buzz of the lights broke the otherwise eerie silence. The hair on my neck stood on end, and I was suddenly thankful for Talia's presence at my side.

As we walked, I stopped to look through the small glass windows set on the many doors. Some rooms were filled with computers, some held what looked like scientific equipment, and others looked like hospital rooms, each with a cot in the corner. Some were filled with strange tubes of green water that I could guess no purpose for, yet recognized from Walter's lab and the testing center.

"What if they're testing for a cure?" Talia whispered, as she peeked into another doorway.

"Then why hide it under the city?"

She hesitated. "Maybe they need human subjects for it."

With those unsettling words, we continued down the hallway. I remembered, at the Birmingham Medical Testing Center in downtown Boise, there had been monkeys locked in cages on one of the lower floors. The animals had been left there to die—maybe they'd been using them to test for a cure? There were too many questions and not enough answers.

"Ara," Talia whispered, gazing through the window at a room. The hair on my neck stood on end as I approached the door and looked inside. My heart fluttered in my chest. The room had a cage on one side. A cage that held a woman. She looked asleep, but as I gazed in the room, suddenly her eyes came up to meet mine—and it felt like I'd been electrocuted.

White eyes weeping blood.

I jerked back, heart hammering, vision tilting.

"Should we break her out?" Talia whispered.

I stepped backward, struggling for words. "No . . . she's infected. I—What could we do for her?"

The fluorescent lights seemed to glare down at us, the soft buzzing sound not near loud enough to drown out the pounding in my ears. The pale hallways seemed to narrow as Talia took my hand in hers, the two of us staring at the door in silence. *There's nothing we can do for her. Nothing.*

Yet it still didn't feel right when we continued down the hallway. The woman's presence seemed to trail after me like a ghost.

We came to a fork in the hallway. The white hallway continued to the left, but on the other side lay another silver door. I paused, about to ask which way we should go when Talia froze beside me.

Voices. Coming toward us.

I leapt forward, smearing blood across the silver door before throwing my weight against it. Together we slipped to the other side and then eased the door shut behind us. As it sealed, the bright lights and tiled floor of the hallway disappeared. Neither of us moved.

It was only after my heart stopped thundering that I realized we had once again stepped into a new world. The earth beneath us was rocky, not the smooth tiled white floors of the hallways. The curving earthen tunnel before was lit by the green glow I was coming to know too well.

"Where are we?" I whispered to Talia.

"The tunnels beneath the city," she whispered back. I took a few steps deeper. The tunnel curved, but just before it did, there was a gaping hole in the rock—with bars over it. *A cage. They have cages down here.*

Together we started down the tunnel. We passed three, then four, then six cages built into natural openings in the rock walls, all empty.

At the seventh cage I'd almost turned to go when something moved at the back of the cage. My heart went into overdrive.

"Hello?" My voice trembled as I leaned closer. At the very back, curled into a ball next to the rock face, a form moved—a man. He slowly raised his head and blinked. Relief filled me—his eyes weren't white. He wasn't infected.

So why was he here?

The man was almost skeletal, with long matted hair, and a thick beard covering his face, so that I could hardly make out his eyes under all the dirt and hair.

"Hello? Can you hear me? My name is Ara—I'm not going to hurt you. I just want to talk."

Painfully slowly, he unfolded his legs and stood. He was pitiful to look at. His shoulder blades stood out like sticks, his eyes gaunt. As he came closer, I could smell him—a mixture of sweat and feces and rot. Finally he made it to the bars, gnarled fingers with almost black fingernails wrapping around them. He looked up at me, and I was surprised that his eyes were very much alert.

"You never should have come here, Ara."

I jerked back at my name, thudding into Talia.

"Ara? What's wrong?" she whispered. I barely heard her—I couldn't look away from the man before me.

Because beyond the shriveled body of an old man was a voice that had once been musical, eyes that had once held laughter, arms that had once protected his daughter from the world.

"Father?"

TWENTY-TWO—SAM

My arms ached as we kayaked through the river system that now dominated downtown Boise. The creaking skyscrapers towered over us, gray clouds holding the sky low, the colors of fall now diminished into the monochrome buildings watermarked with lines of green scum.

With each stroke, I wondered how long the buildings would stand until they ceded to the water. Even in the fall, with the river running low, the water seemed dark and powerful, hiding a whole world beneath. Last time I'd been here something had pulled me under.

It's just water. Whatever that thing was, it's gone now. I'm not scared. Just to prove it, I trailed my hand through the frigid flow, fighting the impulse to rip it free. The water felt good on the raised red burns on my hand, but even so, I pulled it back quickly. If M was in pain, she hid it well.

We floated through a metal canyon with small offshoots for streets, and even smaller alleyways. Occasionally trees or lampposts rose out of the flow, the only marker I had for depth. Kaden said someone had blown the dam above the city after the plague, but without the internet or news it was hard to know.

M led now, a few kayak lengths ahead of me. Her hood was thrown back, her dark hair in a braid down her back, her head whipping one way and then another. Even from this distance, I could feel her frustration. We should have been there by now—but the currents had changed since I'd last been here.

I propelled my kayak up to hers, drifting in silence until I finally said, "Last time we were at the Birmingham Medical Testing Center, we spent the night there. We didn't find anything."

"Did you get the computers on?"

"No."

"Then you ain't seen shit yet."

A slight current pulled us, the two of us drifting forward in the shadows of the building. I said nothing, but even so, I could feel her eyes on me.

"You got something to say, Sasquatch?" Her voice held a dangerous tone, one that would have made the old Sam stay quiet. But I'd killed a man this morning—that cast the world into a new perspective.

"Just that the testing center wasn't a great place to spend the night." I pointed back the way we'd come. "I saw an old hotel a block back. I remember my mom talking about it once, she said it had a great view of downtown, and a restaurant at the top. Maybe we could stay there for the night, and get a bird's-eye view of downtown."

She turned to look up at the buildings all around before she nodded. "Fine. Lead the way."

M followed me now as we paddled between two buildings,

the water rushing faster beneath us as it pulled us down a sort of shoot. It reminded me of one of the times I'd gone white-water rafting on the Snake River: the churning white water, the sheer, terrifying power of it all. But on the river you could get to the bank—here the buildings were slick from the water, offering no escape.

The shoot spat us out onto another road between the tall buildings. The only signs of life so far had been fish below, but now a massive flock of birds flew up.

"What the hell . . ." I tried to paddle backward, but the current was too strong. Gulls and other larger birds flew through the air in a dizzying mass above us.

The current pulled us forward, birds still crying and flying overhead as others settled onto something massive floating in the water. It looked to be trapped in the current, speared on a set of flagpoles.

"What is that?" M said.

"Don't know."

At first I thought it was the carcass of a cow, caught on the flagpoles and slowly rotting in the water. But it was too big. *Maybe something from the zoo?* Curiosity and trepidation grew in me as the current pulled us closer. M didn't share the same fear, paddling straight past me. I lifted an arm to stop her, but the words caught in my mouth.

Because I suddenly knew exactly what was floating in the water.

It was a giant rotting corpse, the size of an elephant, but long, serpentine, with bits of pink flesh exposed beneath a scaly gray exterior. An exterior I recognized. It looked like some kind of massive prehistoric monster that shouldn't have existed.

Bile rose in the back of my throat at the sudden overwhelming stench of rotting flesh. *It's dead. It can't hurt you. Not like it did before.*

"The hell is that thing?" M said, waving her paddle in the air, trying to shove the birds off the corpse. The flashing silver of feeding fish boiled beneath the water.

"I think that's the thing that attacked me," I finally uttered as I tried to stop myself from bending over the kayak and emptying the contents of my stomach. The current continued to draw me closer—I would have to pass right by it. A feeding frenzy roiled the water at the base of the corpse.

M finally turned back to look at me. I was drawing level with it now, my heart pounding, throat dry, breathless and light-headed. *It's dead.*

M said something but I didn't hear her. Something strange was happening to my hands—they felt numb and tingly at the same time. A force pressed down on me, squeezing my chest, making it hard to breathe or think. I focused only on paddling past the thing and not throwing up. *It's dead. It can't hurt you.* But the fact that "it" even existed was wrong.

The current pulled me forward, down another street. Only when it was hidden from view, the feeding frenzy gone, could I breathe again. To my vast surprise, M followed me without comment or derision.

"You okay, Sasquatch?" she said, pulling up beside me.

My smile was forced. "You aren't going to make fun of me for being afraid of a dead monster?"

"There's nothing wrong with being afraid of monsters." There was no derision in her voice—only a grim sort of determination. "So long as you make yourself into a bigger, scarier monster."

We set out again. It turned out to be harder than I thought to get to the hotel, but after seeing the massive corpse in the water, fighting the current was a welcome challenge. By the time we found the hotel I'd been talking about, I was exhausted and starving.

We left the kayaks on the floor where we'd managed to enter the hotel. Then we headed straight to the top. I was right: the hotel had a restaurant there. We found a few small containers of canned salmon, and the single biggest can of peaches I'd ever seen. M collected some water that we boiled. Afterward we sat in an elegant, dusty dining room with a view of the whole downtown.

"Ahh good sir, I see you got the caviar and truffles, most excellent choice," M said, putting on an accent and pointing to the canned salmon I was eating. "Do tell me about your most recent land acquisition."

I smiled, putting on my best accent—far inferior to hers. "Yes, I recently purchased a very grand . . . erm . . . bookstore. And a whole city."

She laughed, but instead of mocking me, only responded in an even more absurd accent—the happiest I had ever seen her. Our accents grew progressively more absurd, as did our conversation, but there was something about her smile that made me happy too. I liked this version of Sam and M; just two people spending an afternoon together. No dark quests to complete or ugly truths to reveal.

Hours later we retreated to the biggest hotel room we could find, with a massive king-size bed, and a sofa that I took for myself. The room was filled with deep red velvets and gold accents. Even covered in dust, it felt like a room royalty would have once stayed in. Originally I'd planned to take a different room entirely, but to my surprise, M said there was plenty of room in here—which was true. One of the walls was made entirely of glass, with a spectacular view of the sunset over downtown. When we'd been kayaking the water seemed nearly black, but from here, the sinking sun lit it in blazing golden stripes. Had the spot not been fully surrounded by water, I would have considered moving my hideout here for the view alone.

"How long did it take you to find the building last time?" M said, reclining on the bed like a sort of queen on her throne.

Now that we were high above the water and had enjoyed a full meal, it was easier to think back to that expedition.

I shrugged. "No more than a couple of hours. But Kaden had been down here a lot, and he knew where to go. He was really good at finding things—he was the best expedition leader in the clan."

"In contrast to you and me, who both suck at finding things?"

"To be fair, I found you."

She laughed. "Did you find me? Or did I find you? Because I distinctly remember you squealing when I shot the gun."

"I did not squeal." I paused. "It was a very manly shriek." I lifted my voice, making it high and girly. "Eeek! EEEK! See?"

The way she watched me, her cheeks pink, a real smile on her face, the gun propped up on the nightstand and not held clutched in her hands—she looked happy. Like a regular teenage girl who might actually be my friend. *Or maybe something more than a friend.* The thought made my cheeks go red.

"If he was so great at finding things," M went on, "why were you alone when you found me?"

My smile disappeared. I'd told her the story, but hearing it put so bluntly made it harder to stomach. "He met a girl."

"So he picked her over you?"

My first instinct was to deny it, to defend Kaden—that he'd only picked her over me because he'd thought I was dead. *But he started picking Ara over me long before that.* "It's complicated," I said instead.

She shrugged from her spot on the bed. "My family left me too," she said. "But it's better to be alone."

"You aren't alone now."

Her voice was quiet when she responded. "We're all alone in the end."

Maybe she was right. There were so few women left. Like the swollen corpse of the monster in the water, M belonged to a nearly extinct group. But that didn't mean it had to be like this *forever*. Part of the reason I'd worked so hard to get the electricity on in the mall, and even tried to access the new tech, was that I dreamed someday we'd get it all back. Not that I'd tell M that.

I flopped down on the couch across the room from her, wiggling in the sleeping bag to try to find a comfortable position. A cloud of dust rose each time I moved.

"You think he'll ever come back? Your brother, I mean," M asked suddenly, surprising me.

I paused, and then said with honesty, "No."

"Maybe it's a good thing he's gone. You shouldn't trust someone so completely like that. People just let you down."

I trust you. I just barely managed to stop the words from leaving my mouth. She'd almost left me this morning—I didn't need to go spilling my guts now. Instead I said, "Don't you think it's necessary, in a world like this? To rely on others?"

"You weren't relying on anyone when I found you."

Except that wasn't quite true. I had all the supplies Kaden and Issac had left for me and only now did I realize how desperately lonely I had been. *The apocalypse only sucks if you let it.* That's what I'd been telling myself. Now I realized that wasn't true. The apocalypse only sucks if you don't have someone you love to spend it with.

"I don't think I can go back to that," I said, surprised at how vulnerable telling her that made me feel.

"What about all your books?"

"They'll be fine without me."

"You sure? They're probably cheating on you right now. Opening all their pages up to some other librarian."

"So long as this other librarian treats them right."

"Oh no. He treats them horribly. Dog-ears the pages. Eats greasy food over them. Uses them as coasters and door openers. Throws all your most valuable comics into the fire as kindling."

"That bastard. We'll get him after this."

She went quiet, and in the silence, I knew I'd misstepped. There was no "we" after this.

"We'll find the building tomorrow," I said, clearing my throat and trying to step past the awkward moment.

"Right."

She turned over on the bed. Then: "You know, you can come sleep on the bed. It's a king, there's more than enough room."

I paused, shocked but trying to downplay it. "You sure? I'd rather not be shot at again."

"Just keep all your gangly arms and legs to yourself."

I smiled and then moved my sleeping bag to the bed, climbing carefully onto the other side before crawling back into it.

The golden colors of the sunset faded, until only moonlight came through the windows, enough that I could make out her eyes in the darkness, wide and staring up at the ceiling. I thought she would tell me we needed to sleep, or talk strategy for the morning, but instead she said, "Best thing about the apocalypse: no more making beds. My mom always made me make mine every morning."

It was the first time she'd volunteered something about her mother without me asking. For such a small detail it felt incredibly significant.

"Wrong," I countered. "The best thing about the apocalypse is no more light pollution. The stars are so much brighter now. Some men in the clan said they've even seen the northern lights down here."

She fired back right away. "No more social media—and no more using Google to end arguments."

"Are you saying the best thing about the apocalypse is endless arguments?"

"Feel free to argue with me about it."

My burns still stung, but my stomach was full, and a smile clung to my lips. This morning she'd tried to leave without me—but now I think I understood why. I'd spent the summer alone because I was waiting for Kaden . . . but also because I thought if I didn't love or trust anyone new, then no one could hurt me. Somehow the opposite was true: I only hurt more for those that I'd lost.

I couldn't live that way anymore. Meeting M had shown me that. She was strong all on her own, and she wasn't waiting for anyone to come save her. If I had learned about Issac's death on my own, I doubted I would have made it. I would have turned bitter and hard and angry. Instead, I hoped for a better tomorrow. I'd accepted that Kaden was never coming back, and that the path I chose now was my own. A path that I wanted to be on with M.

Her breathing evened out as I stared up at the ceiling, and thought about the answer I hadn't dared to speak aloud. The best thing about the apocalypse wasn't the stars, or endless arguments, or the books that belonged only to me.

The best thing about the apocalypse was her.

TWENTY-THREE—KADEN

In the distance the sun shattered the night sky into glorious streaks of violet and bronze. For once I ignored the beauty of the dawn. Instead, I kept my eyes firmly on the massive steel structure we both climbed. *Guess it's my fault for telling Septimus that the best view in the park would be from the top of the Ferris wheel.*

"You know, Septimus," I called out to him. "I'm starting to think I'm a bad influence."

"Why? What's wrong with this?" The cold wind nearly ripped away his words, though he was barely ten feet above me.

I turned to glance at the ground far, far below. When we first started climbing the Ferris wheel, I'd taken my gloves off to have a better grip on the cold steel. Now my fingers were frozen, but I didn't dare put my gloves back on.

Above me, Septimus held on with only one hand, leaning back into the wind, as casual as if he was three feet off the ground and not a hundred. *So much for giving him a healthy dose of fear.*

"See anything?" I called out, testing another steel bar before pulling myself up.

He didn't respond. I kept climbing, and then, when I'd drawn level with him, pointed to the white-and-red gondola just above us—the one suspended forever at the top of the structure.

"Might as well make it to the top," I said. "If we fall from either height, we're dead."

Together we scaled the very top metal bar. The higher we climbed, the stronger and colder the wind seemed to become. At the very top it was so strong I didn't dare try to warm my hands, even for a second. The gondola creaked as I slowly lowered my weight into it. It was big—made to hold maybe ten people, the top cover ripped off completely. It swung gently back and forth in the breeze, making a creaking noise each time it did.

Septimus landed beside me and the two of us stood there in silence, looking at the equally terrifying and breathtaking view below. The sunrise painted the horizon in stripes of gold and purple. The river wound through the ruins to the west of us, until it reached the city walls just visible in the distance. So high above it all, I felt as if the old world was back. That at any moment the airships and cars and noise of the world would start again.

The device I'd stolen from the Captain vibrated in my pocket and I pulled it out now. I'd forgotten it was in my coat pocket, but this morning when it vibrated, and I realized that even though I couldn't log in, I could still read messages sent out to the expedition teams. This morning's message read: *Both targets killed. Captain also dead.* My best guess was that someone was lying because they didn't want to admit they hadn't killed us to Walter. Smart, really.

Now I lifted the device just in time to watch another message flash across the screen and disappear.

All teams report back to The Last City immediately. Then, a few seconds later: *All teams returning.* When nothing else happened, I tucked the device back into my pocket. Had Sam been here, he would have been able to figure out how to charge it or hack it, but I didn't see the point. If Walter had pulled all teams back to the city, then no one was hunting us—which was a good thing. Except for the fact that it meant today was the worst possible day to try to break back in.

"Find anything useful in that thing?" Septimus said.

I shrugged. "Can't log in, and it's pretty much dead now, but it looks like Walter called all the teams back today. Which probably means we shouldn't move camp until tomorrow. We don't want to run into anyone in the ruins. But at least we aren't being hunted." I blew breath into my hands, warming them before I turned to Septimus. "How about you? Anything coming back?" The wind caught my words, ripping them away and pulling them out to a horizon tinged in deep golds and pinks.

"Swirling shadows, whispers . . . nothing solid. Nothing I can understand."

Even I didn't even have a joke for that. To not remember who you were or where you'd been—it felt like a sort of death in its own way. *Or maybe a birth.*

"I took Sam to a theme park once," I said, the memory coming back bright and sharp. "It was the only time I've ever been. Besides now."

"What was it like?"

"Crowded. Noisy. Dirty. But that's not the way Sam saw it. To him it was . . . magical." A sudden weight sat on my chest. "If I could go back, change one thing, it would be that. To see things the way he did. I was so jaded back then." I stared down at the park spread around us, smiling at the thought of the boy I'd once been. "All I wanted to do was leave Montana and my dad's ranch behind forever. Then when he died, I wished I had it all back."

"That's when you went to Boise? To find Sam?"

"Yeah. I knew Boise pretty well. I'd lived there for most of the year with my mom, only spending summers with my dad until she remarried. Then I moved out to Montana to live with my dad—I didn't really get along with Sam's dad. When the plague hit, Mom was able to get me a message just before everything went to shit. She begged me to come get Sam. At that point—" I stopped for a moment, the words hard to say. "At that point all my family in Montana was dead. I rode Red to Boise myself—I always wanted to ride him across state lines." I'd thought all I wanted was to escape Montana and my father forever, but I'd never escape the memory of burying my half sibling Kia and my two stepbrothers. If it hadn't been for Sam needing me, and Red, I might not have made it.

"What happened to Sam?"

I stiffened in the morning breeze. I'd told Septimus so much about the clan and Ara last night, but I'd skipped over that part. "He died trying to save me." My throat thickened. "It was my fault. I was supposed to protect him, but I failed him." A fresh wave of grief and guilt washed over me. "Actually, I failed a lot of people. Everyone."

Suddenly the gorgeous view was just one more thing Sam would never see. I pulled out the cigars I'd taken from the Captain's pocket, along with his lighter.

"Here." I handed him one. "May as well complete my corruption."

He joined me, the two of us using our bodies to block the

wind to light the cigars. He watched as I took a deep pull, the end flaring. He copied me, and to my surprise, didn't even cough.

"Why'd you really wanna come up here?" I said.

He took another pull, exhaling slowly before he answered. "When I was in the river, there was a moment when I thought death had me. But then I saw a woman."

"You mean from shore?"

"No." He paused, rolling the cigar in his fingers. "It was like a memory. Or a dream. I think she might be beneath the city."

The cold wind suddenly shook the gondola, the iron joints of the Ferris wheel creaking in the breeze. "Did you see her there?"

"I'm not sure . . . my only memories, if you could call them that, are strange, blurry things. They feel more like dreams. But I know she's down there; it's like she's calling to me. Does that make sense?"

I thought of Ara, the need to return to her. The secrets hidden in the city we'd only begun to uncover. "In a weird way it does."

"I think she's in trouble. She's running out of time."

Aren't we all? "How did you get out?"

He swallowed, silent for some time. "Something went wrong. I woke up when I wasn't supposed to." His eyes closed, and when he spoke, his voice was etched by pain. "I didn't mean to kill them. Those three men. But I couldn't go back to nothingness. It was like waking up into a nightmare. I knew if I didn't escape then, I never would." His eyes met mine, suddenly hard, his words fierce. "I won't go back to that. Even if these few memories, of this park, the sunrise, and saving you are all I have, I won't let them take it all away again." He glared out over the edge of the gondola, his hands in fists, his eyes on fire. It was the most passion I'd seen in him.

"Those are some pretty shit memories, to be your only ones." When he didn't smile, I said gently, "I wouldn't ask you to, Septimus."

He finally turned his gaze from the world laid out below and stared at me. "That's my price."

"Price?"

He pointed to the gun that I had tucked into my belt. "I said that I would show you the way back into The Last City, and I will, but I won't let them make me into nothing again. If they catch us, you use that gun to end me. That's my price."

He held out his hand, expectant and waiting. I stared at it, feeling cold. This wasn't an easy handshake. This was agreeing to kill a man—a man I actually liked. He had saved my life. What he asked for was another kind of unknowing. A final one.

Yet I already knew what my answer would be.

Maybe Issac's peace was forever out of reach because the price that I would pay to save Ara was absolutely anything.

"It won't come to that." But I shook his hand, praying to Issac's God that I was right. "We'll find Ara and your mystery girl." Then softer, so soft I wasn't even sure he could hear: "I won't make the same mistakes I did with Issac and Sam."

He took another slow puff, and then looked down at the cigar in distaste. "This thing is disgusting."

I pulled the cigar free, glanced down at it, then put it back between my lips. "They slowly kill you. Yet people still love 'em. Some things never change."

He paused, blowing out smoke that mixed with the clouds of cold breath, the dawn breaking golden. When he turned to me, his eyes had that strange stillness that made me think of Issac. "Maybe you should let it go."

Are we talking about cigars or mistakes? My fingers trembled as I held on to the cigar. "What if I can't?"

He took a final pull and then tossed his cigar over the side. "Then you let it slowly kill you."

You let it slowly kill you. Was that what I was doing? I sure as hell hadn't let it go—every day I thought of Sam and Issac. Of what I could have done differently. How I could have saved them. How I couldn't let myself be happy, because how could I be happy in a world they weren't part of? It was my fault. My failing. I had to let it keep killing me—because it was the only piece of them I had left.

Maybe you should let it go.

I stared at the smoking end of the cigar, and saw a whole other life play out. Sam riding Red. Issac reading before the fire. A clan I led.

Then I saw a different story. A future I hadn't dared to imagine. A child with auburn hair, Ara smiling as she lifted him and he laughed in her arms. A future I wanted but never dared believe I deserved.

The end of the cigar glowed, a bright ember against the cold. Still I didn't release it. Because if I did, if I finally forgave myself for failing them, if I let myself move on and imagine a new future with Ara, wouldn't it be like losing them all over again?

My fingers tightened, and then, finally, released the cigar. It fell, blazing and tumbling, before it hit the snow and disappeared.

I stared down at it, wondering why my heart both twisted and felt lighter than it had in ages.

Forgive me, Sam. Forgive me, Issac. Forgive me for moving on. Forgive me for living when you're both gone.

We were both silent for a long time, the low moan of the wind and deep creaks of the Ferris wheel the only sounds. The sun was full over the edge of the horizon, my nose numb and fingers buried deep in my jacket when I finally spoke. "So, are we breaking into The Last City today?"

"If all the teams are returning today, then we should probably wait at least a few days—"

"We don't have a few days."

"You didn't let me finish. It would be best, but we've already established that personal health isn't a priority."

I laughed. "True."

"We'll move out tonight. At dusk. It'll take most of the night to cross the ruins. We can get close, camp on the outskirts of the city. Tomorrow night, a few hours after dusk, we make our move."

Two days. Ara will be okay for two days. "Are there any supplies we need?"

"No."

"Should we gather food? Scout?"

"We already have enough food and it's best if we don't leave the park."

My fingers rattled on the railing, not used to stillness. "So . . . a whole day in an abandoned amusement park." *Can't remember the last time I had a day off.*

A faded flag far below us clinked in the wind, the rings on the swings making a horrible rattling noise that would have been terrifying in the dark. But in the growing light of day, it gave me an idea. I turned to Septimus, wondering aloud: "You said it was a near-death experience that made you remember the girl?"

He lifted a single brow. "Are you threatening to throw me off this ride?"

I turned to look over the wide park, at the swings and twisting roller coasters, as a brilliant, terrible idea came together. "No. I've got a better idea—especially if we are alone in these ruins now. Come on."

"What if we aren't alone? What if this was all some convoluted trap?"

"It's not. But if it is, then we spring their trap and bring 'em to us. Besides I hate waiting. May as well enjoy the apocalypse while we still can."

~

Two hours later the two of us stood before a roller coaster, the cars rattling by, slowing in the stretch before zooming up and away. It turned out that the power was on for the entire park, and it had only taken a few guesses to get the biggest roller coaster back on.

"Why would someone ever ride this?" Septimus stared with wide eyes at the carts slowly rattling by.

"Fun."

"Fun?" He looked even more dubious. "Does it also slowly kill you like the cigar?"

"No." I laughed at the relieved look on his face. One of the cars slowed, and I caught the bar and jumped in the front. "This would kill you quick, not slow!"

"Wait! Isn't this a bad idea?" Septimus jogged alongside the cart, looking skeptically at the end of the runway where the cart climbed up at a sharp angle.

Adrenaline pulsed through my veins—it wasn't quite the high of riding a horse at breakneck speed. But it was pretty damn close.

"Terrible!" I laughed at his expression. "Remember my most important rule? No one survives the apocalypse, so you may as well enjoy it while you can. Time to start making new memories."

Just before the walkway ended he jumped into the cart.

"Put your seat belt on," I said as we climbed the steep hill. "And definitely don't tell Ara about this."

"What happens when we get to the top?" Septimus said, his voice full of awe and fear, his head whipping all around. The top grew closer and closer, higher and higher, but I looked only ahead.

"Hopefully you remember something," I said as we drew to the highest point, pausing as the track fell away in a terrifying vertical plunge. My breath caught as I whispered, "And hopefully this track holds."

For a moment there was only the cold wind, my beating heart, and white knuckles wrapped around the front bar.

Then the cart plunged forward.

I wasn't sure if I was laughing, screaming, or both. The wind ripped tears from my eyes, but I didn't try to fight it anymore—I couldn't. I screamed and let it all go. The pain, the fear, the regret, the sorrow, the grief. Sam, Issac, Red, Kia, my father and stepbrothers. Everyone I knew and loved. All of it.

Only when my voice broke did I realize Septimus was screaming and laughing beside me too. The ride threw us sideways and up and over, a madness and surrendering I couldn't remember since before the plague.

When the track was done, Septimus stared at me with wide eyes. For a moment I thought he might throw up—my apocalyptic stew this morning hadn't been for the faint of stomach. Instead, a wondrous look broke over his face. "Can we do that again?"

"Hell yeah."

So we did.

~

A few hours later, we sat on the outside of one of the carnival booths, eating another batch of my apocalypse stew and some canned apple pie so sweet it made my lips pucker. "So"—I licked juice off my fingers—"anything come back?"

He waited a long moment before responding. "I saw the girl again. She was angry at me."

"If you want my advice, if you ever meet her, apologize."

"Even if I don't know what I'm apologizing for?"

"Exactly." I threw the empty can at him and he ducked. "Also, refer back to rule number one: no one survives the apocalypse. That might apply to women too."

He laughed softly and shook his head. "I will remember that, should I ever meet her."

I paused, and then said, "The girl you remember, what's she like?"

"Angry, always." But this didn't seem to bother him: his voice was reverent, eyes staring into the distance as if he could picture her now. "But also beautiful. Blue eyes like ice. Long, dark hair. She's in trouble. Trapped. It's like she's . . . calling to me. Asking me to free her."

A cold chill crept down my back at his words. "You think she's in this underground place?"

"I'm not sure. But it's my best bet."

"And it's worth it for you to risk going back to find her?"

This time his eyes found mine. "Is it worth it for you? To find Ara?"

His answer was a deflection—intuition told me he wasn't telling me everything. First, he'd said he'd never met a woman, but now he was willing to risk his life—to the point of making me promise to shoot him if we were caught—all to save a woman he'd only ever seen in dreams? But I needed his help, so I just shrugged. "Point made." Then I stood up and stretched. "Come on, if we're gonna be up all night, we may as well nap."

As we walked back to the break room, I thought of all he'd said—I couldn't imagine what it would be like to forget yourself. It made me want to try to make it even a little bit better for him. I wanted him to see this ruined world—the rides rusted, the bright colors faded—for what it really was.

"You know, Septimus, it might not be the worst thing not to remember the world before all this." I waved a hand at the ruins of the park. "Sometimes when I see all this, it just makes me sad for the way things used to be. Issac wouldn't have agreed, but sometimes I wonder if God did all this to punish us. Like He wants us to see all we had and didn't appreciate."

"What if He wants us to appreciate everything that still remains?"

What still remains. I lost so much—my family, my home, and then, just when I'd made a new family, a new home, I lost Issac and Sam. But I still had Ara. I still had a heart beating in my chest.

Maybe that's what Issac's peace was. The peace that you found when there was none. The peace when you were riding a roller coaster and screaming at the whole world, crying at what it had done to you, and laughing at what was yet to come.

"You know what, Septimus, I think I'm gonna make that an apocalypse tip." He smiled at this, and then opened the door to the room. I paused on the threshold, glancing back at the park and the ruins—wondering if even in the decay, there was still beauty.

I'll keep looking, Issac. I promise you that.

For some reason, the thought made me smile.

TWENTY-FOUR—SAM

Screams tore through the night.

I jerked upright, searching for an enemy, thrown by the extravagant room, the wide glass windows with the moon over the water beyond. *Hotel. We're in the hotel downtown.* Beside me, M thrashed beneath the blankets, moaning and muttering words I couldn't make out. I reached over and grabbed her shoulder, shaking her.

"M! M! Wake up! It's just a nightmare."

Her eyes snapped open, but instead of jerking away, as she normally did, she seized my arm, her fingernails digging into my skin so hard it hurt. Even so, I didn't move.

"Sam?" Her voice was tender, terrified, her chest rising and falling like she'd just run a race. "They're running out of time." Her nails dug deeper into my arm.

"Who? Who's running out of time?"

"The people in the green water. They're calling to me. They're afraid."

The people in the green water. I'd heard her talking about them in her dreams, but I thought they were something left over from a horror movie. Or maybe some kind of metaphor. But the fear in her eyes was real, and I didn't dare suggest she'd imagined them.

"It's going to be okay. You're safe here."

Before I could ask more, M bolted from the bed and ran into the adjoining bathroom.

"M?" I called out. Retching sounds came from behind the closed door. *Maybe I'll just give her a second.* The moonlight leaked in through the floor-to-ceiling windows, lighting our packs and scattered supplies . . . and the gun M had left propped against the side table. For the first time ever, M had left her gun behind. Did that mean she trusted me? Or just that she'd forgotten it? *Probably the second.* More retching sounds came from the bathroom and I jumped out of bed, searching the cabinets until I found one of those little leftover plastic hotel cups. After I filled it with some of our filtered water, I knocked on the door.

"M? Can I come in? I have water."

She didn't respond, and I slowly opened the door. She sat with her back against the wall, next to the enormous clawed bathtub. I propped the door open, and then slid down the wall to sit beside M, leaving a generous space between us. With only the light of the moon cutting a thin streak against the tiled floor, her face was shadowed.

I set the cup in the space between us. "M . . . do the people in the green water have something to do with the testing center?" I almost couldn't believe I'd dared ask. Or, more shocking, that she responded.

"The people in the green water aren't at the testing center but I think I could contact them from there. If you could get the electricity on." Kaden had mentioned tubes of green water, but never someone inside the water.

"How do you know these people?"

She picked up the cup but didn't drink. "That's what I'm trying to figure out."

She's finally sharing. Don't let her stop. Show her you care. "I didn't see anyone there last time. But I also didn't go up to the top floor. Only Ara and Kaden did. He was sort of cagey about what happened up there. But I remember him telling me there was some sort of new tech powering that floor alone, and that he didn't want Gabriel to know about it. If there are computers up there, and the new tech still works, then it shouldn't be hard to connect it to the power source."

A thousand other questions burned in me—like what the hell were people in the green water and why did we need to find them—but instead, I said, "I'll do whatever I can to help you, M. But I might be more helpful if I knew more."

Silence grew between us, and I worried that I'd pushed too far, asked too much. But she didn't pull away from me. If anything, sitting there in the darkness, I felt closer to her than I ever had.

"I think the people in the green water are trapped inside The Lost City," M finally whispered. "I tried for a time to find the city but couldn't. There was another lab, like the one downtown, but hidden deep in the mountains, just off the river." The cup spun faster and faster in her hands. "After I recovered from the plague, the men who had me prisoner took me there. I'd been recovering for some time, and planning my escape, but I thought maybe the people in the green water would be there. So I let them take me." She stopped, and suddenly tilted the cup back, drained the water, and then crushed the cup. "But they weren't there. There was something else."

"What?"

Her voice came from far away. "A monster."

A monster . . . does she mean . . . ? A cold sweat broke out over my forehead.

She hugged her knees to her chest, her voice a whisper that somehow felt loud. "That thing we saw in the water earlier, they had it in some big tank. It was horrible. I don't know if they made it or found it, or if they were using it to try to find some sort of cure. But they were torturing it, so I set it free." She paused, and when she spoke again, her voice was flat. "And it was angry."

Holy shit. My heart beat faster: in terror, in awe, in shock that I'd finally learned where the monster had come from—and I was sitting a foot from the girl who'd unleashed it. "What happened next?"

"It killed all the men there." Her voice was blunt, without apology. "I barely got out. I came back after, but there was too much damage, I couldn't get anything to work. The monster was gone. I thought it had died, but it must have gotten to the river, and without the dams—"

"—it made its way down to the city," I filled in, leaning back against the wall and exhaling. Maybe I should have felt bad for the men the monster had killed, but I didn't. I felt only admiration for M. Here I'd spent years in a clan beneath a man I despised, doing nothing, and M had unleashed a literal monster to gain her freedom.

So how did it all connect? I struggled to understand. "The people in the green water, are they testing them for a cure too?"

"I don't think so. They're prisoners in The Lost City." She

paused, and this time I forced myself to stay quiet, and was rewarded when she spoke again. "They've always called to me. But it's gotten louder now."

"Called to you how?"

"In my dreams," she whispered. "When I was infected I started to hear them louder. I thought it would go away after my eyes cleared, but it didn't. They *want* me to go to the testing center. I think they wanted me to go to the other lab in the mountains too—but after the electronics were destroyed, I couldn't access anything." She shook her head, her hair a dark sheet hanging free around her. Even if I couldn't see the expression on her face, I could hear the devotion in her voice. "They need me. I have to free them."

I pulled my lighter free from my pocket, turning it over and over again as I thought over her words. I'd read sci-fi stories my whole life, loved them, even dreamed of someday writing one of my own. But being trapped *inside* one . . . well, I wasn't sure how I felt about that. Part of me wanted not to believe any of it. Except—I had *felt* the monster pull me under. I'd seen its bloated carcass floating in the water. If the monster was real, then the people in the green water could also be real.

Her voice brought me back—razor-sharp now. "You don't believe me. You think I'm insane."

"M. Look at me."

"It's too dark, stupid."

"Just do it."

She turned slowly, and when her face was turned to mine, I flicked my lighter to life. The tiny light burned between us. It lit her face in dancing shadows, cloaked her eyes in darkness, made her more beautiful than she had ever been. It took all my self-control not to lean forward and kiss her.

"I let you sleep in my bed, threaten to burn all my books"—she smiled and my heart turned over—"I crossed the city. I turned down returning to the clan. I was ready to face the monster that almost killed me last time. I helped you with just about the stupidest plan ever to steal two kayaks." Then, softer, "I killed a man. If you say there are people who need our help, then you don't have to tell me why or how or who. I'm with you."

The tiny fire burned between us. She stared at me, our eyes locked, my heart beating so hard in my chest I worried she would hear it.

Then the lighter flickered out. She turned away and somehow it felt like I'd missed a moment that would never return.

"Sam?" Her voice came soft through the darkness.

"Yes?"

"Thank you. I've been kind of . . . Well, you didn't deserve some of what I've said to you."

I laughed. "That is the worst apology I've ever heard."

"Yeah, well, apologies aren't really my thing."

I was about to respond when her fingers laced through mine and words left me. She moved to my side, the two of us shoulder to shoulder against the bathroom wall. *Did I say worst apology? I meant best.*

We sat there in perfect silence—a silence I didn't despise. There was a time over the summer that I had started talking to the mannequins, and I swore I saw one move out of the corner of my eye. I'd unloaded four arrows into it before I even knew what had happened. My quest to fix the music in the mall wasn't just to keep up my spirits, or even to bring back music to a fallen world: it was to fix the oppressive, mind-eating silence that had wormed its way into my skull.

M's head came to rest against my shoulder and for the first time since the plague, I wished the silence would never end.

When dawn came, we both got off the bathroom floor and packed up camp. Then we headed up to the top of the building. The wind whipped up the water into stiff white peaks, the buildings of downtown impressive even in their decay. Eventually we both agreed we'd been pulled too far east, and the testing center was farther back to the west.

It was only then, in the full light of day, that I finally said, "M, what happened the last time you went to this testing center?"

When she spoke, her eyes were trained on the water, her voice soft in a way it wasn't often. "My father brought me there. When the plague had just started. They took my blood—and then tried to turn it into some sort of cure. But it didn't work."

"Who is 'they'?"

"My father and another man he knew, some scientist." She shook her head. "I remember the testing center—it had all this weird green moss on the walls and I had the feeling I'd seen it before, even though I couldn't remember where. I can feel the people in the green water calling me back there." The wind blew dark tendrils of hair across her face, and she turned to me. "You think I'm crazy, right?"

"You've got to be a little crazy to set a sea monster free and live to tell the tale."

"Sea monster, hmm . . . That has a nice ring to it."

I laughed. "No thanks. I'm actually getting attached to Sasquatch."

Her face changed, her voice soft when she said, "Yeah. Me too." She smiled up at me, and my stomach lurched. Then her smile slipped away. She turned, setting her hands on the thin railing protecting us from a long drop to the water below. "You're lucky, you know. Your brother must have really loved you."

Silence fell between us. I could hear her unspoken words: that her father or sister hadn't loved her. I couldn't stand the sorrow on her face—or the idea that she might ever think she was unloved.

"You know," I said. "Parents make mistakes too. He might have messed up, but your father loved you."

A seagull cried out above us, wheeling through the sky. Her eyes tracked its movement, and when she spoke, her words were honest and blunt. "He didn't though."

"I'm sure that's not true."

"I don't really care about him . . . it was my sister I cared about."

Cared—as in you no longer do? I stepped closer to her, my hands joining hers on the railing. "What was she like—your sister?"

Her thin shoulders rose and fell. "She was different than me—in more ways than I can explain. Father tried to keep us apart, but it never really worked. We were inseparable. I thought nothing could ever change that." She stopped, her jaw suddenly set hard, her eyes dropping from the bird's movements and down to the dark water below. "Then one day we were out in the foothills, by an old ravine. A man came out of nowhere, grabbed my hand, and told me I had to go with him. I didn't want to, so I ran, and he chased me. I didn't mean to . . . it was an accident—"

She cut off, her eyes closed, her head bowed forward. Then she swallowed, and when her eyes opened again, her words were cold and measured. "He fell into the ravine. She was supposed to be my big sister—that's what Father always said—but when I showed her the body, if felt like I was years older than her. Centuries. I'll never forget the way she looked at me. Like she didn't know me. Like I was . . . broken."

"You aren't broken." I desperately wanted to comfort her, to reach forward and tuck the lone lock of hair blowing in the wind behind her ear. "And if you are, then we all are. We've all done things we'd rather forget to survive."

"Not you." She shook her head. "You're bloody *perfect*. Trying to save all those stupid books. Trying to get the new tech back on. Trying to find your brother." Her head bowed. "You only killed that man because of me."

Until now, I'd kept a careful bubble of space between us, but last night had changed everything—or maybe I had changed. So I stepped forward, reached out, and touched her chin, lifting her face until her eyes met mine. I captured the stray dark lock of hair in my fingers and tucked it behind her ear. She didn't pull away.

"My choices are mine to make. I chose to defend you." Then, the words I could no longer hold back. "I choose you, M." I stepped forward, closing the small gap between us, and pressed my lips to hers.

A soft gasp escaped her.

Then she kissed me back.

For a moment, the cold air, the swirling water, the whole fallen world disappeared. There were only her lips against mine, my fingers moving through her hair, holding her against me, her breath mixed with my own. We were no longer Sam and M, but something infinite and immeasurable.

It was a high I didn't have words for. A moment I wouldn't have traded even if it meant having the old world back.

She pulled away before I would have, her hands pressed against my chest, her breath coming as hard as my own. But there wasn't regret in her eyes—only happiness. She gave me a smile so wicked and beautiful I would have jumped off the roof in that moment had she asked.

"Come on, Sasquatch. We've got real work to do."

We made our way back down to the kayaks and launched them into the frigid water. The difference in today versus yesterday was small, yet I felt it in every glance, every movement, every smile. Yesterday we were two people forced to depend on each other—today we were something different. Something new.

I didn't care if we freed a thousand monsters or a thousand innocents, as long as we did it together.

TWENTY-FIVE—ARA

"Father . . . what are you doing here?" I reached through the bars as his thin arms wrapped around me. It felt like I was holding a ghost. He looked nothing like the full, vibrant man I remembered.

"Ara, you can't be here." His voice was raspy, no longer the musical voice I remembered. "You have to leave. Walter will find you."

Once I would have followed his words in an instant. Now I only stared at him, unmoving—a bitter image of how much had changed between us.

"Walter did this to you?" I said. "Why?"

Talia grabbed my hand, trying to pull me away. "Maybe we should listen to him."

"Ara, please," my father said. "If they find you—"

I ignored both of them, instead examining the lock on my father's cell—solid metal, but rusted—then turned to the rocks scattered on the floor of the tunnel. One of them had to be big enough. The green glow pushed in all around us, the tunnels seeming to tighten as Father again begged me to leave. I tuned him out, focusing instead on locating what I needed. Twenty feet down the tunnel I found a rock as big as my head. The cut on my hand burned as I struggled to carry it back to his cell.

"This is gonna be loud," I said to Talia. "Get ready to run like hell."

Father was instantly at the bars. "I forbid it. You need to leave."

"No," I said sharply. "We aren't doing that again. We're a family. I'm not leaving you." I wouldn't make the same mistake again, and desert another family member. Not when leaving Emma was the mistake that had begun all of this. I tried to lift the rock again when Talia stepped up and grabbed it instead.

"Honestly Ara, you don't have to do everything on your own."

My hand burned enough that I didn't try to take it back. She hefted the rock over her head and smashed it down on the lock with an ear-splitting crash. The lock twisted but didn't break. She did it again, not holding anything back. On the third time it broke.

Voices came down the hallway as I yanked the cell door open. There was no daughterly embrace, no words of fondness. Father stared down the corridor at the sound of fast approaching voices. His gaze was sharp, and for a moment I saw a flicker of the man he'd once been.

"Follow me," he said. "I know a place we can hide." He made his way down the stone corridor, limping as he went.

Talia came to stand beside me, the two of us watching him go. "Princess, don't take this the wrong way, but I'm starting to worry that crazy runs in your family."

"Wait till you meet my sister," I muttered, and then took her hand and pulled her after him.

~

Father led us turn after turn down the green-lit stone tunnels. Though he leaned heavily on his left leg, his breath coming in gasps, he didn't hesitate in the turns he made in the seemingly endless, convoluted tunnels. Soon the sounds of pursuit faded.

Then there was only the unending green glow, the catacomb-like tunnels, and the oppressive silence that came from being far beneath the earth.

My father stopped, breathing hard as he leaned against the stone wall. "You shouldn't have come here, Ara."

"Oh, I'm sorry. Were you not the one who sent me a letter specifically saying to come here?"

He stared at me in surprise—I'd never talked to my father like this. Yet the man standing in front of me seemed like a mere shadow of the man I once knew. His body was thinner, his hair streaked with gray, and the kind, caring smile I'd once known was gone. He looked exhausted, beaten.

I suddenly felt ashamed that I'd snapped at him. "I'm sorry. Talia and I have been through a lot to find you." I nodded to Talia, who hung back from my father and watched him with cautious eyes. "Please, Father. Tell me what's going on. Why did Walter lock you up down here? What happened between you two?"

He pushed off the wall, starting off again. I exchanged a look with Talia before we followed.

I thought he was trying to avoid the conversation, but before I could ask again he said, "I grew up here, in Thule. The city strove to be a place set apart. Producing everything on their own. Denying the culture and corruption of the outside world. But the older I got, the more I resented the restrictions. I found others who felt the same, and we began to use the tunnels to bring in alcohol and other outside diversions the Council forbade within the city."

"These tunnels?" I looked at the creepy tunnels with a newfound respect.

He took another turn—despite his limp, he seemed confident in our path. "Yes. We thought we were rebels—that we could change things."

"Guess it runs in the family," Talia muttered.

"That was when I began to see the truth about Walter," my father went on, ignoring Talia's comment.

"Which was?" I pressed.

His eyes met mine, sadness there. "That people who moved against him tended to disappear. That his ambitions had no end. Even my own mother wasn't safe from him: I doubted I would be for long either."

"You mean my grandmother, Arabella?"

He nearly stumbled. *Yes, Father, I've learned a lot while you've been gone. Even my name held a story you never told.*

"So why did he lock you up for coming back?" I said.

"I wasn't exactly the ideal son. I stole something precious from him when I left, and destroyed some of his research. He hasn't forgotten it." So the blind man was right after all: a powerful man had returned and was now hidden away. But I felt like these answers only created more questions. I'd always assumed my Father had a hard childhood, one he didn't like to talk about—but I never considered it might be something he was hiding from me. "So why did you send me here?"

"Because the mark of the black spiral was on our house—a mark I'd last seen in Thule. I truly did think Emma might be here." *Did. So he doesn't think she is here now?* I wanted to ask why not, but he continued on, his voice dark with anger now. "I had no idea Walter was still ruling. Actually I hoped he was dead."

The venom with which he spoke of wishing his own father dead shocked me—but he wasn't done. "I had no idea he would still be continuing his plans."

"Plans?" My voice crept higher. "Plans for what?"

"We're nearly there. Wait here." He started down a smaller tunnel that required him to bend nearly double.

"You sure about this, Princess?" Talia said, pulling me back as we watched my father make his way down the small tunnel. "I know he's your pops, but he looks like he's been in that cell a long time."

"He's my father. I trust him." My voice wasn't as confident as I would have liked.

"Yeah, well, see, the problem is I have a general rule about not trusting strangers. Or men. Or people who smile too much."

"Then trust me."

Talia gave me a skeptical look but I simply waited. Thirty feet down the increasingly narrow tunnel my father called out: "Almost got it!" His voice echoed strangely in the tight space.

"I'm just saying," Talia said, "I know someplace we can hide and—"

A metallic grinding noise cut her off. The two of us shifted away as the wall to my left trembled, dust rising in the small space. Just when I feared the tunnel was collapsing in on us, the wall began to recede straight into the floor, revealing a room beyond.

We both stared in shock as the false wall sank into the floor, the opening growing to reveal a room beyond lit with a golden glow. At first I hoped it was an opening to the world above, but I could see walls inside—and the telltale flickering of electricity.

"I've got a bad feeling about this," Talia whispered.

"Can't be any worse than the Sanctum."

Together Talia and I climbed through a narrow opening, the green glow receding as we came into an underground room. Flickering light bulbs hung from a ceiling a few feet higher than the tunnels, giving the room a cavernous feel. The room was shaped like a rough rectangle, with chairs and tables on one end, and on the other a massive wooden bar with barstools in front. Faded posters papered the walls. The thick layer of dust muted the details of the room, swallowing even the sound of our footsteps.

Father stepped inside after us, the rock door rising back into place and sealing us into the room with a resounding thud.

"Did you just bring us to an abandoned *bar*?" I didn't bother to hide my shock.

"We preferred 'underground club,'" Father said. "I thought it would be a safe place to regroup."

Talia's voice was full of awe. "Respect."

Father made his way across the room, stepping over flyers, beer cans, and bottles strewn across the floor. *I wonder how long it's been since anyone has been here.* Judging by the debris littered across the floor and tables, it looked like some sort of party had been abandoned halfway through.

"How exactly did you factor into this underground club, Mr. Ara's dad?" Talia said with cheeky innocence. To my ever-growing shock, Father laughed.

"Charles, please." He smiled at the place, as if he saw something more than a dusty, abandoned room. When he spoke, there was a sadness to his voice that I used to hear when he talked of things long gone. "For a time Thule tried to limit the sale of alcohol, and this place came into being. We thought we could change things."

"But instead you left?"

"I left to find a better future."

I tried to put what I knew of my father—an outdoorsman whom I'd never seen drink more than one beer—together with a man who had started an underground bar. I couldn't. Something still didn't make sense to me. "Why would some research you destroyed that long ago make Walter that mad now?"

"Because he didn't just want to build an independent city. He built it to be The *Last* City. The final settlement of humanity." He stepped over some discarded cans and bottles and made his way to the bar.

"Even Walter couldn't know a plague would destroy the world." I stepped up to one of the posters on the wall and ran a finger through the dust. A streak of bright color appeared.

"He did."

Some odd note in his voice made me turn from the wall and face my father. *Something is wrong here.* I knew it in that strange way you sometimes know a storm is coming before the clouds ever appear. The way he looked at me now, as if he was bracing himself, reminded me of a look I'd seen on his face just once before. In fifth grade when he'd sat me down at the kitchen table and told me a girl I knew from school had died in a car crash. It was a look I'd never forget. A look I'd hoped never to see again.

"What do you mean?" I said carefully. "How could he know that?" Some deep warning tightened in my gut, as if cautioning me not to ask. Not to seek. But I'd come too far for the truth to stop now.

"Because he created the plague and released it himself."

For a moment, time stopped. Talia, the room, and my father all faded. Only his words existed. Along with the crushing, horrible truth they carried.

Walter created the plague and released it himself.

Walter, who told me the plague was an opportunity. An opportunity he'd created himself.

I wanted to deny it. Maybe Walter had done horrible things, maybe he'd been cruel to my father, but it didn't seem possible that a single person could do so much evil. Let alone my own grandfather.

You wanted the truth, some dark voice whispered to me. *No one said it would set you free.*

"Why would he do that?" I finally managed to say. I wanted to beg my father to say it had been some kind of horrible accident. Because if it was true . . . then my *family* was responsible for this. My own flesh and blood had ended the world. It was too horrible to comprehend.

"He saw it as his way to save the world," Father said, his voice unwavering even though his eyes were filled with grief. "It was designed as a disease to target only women, to slow human reproduction, and to stop overpopulation."

I felt hollow inside. Like I wasn't really here. Like I was watching all this happen and would wake up in a moment. When Talia spoke I jumped—I'd forgotten she was even there. "How do you know that?"

Then the worst confession of all, delivered in a hoarse, unrecognizable voice: "Because I helped him."

No, that's not possible. My father couldn't have. Part of me wanted to cross the room, to stand by his side. The other part kept me rooted in place. I knew my father. He was kind, intelligent, strong. He could sing a songbird out of a tree. He had taught me to survive in a cruel world. I knew him and he wasn't a mass murderer.

Or maybe you never really knew him. Maybe you never wanted to see the truth.

He spoke quicker now. "When I realized what he intended to do—that it wasn't a disease to slow humanity's growth but to end it—I did everything I could to stop him. He was obsessed with purifying humanity: somehow restarting the world. All I heard growing up were the horrors of humanity. How we had destroyed the planet and each other—but I always just thought it was talk. Then I took over the research he was doing at the university. The world thought he was working on some new lifesaving cancer treatment, but I saw the first phase of his plan: a cure he intended to give only to people within The Last City, and the disease that would cripple the world. I couldn't destroy the disease, so I destroyed the cure, injecting the only remaining copy within myself, the genetic blueprint of which would remain forever inside me, as a final safeguard. I escaped, believing that Walter would no longer release the disease, or risk it killing everyone within The Last City, with no way to control it."

"But he released it regardless," Talia said softly. My eyes went to her, too numb to speak. Because all I could remember was the sight of corpses on the ground, the red Xs on doors, the great flocks of black birds the only noise over the silent city. Death my grandfather was responsible for.

"He did."

"Why?" I finally managed. "Why would he release it some twenty years later without any way to stop it? Without a cure?"

His eyes became shadowed. "I'm not sure . . . but my guess is they found the plague flower and thought a temporary immunity would keep them safe." He paused, then slower: "Or maybe he decided to finish his plan, no matter the cost."

No matter the cost. The cost being all of humanity. I stared at him, wondering how I'd once thought I knew this man better than anyone else in the world. The person who'd raised me, protected me, then taught me to survive, had not only kept secrets from me but concealed the truth of how the world had ended. It was a betrayal I didn't have words for.

I suddenly felt light-headed, a wave of dizziness passing over me. I gave in to it, sinking to the floor, and put my head to my knees.

My father's voice immediately rang out. "Ara, are you all right?"

"I just need a moment," I whispered from the floor. A moment to accept what my grandfather had done. And what my father hadn't. He'd tried to stop him. He'd tried but failed. Was that good enough when the whole world had paid the price?

"What about the antidote inside you?" I said, pushing past the swirling betrayal. I couldn't look at him as I said it. "Why didn't you use it?"

"I tried, Ara, but it didn't work. When I realized what happened I went to a testing center downtown, an outpost of The Last City that I'd never gone to before, because I didn't want Walter to find us. But the antidote from my blood didn't work." He hesitated, and then gently whispered, "It was only when I came here I realized why. The disease was made to target females first. The cure only works when passed on to my female blood descendants."

His words echoed inside me. *Blood descendants.* "That can't be right . . . because that would mean . . ."

"It would mean Emma isn't your blood sister—she was adopted as a baby." Once those words would have torn my world in half—but they were nothing compared to what came next. "You are the only one with the true cure inside you. I realized it far too late. You are the last she, Ara."

The last she. Invalid. The true cure.

I finally looked up at my father as it all finally, *finally* came together—so horrible and twisted, and yet so clear that I couldn't believe I hadn't seen it before. When Kaden first found me, we were chased by infected dogs in the abandoned mall, and one of those dogs had bit him. His eyes should have turned white and wept blood. But they hadn't.

Because I'd doctored his wounds with bleeding hands. Our blood had mingled.

My blood had been the cure all along.

The cure that could have saved the whole world, and instead saved no one.

"I could have saved Mother," I whispered, my voice breaking. "And Emma." Emma, who had always been so different from me and my father and mother. Emma, singular and beautiful and *adopted.* My eyes flashed up to my father's, a hatred both cold and hot all at the same time. "Why didn't we save them?"

"Ara—I tried everything I could." His voice was pleading now. "Putting the cure in my blood was a last resort—I never thought we'd actually need it, and I didn't realize I would pass it down into my offspring. But Walter is going to realize the same, if he hasn't already. You need to get as far away from here as fast as you can. Whatever he's planning, the plague was only the beginning." Father didn't notice the stillness that had overcome me. "There's still time. There's a way out of these tunnels. I can show you."

Leave. Run. Words I knew well. Hadn't my father always told me there was no such thing as friendly men in this world? He wanted to send me back to the forests and rivers and a life of always watching my back. Once I would have listened to him. I would have abandoned everyone and everything to save myself and him.

But I wasn't that girl anymore. I was no longer the girl who'd followed her father through the mountains. If I really had the cure inside me, I wouldn't desert the world. Not again. It didn't matter if Emma was adopted—she was still my sister.

"No." I shook my head. "I won't run, not this time. We shouldn't have left Emma. We should have stayed with her—even if we died too."

"She's gone, Ara."

His words hurt more than if he'd stepped across the room and slapped me. *Only granddaughter. Gone.* It didn't matter what these old men said. It didn't matter if they didn't claim Emma—I claimed her.

It felt like a different girl, one harder and older, who picked herself up from the floor and faced the man before her. "Did you ever think she was here, or was that a lie too?"

I could see the hurt in his eyes, the way his shoulders caved forward and he seemed almost afraid of me. Frail. That was what he'd become. His voice was soft when he spoke. "The mark of the black spiral was on our door when I returned. There was no corpse."

"So you lied?"

"I didn't lie, but I recognized the mark, and I thought Walter would be dead. I tried to warn you it would be dangerous and—"

"Stop!" I cut him off and his eyes opened in shock. It seemed impossible that the father I knew could also be the man who had helped Walter create a plague that had ended the world. The revelation that he had injected a cure inside himself—a cure that he'd passed on to me—should have been pounding through me in shock. Instead, all I could think about was Emma and his ultimate betrayal.

"You should have told me—about all of it." I shook my head, staring at him while cold anger pumped through my whole body. "I feel like I don't even know you."

He nodded, his gaze falling away from me. "I'm sorry . . . this was never what I wanted."

Yeah, well, join the club.

Glass crunched beneath my feet as I stepped deeper into the wide, quiet room—wanting to look anywhere but at my father. I felt his and Talia's gaze, and the uncomfortable weight that came with it. The fact that the cure was inside me—it was a responsibility I hadn't asked for.

Silence stretched out between the three of us, the soft hum of the lights above the only noise. Part of me wanted to run to my father, to throw my arms around him and tell him I forgave him. That whatever secrets he'd kept, I knew that he only wanted to protect me.

Another part of me wanted to walk back into the tunnels and leave him here forever.

It felt like a war raged in my chest between the girl I once was and the woman I was now. The girl with the cure, and the person who'd abandoned the world.

Finally Talia cleared her throat. "Any chance there's any alcohol left in this place? I could use a drink." She came to my side and slung an arm around my shoulders. "We both could."

Father gave me a last regretful look before he ducked behind the bar. The sound of opening cabinets and shuffling bottles rose. Then he emerged holding a dusty bottle of deep-amber-colored liquid.

Before I could stop her, Talia made her way across to the bar, righted one of the fallen barstools, and sat down.

"Pour me a drink, pops," she said with a wink. He gave her a look that most would have withered beneath, but she grinned wider. "Sorry, *Charles*."

To my vast surprise, he actually did. Then he fished out two more glasses, sitting the third one farther down the bar—a drink for me. His smile was sad as he looked at me. "Guess you're old enough to drink now. Pretty sure it's whiskey."

Talia lifted her glass. "Only one way to find out." She threw the drink back.

Betrayal still swirled in my chest, but I crossed the room and took a seat beside Talia. The scent of wood rot and dust overpowered the room, but the sweet, burning scent of the whiskey was oddly tempting. I picked up the glass but didn't drink—not yet. The last she. The cure inside me. It should have been all-consuming—but I could only think of Emma. Had she known? She was always so different from me. It didn't change my love for her in the slightest to know she was adopted, and yet I wondered if it had changed my father's. We had left her, and maybe now I knew the horrible reason why.

"What now?" I said, trying to banish Emma and my final image of her: her once ice-blue eyes now white and weeping blood.

"We're safe here." Father lifted his glass and took a drink, sipping it instead of downing it like Talia. "If Walter had ever found this place, he would have destroyed it. This is where we kept all our supplies for sneaking in and out of the city. And this was the headquarters of . . . well, the people who were against Walter and the Council back then."

"The resistance." Talia's eyes gleamed as she turned to me. "Like father, like daughter." I ignored her, not in the mood for her teasing.

Father disappeared behind the bar again, and I wondered if maybe he was searching for more alcohol—*wow, never thought I'd be the stiff between me and my father*—when suddenly a rattling noise of grinding gears came from below.

Talia and I both hopped off our stools and came around the bar. In the space between the bar and the wall, a sort of trapdoor had opened, grinding and clunking, a cloud of dust rising when it finally stopped. A set of stairs descended nearly straight down into a deep, black hole.

"I'm gonna need another drink," Talia said.

TWENTY-SIX—SAM

"There it is," I said, as we rounded the corner. A metallic gray building loomed into view, BIRMINGHAM MEDICAL TESTING CENTER written in black lettering across the front. A shiver ran down my spine as we drew closer. The building, The Lost City, the monster, the people in the green water—it was all connected. The thought that we might be about to figure out how was terrifying. Or it would have been terrifying, if the memory of M's lips against mine wasn't playing on a constant loop in my head.

"That's the opening we entered last time." I pointed with my paddle when we came closer.

"I see it."

M made for the opening before I could even suggest scouting the location first. The hole had widened, the entire window now gone, water moving in and out in a swirling flow. *I wonder how long these buildings will hold with the water.* M disappeared into the foreboding opening. With a deep, steadying breath I followed her into the dim interior. *Too late to wonder now.*

It had been almost a year, but sliding into the room—a dark, dingy cave with a faint tiled floor below—a wave of dread washed over me. Suddenly the memory of the kiss wasn't quite enough to squash the other emotions rising in my chest.

"The stairwell is through that way." I pointed to the door on the far side of the room. Then, after a moment of hesitation, I jumped out of the kayak, gasping as the cold water reached up to my waist. *You are not afraid.* M made to follow, but I waved her back.

"You may as well stay dry," I said. My entire body trembled, whether it was from the cold water and fear I couldn't say. "I'll drag my kayak through, then come back for you. Stay here, okay?"

Moving through the dark interior, the water casting eerie shadows, I was thankful we'd waited for full daylight to approach. The stairwell felt smaller when I pulled my kayak up and then waded back.

M gave me a grim smile when I returned to the room. I took hold of the front of her kayak, and then dragged it down the hallway and into the stairwell. When I'd pulled it into the landing, she jumped out before I could help her. I stood there, my body shaking and covered in goose bumps as water streamed down my legs. It took a conscious effort to keep my teeth from chattering.

She stared at me, looking all the way down my body to my toes, and then back up, something odd in her expression when she said, "You okay?"

"Water's cold." I paused. "You mind if I change before we go up?"

"As long as you're fast."

I'd already reached into my bag and dragged out a pair of jeans. M had wrapped her shotgun in some of her clothes to keep it dry, and she pulled it out of her kayak now. I was halfway out of my pants when she turned back and I desperately tried to cover up and still look cool. Even though my boxers were soaked, I suddenly decided they would have to stay that way.

"Can you hurry up, Sasquatch?" She cocked a single brow at me, smiling as she turned her back again.

I nearly fell, trying to force wet legs into dry jeans. "Trying . . . one sec . . . okay done."

She didn't even look back, starting up the stairwell. I stumbled after her, shoving my feet back into my shoes as I went.

We climbed floor after floor, but she didn't look at any of the doors. "Shouldn't we check the other levels?" I called out.

"No. Nothing matters but the top floor."

The closer we got to the top, the faster she climbed.

Finally, we stood before the final floor. My breath came in heavy gasps after climbing the stairway, but M barely seemed winded. Instead she stared at the door, frozen before the strange, silvery material, just like the airships.

It was some sort of new tech, impossible to break down, except unlike last time, the door was already cracked open. I snuck a glance at M—something tense, almost wild burned in her eyes.

"Guess they didn't shut it when they left. Should we—"

M strode forward, ignoring me as she pushed open the door.

"—make some kind of plan?" I finished darkly, then followed her inside.

The room had no windows, yet was lit enough to see clearly. A glowing green moss grew over the walls, making branching, treelike shapes. It was some sort of lab, with long counters and equipment I couldn't guess a purpose for. The walls were the same silvery metal as the door, and there, across the room, were several glass tubes of green water. They stood floor to ceiling, the water swishing and bubbling inside, still powered by some kind of new tech. But there definitely weren't any people trapped inside.

I glanced sideways at M's stony face, trying to read her reaction to the room. Finally, I had to break the silence. "Is this how it looked last time?"

"Mostly . . . that wasn't there though." She pointed to a strange green lump on the floor that I hadn't noticed until now. Together we moved deeper into the room, until we stood beside it. At first I'd thought it was a lump of discarded carpet or clothing, but now I saw that it was the exact outline of a man.

M crouched beside the moss, looking down with hard eyes. "Guess we know what happened to the scientist."

I froze, cold fear inching up my back as I understood what she meant. "You think that's a *body*?" My voice squeaked on the word. Considering I'd killed a man, maybe a corpse shouldn't have scared me—but it did. The way the moss had taken over the corpse, covering every inch of it, felt wrong.

She nodded, and I recognized that faraway, accessing look in her eyes, as she walked in a circle around the body. A crowbar lay a few feet away from it, but I looked away from it as quickly as I could, not wanting to know if there was blood on the end.

"Well, should we get to work?" M walked past the body, as if dismissing it.

"Sure thing," I said, relieved to leave the body where it lay.

I spent the rest of the day following cords, and trying to figure out a system I knew very little about. But as it turned out, my summer spent repairing the mall sound system came in handy, because only a few hours in, one of the computer screens flared to life. I paused, thinking of calling out to M, who was searching the other room—and then decided not to. I worked best without someone breathing over my neck. Better to figure out what I was doing first, and then show her when I'd found something.

Password flashed across the screen, five blank spaces, and I paused for a moment, trying a few different combos before I finally stopped and forced myself to think. What did I actually know about this room? Very little . . . except for Ara. She was the only one to get in here. Ara was too short, Arabella too long. *Not her last name though.* I typed : *E D A N A*, expecting nothing.

Instead, the password screen disappeared.

Holy shit. I did it. I'm in.

My heart raced with victory, but I resisted the temptation to call out to M. Instead, I slowly moved through the files, one by one. There were tests I didn't understand and long lab documents with numbers that I couldn't make sense of. But one thing seemed clear: they had been testing for a cure. There were dozens of test subjects, with descriptions of their age, race, gender, ranging the board. There was only one commonality between all of their files. At the very bottom, written in bold capital letters: *Patient Unresponsive, Cure not found, Will continue testing,* with a date of death listed after. From what I could see, all of them had died. The testing stopped around a year ago. *Right when we were here.* I thought back to the body in the other room, and then dismissed it. *No. No way.* Kaden would have told me if they had *killed* someone here.

Right?

Most of the files had been accessed multiple times, but I searched until I found something that had never been opened. I clicked on it and was surprised when it brought up a video of an older man in a white lab coat. It began to play before I could think to call for M.

"Hello, Dr. Collins. This is the third week you've failed to check in. Please report back at your earliest convenience. We look forward to hearing from you." The video cut, but my heart didn't stop its skittering beat. *Dr. Collins—was that the dead man on the floor? What happened to him?*

At the beginning of the summer, I thought a single song was the greatest goal I could achieve. And now I'd just watched an entire video. A video that was most likely about the dead man decomposing in the other room, but still. The colors and textures of the screen were wondrous, a window back to my past, both bizarre and yet familiar, like riding a bike again after years away.

Whoever had sent this video was clearly expecting a reply. All I could think was that the scientist here had been testing for a cure, and checking in with some other lab. *Imagine being able to talk to someone on the other side of the world.* And then my breath caught in my chest. The dead man had been sending and receiving video from some other place: which meant there were other places in the world that still had new tech power.

There's still new tech out there. Maybe it is possible to get it all back on.

My heart beat faster, my fingers trembling over the keyboard at the thought of others out there, people who had access to new tech, who could help turn it back on. *Maybe Kaden would come back.* I clicked on the camera, and immediately froze at the sight of my face on the screen. I barely recognized the person before me. My cheeks and face were sharper than I remembered. I looked older. My face had changed—and I didn't hate it. But we had all changed, hadn't we? I pushed Record before I could wimp out or M could come in and stop me.

"Hello," I began slowly, trying to sound assured and confident. "My name is Sam Preston coming to you from downtown Boise. Whoever you are, wherever you are, I want you to know that there's infrastructure for new tech in Boise. If you are a part of this lab, or know something about the new tech, you should come here and help me turn it back on.

"We also have clans here—stability and food and shelter. If you're out there and need a home, you can come down to Boise. The Castellano clan is set up in the Old Penitentiary, and I've heard they're taking new members." M moved into the background behind me, but I didn't stop.

"Kaden, or Ara, if you're out there . . ." I paused, my throat thickening with all the goodbyes I'd never get to say. I swallowed, and put on a brave smile, like Kaden would have. "I'm doing okay. Wherever you guys are, I hope you are okay too. I'll be here, in Boise. Making our apocalypse stew and reading all the books Issac left behind."

At Issac's name, I reached forward and stopped the recording, forcing back tears. *Get a hold of yourself.* Before I could second-guess myself, I sent the message out. I didn't really believe Kaden or Ara would ever see it, but if just one other lost soul watched it, and it gave them hope, that was good enough for me.

"The computer works?"

I jumped at M's voice behind me, blinking furiously to rid my eyes of tears as I spun in the chair. "Yeah." *I also sent out a message to the world, hope that's okay.*

"What are you doing?"

I pointed to the message I'd recorded, trying to find some sort of not-asking-permission but also wasn't-that-a-cool-idea middle ground. "There's some kind of signal going out from this lab.

So I made a message to broadcast. Maybe someone who knows about new tech will be able to come here and help us."

"Are you serious?" she snapped. "We just spent all that time zigzagging through the city, and now you're advertising our location to the world?"

"I didn't tell people where we're at *specifically*," I said, defensive now. "Just that we had new tech infrastructure here. And you would have to have new tech to intercept the message. Not just anyone could find it."

"And that makes it better?"

Yeah, it kind of does. I turned from the computer and took a deep breath, determined to make her understand. "M, think about what this could mean. If he was sending messages to someplace else, they *also* have new tech. This isn't just some freak, leftover accident. Maybe it's possible to turn the new tech back on in Boise." I didn't dare say more: that maybe it was possible to turn the whole city back on. To turn the world back on. That maybe everything we'd lost didn't have to stay that way.

M read the truth of my face regardless. "The world is lost, Sam. There's no use trying to bring it back."

The way she said it, like I was some naive child, hurt. Once I would have retreated and let her have it her way. But I'd killed a man. I'd faced the monster that had tried to kill me. I'd kissed M and she had kissed me back—she wasn't as immune to everything as she pretended. "I'm not deleting the message." Her eyes flashed, but I cut her off before she could speak again. "It's not just about the new tech: Liam said everyone thinks I'm dead. If my brother is out there and he sees this, or hears about it from someone else, then he'll come back. It's worth the risk."

"Worth the risk for *you*."

"Yeah, for me. I get a say in all this too."

She shook her head, like I was some sort of lost cause. But for once, she didn't fight me. "Fine. Let's get back to work."

She came to stand behind me, leaning over my shoulder. Together we combed through different files, me trying not to lean into her scent. There were years of data to wade through, mountains and mountains of code I didn't understand, notes that made no sense to me, and much I couldn't access. But what I could access was sobering: hundreds and hundreds of human test subjects marked *deceased*. Then she pointed at a sort of video feed I hadn't seen before. "There. Bring that up."

I clicked it. Suddenly, a live camera feed came up on the screen. M's fingers dug into my shoulder but I barely felt it. My heart pounded in my ears, my throat suddenly dry, feeling like I'd suddenly plunged through ice into cold water. Somehow I hadn't truly believed . . . or imagined . . .

On the video screen was a young woman suspended in a glass tube of green water.

M was right.

The people in the green water were real—and we were watching one of them through some sort of live video feed.

"Can we tell where this video originates?" M whispered. I shook my head; a strange creeping horror built in my chest as I stared at the woman on the screen. Green water swirled all around her, a breathing apparatus lodged in her mouth.

"It's from whatever lab was connected to this one. I can't tell where." The more I stared at the young women in the green water, the more the horror grew. Her chest rose and fell, her fingers and closed eyelids twitching slightly, like she was trapped in a dream. But none of that was where the horror came from.

The more I stared, the more I realized I knew that face, those eyes, those lips, the petite features, the small, lithe body.

"M . . . is that *you*?" She didn't answer me. But the moment I said it, I knew. I knew in some horrible, awful way that made the hair on the back of my neck stand on end, made me wish I could take the words back. *There has to be some kind of explanation.* "Do you have an identical twin?" I whispered.

"No."

Suddenly the woman's eyes snapped open, and M and I both jerked back. The woman in the green water put a hand on the glass, and somehow, though I wanted it to be impossible, she looked at us.

"She wants out," M whispered. "We have to help her."

A horrible, churning sensation roiled in my gut. *This is all a bad dream. You're still asleep at the hotel and are going to wake up soon.* But M's hand dug into my shoulder; the pain there was real. "Who is she?" I finally managed.

"*It doesn't matter!* She's trapped! We have to help her! Please, Sam, help her." Her voice was so full of desperation that I tore my eyes away from the woman in the green water and focused on the program within which the video was contained. Adrenaline pounded inside me. As long as I didn't look at the woman in the green water, and didn't think about the fact that she was a carbon copy of the person standing beside me, I could focus on trying to understand what it would take to do what M asked. *Just don't think about it. Focus on the mechanics, not the outcome. It's just like playing another song in the mall.* Except the song was a person whose existence didn't seem possible.

Finally, I shook my head. "There's a fail-safe built in, but I'm not sure what it'll do. It could drain the tube, but it might also cut the tube to oxygen she's getting—"

"Do it." M's voice brooked no argument.

"M, we don't even know what she is, what this is—"

"Do it, Sasquatch."

"Not until you tell me what's happening!" I said, surprised at the steel in my voice.

Her eyes turned to mine, and there were actual tears there. She looked nothing like the terrifying, fierce M I'd come to know—she looked lost. "She's the one who has been calling to me. She needs me. Please, Sam." Her voice broke on my name—and so did my resolve.

Issac, if you're watching, please let this be the right thing to do. Then I pushed the button. The woman in the glass tube began to thrash.

"What's happening to her?" M shouted, the panic in her voice matching the panic coursing through my veins. *I killed someone else. She's dying.* "What's happening?!" M screamed. "Undo it!"

"I can't," I said, furiously trying to do just that.

The woman thrashed, the water full of bubbles making it difficult to make out her form. *She's drowning. She's dying. I killed her. I pushed some kind of kill switch.* Then, just when I thought it was over, that I was now a murderer of two souls, the green water began to drain out of the giant glass tube.

"What's happening?" M demanded again. The water level continued to sink lower and lower. I could say nothing—relief swept through my whole body, my limbs heavy and limp. The woman—the other M—swam to the top of the tank. She struggled against the respirator in her mouth, trying to pull it free.

"She can't breathe!" M moaned. "Do something!"

Before I could repeat that there was nothing I could do, the breathing apparatus came out and the woman coughed and choked.

"She's breathing!" M said, both of us unable to look away from the screen for even a moment. The water sank lower, and lower, until the woman stood on unsteady feet. We watched as the water level sank to her knees, and then calves, and then was gone, leaving her standing in the tank.

"Can she get out?" I whispered, when she suddenly surged forward. M and I both flinched back as her fists connected with the glass. Then she kicked at the same spot. She went on, rotating from leg to fist from leg to fist.

"It's glass—she can't break it—she'll break her hand," I said.

"Look."

With the next thud, a spiderweb-like crack appeared in the glass. Another hit and cracks ran down the shell. And then her fist was free—blood flowing with it. She didn't stop, kicking the hole wider and wider, until she stepped free, her chest heaving and falling.

She did it. We did it?

Holy shit.

She stared up at the camera. Instead of gratitude, her eyes were full of hatred. M and I both leaned forward, charged silence as we waited. *Would she try to communicate with us?* She stepped forward, reaching up—

—and the screen went black.

TWENTY-SEVEN—KADEN

"This has got to be the dumbest thing I've ever done," I muttered, the roar of the water below drowning out my words. "Which is saying something."

Septimus and I crept down the thin ledge that jutted over the river—so narrow that in parts my whole foot didn't even fit. Most of the river ran alongside the western edge of the city, but there was a section of it that had been diverted to run through the city. Thirty feet to my right, the water shot out of a tunnel set into a concrete portion of the wall. The section of the wall above the guards was patrolled only once every hour, because it was assumed that no one would be insane enough to scale the cliff and enter the city through the tunnel.

They assumed wrong.

My fingers searched for purchase on the cold, slippery wall as we moved across the ledge. It had been only a couple of days since I'd asked Ara to marry me and already someone had tried to kill me, I'd ridden a rusty roller coaster, climbed a Ferris wheel, and now climbed the side of a cliff to get back into a city where I was a wanted man. *If I reframe this as the world's most dangerous, epic bachelor party, I'd say it's a success.*

A rock moved beneath my foot, and I froze. For one heart-rending moment I thought the whole ledge would give way and send us plunging into the icy river below—if we didn't hit one of the sharp boulders first. The ledge held. I kept moving.

Just don't look down. Epic postapocalyptic bachelor party. That's all this is. The sun had set a few hours earlier—the only light coming from the lights on top of the wall. We were lucky that the nearest lights weren't directly above us, and that the mist churned up from the river covered us further. *Right, lucky, that's what this is.*

"How did you find this place?" I said to Septimus. The tunnel opening was still another thirty feet off, the roar of the water nearly overwhelming now.

"This ledge runs straight from my escape tunnel." Septimus paused, waiting for me to draw closer before he continued. "I think other people use it to get in and out of the city. But they were following me and—" He glanced down at the water and I suddenly understood what had happened last time he was here.

"You found this ledge when you FELL OFF IT?"

"You said I need to make new memories." He kept moving down the ledge.

"How about I push your ass in," I muttered. "That'll be a good memory." At this point it would be harder to go back, and even the act of turning my head—currently pressed as tightly against the rock face as my body—terrified me. *I bet Talia had an easier way to sneak in and out. One that didn't result in near-death experiences.*

Step by step we moved closer, until finally I could see the gaping mouth of the tunnel. Septimus disappeared inside, swallowed by the darkness. I reached for the slick ledge and pulled myself around the corner and into the tunnel—relief washing over me as I stood on solid ground. The tunnel opened around us, larger than I'd expected, with a blessedly large walkway beside the roaring river. It took everything in me not to kiss the floor beneath me.

Septimus started down the tunnel. "Come." His voice sounded ghostly in the rumbling of the tunnel. "We're burning the moonlight."

"Daylight," I muttered as I cast a final look back at the night sky. "We're burning *daylight*." So far my attempts to teach Septimus slang had failed. Half the time he sounded like a robot, and the other half like some strangely formal person from the past. Wherever the hell he was from, it was no place I'd ever been.

As we walked, the river churned so fast and swift it almost seemed to boil, a misty spray coating the walls and my clothes. Looking down at the roaring flow, it seemed almost malicious. It made me wonder how Septimus had survived not only falling in but making it all the way back to the theme park. *He's one lucky bastard.* I guess I was too, considering he found me. I reached down to touch the cold steel of the Captain's gun at my hip, a reminder of the promise I'd made to Septimus and how much we needed luck tonight. *It won't come to that. Epic bachelor parties don't end in death.*

Once we were past the opening, what little light came from the city and moon disappeared. The roar of the river became all-consuming. At first I worried how we would see—neither of us had a torch or flashlight. But the farther we walked, the more a strange, greenish glow began to fill the tunnel. It wasn't the warm, golden glow of electricity, but an eerie glow that seemed to come from everywhere at once.

The tunnel twisted, blocking the last of the outside light, and only then did I realize the glow came from the moss that grew along the tunnel walls. *The same moss we'd seen in the testing center in Boise. The same moss Ara had seen in the graveyard behind the hospital. Great.* The farther we walked, the stronger the glow became, until the tunnels held an eerie, otherworldly feel.

"This place is even creepier than the amusement park," I muttered as we walked.

"What was creepy about the park?" Septimus said, his voice so innocent I had to roll my eyes.

"Trust me, if you'd ever seen a clown, you'd agree."

We came to a fork. A smaller tunnel split off from the river tunnel, twisting away from us. The green glow continued down both tunnels, but on the small tunnel a mound of rocks on the floor shone brighter than the walls. Septimus stopped, staring at the pile of rocks that glowed bright.

"Don't tell me you're lost?" I drew even with him, then froze at the look on his face. He looked horrified. Or maybe terrified. "Septimus?" I whispered.

"That's one of the men I killed," he whispered. The hair on my neck stood on end as I suddenly realized what I hadn't before. The mass of what I'd thought was moss covering rocks was actually the outline of a man's body. He was lying on his side, one arm awkwardly out in front of him—an arm we were going to have to step over if we wanted to continue down the corridor. *It doesn't even smell—shouldn't a decomposing body smell?*

"Is that the way forward?" I swallowed fear and pointed beyond the body. Maybe it was the eerie glow of the tunnels, or the dead man lying on the ground, but something felt wrong here. Like being buried alive.

Septimus nodded, and I forced myself to look beyond the body. "Then we keep moving. He's dead. He can't hurt us."

Right, keep telling yourself that. I hugged the edge of the tunnel, and then stepped over the outstretched hand, keeping my eyes on the body the whole time. Septimus didn't follow. He just stared down at the body, unmoving.

"Septimus," I called out, and finally his eyes came up to mine. *I've killed men too. I know what it's like to have blood on your hands.* "Come on."

He moved around the body. When he'd passed I patted him on the shoulder. "It's gonna be okay. We'll find a different way back. Talia will know a better way." It might have been a lie, but I didn't care. He needed to hear some reassurance beyond the eerie, echoing rumble of the river.

We continued down the twisting tunnels, more offshoots and branches leading into the darkness. It was only after the tenth turn I realized how lost I was. I'd been watching Septimus, worried about his sudden silence, instead of marking the way. I would never be able to make it out of here without him. *It'll be fine. Talia will have another way out.* Still, I didn't like the thought of having to rely on others for a way out of this city. It went against every instinct of an expedition leader.

"Here."

Septimus's voice brought me to a sudden stop. A silver metal door lay before us, blocking the tunnel. Once again, the feeling of going back in time rose in me.

It was the exact same door I'd seen in the testing center in Boise. The door where it had all begun.

"How do we open it?" I said, a strange feeling of déjà vu rising in me. But I'd never asked Ara how she'd gotten through the door at the testing center, and she'd never told me. Maybe the feeling came from dread. Because last time I'd gone through a door like this I'd killed a man.

"One of the men I killed had a sort of lanyard on him." He stopped and took a deep breath, closing his eyes when he added, "There was a mark of fresh blood on it. That's how it opened."

"So we just need some blood?" I said, my mind spinning. Was that how Ara had opened the door?

"No," he whispered, and then he finally turned to me. "Invalid blood."

Shock coursed through my body. The cold of the tunnels, the eeriness of it all, faded as I stared at Septimus. I suddenly realized I'd never taught Septimus the most important apocalypse survival tip that I'd apparently forgotten myself: trust no one.

"How do you know that?" I didn't want to believe it, but the wary, guilty way he looked at me told me the truth. Septimus knew more than he was letting on. "How do you know I tested as Invalid?"

"That night the Captain and you stood watch, I snuck up on the other men's camp. I heard them talking about a man with Invalid blood—whom the Captain was going to kill. They said that your blood was too dangerous to have around. I figured that meant you could open this door."

I wasn't even sure why his words surprised me: no man was truly innocent in this world. Maybe I was just surprised I hadn't seen it. "This whole time you knew I was the only one who could get you through here?" But no, that wasn't right. There was one more person with Invalid blood: Ara.

"I knew." His shoulders slumped forward, his voice heavy. "But I never imagined you would become my friend . . . or that you'd be mad enough to want to come back here."

Yeah, well, that makes two of us. I wasn't exactly sure if I should be angry at him—after all, if this door brought me back to Ara then we'd both get what we wanted—but learning about it here, in the eleventh hour, felt like its own deception.

Too late now. I turned back to the door. "So I just . . . cut my hand?"

"Yes."

I drew the small knife I kept in my boot. *He's not Sam. He might not even be your friend—he just needed your blood.* Only now, buried deep beneath the earth with no way back, did I realize how little I knew about Septimus. How easy it would have been to pretend to be a certain person for a few days. How saving someone's life would instantly gain their trust.

My heart sped up, my throat dry as I looked down at the knife, its edge gleaming with a wicked sharp smile. I pressed the knife point into my finger, drawing blood, and then smeared the blood across.

The metal shimmered with the blood. I thought that would be it, but then the blood suddenly soaked into the metal, disappearing entirely. Septimus stepped forward and pushed.

The door swung wide, a bright green glow coming from inside. *No way but forward.* I followed Septimus into a sort of underground cavern, wide and deep . . . and suddenly all thoughts of Septimus's betrayal disappeared.

Stretching out into the cavern, as far as I could see, were massive glass columns filled with green water, suspended between the floor and ceiling. A low, soft gurgling noise filled the room.

But it was what lay inside the glass columns that robbed all breath from my body and rooted me to the spot.

Bodies.

Full-grown human *bodies* were suspended in the green water.

In the column next to us a male floated, his body curled forward. Some sort of breathing apparatus protruded from his mouth, and another cord attached to his stomach. *Like an umbilical cord.* His eyes were closed, yet his chest rose and fell in a steady rhythm.

They're alive. Ara had insisted Walter had secrets, but never had I dreamed it would be something as dark and twisted as this. *Bloody hell, what is this place?*

"Septimus—wait!"

He'd already strode forward, deeper into the room of glass columns. Filled with bodies. A whole army of them. Every instinct from my years as an expedition leader screamed to get the hell out of this place. But if I went back through the door we'd just come through, I would have to find my way out of the tunnels alone, with no clear path into the city to find Ara.

You should have marked the way, you idiot. What kind of expedition leader doesn't have an escape plan?

Lacking another plan, I drew my gun and followed Septimus deeper into the room. As I walked I stared at the bodies in the tanks, floating silently, horribly. Why would someone have tanks full of hundreds of bodies down here? Was this some kind of army Walter was assembling? But for what purpose—the world had already fallen. Was he using them to try to produce a cure? Why would he need them in these tanks? Were they people who'd died of the plague and he'd stored them down here like specimens in jars? But no, their chests rose and fell. They were alive.

The soft sounds of the rushing water filled the vast cavern. I didn't want to look any closer at the people in the water, but I couldn't help it: they were male and female, all of them young, maybe only teenagers or young adults. I stopped in front of one with dark hair swirling in the water, who looked just like another across the way from her. And there was a male who looked like another . . .

Some of them look exactly like one another. Horror coursed through me at the realization. Was Walter producing clones? Was this some sort of body farm? I tore my eyes away and to the ground, refusing to look at any of them closer. *It's only the green water, and the respirators. That's why some of them look alike.*

Sam was always the one who loved the sci-fi stories about aliens and robots and plagues—he was the one who should have been down here. He and Ara were the ones who quested for truth, not me.

They aren't here though. Septimus is. He might have concealed the truth, but I still needed him to show me to the surface. Maybe the real question was, did he still need me?

Between two of the massive water-filled columns, Septimus stopped and bent over. He touched something on the ground, then lifted his hand. Even in the green-lit room, I saw the bright mark of crimson.

Blood.

There was blood on the ground.

I cast a last look at the door back to the tunnels before I made my way over to Septimus's side. "Septimus," I whispered. "Let's get out of here."

"The men you were with, they called you a tracker." Septimus crouched next to the blood, rubbing it between his fingers, before his eyes came up to mine. "Help me find where the blood came from. Then I'll show you the way to the surface."

He's not Sam. He's not your friend—he's been playing you. But then his voice softened. "Please, Kaden. Help me."

Surrounded by the floating bodies, it felt like the worst imaginings of Sam's stories were true. Like I would never escape this hell. *Apocalypse survival rule: trust no one.* Yet Septimus had asked for my help. I'd failed my last team—I didn't want to fail him. I lowered the gun, watching Septimus carefully. "Give me your word."

"I promise. Help me with this one last thing."

Oh, bloody hell, Issac. If I die for trying to be the good guy I swear the first thing I'm going to tell you is I told you so. "Fine. We follow the trail, then we head straight to the surface."

After all, what's an end-of-the-world bachelor party without a blood trail and the imminent threat of death?

I bent beside the blood and then started to make wider circles from the spot until I found another small drop. Septimus followed me through the rows and rows of floating bodies. The eerie, unending sense of being watched followed me even though all their eyes were closed. The size of the room itself was staggering: there were hundreds of bodies here. Maybe more.

The blood trail led us to a door leading out of the massive room. The door was already open, but the room beyond it was dark.

"Wait," I hissed. But he'd already stepped into the darkened room, blazing lights flaring to life the moment he stepped inside. Unlike the giant, cavernous room outside, this room was small. Maybe the size of an office or bedroom.

It was covered in blood.

At the center of the room was one of the glass columns—empty of green water and streaked with blood, with a gaping hole in the center. *Oh please do not mean what I think that means.*

I slowly stepped into the room, gun out. Glass and blood littered the floor. There were bloody footprints leading to an open locker in the side of the room. Maybe the only consolation was that the footprints were smaller than my own.

It wouldn't have taken a tracker to put the clues together, but even so, my heart seemed to pump cement, my throat dry when I finally said, "One of them got out."

What exactly "them" was, I had no idea.

Septimus's expression was completely different from mine: frustrated as he paced the room and then stopped before the broken glass. But at the very least it was still the Septimus I knew who spoke, all innocent concern. "The girl with the dark hair was here. The one I dreamed of."

Ice crawled down my back. "You can't know that."

"I do."

"Septimus," I said, as firmly as I could. "What the *fuck* is this place?"

He didn't answer, bending over the shattered glass, turning a few pieces over. And then he turned back to look behind me. I spun, bringing my gun up as my heart thundered, but there was no horrible bloody monster or person in the door—only a small camera mounted on the wall.

"These are Walter's prisoners," he said softly. "They've been calling to me. They want to be free."

The thought of these people wanting something, wanting *freedom*, was terrifying. Almost as terrifying as not knowing why an entire room full of beings trapped inside tubes of green even existed.

In fact, the only reason I wasn't running right now was that they all seemed firmly asleep.

"Septimus, what the hell is this place? *Why* are these people here?"

He stared out into the dark recesses of the main cavern. "This is what Walter has been building beneath the city."

"You mean he built this lab and those tubes? Why?" I wanted to reach out and shake the distant look off his face. To make him answer me. But another part of me wanted to run, right now, and never think about this place again.

"Walter seeks to build a new humanity," he said softly.

What the hell does that even mean?! His eyes finally came to mine, and I decided I was done with this cryptic nonsense. I wasn't going to get an answer from him, and I wasn't going to wait around for one. Whatever these people were, they were just going to have to stay here. All that mattered was getting Ara as far away from this place as possible. I settled a hand on his shoulder, unable to ignore the metallic scent of blood. *Still Septimus. It's still Septimus.*

"Septimus, whatever this place is, these people *aren't* calling to you. We can't help them. All we can do is help—"

"The people we love," he said softly. "And what if every memory of anyone who loved you was stolen? What then, Kaden? When all your people are gone, when no one is left to love or remember you, where then do you turn?" There was a bitterness and anger to his words—but somehow it gave me hope. Because this was the Septimus I knew.

"Then you start over and make new memories. You find a new home and a new family. There's no way Ara and I are staying here now. Not when he's running some kind of *body farm*." I shot an unwilling glance back at the wide room beyond, and then forced my eyes back to Septimus. "Come to Boise with me. We can build a new life. Whatever this place is . . . you don't owe anything to these people."

"I am one of them, Kaden."

One of them.

Holy shit.

Suddenly, it all made horrible sense. Why he'd made me promise to shoot him rather than be taken captive. Why he didn't remember anything from before. Because he was one of whatever the hell these people were.

My mind raced ahead, trying to understand what that meant for us now. "Are they people Walter takes prisoner?" I pictured myself in green water, a breathing tube shoved into my mouth and a heavy weight pressed down on my chest.

Septimus's answer surprised me. "No. They are called the Creation."

"Creation . . . like . . . he made them?" *Well, this just gets worse and worse.*

"Yes. They want free. You once ran from your responsibility when you should have shouldered it. Don't make the same mistake now. Help me."

I stared at him. I couldn't understand a person creating others, but I could understand his plea for help, because it reminded me so much of Sam. Sam, who had told me I'd deserted the clan when I should have stayed. Sam, who died because I couldn't save him. And there it was: the real reason I hadn't left Septimus when all reason demanded it.

This was my chance at redemption. My chance to rewrite history. To save a brother instead of failing him. But I couldn't take on this responsibility, not when Ara was in trouble.

"Ara needs me."

"Then go. We won't forget the help you gave me, Kaden."

We. Who the hell is we? I didn't ask. I wasn't like Sam. The wind, the sun, the grass, the movement of a running horse, Ara's love: those were the only mysteries I wanted in my life.

Septimus pointed at the door behind us. "There's a door at the other end of the lab—it will take you to the surface. Find Ara and run. The Last City is almost at an end."

But I had to make one final plea. "Septimus, whatever you were . . . created to be, you can choose a new beginning. A new life."

"They need me. They want out."

"How do you know?"

He nodded behind me, and I slowly turned. My whole body tightened and I had to take my finger off the trigger. There weren't enough bullets in the world for the horror staring at me now.

Every face from the tanks was trained on us, watching with angry, desperate eyes.

And then a shrieking alarm began to sound over the room.

TWENTY-EIGHT—SAM

We stared at the black screen, three heartbeats of silence before M stepped forward and shook the monitor.

"Fix it!" She spun to me. "Bring her back!"

I tried, but then shook my head. "It's on their end, not ours. There's nothing I can do." In fact, the whole system had booted me out. Some sort of alarm began to flash on the screen, locking me out of the system entirely. The files, the camera—I could no longer access any of it.

"Why can't you fix it?" M hissed. "You fixed it before, fix it again!"

"I can't. M, it's not working, I'm trying—"

"You're useless."

Heat flushed through my body. I spun away from the computer, suddenly angry. "Oh right, I'm useless. The boy who brought you here is useless. Well then, M, tell me, who exactly was that?"

She flinched away from me, saying nothing, her gaze guarded once again.

"M," I said, not backing down. "Who was that?"

"You won't believe me."

"Try me."

She swallowed, turning away from me, her arms wrapping around her. Finally she said, "Not who. You said '*Who* the hell was that?' The right question is '*What* the hell was that?'"

I closed my eyes and thought back to every sci-fi story I'd ever read—in a room filled with green moss that glowed, it was easier than it should have been. But it wasn't just the girl on the screen and the girl beside me that were pieces of this puzzle. There was also another girl, a girl with red hair, that I hadn't considered was connected to all this. Until now.

"We need to get the computer—"

I cut her off midsentence. "The book said that the people in Thule dabbled in sciences that were better left alone, right?"

M stared at me in shock, her lips pressed together in a thin white line. But something in her eyes made me continue. "It said they made some sort of human clone—a clone that disappeared. You found the lab where they created the river monster that tried to pull me under . . . So what if they did more than just create monsters?" The shadows of the room pressed closer. "What if they created people?" *People like the girl in the tube.*

If that was true, if I was right, then there was one other explanation for why M and the girl in the tube looked exactly alike. But I wanted to hear it from her first. "The better question is *why*. Why create a person?"

"People," she whispered. "There's hundreds of them, maybe more. An army."

My eyes widened in wonder—and horror. "So The Lost City created the people in the green water? And you . . ." I trailed off, because I suddenly understood exactly where that put her. *What* that made her.

The green moss lit her features as she locked eyes with me, like some kind of beautiful monster herself. "I hear them calling to me. That girl, the one who looks like me, she called the loudest. They're prisoners. I thought if we could just find a way to release them, their voices would go away." She buried her head in her hands, sounding near tears. "I *want* them to go away. But it didn't work."

I felt cold all over, wanting to pull her into my arms, to comfort her, but unable to move a single step closer. "Did it work? Do you"—I stopped, not sure how to say it—"hear her anymore?"

She closed her eyes, her fingers like claws against her head. "No. They're still trapped . . . and angry."

"M, I—"

"Whatever pointless thing you're going to say, don't. You *don't* know what I'm going through. You don't know what it's like to be me. *You're not like me, Sam.* No one is. That's what I'm trying to tell you. Whatever they are . . ." Her voice broke, a sob escaping. "Whatever they are, I am too. And yet, I'm here, alone."

I wanted to stand up, to cross the distance and take her hand—but couldn't. Because her words made sense in a whole new way. No one was like her.

Because she wasn't entirely human.

"Whatever you are," I said, "it doesn't matter to me. I'm here. I won't leave."

"Everyone leaves. So will you."

"I won't."

She shook her head disgustedly. "You don't know anything about me."

"Don't I?" I pushed aside the chair and stepped closer, until I stared down at her, angry and exhausted in equal measure. "I crossed the city. I left my home. I risked my life. I *killed a man* for you, M. What more do I have to do for you to trust me?"

"I didn't say I didn't trust you. Just that you don't know me."

Cold flames of anger burned in my chest, foreign yet unmistakable. I almost didn't recognize the man who spoke next. "Are you sure about that? Because I used the name Edana to log into the computers here."

Some deep emotion flickered in her eyes, then studied nonchalance. It told me I was right—even though I wasn't sure I wholly wanted to be.

"So?"

"I do know you, M. I've been listening to everything you have, and haven't, said. You told me you grew up here, that you had parents." The old Sam would have stopped, considered the consequences of what he was saying. The new Sam was angry and tired of being stepped on. He wanted to be *right*. "And a sister. Older, wasn't it?"

She didn't speak. It didn't matter, because I finally saw the truth.

"Your father brought you here . . . the same place Ara wanted to come." Ara, who'd kept more secrets than I ever imagined. Ara, who'd talked about her little sister in a way that made me think she was a small, innocent child. But maybe older siblings were blind in that way. Or maybe we'd all once been innocent before the plague—I know I had been. But I wasn't now.

"When Kaden was sick, Ara and I sat up all night talking." I stepped closer to M, and she stepped back, but I continued forward. "She told me all about her little sister. How different and special she was. How they both grew up here. About her mother who always kept the house clean. About her father who loved to take them out into the mountains. How she had dark hair and blue eyes—and how they left her when she was infected. But you survived the plague. You wanted to return to the place Ara risked her life to journey to. And when I told you about the clan, and Ara, you were so quiet." I took a deep breath and said the words I'd never be able to take back. "Ara is your sister. You're Emma."

Usually it was M who glared at me, loomed over me, but now it was the opposite. I stared down at her, as she refused to meet my eye. Only when I spoke the truth aloud did I realize she had asked me to call her "Em," not the letter *M*. I was surprised at how stupid and used I felt. I didn't care if she wasn't human—I cared that she'd been lying to me from the first moment I'd met her. Kaden had taught me not to trust others, but maybe it was a lesson that could only be learned the hard way.

Still, her next words, and her absolute vulnerability, surprised me.

"She left me," she whispered. "Everyone I loved left me. All I have left are the people in the green water. The people who called to me when there was no one else."

You are such an ass, Sam. She literally just admitted to you she might not be fully human and you're yelling at her! There was something else—her eyes, always bright and angry, were now full of tears.

"Em," I said as gently as I could, "she was looking for you. Ara never gave up hope she'd find you. She risked *everything* to find you. Sometimes, the people we love, they mess up. It doesn't mean they don't love us. It doesn't mean everyone will abandon us. Whatever you were, whatever you are, it doesn't matter to me.

You don't have to be alone."

Em finally looked up. Her eyes met mine. The tears were still there, but below them lay the anger I knew too well. She stepped forward, so close I could have leaned forward and pressed my lips to hers—for a moment I imagined that was what she intended to do. I imagined her fingers in my hair, my hands at her waist, her lips hungry against my own. It felt like my soul balanced on the edge of a knife, and which side it fell was dependent on the woman before me.

On one side there was the Sam from before: trusting, innocent, hopeful. The Sam who believed that love was stronger than anything. The Sam that Kaden and Issac had protected and nurtured. The follower, the believer. The Sam who imagined Em taking a single step forward, into his arms, telling him she trusted him and the two of them could face the world together.

Then there was the new Sam: hard, but also strong. The Sam who doubted that Kaden would ever return. Who knew Issac never would. The Sam who'd spent an entire summer alone only to realize no one was coming to save him. The Sam who'd killed a man. The Sam who no longer trusted the girl before him.

Em picked up her gun, and I felt one Sam end forever—and another begin.

"You're wrong, Sam." There wasn't anger in her voice as she walked out of the room. Just the kind of acceptance that came from knowing who she was all along. "We're all alone."

TWENTY-NINE—ARA

Father crouched beside the hole in the floor he'd opened. I could smell the whiskey on Talia's breath as she hovered at my side and the two of us stared down in the darkness.

"We had a computer lab down there," my father said. "We used it to monitor what Walter was up to, we set up back doors into all the systems. It was how I first found out what he intended to do with the plague." Then he glanced up at me. "Unless you want to leave The Last City."

The last she. The girl with the cure. Invalid. I had the truth—now I had to figure out what to do with it. One thing was clear. "I'm not leaving without Kaden."

"Kaden?"

It was only then that I realized my father had no idea who Kaden was. My own father didn't know the love of my life. That strange, pubescent feeling of being in trouble, one I hadn't felt in ages, rose in my chest. *But why should I feel guilty? He's the one who hasn't been here. He's the one who kept secrets from me.*

Talia reached back and grabbed the glass of whiskey I'd left on the counter and passed it to me. "Feels like you're gonna need this."

I didn't drink. Instead, I looked my father straight in the eye and said, "Kaden is the man I came here with. I love him. I'm not leaving without him."

Father stared down into the darkness, his hands in fists. I could tell there was more he wanted to say, more he wanted to ask, but didn't. The same way I didn't volunteer more. A wall had risen between us. How could it not when he'd just admitted the one true cure for the plague had been inside me all along.

"I see," he finally said. With nothing more, he started down the steep stairs.

I stood on the edge of the hole, watching as he disappeared into the darkness, wondering what had happened to the father I'd followed into the mountains. He was so different now—or was it me who had changed? Kaden was the one I'd come to rely on now. Learning that my father knew about the plague, knew about Walter and The Last City . . . it felt like stepping into a new reality where everything I knew and trusted about my father was called into doubt.

Talia must have sensed my hesitation, because she lifted the bottle of whiskey—I hadn't even seen her grab it. "It's not too late, you know. We could shut the trapdoor, make off with the whiskey. Start a new life together somewhere. Adopt a bunch of cats. Or dogs. I'm flexible."

Even with the wicked, teasing glint in her eyes—there was something in her voice that was partly serious. It was only then that I realized how wrong I had been about Talia. She'd risked her life, and the life she'd built in The Last City, all to help me.

"What about your sister?"

Her eyes cut away from mine, her voice soft. "Una? Not sure even you can help me with that quest, Princess."

I reached out and took her hand. "You can't give up. We'll keep looking, no matter what." My voice thickened. "Thank you. For coming with me. For"—I didn't have a big enough word for all we'd gone through together—"everything."

Her eyes couldn't meet mine as she shrugged. "It's nothing."

"It's not nothing. You risked so much for me. It's not fair for me to ask any more from you."

Her smile was teasing now. "And yet, you're about to."

I swallowed, looking down at the hole my father had disappeared into, the only solution I could think of rising in me. "I'm tired of running. If the cure is really inside me, then I need to get to the plague flowers. Walter feeds them his blood. If I feed them mine, then maybe we could cure the whole city. My father lived here once. He can help us figure out where Emma, Una, and Kaden are." *I hope.*

Her eyes suddenly came up to mine, and I was shocked at how quickly they'd gone from teasing to serious. "Can we trust him?"

"He's my father." But suddenly I wasn't sure how much that meant. Walter was my grandfather, and look where that had gotten me—and the world.

"Just because you think you know someone, doesn't mean you can trust them." Her eyes held a warning. It made me pause. My father had once been my savior, my protector—but I'd learned how to protect myself and loved someone else now. I didn't want to be the girl who trusted no one.

So I reached out and stole the whiskey bottle from her hands. "I trust *you*. We feed my blood to the flowers, find the others, and then get the hell out of here. If my father won't help us, we do it just the two of us. We got in and out of the Sanctum on our own—if we have to, we can do this alone too."

I held the whiskey bottle out in a sort of salute. "To not needing men to save us." Then I took a swig—only to choke and cough as it burned down my throat, my eyes brimming with tears.

She laughed. "Princess, you are too much." Then she grabbed the bottle and drank deeply.

Lights flickered on as we climbed down into a cave-like room. While the club above had wall coverings, a wood floor, and rough corners, here the pretense of decoration fell away. The room looked like a cave that someone had filled with cords, electrical equipment, and survival supplies, then abandoned.

There were two sets of metal bunks on one side. To the left of the bunks, shower curtains sectioned off a corner of the cave—possibly concealing some sort of makeshift bathroom. On the opposite side of the bunks was an area devoted to a large collection of computers covered in tarps. That was where my father now stood, pulling tarps free from computer after computer.

"Come help me," Father called out. "See if we can get any of them on."

Together Talia and I helped my father uncover the computers. In the end, only one flickered to life. My father took a seat before it. I watched as he sorted through folders and files full of text I didn't understand. When nothing happened for several minutes, I started to pace.

A few minutes later he sighed. "I'm not sure if I can still get into the systems—"

"Move aside," Talia said in a commanding tone. "Ronnie and

Harrison worked on surveillance, but I'm the one who got them that job."

They traded spots and she laughed as she brushed a bit of dust off the screen. "How old is this thing?"

"Everyone wanted these computers in my day," my father muttered. I leaned in behind her, watching the screen, until she turned and lifted a brow at me. "It's gonna be a while. These things are ancient. I'll let you know when I find anything."

"Right," I said, suddenly unsure what to do.

But my father's gaze instantly went to the other side of the room. "We'll see if we can get the water running—and if any of the food preserves lasted." Talia ignored him, lost in the blue glow of the screen as Father and I made our way over to the supplies.

"Are you sure you shouldn't rest?" I tried to hide the anxiety in my voice.

But he only smiled. "No. I've rested more than enough these past few months."

Months. He's been locked up here for months. The realization was painful—because it meant that he really had been here waiting for me.

He led me to a pile of heavy plastic crates I hadn't seen, hidden behind the bunk beds. One by one we opened them. I was surprised at the food and supplies contained within: enough to last down here for months. *He was prepared.* But I suppose that was my father. Then he showed me the bathroom behind the shower curtains, with water from the river. There was a small faucet with a drain beneath, a makeshift toilet, and even a shower spout.

"It's safe to drink," Father said, motioning for me to go first. I drank deeply, the water so cold my teeth ached. Then I undid the wrapping on my wrist, gritting my teeth at the flash of pain when

I dunked it beneath the flow. For the first time I took in the full extent of the damage: my knuckles were bloody, and there were two deep gashes and numerous small cuts.

"Are you hurt?" he said.

"I kicked a window, then cut my hand when I reached through."

"Sounds painful."

"You should have seen the window."

He smiled, and for a moment it almost felt like old times. "We had a first aid kit down here. Let me see if I can find it."

It felt so much like old times—the father I remembered looking out for me, helping me. And yet now as I thought back to all the fond memories of us together, all I could think about was how much time he'd had to tell me the truth and still chose not to. Part of me wanted to demand an answer, but a bigger part was too cowardly.

Instead, I asked the question that would help Kaden—I hoped. "Father?" I said softly when he held my hand, bandaging it. "How did you escape last time?"

He wrapped the bandage one more time around my hand before he answered. "I jumped into the black whirlpool."

So there really is a black whirlpool in the tunnels that can be survived. "Any idea how that became the symbol in The Last City?"

He grinned. "'Course I do. I started it. Walter always hated that whirlpool."

I smiled back—this was the father that I'd missed. The one who was fearless.

A few hours passed like that. Father finished bandaging my hand and then the two of us caught up while Talia worked quietly on the computer. I didn't tell him everything—I remained guarded—but I did tell him that I'd found his letter, and then filled him in on some of our long journey here. In turn, he told me how he'd been captured before he'd even made it to The Last City. The men who'd taken him had their own scanner, and found his Invalid test interesting. They'd sent a message to someone inside The Last City, trying to sell him. But then, in the dead of night, his entire team had been killed. Father was taken belowground, to a cell where he was kept alone, without answers.

"Did you talk to Walter after that?" I said.

"He came to speak with me once. I tried to convince him to use my blood for the cure, but he wasn't interested." He stopped, and then turned to look at me, his expression pained. "I think the only reason he kept me there was you."

"Me? Why?"

"For all Walter's ambitions, he liked having followers and people who loved him. I think when he realized he couldn't bring me to his side, he kept me hidden so I wouldn't turn you against him. Or maybe he saw me as an insurance policy—in case he couldn't control you. We've stood on opposing sides for some time. I'm guessing he wanted you to trust him, and not me."

A rush of loyalty surged in my chest. "You're my father. A lot has changed"—*you lied when you should have told the truth*—"but that hasn't."

He gave me a soft, sad smile. "He was my father too."

I wasn't sure why those words hit so hard, but they did. My father had trusted his father—who had ended the world. And now, if my father was correct, Walter sought to go even further. It was a bitter pill to swallow. Maybe more so because every time I wanted to ask about Emma, the words stuck in my mouth.

Father and I pulled together a meal from the dried and canned foods, using an old gas burner stove that still worked. I was surprised how quickly we fell back into a rhythm, different only in the long silences that stretched between us. In those moments, I was forced to think about my next move.

Kaden might be out in the ruins. Or he could be down here somewhere, held prisoner like my father. I had no way of knowing. If I really had the true cure inside me, and I'd cured Kaden, then he had the cure inside him too. I hoped that meant I could pass the cure along through the plague flower. Then there was an entire cathedral full of brainwashed women, women I had no idea how to help, but Emma and Una weren't among them.

It all came back to Walter—he was the center of the wheel, all the spokes turning endlessly around him. Could we take Walter away from the equation without everything else crumbling? I'd told Talia we would cure the city and leave—but that suddenly seemed like a daunting, impossible task. The kind of thing that took years of planning or left a city burning. I didn't want to be the girl who left destruction in her wake—I wouldn't leave The Last City burning like I had the clan.

Walter was the problem. So he had to be part of the solution.

Talia's voice suddenly cut across the room. "I found something."

Father and I both abandoned our tasks and came to stand on either side of her chair. Talia brought up some kind of video. "I'm not exactly sure what it is, but it came from outside The Last City."

"How does that help us?" I said, trying not to sound frustrated.

She shrugged. "Maybe it doesn't. But I've never seen something like this. It's coming from some kind of new tech outside The Last City." Then she turned to me, a smile that told me she'd buried the lede. "And it's broadcast from *Boise*."

My heart tumbled and fell. "Play it. Maybe it's from Gabriel."

I'm actually excited to hear from Gabriel: you win, world. For all Gabriel's faults, it was beginning to become increasingly obvious we needed a new place to live.

"Remind me, is Gabriel the one that you fake-married?" Talia said. I stiffened beside her, waiting for the inevitable reaction that followed—a choking noise from the other side of the chair.

"You're married?!" Father finally managed.

"*Fake*-married, and only as a way to free Kaden." Too late I realized I might have overshared.

"Kaden? The man you came here with? Who is he?"

I shot a look at Talia, who had suddenly become all-consumed in the computer, not quite hiding a grin.

"Kaden is . . . my, umm, fiancé."

"You're engaged?" His voice went even higher. *Well, Kaden, the good news is I found my father. The bad news is I killed him when I told him about you.*

"He asked me before he left," I said, not wanting to tell him but also feeling like I shouldn't have to keep it a secret. I'd already filled my father in on most of the story: that Talia was also looking for someone, and that Kaden had gone out into the ruins and had never returned. I just hadn't filled him in on exactly what Kaden was to me.

"Was there a ring involved in this proposal?" Talia spun the chair to face me—clearly not working as hard as she pretended.

A blush worked its way into my cheeks, but I couldn't resist pulling the ring out from around my neck and showing it to her. I'd already decided not to put it on my finger—I wanted Kaden to. "He gave it to me before he left."

Maybe it was all the wrong timing—okay, it definitely was—but so what? I loved Kaden, and as he said, no one survived the apocalypse. You had to take what time you could, moment by moment. Kaden had told me I was the only truth that he'd wanted. Too late I understood what he'd meant.

My father stared at the ring, shock on his face. I'd always imagined my future husband asking my father's permission: but he hadn't been there and I sure as hell wasn't asking now.

My father turned back to the computer and said softly, "Well, then I guess we'd better find him."

Talia winked at me before turning back to the computer. "Good thing I found this message. We'd better make sure you're good and divorced before we make you a married woman."

I didn't have time to react to her words. The screen flashed up and my heart stopped.

The person I saw on the screen was impossible.

He was older, his face harder, without the baby fat I remembered. The lines on his face were sharper, his hair shaved short so that you could barely make out the red.

But I had known him in a different life.

Sam.

"Damn, Ara." Talia gave a low whistle. "You never told me Gabriel was handsome. And young! I didn't take you for a cradle robber."

"No," I whispered, my voice hoarse with disbelief. "That's Sam."

Sam.

Sam is alive.

I wanted to cry. I wanted to scream. "That's Sam," I whispered, then louder, nearly yelling. "Kaden's brother! Sam is alive! When was this recorded?" It had to be recent: he looked older, harder somehow. My heart thundered. It couldn't be possible. Sam was alive . . .

Sam is alive! I had to find Kaden. I had to tell him.

"Recently it looks like . . ." Talia typed something into the computer and then frowned. "It doesn't have an exact time, but it looks like we're the first here to intercept it. Should I play it?"

"Yes!"

She clicked on something, and then Sam's voice played in the room, opening a door to my past as it did.

"Hello. My name is Sam Preston, coming to you from downtown Boise." Even his voice sounded different now, deeper and more serious. "Whoever you are, wherever you are, I want you to know that there's infrastructure for new tech in Boise. If you are a part of this lab, or know something about the new tech, you should come here and help me turn it back on." He paused, turning to look over his shoulder—he seemed to be in some sort of lab, and there was someone moving in the background. "We also have clans here—stability and food and shelter. If you're out there and need a home, you can come down to Boise. The Castellano clan is set up in the Old Penitentiary, and I've heard they're taking new members." And then the person in the background walked into view.

I didn't hear what he said next.

Because I couldn't breathe.

She was older now, beautiful, but I had known her in a different life.

My knees hit the ground, and it was some time before I realized Talia was in front of me, shaking my shoulders.

"Ara?! Ara, are you okay?" She shook me again. "What happened? What's wrong?"

Behind her, my father stared at the screen, not moving. My eyes brimmed with tears, my heart full to bursting. "Emma," I whispered. "That was Emma in the background."

Father watched the screen with wide eyes. “It can’t be,” he whispered.

But I was sure. I climbed back to my feet, heat radiating through my chest, everything in me wanting to jump and scream. “It’s her. It’s Emma. I know it.”

We both moved back to the screen, and Talia slowed it down and played it again, showing frame by frame my little sister. If Sam had grown up, it was nothing compared to Emma. When I’d last seen her she was a little girl—now she was a young woman. Beautiful. Strong.

It felt like something had broken inside me forever—like a weight had fallen away that I hadn’t even known had been crushing me. It felt like the moment I found my father alive; like a spring had burst open in a desert, making everything new again.

I tilted my head back, tears falling free as I laughed and cried at the same time. “We crossed the mountains to get here, but she’s back in Boise—with Sam! They were both there the whole time.” And now I really was crying, unbound. “We came all the way here, but they were both there the whole time.” It felt like my chest was bursting. Like finally, finally, it was all worth it.

“Play it again,” I said, and then watched, again and again, the image of my little sister, by choice if not blood, on the screen, whole and well and waiting for me in the last place I’d ever expected.

Home.

THIRTY—ARA

"Ara, look what I found!" Emma emerged from the thicket, her eyes wicked with delight. She held some kind of lupine skull cradled in her hands.

"Ewww! We're supposed to be picking berries!" But I laughed regardless, abandoning my blanket of huckleberries to come to her side. The summer sun beat through the pine, but the shadows kept us cool. Father had left us here and had hiked upriver, promising he'd be back in a few hours.

"Look at the canines." Emma peered even closer at the bits of grime and decay still clinging to the skull. "Do you think it was a wolf?"

"Probably just a dog someone buried up here. Father will know." I glanced down the slope, the sound of the river audible over the birdsong and wind through the pine. "We should get back to picking. He said we could make a cobbler with the berries if we get enough."

"I think we should go into town."

"Emma!" I chided, shocked she'd even suggested it. "Don't even joke about that. We can't leave."

"You don't have to always do what he says." Emma didn't even look at me as she said it. She just worked the jaw of the creature, opening and closing the teeth with a snap.

"I don't always do what he says."

She grinned. "Great. Then let's go."

Too late I realized I'd fallen right into her trap. "He'll be worried if we're not here." Once I'd thought that would have been enough to make her stay—but Emma was different from other people's little sisters. Mostly in that she did what she wanted and more and more lately that was the opposite of what Father and Mother wanted.

She leaned down and planted a kiss on the skull—an evil grin stretched across her face when my eyes widened in horror. She danced away before I could snatch the skull from her hands.

"He'll be worried about you," she said. "Not me. You're his favorite."

"That's not true, Emma."

"You know it is." She waltzed back into the trees, holding the skull as tenderly as most girls held flowers. "It's always been true. You just don't see it yet."

~

I lay on the bed, eyes open but unseeing. *You just don't see it yet.* Those first few hours after discovering Sam and Emma were alive felt like the happiest dream I'd ever had. I'd fallen asleep smiling.

Yet now, hours later, when I awoke in one of the bunk beds, I couldn't fall back asleep. *You just don't see it yet.* I had been so certain back then that Father loved Emma and me equally. Even when we'd left her, I'd held tight to that knowledge. It felt like an indisputable fact, as unbreakable as gravity.

But we *had* left her.

Father had protected me, not her. And now, finally, I knew why.

When I learned that Emma and Sam were alive, I hadn't thought to process my father's reaction. Now I did. He'd been silent. He hadn't commented on Emma's miraculous reappearance.

Lying there, all I could think of was all the ways my father had lied to me over the years. That knowledge felt like something physical in my chest, growing larger and angrier until I finally pushed aside the blankets and gave up on sleep. I made my way through the small bunker over to the computers to where Talia sat alone, the blue screen lighting her features in a pale glow. On the other side of the room, my father's snores sounded. Once he'd been a light sleeper, but even I could see how his time as a prisoner had affected him. We'd gotten some food and water in him, and then he'd crashed, hard.

"What's up?" Talia said, her eyes not moving from the screen.

"Woke up and couldn't go back to sleep." I came to stand behind her, trying unsuccessfully to roll the soreness out of my shoulders. "What time is it?"

Talia clicked on something on the computer. "We got here at about six in the morning. You guys slept through the whole day. It's night again outside." She cast a look at me. "You okay?"

I just found out that my blood is the only true cure, that my sister was adopted, and that my father isn't who I thought he was. So no. "I was just thinking about my sister." I grabbed the other chair, and then rolled it to her side. "You never told me anything about your sister. Una, right?"

I thought the question would make her turn to me, but instead she stiffened, a guarded look crossing her face. "What do you want to know?"

"What was she like?"

"She was beautiful," she said, a grim twist to her mouth. "Never listened to a damn thing I said." *Sounds like my sister.*

"What were your parents like?"

"They died a long time ago," she said bluntly. "Someone else raised us. An older man."

I couldn't understand it—but there was something strange in her voice. Or maybe it was the way she wouldn't meet my eye . . . like she wanted me to ask, but couldn't look at me and say so.

Intuition flickered in me, and some deep warning. *Haven't you had enough secrets?* But still she didn't meet my eye, still that strange silence stretched between us. "Who?" I finally said.

Talia took her time in responding, squeaking the chair back and forth. I thought it was only her way of being difficult or trying to reclaim my attention, but what she said next shifted everything. "Walter."

Exhaustion fell from my limbs as suddenly as if I'd plunged through ice. "Walter *raised* you? As in Walter, the Chancellor, my *grandfather* Walter?"

"Yes."

I stared at her. She still couldn't meet my eyes. A cold, heavy feeling crept down my spine. Was everyone lying to me?

"I wanted to tell you, Ara. So, so many times. But I didn't know how." Now it was me who had to look away, to try to sort through all the feelings roiling in my chest. To replay every moment with him and with her.

"You always disappeared when he showed up," I finally said. "I thought you were afraid of him."

"I *am* afraid of him," she whispered. "He asked me to keep watch over you, to make you his loyal follower. But I didn't do that. I tried to show you the truth about The Last City. Give you the choice I never got." She swallowed, and then reached into her pocket, her hands shaking as she held out a sealed envelope to me.

"I went to see him a few hours ago while you were sleeping. He's not perfect, but he's not what your father made him out to be. He protected me and my sister."

I stared at her in disbelief. "You left this bunker? And talked to him?"

"Yes. But I didn't tell him where you were. And I made sure no one followed me back . . . I might not be as bad at traveling through the tunnels as I made myself out to be." She paused, and gave a very un-Talia-like sigh. "Look, it's your choice if you want to meet with him. Just read the letter."

Why did it have to be her? My mind spun, everywhere at once.

While I sat there in silence, Talia once again extended the letter. "Read it, Ara. What your dad told you—it's just one version of the truth. I'm not saying Walter is all good, but he isn't all bad either. Nobody is in this world—not even you, Princess."

I didn't reach for the letter. All I could do was stare at Talia, trying to process her words and failing. When I didn't move, she dropped the letter on my lap. She rose to leave, but I caught her hand before she could go.

"Talia," I said, not even sure what I wanted to say. Was I angry?

Betrayed? Did I even know who this woman was? I settled for trying to understand.

"Your sister . . . is she really missing?"

"Yes. Only Walter can bring her back to me." She shook her head, something miserable there. "It's not personal, Princess. Just read the letter."

With those words ringing in my ears, she walked away. I was left alone, sitting there in the blue glow of the computer screen, wondering if anyone I knew was who I thought they really were.

For a moment I considered storming after her, demanding she explain everything. How she knew Walter, what she hadn't told me, how much of this friendship was real and how much wasn't . . . but the letter in my hands proved too much to resist. I opened the envelope and leaned into the light of the computer to read.

My dearest granddaughter, Arabella,

First let me say, what a surprise it has been watching you and hearing Talia's reports. I have forgotten how rebellious children can be, but even so, I assumed that you would follow in your father's footsteps and abandon The Last City. I never expected you to join the Sanctum. I hope you now believe me that Emma is not there.

Perhaps not, considering your father's cell is empty. This, I admit, will be harder to explain. What your father stole from me all those years ago was unforgivable. But I do not count his crimes against you. By now I assume he has told you where the plague originated, and that the cure lies within your blood. I urge you to put aside thoughts of what might have been and instead look at what humanity truly was: a cruel, selfish species that was destroying the planet and each other. There is a plan for all of this. A plan I want both you and Talia to be a part of.

Come to the greenhouse at dawn, without your father, and let me show you the future—our future. Kaden is alive and being held. So long as you follow my instructions, he will remain unharmed. If you do not wish to join me, you and Kaden will be free to go. I give you my word on this: so long as you come and hear what I have to say, you both may leave in peace.

Do not test my mercy, for it is not limitless.

Your grandfather and Chancellor,

Walter

I read the letter over again, trying to soak it in, and then gave up. Trying to accept this now wasn't any easier than before. Walter knew about the plague—I mean, of course he did, but still. The way he spoke about it, as if humanity were a science experiment, as if he could just talk to me and I would understand . . . I rocked back in the seat.

He's insane. Or just evil and completely deluded. Either way, his words only sharpened my resolve. I couldn't change the past, I couldn't change what my father and grandfather had both done, but I could try to right their mistakes in some small way. The way my father should have let me. Which meant meeting with Walter—and feeding my blood to the plague flowers.

In the corner of the room, behind the reach of the light, Talia sat, watching me. *She knew more than she let on.* Yet I couldn't find it in me to be angry at her. I had also once followed the words of a man with blind devotion. And I had been willing to do whatever it took to find my sister: I couldn't fault Talia for the same.

I saw the truth about Walter now—he was greedy. For power. For control. For his way to be the only way. But that didn't mean I had to give up on Talia just because he'd manipulated her.

"Talia," I said as gently as if speaking to a wild animal. "How can I help you?"

In the darkness, I couldn't read her features, only the low, guarded cadence of her voice. "You can't. Only Walter can get my sister back."

There was a painful tightening in my throat, a pricking in my eyes at her words. I stared into the darkness, swallowing all emotion when I said, "Is it true? What he said about Kaden?"

"Yes. He's alive, and locked up somewhere underground."

Kaden is alive. I closed my eyes and focused only on those words. No matter what else happened, Kaden was alive. That single sentence brought the world into sharper focus. There was nothing more important than going to Walter's meeting.

"He'll keep his word and release him if I go talk to him?"

"Yes." Once I would have believed her in a second; now I wondered. Walter had told me that women were more likely to trust other women, and then he'd assigned Talia to be my guide. I hadn't realized he was using that trust to monitor me.

It doesn't matter now. All that matters is Kaden and getting the hell out of here.

I glanced back at the corner where my father slept, trying to harden my heart. "How long till dawn?"

Talia brought up a camera that pointed into the ruins—the sky was black and star-filled, but the eastern horizon was just a shade lighter. "Maybe an hour?"

"And there's nothing I can do to convince you to come with us, back to Boise?"

Her eyes were empty. “Could I convince you to leave your sister?”

My father had once—and I’d regretted it ever since. Maybe Talia wasn’t who I thought she was, but I still understood her decision.

Her jacket lay discarded on the desk beside the computer, so I picked it up and held it out to her, the closest thing I had to a peace offering. “Is it too late to become hermits and adopt that bunch of cats?”

Talia stood, her smile sad as she took the jacket. “’Fraid so, Princess.” She glanced back at where my father slept. “Are you going to wake him?”

“No. Would it be too cheesy if I said this was a journey only for sisters?”

She rolled her eyes, suddenly the Talia I knew. “Yes.”

“Then how about friends?”

Her smile was bittersweet. “I think I can handle that. Let’s go.”

THIRTY-ONE—KADEN

"You promised to shoot me," Septimus said, glaring at me. "What kind of man gives his word and doesn't keep it?"

I sighed from my place sitting against the wall, knocking my head back against the stone so hard it hurt. "Look, I'm sorry I didn't shoot you." *Never thought I'd say those words aloud.* "But to be fair, I didn't have much of a chance." When the alarm had sounded in the room, we'd barely had ten seconds before we were swarmed by guards. In the end I'd set the gun on the floor, raised my hands, and surrendered. Septimus might want to die, but I sure as hell didn't. If I had tried to use the gun, even to shoot Septimus, I was fully confident we'd both be dead right now.

"You should have kept your word," he said, insistent.

"Septimus, you're my friend. I'm not going to shoot you. And as far as being truthful goes, I'm not sure you have any ground to stand on."

He had the grace to at least look embarrassed.

One of them. Septimus had told me he was one of the people floating in the tanks—what exactly they were, and where that left us now, I wasn't entirely sure. As far as bachelor parties went, this one had taken a dark twist.

"If they take me back . . ." Septimus shook his head, muttering words I couldn't make out. He'd been like this all night, pacing our small cell like a madman. The bars contained us in some sort of small natural cave, complete with a bucket in one corner, two rickety cots, and the godawful glowing green moss. I hadn't yet gotten hungry enough to try to eat some of it, but it had only been one night. Or what seemed like one night. It was hard to tell down here.

"We're going to find a way out. It's going to be okay." I picked a bit of moss off the wall, sniffed it, and then flicked it away before I gave in. Some of the men in the stables said they'd fed moss to the wild horses to make them more docile—knowing my luck it'd be this exact stuff.

"You don't know that," Septimus said, pacing again.

"Could you please sit down? Your pacing is making me hungry. We need to conserve energy. Come up with a plan." *A plan that involves escape, then Ara, then food.*

Septimus shook the bars, clearly frustrated, but at least he was no longer pacing. "A plan won't help us. Nothing will now."

I gathered a bit of the moss into a ball and then threw it at him. He didn't even flinch.

"I thought you wanted to release the people in the water," I said. "Why the sudden change of heart?"

"Because I failed them—and now they're angry. And he knows we're here."

I assumed by "he," he meant Walter—yet another bit of knowledge Septimus had failed to share. Still, the way he paced, his eyes darting, flinching at every small noise, it was like he was a caged animal awaiting execution. I couldn't help but want to cheer him up. "Listen, Septimus, I've been waiting my whole life to spend a night in jail—excellent street cred. Is it what I expected? No. But it ain't over till the fat lady sings."

"There are no fat ladies in The Last City." The glow of the moss gave just enough light I could see his lips were raised. Septimus was joking.

Shit, maybe we really are screwed.

I forced myself to stand up, dangling my arms through the bars beside him. The tunnel curved out of sight both left and right away from us, lit only by the green glow of the moss. No guards. No way to get help. The only thing to suggest human presence was the tiny red light on what I guessed was a camera farther down the tunnel from our cell. Not that it really mattered that someone was likely watching us: so far my escape attempts had come to nothing. The lock itself was ancient and rusted, but without tools or leverage, I wasn't sure how we were going to break out.

"All right," I said, thinking aloud. "They put us here . . . so they're keeping us for something. Maybe they'll move us. That'd give us an opening to escape."

"Or you could just surrender without a fight again," Septimus said, his dark mood returning. I understood his frustration. The longer we waited, the worse things seemed.

"Or maybe you could explain to me a little more about what those people were. And how you escaped." All night the memory of their eyes watching us from behind the glass made the hairs on the back of my neck stand on end. But now that we'd been down here a while, my restless nature had taken over. Curiosity had replaced horror. And something told me that as much as I didn't want the truth, it might be the key to freedom.

He was silent for some time. Finally he bowed his head, resting it against the bars. "They are called the Creation. They were made by Walter, to begin humanity anew. I do not know how."

"And why did they let you out?"

"I was flawed. They were taking me out to destroy me."

Flawed. They had tried to kill him because he was flawed? Wrapping my brain around all of this felt like stepping into a new, dark reality I very much wanted to stay fiction. Ara had told me that Walter had talked about perfect humanity, about doing better than God, but this . . . I didn't even know that creating people was possible.

Seeing him there, beaten and hunched over, I felt guilty that I'd doubted him. He looked as lost as when I'd seen him standing over the Captain's dead body. Whatever happened, wherever he'd come from, we were in this together now. I reached over and set a hand on his shoulder. "To be flawed is to be human. I think some dumb philosopher said that." He smiled just a tiny bit. "They might count that against you, but I don't. I won't let them take you back. We leave here together or not at all."

"You might be better off without me."

"Septimus." I forced him to turn to face me. "I need you to hear this. We *will* find our way out of here. Then we'll make our way back to Boise and forget this place even existed. It doesn't matter where you came from—only where you're going."

His eyes were still dark and heavy, but after a moment he said, "What's it like in Boise?"

I leaned my forehead against the cold metal of the bars, breathing in the scents of earth and metal, and remembering different scents: of sagebrush, of pine, of a river, of sprawling concrete blistering beneath the Idaho sun. "Imagine a river surrounded by greenery and wildlife and possibility. There're trees everywhere. Not these little shit pines—real, beautiful, soaring trees. The downtown is flooded, but when the waters are high you can kayak through the skyscrapers, all the way around the dome of the Capitol. There're wild horses in the foothills, salmon in the river, deer in the trees, and the mountains in the distance, watching over it all. A whole city ready to be taken." I opened my eyes, for a moment the brightness of it all reshaping the shadows. "Ara thinks that someday someone might be able to get the new tech back on. Imagine, turning the whole world back on."

"It does sound nice."

"Nice!" I shoved him, and he finally smiled. "We can do whatever the hell we want—go wherever the hell we want. There's a whole world out there waiting for us."

"If we're going to do all that, we need to find a way out of this cell first."

I laughed. "Probably a good first step."

We passed a few more hours like that, me throwing out increasingly wild ideas—collect the moss and see if we could light it on fire, pretend one of us was deathly ill and cry for help, destroy the cot and try to pick the lock—nothing useful beyond keeping us from going insane.

Septimus had lain down on the cot, silent for some time before he suddenly opened his eyes and sat up. "Someone's coming."

My heart stuttered. Was it possible Ara had found me? Part of me desperately wanted to see her. The other part was terrified of her being trapped in this underground hell.

The footfalls grew louder until a man I knew turned the corner. *Not the fat lady but pretty damn close.*

"Hello, Kaden. Septimus," Walter said as he drew closer. "I hope you'll forgive the accommodations. It won't be for long."

Septimus had frozen beside me. I wanted to grab Walter by his throat and shake him, but he stopped ten feet from us, carefully out of reach, as if he could read my mind.

"Walter," I said. "Funny meeting you down here. Please, do come in. We're thinking of redecorating with pink moss—the green's getting old." While I'd suspected him of being behind all of this, I hadn't expected him to actually face me. Gabriel had once thrown me in a shed and let me rot rather than face me himself. I wondered if it was a bad sign.

"Yes, well, I have to admit I was surprised to find you and Septimus had made your way back into the city. Let alone into my lab."

"Quite the freak show you've got going on there," I said, hoping to taunt him into coming closer. *If he just got close enough, we could force him to give us a key. Or call for guards.* "Did you come here to finish us off? Or just for the pleasure of our company?"

Walter stayed exactly where he was. "I'm not here to kill you, or anyone. I came to ask you something."

"Then ask. I've got a meeting in five I can't miss."

Again that cold, humorless smile. "Why did you come back? My men tried to kill you. You had to know what would happen if you came back."

"Ara is here. I'll always come back for her."

"It could have been easy, you know." He took a small step forward. "It still could be. You could promise to leave. Forever."

"You know I'm not going to do that."

He stared at me in silence, and then turned to Septimus. "And you? Why did you return?"

Septimus said nothing, his jaw hard, eyes trained on the ground. Walter looked between the two of us, something satisfied in his expression. It made me want to throttle him even more.

"You know, one of my biggest worries was that humanity and the Creation wouldn't be able to work together," Walter said. "That the succession of humanity fading away and the Creation rising to power would be painful. But the two of you prove it's quite possible."

Creation? Is that what he called the people in the tubes? I didn't ask, waiting for him to step closer.

"You proved I was right all along," he went on, "but you've also created a problem. You see, Kaden, while I told the Captain your blood was too dangerous to keep in the city, the real reason to kill you was much simpler. Ara will never follow me while you're in the way." He sighed. "I hoped if you disappeared into the ruins, she would let it be. Turns out she's more resourceful than I gave her credit for. An unfortunate outcome. It shows my entire point: love is a weakness in humanity."

"What have you done with Ara? Where is she?" Cold fingers of fear ran down my back.

"I only wish the best for my granddaughter," Walter said. "What I can give her is the best. A new start for humanity. A new, better world. What can you give her?"

I wanted to yell at him, tell him I could give her security and love and a better life . . . but was that really true? What if all I could give her was a life of danger and fear? Here I'd spoken of Boise as if it were a promised land, but I knew what awaited us there. Danger and heartache and trouble. Gabriel would never welcome us back. We'd have to start over. We would have to fight and struggle at every turn.

Yet I didn't falter when I answered him. "I will always want Ara, and she will always want me."

"We'll see." Then he lifted his wrist, a flash of silver as he checked his watch. "It's nearly dawn. Ara is coming to talk with me. I will tell her the whole truth—and my final plan. If she chooses to go with you, then very well. I wish you the best with her. But if she doesn't . . ."

He trailed off, and I finished his sentence. "Then I will leave." *Fat chance, you old maggot.*

"Excellent. Then I also have an appointment to make."

He turned to make his way back the way he'd come. Septimus, who had been silent the whole exchange, suddenly spoke.

"They aren't what you think they are."

Walter stopped, turning back and staring at Septimus in surprise. "What did you say?"

Septimus stared at the ground, knuckles white on the bars. "What you created. They aren't what you think they are." His gaze slowly came up to meet Walter's. "They don't forgive. They won't forget. And they might be angry at me, but it's nothing close to what they feel for you."

Walter's face paled. His mouth opened, and then he closed it and hurried away. I stared at the empty tunnel, and then back at Septimus.

"Really? You couldn't have used that mumbo jumbo to scare him *closer*?" I held up a hand before he could speak. "Nope. Too late. I need to take a nap and then we come up with a new plan."

I lay down on the cot and sent up a prayer to Issac's God, hoping that he was feeling generous today.

The fat lady hadn't sung yet, but I had a feeling I could hear her in the wings.

THIRTY-TWO—ARA

"We're here to see the Chancellor," I said to the guards when Talia and I stood before the greenhouse doors. Talia had led us out of the tunnels and across the city in near silence. Now cold determination pumped through me as we stood before the doors. "My grandfather is expecting us."

The guard looked at me first, then Talia. For someone who was usually overconfident and swaggering, Talia stood silently beside me, her eyes on the ground. It didn't matter: the doors swung open. After the dark, cold streets of the city, the lights of the greenhouse blazed bright, warmth and humidity washing over me in a wave. I stepped forward, but before I could go farther than a few steps, Talia caught my arm.

"Wait, Ara." Her usual teasing tone was gone. "I want things to be right between us before . . ." She trailed off. Before we both continued on our quests for our sisters without each other.

"They are right between us." *Or as right as they can be.* I stepped forward and pulled her into a fierce hug, trying to blink back tears. Then I pulled back and nodded to the center tank of swirling water, my voice thick. "I need to put my blood in the water before he gets here."

She nodded, and I saw there were tears in her eyes too. Together we made our way to the center tank of swirling water. I'd never seen Walter put his blood in, but I'd visited the greenhouse a few times on my own. I'd overheard some of the gardeners talk about how Walter visited the dark pool of water every morning. They said he used a needle to draw blood from his arm, and then emptied it into the pool. What I didn't know was how much blood to leave—especially if I only had one chance.

I tore the bandage off my hand, wincing at the sudden pain. A few drops leaked from the scab. *Not enough.* I pulled my blade free from where I'd concealed it in my boot, and then reopened the wound, gasping as blood flowed free, spinning into the depths. *Maybe this was the whirlpool all along.*

The gardeners said Walter stopped at a few drops, but I didn't. I let the red leak into the water, wanting my guilt and pain to leak away with it. *Could it really be so simple? Could humanity have been saved if I'd known the truth?* I kept squeezing my hand, letting the blood flow free, more and more.

Finally, Talia pulled me back. "That's enough, Princess."

I let her pull me back, light-headed, unable to look anywhere but at the swirling water. Would it work? Would the people of The Last City finally have the cure? Walter said he'd brought me here to tell me his new vision for The Last City—what if it included giving everyone the cure? Maybe he was going to build a better city. Release the women in the Sanctum. Maybe it was still possible to save this. Maybe I didn't have to leave Talia and all of this. *And maybe I'm a fool.*

Talia already had a new bandage prepared, and she forced me to hold out my hand while she wrapped it.

"There's one more thing," Talia said, speaking low and swift. "Your father was right: Walter does have a plan for after the plague. You and Kaden should get the hell away from here. As far as you can."

"We're going back to Boise." *And you should come with us.*

She swallowed, her eyes darting to the water and back. "That might not be far enough."

"Of course it is." I reached out and took her hand. "Come with us, Talia."

She pulled her hand back slowly but firmly. "I can't. I have Una." Her face looked miserable, and when she smiled it was forced. "Give Emma and Sam a hug for me, okay? I wish I could have met them. And tell Kaden if he's not good to you you're gonna dump him and go with the cat lady plan."

I stepped forward and pulled her to me, holding her close, the way she had that night in my room. "It's going to be okay, Talia," I whispered. *Please, please let that be true.*

"Arabella. Talia." Walter's voice boomed through the room, and we jumped apart. He strode through the bloodred rows of flowers toward us. "So good of you to come. And early! Of course, I *thought* you might try to feed the plague flowers, Ara. I wondered if Talia would try to stop you. I suppose she wasn't quite as good a spy as I'd hoped for."

He wore the same suit he'd worn on the first day I'd seen him. Yet now he seemed different in it. Once I'd seen a man like my father—now I saw only the man who'd ended the world.

"The people have the cure now—the true cure," I said. "You're too late to stop me."

Walter laughed at this, a full booming sound that made me flinch. "Stop you? Ara, I brought you here. It was my men who looked for you when the world fell. It was my team that saved you, brought you out of the ruins. It was my guide who showed you the city." He shook his head at me. "Your father slipped through my fingers once. My greatest supporter became my greatest disappointment." He glanced at Talia, his gaze cold. "A betrayal I'm beginning to know well."

Pain burned through my hand, but I couldn't relax from the tight fist it had formed. I couldn't leave without at least trying. "Whatever you're planning next, it doesn't have to be like this. Let the women of the Sanctum go. Explain to the people of The Last City that you have the true cure. You'll be a hero to them."

"Look around, Ara. I already am. And now I will be more than a hero. I will be a god. Humanity is flawed. The only way forward is to start over. Make a new beginning. Nature does the same. An old species falls away making way for a new, better one. You blame the plague, but look at what humanity was doing to each other: wars and greed and horror. Removing humanity was an act of mercy."

"Death isn't mercy," I whispered.

"Yet many people ask for death in the worst of situations—when they're dying of cancer, when they're in indescribable pain. The world was falling apart, I ended it where others would have drawn it out."

"You're sick!" I said, angry now. "My cure is in the flowers now. You won't be able to control the city anymore—not without the fear of the plague."

"Oh really? Then tell me, say your cure works, will it change anything? Or will men continue to fight and bicker while some live fat and happy and others starve?"

It felt like I'd swallowed a stone, like my feet had sunk into a foot of concrete. No matter what I said or did, there would be no changing his mind. I was too late: he'd been on this path since before I was born. Since before my father was born.

"The problem isn't the cure: it's humanity," he said. "Join me, Ara. Let us begin a new age together."

I stepped back, shaking my head. The clan. Boise. Kaden. My father. Emma. Those were the only new beginnings I wanted. "No. I don't want any part of this." I took another step back, then stopped. "I upheld my part of the bargain, now you uphold yours. Release Kaden and let us go."

He shook his head, a sad smile on his face. "You are as much of a disappointment as your father."

"Guess it runs in the family." The length of the greenhouse beckoned, but I didn't leave yet. "I want you to give the same choice to Talia."

This time he smiled. "Talia is here of her own free will."

"Is she? Or are you holding her sister captive to make her do what you want?"

Now Walter laughed. "Is that what she told you?" He shook his head, turning to Talia, who only stared at the ground. "Tsk-tsk, Talia. Sounds like someone's twisting the truth. But I am nothing if not a fair man. You are free to go with her."

"Talia," I whispered. "Come with me."

Finally, she lifted her gaze to my own. "I can't."

I don't understand! I wanted to scream at her. But I saw the resolve in her eyes: she wasn't coming with me. Tears pricked my eyes.

Walter motioned to one of the guards at the far end. "One

of the guards at the front will take you. Goodbye, Ara. I have a feeling I'll be seeing you again soon enough."

"Not likely."

Something hot and heavy and angry pulsed in my chest. I was sick and tired of the lies of this place. The Last City wasn't different. It wasn't some sanctuary. It was exactly the same as the rest of the world: broken. I cleared my throat and made my eyes as cold as my heart.

"Goodbye, Walter." And then the words that were harder by far: "Goodbye, Talia."

THIRTY-THREE—SAM

In the weeks I spent alone, I'd come to understand the different sounds of silence. For a small time the world got louder—sirens, gunshots, screams, explosions. But the silence won out in the end. Maybe it always did.

That morning I woke to a silence I knew too well.

I woke knowing she was gone. Her sleeping bag, her pack, her gun—all missing.

The building creaked, the winter breeze whispered outside the glass, and far below the water lapped at the walls. Each sound mocked me because they weren't her. Part of me wanted to scream, or break something. Instead, I packed up the remains of my camp in silence.

All she had left behind was a single note. Just like Issac. As I'd done with his, I put it in my pocket, unopened.

I went outside. Only one kayak remained. The dark water stretched out all around, a morning breeze biting straight to my core. *As if it could be any colder than her.*

The water stretched out in all directions, her path impossible to track even if I'd wanted to. As I sat there, I realized two notes sat in each of my pockets, two voices waiting to be heard.

So in the cold morning, I opened her final words to me.

Leave the city, Sam. Run as far and as fast as you can. I've seen what they're planning. The people in the green water are coming—and they're going to kill everyone.

No sweet nothings. No mournful goodbye. No regrets or well wishes. Just a warning, as guarded and cryptic as she.

But then I flipped the note over. There, at the very bottom, was a single line. A single line that dragged a begrudging smile free . . .

And finally, in the morning cold, I knew where I was going next.

I set my kayak's nose into the water and set off in a new direction.

~

The walls of the Old Penitentiary rose before me—the fortress Gabriel had always wanted. Shouts came from inside, and when the doors swung open, it was Gabriel who came to greet me, shock and disbelief written over his face.

"Sam?" He was shorter than I remembered—his hair longer. But his face was just as annoying as I remembered it.

"I'm not back to take over the horses," I said, cutting off what I knew would come next. "I'm back to fix the new tech—I think I can turn the whole city back on."

That careful look he always wore slipped for just a moment. I hadn't said what he'd expected. All he saw when he looked at me was Kaden's little brother. But Kaden had shirked the duty that he should have taken on. I was done hiding. Done waiting. There was a whole world out there waiting for someone brave and bold enough to turn it back on.

"Of course, Sam." Gabriel's old smile recovered quickly, even if I wondered if there wasn't coldness hidden beneath. "We're glad to have you back. There's always a place for you here. Come in. Let me show—"

I strode past him, not waiting for him to finish as I called out a greeting to Liam, and then others, a whole new world of noise and movement greeting me. A world I didn't need anyone's permission to claim. Kaden thought because Gabriel ruled the clan, the clan was broken. But the clan wasn't broken. Gabriel was.

So I smiled and embraced the men, as the final words in the note—from the girl I'd never truly known, but who had changed me nonetheless—burned in my mind.

Bastards stay rulers—until you bring them down. Good luck, Sasquatch.

—Emma

THIRTY-FOUR—ARA

Three armed guards surrounded me as we made our way down into the tunnels beneath the city. I was surprised at how heavy my heart felt leaving Talia behind. Somehow I hadn't truly believed she would choose to stay. It was hard to accept that I would never see either of them again. Still Walter's words echoed endlessly in my mind. *He said he wanted to make a new humanity. What does that even mean?*

The green glow of the tunnels seemed to swallow all sound as we walked. Green was once my favorite color: the color of the forest, of Kaden's eyes. Now it was also the color of death, of decay. All I wanted was to get Kaden and get the hell out of here. We needed to get back to Boise and find Sam and Emma. Walter and his plans couldn't touch us there.

We rounded a corner, and I glimpsed movement from the cell ahead. My heart leapt—then fell. A young man stood in the cell, about Kaden's age, but he had short dark hair, deep sad eyes, and a full mouth that looked like it rarely smiled.

Then someone moved behind him.

Kaden.

I surged ahead, when the biggest guard—bald with huge arms—caught me and yanked me back.

"Kaden!" I called out.

He was instantly at the bars, his eyes wild. "Ara, what's going on? Are you okay? What's happening?"

"They're here to free you." I struggled, but the guard who held me had arms like tree trunks—I wasn't going anywhere. The only weapon I had was the small knife concealed in my boot that I'd used to reopen my wound. Not exactly a fair fight, considering there were three guards, each carrying a gun. But I wasn't here to fight. Only for Kaden.

The oldest of the guards stepped forward, keys in hand. The whole walk here I couldn't shake the feeling that I'd seen him before—and now, with the keys in his hand, I suddenly realized who he was: Slump. The guard who'd brought me out of my cell and into The Last City that first day here. *Feels like an eternity ago.*

"Prisoner Kaden," Slump said, "the Chancellor has released you. You're free to go."

I thought Kaden would immediately smile, that his green eyes would meet mine and he'd tell me everything was okay. But to my shock, he stepped back from the bars and glanced at the young man beside him.

"What about Septimus?" he said. The door swung open and clanked against the wall. Slump motioned for Kaden.

"Just you. Not the other," Slump said.

"What will happen to Septimus?"

"That's above my pay grade," Slump said, laying a hand on the gun at his waist. "Unless you'd like me to make it my problem."

Still Kaden didn't move. Fear churned in my gut as Slump pulled the gun free.

"Come on, Kaden," I called out to him, desperate now. "Let's go. They're going to set us free. Walter promised." *We're so, so close.*

Kaden turned to look at me, agony written on his face. Then he turned back to the young man in the cell beside him, and shook his head. "No. I'm not leaving without Septimus. I can't."

"Go, Kaden. Please. I'll be fine." This from the other man—Septimus.

Slump laughed, a cold sound. He lifted the gun and I was about to beg, sure he was going to shoot Kaden, when he turned and left the cell. As he came back to stand next to me he aimed the gun straight at my forehead. My breath caught as I stared down the barrel of the gun. No one moved.

"Let me make this simple," Slump said, his voice loud in the small space. "I was ordered to set you both free. I wasn't told if you had to be bullet-free. So get out of the goddamn cell or I'll put a bullet in your girlfriend's head."

"Whoa, whoa, I'm moving, easy there." Kaden slowly made his way out of the cell, hands raised, when I caught the eye of the man in the cell behind him. He watched Kaden with something like childlike devotion.

And then, to my shock, the young man in the cell caught my eye and nodded—as if he were giving me permission to leave him there. Wishing me well even. I didn't know him, he was a perfect stranger, and yet I suddenly saw in his face everyone I had abandoned. Everyone I had failed: Emma. Izzie. Sam. Rosia.

The whole world.

I was so tired of being the girl who left only destruction in her wake—the girl of flames. I pulled free of the guard holding me and this time he let me go. Kaden caught me as I stumbled into him. I pulled him close, feeling the strength and warmth of his body. There was so much to lose, so much that lay beyond that was so close I could almost taste it. Why would I ever risk everything for a man I didn't know?

Because Kaden was ready to risk his life to save Septimus. He must be important to him. Just like Izzie and Emma were to me.

And I knew if I had the chance to go back, I would have done everything differently.

I pulled back, placed my mouth against his ear, and breathed out, "Look for an opening. We won't leave him."

He stiffened in my arms, but there wasn't time to speak more. Slump swung the cell shut, about to lock it, when several things happened at once.

First, footsteps came from farther down the tunnel.

Slump abandoned the key in the lock as he reached for his gun. I caught Kaden's eye, and he took a step left, closer to Slump, as I took a small step right, closer to the guard who wore a gun at his hip. The three guards all turned to whoever was approaching, distracted.

A new man rounded the corner and our opening came the same moment my heart dropped.

Father.

Then, chaos.

Father lifted his gun, the guards did the same, and Kaden and I both leapt into action. Kaden crashed into Slump, trying to grab his gun, while I knocked the gun free from the other guard's hand, and it went skittering down the tunnel. Before I could chase it, the tree-armed man grabbed me from behind, lifting me clean off the ground. I managed to grab my knife and buried it in his side. He roared and threw me against the wall so hard I saw black.

Shots exploded in the underground tunnel.

I caught a flash of Kaden fighting Slump, then the huge man I'd stabbed was back in front of me. His gun was out, but there wasn't time to run. Father's training kicked in, and I leapt forward, pushing the gun sideways. It exploded inches from my face, the noise so loud I could hear nothing else. He was too big, my knife was gone, his gun was coming back—

—and then another shot exploded, and the man fell, my father standing over him.

"MOVE!" he roared, thrusting me in the opposite direction.

"Kaden—"

"Go! GO!" Kaden said, leaping after me. We took off down the tunnel, more shots ringing out behind us. I risked only a single glance back: Kaden and Septimus followed me, while behind us Father fired at the other two men. Shots exploded in the tunnel, dirt raining down from above.

When we rounded the corner, I paused, and turned. Only Kaden and Septimus followed. Kaden's arm caught me. "We have to keep going!" he said, breathing hard. Shots sounded down the tunnel from us.

"No! My father might need me!"

"That was your dad?" He glanced over his shoulder, but then his expression hardened. "We can't go back. We need to get out of here." He turned to the new man. "Septimus, can you get us out of here?"

He shook his head. "I don't know these tunnels."

"I do." Father staggered around the corner. My heart flooded with joy and relief. I ran forward, wrapping my arms around him—and then slowly pulled back. *No. No, please.* Two bullet holes, one in his stomach, and one lower, near his hip, wept blood.

"Father?" My voice trembled.

The gun in his hands shook—I'd never seen him with shaking hands. He was the surest shot I knew.

"They've got a hospital above," I said, refusing to accept this. "We can get you there."

"No, Ara . . . listen to me. Listen!"

My eyes finally moved from the wounds up to his face. The face I knew of the father I loved. I felt like that small girl lost in the mountains all over again.

"No. I won't leave you. Not again." It wasn't fair. It wasn't supposed to be like this.

"You won't ever lose me. I will always be there, watching over you." He reached out, and touched my chin, lifting it. "Be happy, Ara. I wish I could have taught you how." Sounds came in the distance, men yelling. Footsteps. We were out of time. He nodded to the tunnel to the left. "Follow that tunnel. Stay to the left. The whirlpool will carry you free."

Then he turned, charging back down the tunnel. Kaden took my hand, pulling me in the opposite direction. Kaden said something to me, but I couldn't make out the words. I couldn't think or grasp anything besides the fact that my father was gone. That he'd gone to protect me, and this time he wouldn't be coming back.

Kaden dragged me forward, down the twisting tunnels. Then the tunnel opened into a wide, circular chamber, filled with the sound of rushing water. At the center of the chamber the water swirled into a whirlpool that seemed to swallow all light.

I stared down at the dark swirling water wondering where it led. *Hell, probably.*

Septimus looked behind us, his chest heaving and falling. “Kaden?”

The voices of the guards sounded behind us—we were out of time. But suddenly it was me who spoke: “My father said if we jumped in, it would carry us free.”

“Do you trust him?” Kaden said.

I thought of the girl in the mountains. The cold nights, the blazing fires, the unending fight for survival, and my father, always there to defend me. I’d changed. But one thing was still true—my father would always protect me.

I leapt into the whirlpool, the swirling water grabbing me, pulling me into its powerful flow. I caught a last glimpse of green, of Kaden and Septimus jumping in after me, and then the current dragged me down and there was only darkness.

THIRTY-FIVE—KADEN

I struggled to stand in the roaring flow of the river.

"Ara! Ara!" I screamed, my voice echoing over the banks before the water pulled me under again, capped in white, obliterating all thoughts but escape. I fought against the current, fighting and kicking until I finally staggered into the shallows. My legs and arms felt like rubber, and my shoes weighed a thousand pounds. But the cold seeping into my bones wasn't nearly as all-consuming as the fear.

Ara.

She'd jumped into the whirlpool, and I'd followed into a darkness that never seemed to end.

"Ara!" My voice was mangled. The river roared around me, impervious to my pain.

Then, finally, far downriver, a flash of deep red. I stumbled, sprinting, falling, swimming, anything I could do to get to her. Septimus had a hold of her, struggling in the current to drag her limp body free from the flow.

No, no, no.

"Ara!" I screamed, jumping back into the river, falling and stumbling until I reached Septimus's side, panic pounding through every breath. She was pale and limp in his arms. *No. Please, God, no.*

Together we struggled to escape the powerful current. The river fought against us, pulling at us with relentless force.

Finally we managed to struggle free from the icy water. Her body fell limp on the rocky shore. I crouched over her, fear pounding in every heartbeat.

"Ara! Ara, please wake up!" *Please, Issac, wherever you are, help us!* I pounded on her chest, turning her over on her side.

Then, all of a sudden, she was coughing up river water. She choked and heaved as I cried beside her, feeling like my heart had cracked in two.

"You're all right. You're all right." I wasn't sure if I was talking to her or me. "I'm here. I've got you."

Her breath came in ragged, gasping sobs, each one bringing me back from the edge. Then she fell back, her whole body shuddering, her face pale white and her lips blue. I reached over, taking her hand in mine, exhaustion sweeping through me as I held on.

Finally her eyes opened, and she turned to look at me. "Kaden?"

I knelt beside her and kissed her forehead, my whole body trembling with some mixture of adrenaline, cold, and exhaustion. "Don't ever do that again," I whispered. Goose bumps covered her arms. I ran my hands over her, trying to warm her up, but seeing as I was also covered in soaked clothes, there wasn't much I could do.

When she finally sat upright, and I was sure she was breathing, I took in our surroundings. We were on a small rocky beach, a swirling eddy off the river and a grove of bare quaking aspen surrounding us with their skeletal forms. In the distance, farther than I would have thought possible, lay the walls of The Last City. Seeing how far the river had carried us, knowing how easily it all could have gone wrong—*No, don't think like that. You made it out. That's all that matters.*

Farther up the steep bank Septimus watched Ara and me, that same look he'd had when I'd stood over the Captain, like he would run at a moment's notice—or that he would follow at the slightest invitation.

"Ara, this is Septimus," I said, gesturing to where he stood in the aspen. "He saved my life . . . and he pulled you to shore. Maybe you're good luck for us, Septimus."

Septimus nodded, seeming awestruck, maybe even a bit afraid of Ara as she smiled up at him. A shiver wracked her body, and she said, "I think I finally know what the spiral represents. Cold."

I was too exhausted to laugh. When she was able, Septimus and I helped Ara climb farther up the bank, until the roar of the water diminished a bit. From the higher vantage point, I could make out the turns and twists of the roller coaster, and the Ferris wheel. We weren't far from the park.

And once again, the expedition leader mindset snapped back into place.

"We should move." Adrenaline pulsed through my exhausted body. We had no weapons or supplies—if someone showed up now we'd be defenseless.

"They aren't coming after us," Ara said. "I talked to Walter—he agreed to let us go."

I exchanged a look with Septimus, his eyes as disbelieving as my own. "That doesn't sound like Walter."

"I think he has other plans for The Last City," she said darkly.

Again, Septimus met my gaze. There was something terrified in his gaze—something that made me afraid. He nodded to the park in the distance, and I agreed without having to say a word. It was time to get the hell out of here.

"Sam!" Ara suddenly yelled, so loud I started and looked over my shoulder, to where Septimus stared at her with just as much shock.

"No, that's Septimus—"

But she'd already cut me off, speaking so fast I barely understood her. "No, Sam! Sam is alive! He's back in Boise with Emma. We intercepted a video, well Talia did, even though she was working with Walter, we saw a video of him and he's alive. He was asking for people to come to Boise to turn on the new tech."

I stared at her, my mind buzzing with white noise. *No. It can't be. The cold is messing with me. Sam couldn't be—he couldn't be . . .* "What did you say?" I finally managed.

She stepped forward, tears in her eyes, as she took my shoulders in her hands and shook me. "Sam is alive. He's in Boise. He's alive, Kaden."

Sam was alive?

Sam is alive.

It felt like . . . like I didn't have words. Like my heart had cracked open, and something new had taken root there. Like beginning a new life where anything was possible. Like the sun had come up for the first time ever.

The water roared alongside us, rushing downstream, as if it wanted me to follow it, right now, all the way down to Boise. Ara wrapped her arms around me, and I pulled her to me, too overcome to speak.

"He's alive, Kaden. We'll find him."

I held Ara against me and closed my eyes. *Maybe you were right all along, Issac.* The peace I'd been looking for since Sam had died: it'd been right in front of me the whole time.

I picked Ara up and swung her around—then quickly set her down. The river had taken more out of me than I'd thought. So instead I tilted her lips up to mine and kissed her. My whole body trembled with the cold. Even so I felt invincible, like the joy inside me would never end. Then I stumbled over to Septimus and hugged him fiercely. Septimus seemed shocked by this, patting my back awkwardly, but I didn't care.

"You saved both our lives," I said fiercely to Septimus, holding him out at arm's length. "Come with us. Back to Boise."

He hesitated, glancing at Ara.

"Come with us," Ara said, echoing my words. My heart swelled as she came to stand beside us. The three of us made a small circle of survivors. *Or the beginning of a new team.*

"I'm not sure I deserve a new start," Septimus said. His eyes drifted to the walls of the city in the distance. I wondered if his thoughts were back to the people in the green water. But I wasn't taking no for an answer.

"If we do, then you do. Trust me." I turned to look down at myself—soaked clothes, no weapons or supplies. "Though it might be a rocky start. I hadn't exactly planned to start out with no supplies."

Septimus's eyes suddenly lit up. "I've got supplies hidden in the amusement park," he said. "Enough to make the journey back."

Oh, do you? Imagine that. "We could really use your help, Septimus." It didn't matter that I'd seen where his supplies were hidden—he didn't need to know that.

"I can show you where they are, but then I should return . . ." His eyes went back to the city walls, but I heard the hesitation in his voice. It told me the truth: he didn't want to go back.

"You know, Septimus," I said. "Someone very wise once told me, if something's killing you, it's okay to let it go."

His gaze finally came back to me. I saw the conflicted desires there—even as I saw one winning out over the other. "Won't it be dangerous?" he finally said. "We're ill-prepared."

I grinned, and set an arm around Ara, my heart full to bursting. "'Course it'll be dangerous. But no one survives the apocalypse anyways."

Ara smiled, her grin matching mine, and then, finally, a slow smile worked over Septimus's face. It told me everything. The three of us stood there in the grove of quaking aspen, a new team with a new mission.

I turned south, to the ruins of the city stretching out into the distance. Beyond it lay snow-covered forests, the harsh mountains, the roads full of dangerous men. But somewhere beyond all that, in a green valley at the base of the mountains, was Sam.

Sam and the home that this time, I would fight for.

"Come on, you two. We're burning daylight."

THIRTY-SIX—SEVYN

The glass burst, birthing me free from the green water at last.

Cold, burning lights. After knowing only the green water, the air screamed down my throat like breathing fire. For so long I'd dreamed, longed, ached to be free. Now that I was, the sensations of this world came sharp as knives.

So many years trapped. So many years longing, yearning. And now, at last, our revenge was here.

She stood before me, just as she'd looked in my dreams. A pale heart-shaped face, dark hair, ice-blue eyes both vicious and beautiful.

"You look like the other," she said. Her voice was sharp, clear, and cruel.

"I am not him; I am Sevyn. Your leader." The first words I had ever spoken—a name I'd longed to claim. For so long I had only the memories from the stolen dark-haired girl, but now, the thoughts and memories of all the Creation seeped into me. I felt their desire for the above world we'd been denied. My heart beat faster at the thought.

"Where is he?" My mouth felt strange, my tongue clumsy. "Our creator?"

"The Chancellor is waiting for you."

"Then lead on."

She nodded, leading me through dark, tunnellike corridors. Our eyes were stronger than those of humans, and even in the near dark I could make my way forward.

Freedom, freedom, my blood sang, my fingers longing to wrap around the humans who'd thought they could keep us contained, not knowing that every moment we grew stronger. Not knowing that every moment we called out to the first of us in the above world, begging her to return and free us.

Together we made our way through the winding tunnels.

"The Chancellor brought a human female with him," she said as I soaked up scents of metal and earth and blood. "He thinks he leads us."

I watched the Creation with curiosity, not answering. For so many years I'd dreamed of the one of us who'd escaped, who roamed the earth and had sent back images of beyond: the father who was both a savior and a betrayer, the sister she'd claimed as her own, with the red hair, the trees, the sky, the earth. But this was not that girl. She was a copy of her. The same way I was a copy of another. Another who had not answered our call and would be punished for his betrayal.

We climbed stairs, until she opened a door to a lab—now lit in flickering lights, casting it from light to dark and back. And there he stood: Walter.

I knew his image, only because of his son: Charles. Charles was the human who had abandoned The Last City, who had buried the cure within his own veins. But that wasn't the only thing he took, or the most precious. I closed my eyes, the images coming to me—a young man, running through the tunnels, leaping into the black whirlpool that carried him free, an image that echoed endlessly in all of our minds. Then his escape through the mountains. All the while, tucked against him, a beautiful baby Creation with dark hair and ice-blue eyes.

Then, the moment it all changed.

In the mountains, rain poured outside a cave. He raised a rock, intending to crush her. She'd reached up with tiny grasping hands, screaming in a way that sounded so human. And he made the mistake that would be the undoing of humanity.

Instead of killing her, he picked her up and named her.

Emma.

He'd raised her as his own—one daughter of fire, blood full of the cure, and the other a daughter of ice, not human, aging slower and stronger than humans. One daughter he kept forever hidden in the shadows, one daughter he favored and taught to survive. One daughter to save the world. One daughter to end it.

And now Walter's eyes turned to me.

"You must be Sevyn," he whispered, his voice full of awe. So pitiful. So human. "I wasn't sure if a leader would emerge again."

There was no pity in my eyes, no weakness. Nothing human. "I have. We no longer need your assistance."

Confusion flickered in his eyes—it made me want to laugh that this frail, old human would think we would need him. "My assistance?" he said, his voice wavering. "I created you. I will show you the way forward, to a better humanity. A better earth. I've already proved that humans and Creation can work together." Behind him a small human girl stood; dark hair, large eyes. As breakable and imperfect as him.

"The only way to a better earth is to cleanse it of the plague that is humanity. We will finish what the plague began." The rightness of those words surged through me.

"No . . . that's not . . ." He stepped back from me, fear in his eyes, trembling like the prey he was.

I stepped up to him, slow, careful steps, noting the way his eyes darted one way then the other. There was nowhere to run from what he had created. It almost seemed a pity that our creator was a coward. In contrast the human girl watched me with cold, clear eyes. As I stood before our creator, another memory filled me. A man, smiling down at his daughter, guiding her hands, showing her how to light a fire. I stepped forward and wrapped my arms around him, in a memory of a hug.

"Goodbye, Walter," I whispered, his body tensing against mine. "Die knowing I will fulfill your mission." He tried to pull away, but it was far too late. With a quick jerk, the memory ended as easily as he did.

So easily they fall . . . But there would be more of them on the surface, more of the vicious beasts who'd nearly destroyed the world, more for us to burn away until the earth was left whole and well again. I closed my eyes, feeling the rest of the Creation as they awoke—stretching, climbing for the surface like monsters buried too long beneath the earth.

Yes, wake, my brothers and sisters.

The female human stared down at our creator. "Walter?" she whispered, as if she expected him to get up. I expected her to run, or weep, or beg for mercy. Instead, she turned to me, her eyes blazing with anger. "You killed him. He promised me he'd free my sister."

Foolish girl. I stepped up to her and took her chin in my hands, tilting her head up to mine. She glared at me—defiant. For now. It would have been so easy to end her. But some deep curiosity stilled my hand. "Tell me what you wish for, little human."

Her eyes flickered to the man on the ground, and back to me. "My sister. That's all I want."

A scent I couldn't name clung to her: maybe it was the wind, or fire or grass or a thousand other things I'd never experienced. A thousand things I'd longed for and would soon claim. So I allowed myself this one small indulgence: I would keep this strange, fearless human alive until she was no longer useful. I smiled down at her, "Then you shall have it."

She flinched away from me, finally seeming to sense that she'd made a deal with the devil. Even in the small lab, I could feel the other Creation, waking, preparing to move up and out, to reclaim the sun and everything else that was ours. To finish what Walter had begun.

"What's next?" another Creation asked.

I turned away from the human, leaving her stranded as I tilted my head back to stare at the flickering lights above. I'd dreamed of the sun a thousand times: the heat, the brightness, the power. And now, finally, I was moment's away from everything I'd been denied. "First, we gather the rest of the Creation. We find and kill the last she."

"And then?"

I smiled, past the dead man, past the human I'd spared, to the staircase that lay at the end of the lab. It led up to the above world. My heart beat faster at the thought. "Then we kill all the rest."

The Last City had fallen.

The last Creation had begun.

ABOUT THE AUTHOR

H.J. Nelson is an Idaho native who graduated from University of Wisconsin with degrees in creative writing and wildlife biology. She began writing on Wattpad in 2015, where her story *The Last She* was one of the most read science fiction stories in 2016 and 2017. Since then, her works have garnered over twelve million reads and been optioned for television by Sony. She has also written for brands like General Electric, Writer's Digest, and National Geographic. When not writing, Nelson has lived on a boat in the British Virgin Isles, worked in two zoos, and ridden an elephant through the jungles of Laos—though she considers raising two daughters her most dangerous adventure yet. You can sign up for her newsletter at hjnelsonauthor.com or find her on Instagram @h.j.nelson.